IN HIS MAJESTY'S SERVICE

ELIZABETH SILVER
JENNY URBAN

I0563576

RIPTIDE
PUBLISHING

Riptide Publishing
PO Box 1537
Burnsville, NC 28714
www.riptidepublishing.com

In His Majesty's Service

Cover art: Lou Harper, louharper.com/Design.html
Editor: Carole-ann Galloway
Layout: L.C. Chase, lcchase.com/design.htm

ISBN: 978-1-62649-649-1

First edition
September, 2017

Also available in ebook:
ISBN: 978-1-62649-648-4

IN HIS MAJESTY'S SERVICE

ELIZABETH SILVER
JENNY URBAN

Here's to us. We never could have done it alone
and
for Steve, who pushed me to keep writing even when I didn't have the words.

"Whatever our souls are made of, his and mine are the same."
—Emily Brontë

TABLE OF CONTENTS

PROLOGUE

*I n celebration of the Great Compromise, Dryos Cycle 3046 was
renamed Drion Cycle 1, in honor of King Drion Ands, the first and
greatest king of our people, Unifier of the System, Protector of Our Way of
Life, and Father to a long line of great kings and queens, beginning with
his firstborn son and general of his armies . . .*

"My lord."

Anders ignored the intrusion, gloved fingers tracing the lines of
faded text, moving on to the next passage.

*Ciebos declined to be renamed, passing on the honor of bearing the
name Gloria after King Drion's first wife, she who had first proposed
the Great Compromise, and she from whence peace had forever radiated.
It was at Queen Gloria's tomb where the final signature was added to the
Compromise and the first five-cycle rotation began . . .*

"Anders."

He scowled, hunching his shoulders. This dialect was just old
enough that translating as he went was no small feat. Still, Anders was
up to the task, if only people would stop interrupting him.

*The first rotation held many challenges. Laws and gods from twelve
planets needed reconciling after three hundred cycles apart. It was only
through the steady guidance of King Drion, he for whom our great planet
is called, that those difficult cycles were navigated. King Drion was the
one to establish the first Temple of the Many, and it was he who also
drafted the first law of the Collective, establishing the law of succession
and ensuring his line's right to the throne from that day onward . . .*

"Ground Command to Lord Hawthorne, your signal's scrambled.
Anders!"

Anders glanced up from the dusty pages of the ancient tome,
blinking rapidly as his eyes adjusted. Bern, one of his loyal guards,

cocked a blond eyebrow and gave him his best and flattest look. Anders smiled back; Bern was more bark than bite, regardless of how long he'd been trying to get Anders's attention.

"Sorry," Anders said, carefully slipping a piece of silk between the pages to mark his spot. "Sometimes the family history can be a bit hypnotic, if obnoxiously redundant."

Bern, as ever, was entirely unmoved. "You're the one writing a book about your own genealogy," he said. "Don't even try to tell me it doesn't get you going to read about how great your ancestors were."

Anders laughed. "Maybe a little," he admitted. He lifted the tome with gentle, gloved hands, and secured it in the preservation box. There were digital copies on the network, of course, but there was something about holding a book in his hands that settled a part of Anders like nothing else. Book safely tucked away, he turned back to Bern.

"What can I do for you?" he asked. "Or did you just come in to admire my work?"

Bern huffed a laugh through his nose. "Not precisely. I wanted to let you know that Daniel is in your office and is asking to see you right away."

Daniel. Anders couldn't help the little thrill in his stomach at the thought of his friend. They hadn't spoken in weeks, and a part of Anders couldn't help wondering now if that meant their friendly arrangement of convenient sex and welcome companionship had run its course. He hoped not; it wasn't love, but he was quite fond of Daniel and had been considering possibly deepening their relationship.

They had met at the library two years earlier and had been friends ever since. The sex, a relatively recent addition, had only started when Anders had flat-out propositioned Daniel, half curious to see what his buttoned-up history-professor friend would say to a blatant come-on. It wasn't the most spectacular sex in the Collective, sure, but it was certainly better than going home alone every night without fail.

Anders smiled over his shoulder at his guard. "Why don't we call it a day? You can contact Jackson and tell him our change in schedule while I talk to Daniel, and then we can all get out of here."

"Sounds like a solid plan to me, my lord," Bern said, smoothing his close-cropped blond hair. Being a military man down to the core, just like his partner Jackson, Bern hated when it was his turn to watch over Anders at work. He also had far less patience than Jackson, so Anders was careful to take pity on him whenever possible.

Anders tidied up his workspace, wanting to have everything in its place when he came back in the morning. As much of an absentminded academic some people might think him at times, Anders strictly enforced neatness and order in his offices. It was one of the many things he'd learned from his father, though not the most important.

Finally satisfied, Anders headed down the hall. Bern trailed after him as usual, but didn't follow him into his office; fortunately for everyone's sanity, Daniel had been cleared for private interactions a long time ago.

"Daniel," Anders said warmly, the office door shutting behind him.

Daniel jumped up out of his chair and swept Anders into his arms, kissing him firmly. When Anders tried to deepen the kiss, however, Daniel pulled back. His tanned face shone bright with excitement and barely-contained happiness.

"The most amazing thing has happened, Anders," he said. "And you're the first person I want to know."

"Does this have anything to do with why you've been off the grid for three weeks?" Anders asked with a laugh, catching Daniel's hand and guiding them both to the sofa.

Daniel flushed. "I'm truly sorry about that. Time just got away from me." He outright giggled; solid, staid Daniel had *giggled*, and Anders blinked at him for several seconds.

"This must be one incredible story," he said at last. "So tell me, what's your fantastic news?"

"I matched!" Daniel flung himself back on the couch, arms wide as he nearly shouted. "I went to that dreadful staff party because my supervisor all but ordered me there, and I came out with my match!"

"You . . . matched?"

Daniel pulled up his sleeve to show off his soul mark, nestled in the crook of his elbow. Anders had teased him once that the plain black square was a book, a terribly unhelpful indicator of who his match would be, academia being Daniel's whole world and all.

"Jane's is on her chest." He touched his own collarbone, a distant look in his pale eyes. "I'd never have seen it if she weren't wearing a dress for the party."

Anders rubbed his own mark, hidden under a privacy patch firmly affixed to his left wrist. No one but Anders, his parents, and a very few physicians had even seen his mark. It made the possibility of matching much more remote, but it was standard practice for members of the royal family to hide their marks in order to prevent attempts at fraud. The last thing a person of Anders's standing needed was to be tricked into an unnecessary and unmatched bonding. Anders had never considered that anyone around him might do something as random as meet their match at a staff party. His chest ached, and he wasn't sure if it was disappointment or jealousy.

"And the past few weeks?" Anders prompted, because clearly he was a glutton for punishment.

"Getting to know each other and using up as much personal time as we dared." Daniel sighed happily and leaned back again. "I've never met someone I meshed with so perfectly, Anders. I get it's largely biology, complementary hormones and all that, but she makes me *laugh*. That's something more than science, you know? Now I understand why they call them *soul* marks; because we really do match, right down to our souls. Also," he added, a wicked grin spreading across his face, "the sex is *unbelievable*."

"Always good," Anders said quietly.

"We're bonding next week," Daniel said suddenly. "I recognize it might be a bit awkward, all things considered, but I'd really like to have you there." He sobered. "It would mean a lot to me to have my friend with us. And Jane wants to meet you."

Anders arched an eyebrow. "I take it you haven't told her how you and I spent the entire weekend of the last staff function, then?" The words were a little bitter, but Anders deserved to be a touch petty, if only for a few moments. It wasn't every day someone like him got dumped, after all.

Daniel flushed. "Not yet, no," he admitted. "Although she knows about our arrangement. She's had her own fair share of arrangements in the past too, so she's fine with knowing you and I used to . . ."

"Fuck on a semiregular basis?"

He coughed. "Yes. That."

Used to. Well, this wasn't unexpected, all things considered. It was rare that people would match and not immediately enter into an exclusive, monogamous relationship, and virtually unheard of for bonded couples to see other people. Likely it had to do with the empathic connection activated by the bonding ceremony, one that often deepened into a telepathic connection, allowing bonded matches to communicate with each other over great distances. Jackson and Bern had such a connection. It was part of why they'd been recruited right out from under the Navy and into the Royal Guard.

Still, it stung to be so summarily dismissed by a lover as a *used to*.

"Will you?" Daniel was asking. "Will you come?"

Anders couldn't think of anything he wanted to do less. But. "You couldn't keep me away," he said instead. Certainly he'd be able to find a solid excuse within a week.

Daniel laughed again, pulling him in for a hug. "Thank you, friend," he said in Anders's ear. "Thank you for being so understanding."

Anders returned the hug, but only for a handful of seconds. Then he gently pushed Daniel back, careful to keep his smile as close to real as possible. "Now go back to your match and let me work," he said. "I was in the middle of a particularly difficult translation before you and your love life interrupted."

With a snort, Daniel stood and snatched up his coat. "Are you sure I can't tempt you to dinner?" he asked. "Jane and I have reservations at that café you showed me. We can easily add a third."

"Tempting, but no," Anders said, manfully resisting the urge to shudder at how terrifically awkward *that* meal would be. "So much work, so little time."

He could have done without the look of obvious pity, but at least Daniel finally left, giving Anders a moment alone.

This wasn't a heartbreak, Anders decided. More like a bruise. Honestly, matching caused more problems for people on the periphery than the supposed benefits to the pair. Why people went so absolutely mad over finding someone with the same birthmark, Anders would never know. Besides, it wasn't as though most people didn't bond with imperfect matches. As a people, they were so spread out across the stars, it was unrealistic to wait for that one special person. From not-quite exact matches to outright mismatching, bonding had never truly been just for matches, even if it was supposedly best that way. Why, Anders's own ancestor, King Drion Ands, had bonded and buried a total of three wives in his lifetime.

Someone knocked on the doorframe, and Anders looked up to see both Jackson and Bern standing there, with identical somber expressions. *Speaking of matching pairs.*

"I'm fine," he said. "Daniel matched." He took a great lungful of air and released it all at once. "Maybe I should go home for a while. Spend some time with Father. He didn't seem very well in our last video call."

Their faces went more troubled. "Anders," Bern said, stepping into the room. "My lord . . ." Jackson followed him, carefully closing the door behind him.

Something similar to anxiety started brewing low in Anders's stomach. "What's wrong?"

Jackson knelt at his feet and gently took both of Anders's hands in his own meaty ones. "Your father," he said at last. "We've just received word from home."

"What about him?" The anxiety was rising up and into his throat, threatening to become full-blown hysteria.

"Anders," Jackson said, still in that gentle voice of his, "Anders, your father is dead."

CHAPTER ONE

Anders rolled his shoulders back, sighed, then adjusted his cuffs to stop himself from checking his wrist chrono for the third time in under five minutes. The chair, curved in the wrong places for anything resembling comfort, pressed awkwardly against Anders's back and legs like a plastic torture device. There had to be some explanation, at the very least, for why he had yet to find a single chair worth sitting on in the entire space station.

The media screen overhead kept reporting the same news over and over. King James, the leader of the Drion Collective, was dead after a brief but fierce illness. Some commentators were debating if he might have had a fighting chance if his bonded hadn't died so many years ago, but it was more of a passing mention than anything else while the media streams continually fussed over the transition period. A transition period that was currently full of far too many questions for anyone's peace of mind; according to tradition, the king was supposed to pass on the crown to his appointed successor, but no one had seen Crown Prince Philip since long before his father's death.

"He's in mourning," the liberal commentator pointed out. "I'd be concerned if he went about business as usual."

"He has a job to do," the conservative shot back. "The Collective is without leadership right now for the first time in nearly two hundred years. He can grieve on his own time. Besides, it's high time Prince Philip came back to the public eye. He's been hiding for fifteen years, and it's time to man up. The market is unsteady with the recent flood of substandard black market goods, not to mention the recent wave of recalls all across the technical sector. We need a leader who will step up and do something. Stop hiding in the shadows like a child."

"You know it's protocol to protect the crown prince's identity when there are no other royal children. For someone so fond of tradition, you're sure quick to dismiss it when it's inconvenient for you."

Anders shifted, tugging at the chin-high collar of his new jacket. Dressed all in black, like the rest of the royal family would until the new king was crowned, Anders couldn't help wondering if those damn talking heads had ever lost someone they cared about, and then been told they were supposed to grieve, but only a little and only so it didn't inconvenience everyone else.

Beside him, Jackson stilled Anders with a light touch to the knee. "The ship will be here soon, my lord," he said, never once pausing in his constant scan over all the comings and goings of the room.

Just then, Bern returned from securing their luggage. "The RDC *Pallas* is on final approach now," he said without preamble. "They're waiting on docking clearance; it should only be a few minutes more."

"It's about time," Anders huffed. To be honest, the *Pallas* had made remarkable time, considering what little notice she'd been given to change course. But knowing that didn't help Anders get home any faster. The sight of the Royal Navy ship docking right outside the window made him tremble with anxiety merely thinking about where it would take him and why. Still, he made a better effort to contain himself for the next few minutes. *Just get home. Worry about the rest later.*

The RDC *Pallas* was a war-class vessel, imposing even against the sizeable space port. Her sleek main body gleamed in the station lights, and the modular sections for guest quarters, cargo, and additional weaponry only added to her massive bulk. Some people were intimidated by the rare ships of the *Pallas*'s caliber, but Anders had spent enough of his life in space to know there were few places safer for him to be, surrounded by the best and brightest of the king's Navy.

Still, by the time Anders and his guards were allowed down the gangway to the airlock, it was all he could do not to blow right past the brown-haired officer sent to greet them. Dimly, Anders registered that the man had not only been sporting a crisp uniform with the traditional high-waisted black trousers and the short, open-front jacket of an officer, he also had three blue jeweled pips on his bright-white collar, indicating he was the first officer. Anders didn't care. All he could think about was getting onboard without letting anyone see how his hands were shaking and that he was perilously close to losing the meager lunch he'd managed to choke down earlier.

Anders heard Jackson greeting the first officer and accepting an offer to show them to their quarters. It was enough of a reminder of where he was—aboard one of His Majesty's finest ships, detoured specifically to collect a single royal cousin and his two guards—to slow Anders's stride and allow the others to catch up. His mother would have been appalled at her only son's behavior, had she lived to see it, but Anders couldn't let himself relax. He didn't dare, not yet and certainly not in the open.

At the door to his quarters, Anders at last remembered his manners. "Thank you," he said, turning to the officer by his side. "And thank your captain for me, as well. I know it can't have been easy to delay your journey on such short notice."

The first officer—a young man a few years older than Anders, though not by much—sketched a vaguely formal bow. "You'll be able to tell him yourself over dinner, my lord," he said, not quite making eye contact and posture at full attention. "Captain O'Connell asked me to extend an invitation to you and your party to join him at his private table tonight, as is customary."

Anders acknowledged the offer with a nod of his head, cringing inwardly at the notion of eating shipside rations and making small talk. "Until tonight, then," he said instead, and swept into his quarters.

Door closed behind him, Anders wasted little time in crossing the small sitting room to the equally cramped bedroom, pulling off his boots and collapsing on the comfortable bed nestled in the corner. Maybe he'd get lucky and Jackson and Bern would forget to wake him until they landed in Drion.

Anders snorted to himself. *Dare to dream.*

Zach turned as the door to the bridge *shh*-ed open behind him. "We good to go yet?" he asked Oliver. His first officer gave him a wry look.

"They're settled in, if that's what you mean." Oliver shook his head. "Not terribly friendly, and there's only three of them."

"Well, we were told it would be," Zach said. He gave the ensign a nod, and the young man began preparations to detach from the station. "That seems like a small entourage for a royal cousin."

Oliver nodded. "And I got the distinct impression that they had been waiting for a while."

Zach smirked. "So, what you're saying is that the guy was a dick and you just didn't want to actually say that about royalty, however distant the cousin."

"I didn't say that," Oliver said mildly. "Sir." He crossed to his chair and sat.

The ensign looked at Zach, who walked to the captain's seat and settled in. "We're ready, Peters, lift off."

With a growl of the engines, the *Pallas* slowly detached and turned, then smoothly pushed free of Gloria Station's orbit. Zach watched the planet fall away, subtly relaxing as they moved farther and farther into space.

"I invited them to eat at the captain's table tonight," Oliver said suddenly.

"Fucking hell, Oliver—"

"You know it's protocol, Zach. Even if he is just a cousin. Royal family and dignitaries are always afforded the opportunity to dine with the captain their first night on board."

Zach grumbled under his breath and then sighed. "That means *I* have to eat at the captain's table."

The ensign snorted a laugh and tried to cover it up with a cough. Zach shot him a dirty look but didn't say anything to the kid. He'd have laughed too, and as he thought it, a smile pulled at the corners of his mouth.

"I know," Oliver said somberly. "It's tragic that you can't eat in your quarters tonight."

"Oh, shut up," Zach said.

Zach strode into the formal dining area. He'd briefly debated wearing his dress uniform, just to be obnoxious, but decided it wasn't worth the discomfort. Of course, dressing up would be required for an immediate member of the royal family, but a cousin didn't warrant the honor, especially since he'd been rude to Zach's people and delayed their mission—they needed to reach Drion in time for the royal funeral, and Zach still had another stop to make on the way. There were too many high-ranking assholes that had to attend, and they all needed a ride.

Glancing over to the slightly raised area where the captain's table sat, Zach was relieved to see it still empty. He really should be there to welcome his guests whether he wanted to or not. Settling into his seat, Zach ordered a drink from the in-table menu and told himself to relax. He could make up the time on the way to Ciebos, and he could deal with this cousin for the length of a short dinner.

There was a slight commotion at the door, and Zach looked up to see a seriously hot guy with a seriously disgruntled expression on his face. There were two mountain-sized men with him, all three in solid black. The hot guy had a sharp, straight jaw with only the faintest of clefts in his chin, and his mouth might have been soft and kissable when he wasn't scowling so hard. His skin was the same golden-brown as the late king's, and his dark hair was slicked back and still damp enough that Zach couldn't quite tell what color it was. His snug trousers were tucked into knee-high boots, and his high-collared black jacket hit midthigh. Zach was vaguely disappointed that he wasn't going to be able to see the guy's ass, not while he was wearing that jacket.

He stood and pasted a smile on his face. Yeah, the guy was hot, but between what Oliver hadn't said and the sour expression spoiling the beauty of that face, Zach was sure the evening was already headed straight downhill, and it hadn't even started yet.

The taller of the two guards flanking the hot guy stepped forward. Broad-shouldered and as fair as his partner was dark, he executed a crisp salute before speaking. "Captain O'Connell, might I present Lord Anders Hawthorne of Gloria, tenth in line."

"Thank you, Bern," Lord Anders murmured, his face finally smoothing in a loose approximation of a polite smile. He stepped forward and gave a shallow nod. "Captain."

"Zachary O'Connell, at your service. Welcome on board the *Pallas*, my lord," Zach said with a bow. "I am deeply sorry for your loss, and shall endeavor to see you safely to Drion." He gestured at the seats nearest the three. "Please, sit."

"Thank you," Lord Anders said, sitting on the very edge of his chair, as though he planned to leave at a moment's notice. The two guards followed suit, their military-short haircuts giving Zach a clear view of the matching bond marks behind their right ears. A quick glance to Lord Anders's neck gave nothing away; his hair, only now starting to dry into thick curls, was barely long enough to theoretically hide a bond mark.

They sat in near-perfect silence for several minutes after ordering, Lord Anders barely lifting his eyes from the table. The guards shifted, tense and awkward and obviously having a better grasp of manners than the royal brat.

Zach eventually cleared his throat. "I have heard good things of Gloria," he finally said into the stilted atmosphere. "How did you find your time there? I hope you enjoyed yourself."

Lord Anders started, blinking at Zach as though he'd forgotten he was here. "I was in university until recently," he said. "It was educational." Another long pause, and then he added, "Will your bonded be joining us tonight?"

"I have yet to find a match," Zach said, not explaining that he had no intention of matching anytime soon. He'd heard people talk of the advantages of bonding their match, but nothing he'd heard sounded worth the hassle of being attached to one person for the rest of his life. "And you? Will your bonded be waiting for you on Drion?"

"I also have no match." Lord Anders's smooth expression crumpled back into that scowl. "Frankly, I have no desire to find them. Or to bond without a match, either. It's an archaic institution that rarely yields happy results in my experience." His guilty gaze slid sideways to his guards, and snapped back to Zach. "Though I suppose it's a positive experience for some."

Zach raised an eyebrow at the outburst but said nothing in response. Instead he looked at the guards. "I noticed your marks," he said to them. "Have you been together long?"

The fair guard smiled ever-so-slightly and nodded. "We met on our first posting as ensigns," he said. "Somehow I never ran into Jackson at the academy."

"Probably because you were on KP more often than not," Jackson said, also cracking a smile. "I never gave much thought to bonding before I met Bern, but somehow we were bonded within a month of matching."

Bern snorted. "*Somehow*, he says. I'm pretty sure our CO started planning the ceremony the day we matched."

"Did you have a big ceremony?" Zach couldn't imagine the aggravation of a big bonding ceremony. His own mom would laugh at him and then leave it to him to plan, which would actually be a little frightening. He accidentally met Lord Anders's eyes and thought he saw a shadow of the same kind of fear.

"No, thank goodness," Bern said. "There are some advantages to being nobodies from families no one cares about—" He stopped short at a pointed look from his partner. "Well, let's just say we're better off being in the background of more important lives."

Right. Guards for a royal cousin. Lord Anders's family had probably been planning his bonding ceremony since the day he was born. It was almost enough to make Zach feel sorry for him. Almost.

"Is your kitchen always this slow?" Lord Anders put in suddenly. "Honestly, this is bordering on ridiculous."

"I don't actually know," Zach admitted. "I don't usually eat in here." Just then, the table shifted, and their plates slid into place. "Well, they must have heard you," he said, grinning at Anders.

He took a bite of his steak and almost moaned. He might have to eat in here more often, because as good as the burgers in the other dining areas were, they were nothing compared to the steak on his plate now. The vegetables were crisp and full of flavor, cooked to perfection. Swallowing, Zach turned to his guests. "I hope your meal tastes as good as mine does."

Anders took a neat bite of his steak, and managed what might have been an honest smile. "It's excellent," he conceded. "Much better than I expected. My compliments."

Zach was glad he didn't have any food in his mouth when Anders smiled like that, because he almost swallowed his tongue. The smile lit up Anders's face, dark-brown eyes crinkling slightly at the corners, and Zach smiled back without thinking about it. "I'm glad," he said. Then his eyes narrowed. "What were you expecting?"

"Well." Anders blushed, a faint pink staining his sepia complexion. "To be honest, I was dreading ship rations." He laughed softly and glanced away for a second. "This is much better than that. My apologies."

"We're a star cruiser war-class ship," Zach said. "I haven't had rations since I came on board." He forced himself to stop staring at the pink in Anders's cheeks. "I've been lucky."

Anders hummed, a nonspecific response in and of itself, but immediately tucked into his meal. The rest of dinner passed in a much more comfortable silence, and before long all the plates were cleared away.

"My lord," Jackson murmured, placing a velvet-wrapped bottle on the table.

"Thank you." Anders touched his bodyguard's forearm lightly before turning and offering the bottle to Zach. "A small token of gratitude for opening your ship to us. Glorianna Fire Wine, from the finest winery on all of Gloria. This particular bottle comes from my personal collection, with my compliments."

Zach started at the reminder that Anders was *Lord* Anders, thinking even as he accepted the bottle that he hadn't really had a choice about opening his ship to them. "Thank you," he said, then heard himself add, "Would you care to share a glass with me?"

"I would, thank you," Anders said. A shadow passed over his face. "If nothing else, I've earned it the past two days."

"You have, and I'm sorry for it." Zach smiled faintly at the guards. "You're invited too, of course. However, I suggest we adjourn to my quarters. My rooms have a stunning view of the stars."

As one, Bern and Jackson shook their heads. "Thank you, but no," Jackson said. "We don't drink when we're working."

Lord Anders stood; his shadows followed suit, looming over him protectively. "Why don't the two of you head back to your quarters, then?" he offered. When they hesitated, he pushed harder, clearly having had practice. "We're on a royal vessel in the middle of deep space. I couldn't be safer if I were in the middle of the king's palace."

Finally, Bern relented. "If my lord insists," he said, though he seemed more than a little relieved. If he had to follow Lord Anders around all day, Zach could hardly blame him. Then Zach imagined what the view might be from behind Lord Anders, and reconsidered.

The guards accompanied them as far as Zach's quarters, and quickly checked the rooms, before wishing them good night. As the door slid shut behind them, Zach gestured to the low table near the wall of stars. "I love that I have full windows instead of just viewports."

Lord Anders stared out at the stars for a long moment before turning back to Zach and smiling that real smile once more. "Ever since I was a boy, I've loved the stars. If I'd had my choice, I'd have joined the Navy. Father . . . well, let's say he didn't approve." Again, his face darkened for a moment before he turned away, shrugging out of his dinner jacket and draping it over the nearest chair. "It's a lovely view."

Zach was momentarily stunned by the way Anders's pants clung to his ass. His imagination hadn't done the other man justice. "Yes, it really *is* a lovely view."

He shook the sudden flare of desire off even as Anders shot him a knowing look, a hint of a smirk tugging at his full lips. Zach crossed the room, bottle in hand, to get glasses. He opened the bottle and poured them each a healthy swallow. "What did your father want you to do instead of joining the Navy?"

"Study law," Anders said, his smile going a bit frayed at the edges. "Who we are is the family business, so to speak, but he wanted me to do well at it." He sipped his drink and took a seat at one end of the couch, legs stretched out and crossed at the ankles. "He passed away recently."

"So you've lost your father and the king in a short amount of time," Zach said. He sat down a little closer to Anders than he'd meant to. "I'm sorry."

Anders nodded and buried himself in his glass, finishing off the drink swiftly. "How long have you been with the Navy? You seem a bit young to have the helm of one of His Majesty's finest ships."

Zach flashed him a quick grin. "I joined the academy right after I graduated school, so about twenty cycles, I guess? Time sure flies."

"Still," Anders reached to refill his glass, then offered the same to Zach with an arched brow, "you must have been quite the prodigy.

I feel like an underachiever next to you with my two graduate degrees, and I must be nearly ten cycles younger."

"I worked hard and have an aptitude for flying." Zach shrugged. "You don't look old enough for two graduate degrees; then again, you must be a little older than you look. I'd've pegged you for a few cycles younger than that."

"I'll be thirty next cycle," Anders said. His smirk returned in full force as he licked his upper lip. "I'm all grown-up, I assure you."

Zach let his eyes travel slowly over Anders's body. "Trust me, I've noticed," he said, voice dropping into a deep murmur.

Anders reached out again, this time to set his glass on the table. Sitting back, he slid his arm along the back of the sofa, fingers brushing the small strip of bare skin above Zach's shirt collar. His eyes fell to Zach's mouth for a long second. "I'm glad I'm not the only observant one here."

"Are you flirting with me, my lord?" Zach turned his body toward Anders and slid closer, leaning across Anders to put his own glass down.

"I most certainly am." Anders followed Zach as he straightened, and in a heartbeat, was up and straddling Zach, settling his firm ass right on Zach's lap. "Are you objecting, *Zachary*?"

Zach stroked up Anders's back. "Absolutely not, Anders." His hand slid into Anders's hair, fingers tangling in the thick black curls. Holding Anders's head still, Zach took his mouth in a rough kiss, biting Anders's lip, soothing the sting with his tongue, tasting the liquor in Anders's mouth as he laid claim.

Anders opened for him immediately, groaning softly as he cupped Zach's jaw in one hand, kissing back as good as he got. The other hand slid around Zach's waist, hot even through the layers of fabric. Anders broke the kiss at last, but only to mouth his way to Zach's ear and nip the lobe. "I want to taste you all over," he whispered, then licked behind Zach's ear. "Every. Last. Inch."

Zach tilted his head to give Anders plenty of room. "I think that can be arranged." Keeping one hand fisted in Anders's hair, Zach slid the other down to cup and squeeze his ass. "As long as you let me return the favor."

"Gladly." Anders made quick work of the fastenings along the side of Zach's trousers, pulling the front panel aside to reach in and wrap long, smooth fingers around his cock.

"Oh fuck," Zach gasped. His hips lifted into Anders's touch. "God, that's— God." He slammed his head back against the sofa, making a last-ditch effort not to lose his fucking mind. He hadn't had someone else's hand on his dick for far too long, but Anders had seemed almost fragile for a moment there and Zach didn't want to take advantage of his grief. "We're moving pretty fast, here. You sure—"

"Yes." Anders tightened his grip, stroking relentlessly, wrist twisting. At the same time, he was hovering just above Zach's mouth, panting wetly against his lips. "Come on. Let me see what you've got for me."

Zach surged up and took Anders's mouth again, tongue thrusting between his lips in rhythm with his hand. He maneuvered Anders onto his back and braced himself on one forearm so he could reach down and rub a hand hard against Anders's cock. "How much do you want?"

"Your—your hand," Anders gasped, throwing his head back and exposing the long column of his neck. "Or your mouth. Either." He swallowed heavily, hands flailing until he found Zach's back, pulling his shirt up to touch skin. "I'm not picky right now."

"You said you wanted to taste me," Zach growled. "Me first." With a last bite at Anders's lips, Zach moved between Anders's legs and opened his pants, freeing his cock and swallowing him down. God. Zach moaned around the thick length, savoring the taste and smell and *feel* as he licked and sucked, alternating hard suction with teasing swipes of tongue, pulling away to lick his balls.

Above Zach's head, Anders was outright whimpering, his fingers knotted in the stiff fabric of Zach's uniform jacket. He kept squirming, back arching as though he was trying to resist the urge to thrust, and every so often one of his whimpers formed a broken and desperate sob of Zach's name.

Zach began rolling his hips, rubbing his dick against the sofa. He sucked kisses along the shaft of Anders's cock. "C'mon," he breathed over the leaking tip, "c'mon. You know you want to, Anders, just let go."

Anders gasped, lifting his hips and pushing deeper into Zach's mouth as Zach took him back down. "Your mouth," he finally managed. "Fucking . . . your mouth. I can't hold off much longer. I can't—"

"Do it." Zach took Anders even deeper than before, into his throat, and swallowed around the head of his cock. He grabbed Anders's ass and dug his fingers into the flesh, vaguely wishing the pants were completely gone. He wanted to feel skin, wanted to pull Anders's cheeks apart and push his fingers inside. Wanted more than just his fingers in there. He swallowed again and then again as Anders came, spilling down his throat.

He kept sucking as he pulled back slowly, tongue moving over Anders's dick until Anders twitched away.

"Too much," he groaned.

"Your turn," Zach rasped, voice harsh and jaw sore. "Make me come."

Surprisingly smooth, Anders shifted them so Zach was sitting up, with Anders back in his lap. This time, he licked a filthy strip up his own palm before grasping Zach's shaft in a sure grip. He didn't bother with teasing, jerking Zach at a steady pace as he leaned in, growling in Zach's ear.

"I wanted to fuck you all through dinner. Bend you right over the table, door wide open and half the ship walking by. I wanted to spread you out and fuck myself on you again and again. See what your face looks like when you come with my name on your lips."

"Yeah?" Zach was breathing hard. "You sure hid it well." He rolled his head on the back of the sofa, then tangled both hands in Anders's hair to pull him into a kiss that was rough, teeth and tongues clashing until Zach couldn't keep it together anymore, pressing his forehead to Anders's and panting against his mouth. "C'mon, faster, squeeze me harder, I won't break."

And Anders gave him exactly what he wanted, grip going to just the right side of punishing. "Let me have it, Zach," he ordered. "Let go for me and maybe I'll let you fuck me later."

Zach fought a moment more, desperate to ride the edge of pleasure as long as he could, but Anders's hand was perfect, almost too much, and he cried out as his body arched up hard enough to lift Anders briefly before he curled in. His forehead fell to Anders's shoulder, and his hips kept jerking as he spilled over Anders's hand and Anders kept tugging, milking him dry until it was too much. "Stop, fuck."

"I've got you." Anders ran his clean hand soothingly down Zach's back, easing his shaking. "I've got you."

Somehow, they managed to lie down on the sofa together, Anders wiping his hand clean on the hem of his shirt. It was quiet for a moment or two, and then Anders laughed softly, his face tucked against Zach's neck. "I hope you don't expect me to leave right away. I don't think I could walk if my life depended on it."

Zach laughed. "That would be really rude, my lord. Besides," he smirked, "you still owe me a blowjob. Maybe we can get out of our clothes next time too."

Anders yawned and curled even closer. "Maybe," he said, voice drifting as sleep pulled him under.

Anders woke gradually, aware first that his arm was asleep, and second that this was because it was pinned by a trim but muscular body beneath him on the bed. No, not a bed: the couch in Zach's quarters. With that observation came all the memories of the night before, and Anders bit back a groan as he buried his face against Zach's bare shoulder. Dimly, Anders remembered them struggling out of their clothes at some point in the night, and now they were wearing nothing more than their undershorts.

Jackson was going to have his *head* when he found out. Not only had Zach not been cleared for this kind of interaction with Anders's royal person, but Anders no longer had the luxury of indulging in casual sexual encounters like normal people. Several years ago, when his responsibilities had been little more than a vague notion on a distant horizon, Anders had been able to get away with falling into bed with the odd stranger. But now, with his obligations to the crown coming to bear at full force, Anders was obliged to admit that his sex life was far from his own business any more.

Still. As a distraction from what Anders had lost as well as what he was facing, Zach was probably the best Anders could have hoped for. There would be time enough for facing reality once they reached Drion, but in the meantime, Anders couldn't help but wonder if Zach would be interested in that promised repeat performance right away—this time without the Glorianna Fire Wine.

Zach shifted under Anders, stiffening briefly before relaxing into the sofa and running a hand down Anders's back. "Hey," he rasped. "You awake?"

"I am." Anders kissed Zach's shoulder, a lazy press of lips. "Just drafting a letter to the Navy, insisting they provide their captains with bigger beds."

"Trust me, I have a big bed." Zach laughed softly. "Would you like to see it?"

Anders chuckled. "I'm pretty sure that's a line, Captain."

"You have a filthy mind, my lord." Zach's hand drifted down over Anders's ass.

"You have no idea." Anders grinned and lifted his head enough to kiss Zach properly.

Zach kissed Anders again, then again, pulling him into a harder embrace, tangling their legs together. "C'mon then," he murmured against Anders's lips, "let's go look at it."

"In a minute." Anders surrendered himself to Zach's kisses, enjoying himself far too much to consider stopping. And judging by the way Zach was firming up against his hip, Anders was willing to bet he wasn't the only one. "Just another minute."

A sharp knock sounded at the door, startling them both as the door intercom buzzed. "My lord," Bern said through the speaker. "The crew will be changing shifts soon, and the halls will be quite busy. Now would be the best time to retire to the correct quarters."

Zach's arms tightened reflexively, then relaxed. He lifted his arm to check his wrist unit. "He's right, unless you want to be seen wearing the same clothes you wore last night. And at least some of the crew will notice; it's not often we have royalty on board."

Anders sighed. "I know." Still, he couldn't help admiring the flex of Zach's arm, the firm muscles of his chest, the way his torso narrowed down in a perfect vee—a black mark on Zach's torso, just under his left nipple, caught Anders's eye, and he froze in recognition. *It can't be.*

"My lord?" Bern's voice was a bit louder, and as far from amused as he had ever been.

"Yes," Anders said, his voice not nearly as steady as he wanted it to be. "Give me a moment, please."

Careful not to elbow or knee Zach anywhere tender, Anders climbed up and off the sofa with as much grace as he could muster. Their clothes were in a heap on the floor, and Anders fumbled with them for a moment, trying to buy time to get his act together.

"We need to do this again," Zach said, rustling behind Anders as he rose, before his hand reached in to help separate their clothes. His voice was amused as he added, "You still owe me a blowjob."

Anders laughed as he slipped on his shirt, the tail stiff with spunk. "I didn't realize we were keeping score," he said, forcing his voice to stay light. It took a moment to determine whose black pants were whose, but Anders's were, of course, made of much finer material. He stepped into them and stood, pulling them up quickly before tugging on his boots with smooth, practiced motions.

Dressed very nearly decently, Anders chanced a look at Zach. Still mostly naked, the captain was gathering his own clothes into a neat bundle. Despite everything, despite knowing it was in all of their best interests if Anders were to walk away and never look back, he couldn't help giving Zach a long, slow once-over, followed by a promising smile. Zach really was a gorgeous man, his black hair mussed from a night of sleep and the faint wrinkles at the corners of his vibrant blue eyes deepening with his wide, kissable smile.

"Still," Anders said, stepping in and kissing Zach softly, "we wouldn't want anyone to say the royal family doesn't pay their debts."

"And you can be sure I'll collect." Zach's kiss was slow but firm. "Plus, you haven't seen my bed yet."

"Wouldn't want to miss that," Anders whispered against Zach's mouth. Bern knocked on the door again, two sharp raps, and Anders knew they were out of time. He sighed. "You'll have to show me later."

"Until then, my lord." Zach's somber voice held no hint of the lazy smirk on his face.

"Good day, Captain," Anders said, sketching a full and formal bow, with an added wink at the end for flourish. Then he slipped out the door and back under Bern's watchful gaze.

Jackson was standing across the hall, face dark and thunderous. Anders held up one tired hand and sighed. "I know. I know everything you're going to say, because you're right. I need to start acting like a man with responsibilities and not like an oversexed teenager. But it's a bit late to start behaving now, so let's go back to my rooms so I can shower and sleep, and you can yell at me later."

Bern curled one solid hand over Anders's shoulder with a supportive squeeze. For a moment, Bern and Jackson stared at each other, clearly having a private conversation across their bond. Then Jackson deflated, nodding slightly.

"We worry about you," he said as Bern steered all three of them down the hall and back toward their respective quarters. "After losing your father like that, we don't want to see you get your heart broken on top of everything else."

Anders stifled an inappropriate laugh, right hand wrapping around his left wrist, worrying at the edges of the privacy patch. Marks were supposed to give you a clue as to how you might meet your match; Anders's was a crown with a single star cut out of the front.

Just like the mark he'd seen on Zach moments before.

Swallowing down the hysteria threatening in the back of his throat, Anders smiled and nodded to whatever Bern was saying until he could slip away into the blessed isolation of his own room.

He was so completely fucked.

CHAPTER TWO

Zach scratched absently at his mark as the door slid shut behind Anders. That had been unexpected but definitely not unwelcome. He wished Oliver had told him how hot the royal cousin was instead of how rude he'd been, because one, Anders was tired and grieving which put his behavior in a different light, and two, Zach would have liked to have had some warning before being confronted with the gorgeous Lord Anders. Then again, he wasn't sure he would have believed Oliver anyway.

He wandered through his bedroom and into the shower, dropping his clothes on the floor along the way. Nude, he stepped under the spray and groaned as the water pounded his shoulders and back. Anders had been hot, all right, hot like burning, and Zach still felt a little singed.

The water sluiced over his body, rinsing the suds away as he washed himself. He left his cock for last, because Anders still owed him a blowjob and Zach's body didn't seem to realize it wasn't happening right away. Zach wrapped his hand around himself and closed his eyes, letting his head fall back as he remembered exactly what it had been like to have Anders's dick in his mouth, to look up Anders's body and see his face as he came. Zach's hand slowly stroked over his cock, the other sliding down to cup his balls. He let the feeling, the need, build as long as he could, but he couldn't hold out for long. His hand started moving faster, up and down, thumb rubbing over the head on each upward stroke. He was panting now too, a soft hitch in his breath every time his thumb brushed his leaking slit. His other hand pushed lower, between his legs, and he widened his stance enough that he could press his fingers against his hole, work two inside, and that was all he could take. His body arched and stiffened as he came, spurting again and again until he was left shaking, propped up against the shower wall.

Eventually he turned off the water and dried himself, profoundly grateful that he wasn't needed on the bridge for a while. Orgasms always wiped him out, but the two Anders-induced orgasms seemed to have hit him harder than usual.

He wasn't complaining.

Zach found Anders in one of the viewing areas that night, Jackson and Bern standing guard in the hallway. He was at the window, staring out at the stars, and Zach wanted to walk up behind him and wrap both arms around him. The urge didn't surprise him—he wasn't a relationship guy, not really, but when he was with somebody, he had the tendency to be a cuddler. But it wasn't appropriate, not here and not with Anders. He could stand next to him, though.

Anders glanced at Zach briefly, his dark eyes sad for a moment before a neat, blank mask covered his features. "Captain," he said turning back to the stars. "I trust you are well?"

Moving closer than was strictly proper, Zach whispered in Anders's ear, "I was well when I had your dick in my mouth. Now I'm hungry." He stood straight and continued in a normal voice, "I've been looking for you. I wanted to ask if you would care to dine at the captain's table tonight."

"Did you now?" Anders put his hands behind his back, one wrist grasped lightly in the other hand.

Zach took a small step back, both amused and a little confused. Anders certainly hadn't seemed to have any problem with last night. Now, though, there was something a little stiff in his attitude, and not the kind of stiff that Zach was hoping for.

"I'm curious what you're hoping for, Captain." Anders still didn't look away from the stars, his shoulders rigid and pulled back to parade rest.

"Dinner, to start." Zach's voice was slightly more formal as he straightened to match Anders's posture.

There was a pause, just a few moments while Anders seemed to be working over whatever was bothering him, and then he relaxed by fractions. "Will there be drinks in your quarters again after?" he finally asked, voice as smooth as glass. "I'd hate to miss out on any of the experience now that I've had quite the royal treatment."

Zach raised an eyebrow but didn't comment, willing to go with the flow if it meant Anders in his quarters. "I expect so," he said instead, "as I meant my actual table in my rooms."

Anders laughed softly. "I don't recall there being enough room for four at that particular table," he said, and turned. The move caused the backs of their hands to brush together, fingers nearly tangling.

"No, there isn't." Zach stroked his finger between two of Anders's as their hands touched. "But, then again, I wasn't planning on four people."

"Well then," Anders said, voice low and intimate. "How could I refuse? Besides, I believe we have an account to settle."

Zach took a deep breath in an attempt to keep from grabbing Anders right there. Damn it, he had more control than this! The deep breath only made things worse; it filled his lungs with the rich scent of Anders's cologne and that small something that was just Anders. He curled his hands into fists and then slowly, deliberately, relaxed them. He gestured back toward the door. "Shall we?"

They walked side by side all the way to Zach's quarters, shoulders bumping innocently now and then. Anders kept his hands clasped behind his back and his expression politely blank the whole way, but never once raised his voice above the quietest murmur, giving Zach the perfect excuse to be far closer than would normally be considered appropriate.

The instant the door shut behind them in Zach's cabin, Anders spun, pushing him against the door. "Dinner can wait," he purred, and pulled Zach down into a hard, demanding kiss.

Zach willingly opened to Anders's tongue, kissing him back just as hard. He shoved his leg between Anders's and pressed up, rubbing his thigh against Anders's dick. Anders rocked into him, hands pushing into the open front of his uniform jacket to grab his shoulders from behind.

They kissed like that for a while, grinding and nipping at each other. It was slower than the night before, but somehow hotter. Probably because they both knew where this was leading, and how fucking amazing it was going to be. Then Anders shifted, hands sliding down, lips kissing what little of Zach's neck was left exposed by his collar.

"Take your jacket off," Anders ordered, then sank to his knees, hands going for Zach's pants and pulling them open.

Zach immediately wrestled himself out of his jacket and threw it aside, then slid his hands into Anders's curls. "God, yeah, I want your mouth."

Anders grinned up at him and ran the tip of his tongue over his upper lip. "Wouldn't want to let you down, now would I?" He nuzzled Zach through his shorts. "Besides," he added, kissing up Zach's shaft, "as you keep reminding me, I owe you."

"Hey," Zach said, "you're the one who offered to settle our account." He sucked in a harsh breath. He dropped his head back against the wall with a *thunk* and tightened his fingers in Anders's hair, hips rolling up into Anders's face with an involuntary jerk. "So do it."

"Don't rush perfection," Anders said with a laugh, tugging Zach's pants and shorts down to midthigh. "You know," he went on in a maddeningly conversational tone as he wrapped those long fingers around Zach's prick and stroked, "one of these times we should actually get naked. I'd love to see all of you at once."

Zach groaned. "We should. Tonight, even— *Fuck*," he gasped. Anders had licked the head of his dick before digging the tip of his tongue into Zach's slit. "Do that again."

Anders did as ordered, following up with a wet, sucking kiss on his crown. Then he ducked his head and licked teasingly up Zach's entire length, humming softly in pleasure the whole way. Back up where he'd started, Anders parted his full lips and sucked Zach in; first the head, then more and more until Zach was halfway down Ander's throat, Anders's hand curled around his base, squeezing once.

Zach couldn't help himself. He began thrusting, slow and steady, eyes almost crossing with pleasure as the head of his dick rubbed against the inside of Anders's mouth. "Fuck, so good, baby, so good.

Wanna come down your throat and then ride your dick until I come again."

At that, Anders groaned and swallowed Zach down completely, hand dropping to cradle Zach's balls, one finger reaching back to rub over his perineum. Then he swallowed once, twice, and started bobbing his head in time to Zach's thrusts, an encouragement for face-fucking if Zach had ever seen one.

Zach took the invitation, thrusting harder, rubbing away the tears at the corners of Anders's eyes even as he moved faster, choking him on each shove in. And Anders just knelt there, looking up at Zach's face the whole time, pupils blown wide and mouth wet and ready and open. Anders's hands worked furiously on his trousers, yanking them open with jerky motions and pulling out his flushed cock with a broken sound that vibrated down Zach's entire length.

"Don't you *dare* come," Zach growled, tugging Anders's hair. "I want you to fuck me."

Anders let go of his own cock like he'd been burned, slapping his hands on the wall on either side of Zach's hips. Then he pulled away from Zach's cock, holding eye contact until he was sitting back on his heels. Swiftly, Anders yanked his shirt off and tossed it across the room before sucking briefly on Zach's crown again.

"Fuck my mouth," he ordered, voice rough and fucked out from the punishment Zach's cock had given him. "Fuck my mouth and come on my face."

Zach moaned at the thought of his come all over Anders's face, marking him, making him *his*. He shifted back, unsettled by the possessiveness of the feeling, but then Anders dug his tongue into Zach's slit before sucking hard, and every thought flew right out of Zach's head, leaving only the primal drive to come.

He fucked into Anders's mouth again and again, the head of his cock rubbing against the roof of Anders's mouth, the insides of his cheeks and into his throat, not stopping even when Anders gagged on his thick length. He could feel the orgasm building, fed the pleasure with images of Anders buried deep in his ass and the gorgeous picture Anders made on his knees with his mouth stretched wide. It was finally too much, and Zach pulled free, stripping his own dick with rough, quick strokes until he came, spurting on Anders's face, spunk spilling onto flushed skin, eyelashes sticking together.

"Oh my god," Zach groaned. "Oh my fucking god, you're pretty." He tugged Anders up and kissed him, ignoring the fact that Anders's face was a mess and that it was getting all over his own.

Anders nipped at Zach's mouth, rough and eager and barely able to choke out a single word. "Bedroom," he managed. "*Now.*"

Anders couldn't get undressed fast enough once they were in Zach's bedroom. Still, he took the time to grab a wet cloth from the small attached bath, cleaning both of their faces first. Once he'd wrangled off every last stitch of clothing, Anders nearly pounced on Zach, who had sprawled across the bed, his miles and miles of gorgeous, pale skin on display and ready to be touched. If Zach thought Anders was beautiful, then he clearly needed to take a look in the mirror more often.

He kissed up Zach's body, fingers skirting around the soul mark on his ribs as he went by. He pushed away the jagged, confusing tangle of emotions that little mark caused in favor of kissing Zach's mouth, which was soft and pliable in the wake of his recent orgasm. "Lube?"

Zach waved lazily at the drawer built into the wall, just out of his reach. "In there," he said. "It's all in there."

Anders crawled over to the drawer, finding not only the lube but a nice assortment of dildos and butt plugs, a few with remote controls. Nothing too kinky, but plenty to make their time together more than a little spicy. He groaned and lightly knocked his forehead against the wall. God, but Zach really was *perfect*.

Back over to Zach, Anders kissed him hard. "I might never let you out of this bed," he promised, and knelt between Zach's spread legs, opening the lube in a rush. The walk to Zach's room and cleaning up had given him time to cool off, and he was going to make the most of the calm while it lasted. "Open up for me, darling."

Zach lifted his legs, planting his feet on the bed and letting his knees fall apart. "Open me up yourself," he said, raising an eyebrow. "Slick up your fingers and put them inside me, stretch me wide."

"As you command," Anders said, circling one slick finger around Zach's entrance before bending to kiss up Zach's inner thigh, nose nudging at his soft cock. He pushed the tip of his finger in, just enough to curl and tug, while at the same time he gently sucked Zach's cock into his mouth. Zach *had* said he wanted to come again, after all.

Widening his knees even farther, Zach moaned. "God, that feels good. Give me another finger. I can take it. I want you to fuck me."

Releasing Zach's still-flaccid cock, Anders laughed quietly. "That's the idea," he said, kissing Zach's scrotum lightly. He wanted Zach, obviously, but the depth of that want was more surprising than he cared to admit. Maybe it was the matching marks, maybe it was the emotional strain of the past few days, or maybe it was just that Anders couldn't remember the last time he'd fucked someone who made his stomach flip like Zach did with each kiss. Either way, he wanted to make Zach feel as desperate as he was, wanted to worship his body until Zach was a shaking, pleading mess.

"Next time, you're fucking me," was what Anders said, however. "And don't think I won't collect."

"I'm counting on it," Zach said. "I'll eat you out first, get you all wet and loose before I slide my fingers into you, stretch you wide, so you're ready to take my cock." His hips arched up into Anders's hand, forcing his finger farther into Zach's body. "Get me ready to take yours."

In answer, Anders sucked a dark mark into Zach's leg, swirling his tongue like he was leaving his signature. A stamp upon royal property, not for anyone else to have ever again. It was foolish, but he didn't care. Not in the privacy of his own mind.

When Anders added a third finger, he grinned at the feel of Zach twitching against his cheek. "Glad you could join us," he rasped, and carefully took Zach, still mostly soft, back into his mouth, coaxing him with lips and tongue.

Zach cupped Anders's head, fingers tangling in his curls again. He hummed softly and then said, "Just like that, baby, it feels so good to have your mouth on me."

No one had ever before presumed to give Anders an endearment, and when Zach did, it made a part of him melt a little. If it meant hearing Zach call him *baby* each time, then Anders would gladly suck his cock at every opportunity, if only so he'd never stop.

Feeling ridiculous even for thinking that, Anders lost himself in the pure, mindless pleasure of opening Zach up, of sucking his cock to gradual, perfect hardness. He lost track of time, only focusing on Zach beneath him, around him, inside him, and he couldn't help but moan in anticipation.

Zach writhed under Anders's hands and tongue, his own hands tightening in Anders's hair and his hips rolling in rhythm. He was reduced to groans, breath hitching and body trembling until he finally cried out. "Baby, *please*, I— Fuck. Fuck me already, I need you inside me."

Anders released Zach with a curse, fumbling for the lube to slick himself up. "How—" He swallowed, tried again. "How do you want it?"

Hooking his hands under his knees, Zach pulled up and out, opening himself completely to Anders. "Just like this."

"You're going to be the death of me," Anders groaned, swooping in for a quick, hard kiss. Then he was pushing in, slow and steady and completely forgetting to breathe. Buried all the way in Zach's perfect, tight body, Anders could only brace himself on shaking arms as he tried to get a hold of himself enough to keep from shooting off then and there.

Zach moved underneath him, hooking his knees on Anders's shoulders so he could tease Anders's nipples, rubbing and pinching. His body clenched down on Anders's dick, the muscles in his ass squeezing hard at the intrusion. "Stretch me so good, god. Give me a minute."

Anders laughed, still shaky but not nearly as overwhelmed as he'd been at first. "It's been a damned long time for me," he whispered, shifting side to side just enough to take the edge off his growing need to move. "Normally I'm in your position. And you are far too good-looking for my sanity. Consider this your fair warning."

"I consider myself warned." Zach grinned. "So, you think I'm good-looking? I never would have guessed."

"Don't fish for compliments," Anders said. He turned his head to kiss the side of Zach's knee, then slid back slowly. "It's unbecoming."

Zach met Anders's slow thrusts in perfect rhythm. "I don't need to fish," he said with a laugh in his voice. "I can tell by the way you move against me."

Apparently, cocky teasing really did it for Anders, because he couldn't resist moving a little harder, a little faster. Under him, Zach continued to keep pace. Of course he did, because he was hell bent on ruining Anders for anyone else, ever.

Dropping one of Zach's legs, Anders leaned in and kissed him. "I don't know how much of this I can take," he admitted breathlessly, kissing Zach once more for good measure.

"Then let go," Zach said simply. He rubbed his nose against Anders's even as he squeezed hard on Anders's cock. "Just let go."

"*Fuck*," Anders gasped, and then gave in, rearing back as he started pounding into Zach's body in earnest. He'd been running hot since about thirty seconds after he'd first gotten his mouth on Zach's cock in the other room, and now fucking Zach, he was *finally* going to come—it wiped out what remained of Anders's usual careful control during sex.

Zach strained against Anders, meeting him thrust for thrust, circling his hips and crying out when Anders hit his prostate. He reached between them and, making a loose fist, began stroking his dick, managing a contrasting rhythm that rubbed his knuckles against Anders's stomach. After several strokes, he stiffened and came, spilling over his fist and stomach, body clenching again and again on Anders's dick.

Anders cried out, hips stuttering. "God, Zach—" he said, and then came so hard his vision filled with stars. He thrust in once more, deep, and held it while he shook with the overwhelming sensations. *Yes. Definitely ruined.*

After a few shaking seconds, he collapsed on top of Zach, moving to the side a touch to slip free of him with a sigh. "Don't think this means you get out of feeding me dinner, you know," he said, lazy and happy. "I fully expect another of those amazing steaks when I can walk again."

Zach stroked a hand lightly down Anders's back. "I can totally get behind that," Zach said, voice slurred. "Once my brain kicks in."

Anders grinned, eyelids heavy. "Wake me when you've provided for me," he managed, slipping off to sleep.

CHAPTER THREE

Three days later, it was Anders who found Zach in the viewing area. After a careful glance up and down the hallway, Anders shut the door and locked it before coming up behind Zach and kissing the nape of his neck. It was risky as hell outside of their quarters, but he hadn't seen Zach all day, and was nearly burning with the need to touch him.

"See something interesting out there?" he asked, sliding his hands down over tense shoulders and arms.

"Freedom," Zach said shortly. Then he sighed and relaxed minutely. "Sorry, I shouldn't snap at you. It's not your fault I'm losing one of my ensigns."

Anders raised an eyebrow at that. Even including that somewhat awkward dinner his first night on board, he'd not seen Zach in a foul mood before. "What's going on, then?"

Zach shook his head. "Stupid kid is *bonding*. With one of the fucking officers I picked up before I stopped for you. Clearly I should have kept them away from my people."

"Ah." Anders tried to sound understanding, because he knew Zach's anger. Hell, before this, Anders hadn't *ever* wanted to bond with anyone, not after watching his father waste away. But regardless of what they wanted or the fact that they barely knew each other, he and Zach would find themselves shuttled straight to the nearest temple if anyone found out about their match. And Zach might be a virtual stranger, but Anders couldn't imagine Zach would be very happy about giving up everything. And give it all up, Zach would have to, because it wasn't as though a member of the royal family could fuck off and live on a Navy ship, now was it?

Then again, everyone was always on about how a match was a true blessing, the sort of gift you shouldn't ignore. Daniel had certainly seemed happy with his. Maybe he and Zach could find a happy medium, maybe Zach was hiding a poet's soul under that unfairly sexy uniform . . . Anders ruthlessly squashed the idea that maybe they could make it work. He had never once needed romance before, and he sure as hell didn't have time for it now. Just a few more days, and they'd be on Drion, and he could pretend he'd never seen that damn soul mark. Zach could move on to his next assignment, and Anders . . . well, Anders would be right where he'd always meant to be.

The ache in his chest was unexpected. "Still, considering how rare matching is these days—"

"Maybe it should be more rare." Zach turned to face Anders. "They're going to tie themselves together for the rest of their lives, and I'm going to lose a girl with a great future ahead of her in the Navy, a future that's now completely wasted."

"Is it wasted?" Anders flexed his fingers, resisting the urge to reach for Zach. God, this was worse than he'd imagined it would be. "Just because everything is changing doesn't mean she won't have a new future, something even better for having someone to share it with."

"Her match is a ranking officer." Zach ran a hand through his hair in frustration. "She's going to have to sublimate everything she wanted and worked for to accommodate her match's assignments. How is that not wasting her own naval future?"

A knot formed in Anders's stomach; his mark burned beneath his privacy patch. "Still, if they're willing to bond this quickly, it must be a very solid match. I've heard of some that never bond out of sheer personal incompatibility."

Zach raised an eyebrow. "And matching? Made for one another because you have the same birthmark?" He shook his head. "These girls are just hot for each other. They should get married instead of bonding; that way they can end it when they get sick of each other."

"I take it you have no plans to bond in the near future, then?" Anders was pretty sure he'd kept his voice light. If not, Zach was probably too angry to notice. Still, he couldn't help the small ache growing in his chest where he was ashamed to admit hope had been slowly growing.

"Near future, far future, doesn't matter." Zach shrugged and scratched absently at his ribs. Left side, right where his mark was. "I have no plans to even look for my match, much less bond. I won't risk my career nor force someone else to give up theirs."

Anders turned away to hide his guilt. Bonding with Anders would certainly be the end to Zach's career, no doubt. Anders had known that from the beginning. Still, after the past few days, Anders had dared to wonder if they might make it work anyhow. He *ached* for Zach when they were apart, and wasn't sure how much was the match and how much was a natural development after spending so much time together. It was odd to want something so intimate with a man he scarcely knew, but stranger still for how natural it felt now that Anders recognized the hollow feeling in his chest as affection. Shaking the thought off, Anders crossed the room to a sofa and sat, patting the cushion next to him in invitation.

"I take it they want the captain to officiate the bonding?" he asked, when what he really wanted to say was, *Please let me change your mind.*

"Of course," Zach said, walking over to join Anders on the sofa. "It's one of my responsibilities as captain. Not everyone can officiate a bonding. And they're so excited about it too."

Seeing that Zach had calmed a little, Anders chanced sliding closer, kissing him behind the right ear, where a bonding mark would show. The soul mark on his wrist burned under the patch, but Anders ignored it and pushed on. "Young love," he said softly, proud when he didn't choke on the words.

Zach snorted. "I suppose." He absently curled an arm around Anders's shoulders. "Why can't they be satisfied with fucking each other's brains out?" He grinned at Anders. "It sure works for us."

Something suspiciously like tears pricked at Anders's eyes, and he buried his face against Zach's shoulder, slowly breathing in the scent of fabric, cologne, and skin. "We're a special case," he said at last, "obviously."

"Obviously," Zach echoed. He turned to press a kiss to Anders's head. "Well. It's not until tomorrow. Let's stop talking about them and talk about what I'm going to do to you after dinner instead."

The words were inviting on the surface, but Zach's voice was more morose than randy, and Anders wasn't in the mood for anything beyond curling up and feeling sorry for himself. He shook his head slightly and burrowed closer. "Do you mind if we just sit here for a while? I locked the door; we can claim we were discussing top-secret military matters if anyone asks."

Zach sat back on the sofa, settling Anders more comfortably against him. "Sure, baby," he said absently. "But we'll have to come up with another excuse. You don't have top-secret clearance."

Anders snorted but didn't contradict him. That would take too much explaining. And besides, Zach would know soon enough. Drion was only a couple of days away, and all the unpleasant realities of Anders's life waited there for him. He clung a little closer to Zach. Just two more days, and then this would all be over and the small measure of peace he'd stolen would be gone.

CHAPTER FOUR

Trying to keep his face bland, Zach gestured to the two women kneeling a few feet away. "Arise," he said, "and bring me your cloth."

Obediently the women rose and walked with a slow, measured pace toward him, the trains on their simple white dresses whispering across the floor behind them. When they reached him, they bowed their heads and held out their hands, the teal sash spread across their fingers. Zach took the cloth and, holding it in one hand, picked up the ceremonial knife with the other.

"You are matched?" he asked.

"Yes, Captain," they said in unison.

"You wish to bond, to join your lives, to be ever faithful to one another? You wish to link your minds, hearts, and souls ever more tightly together as you age, to care for one another and live for one another for the rest of your days?"

"Yes, Captain," they said again. Thalia turned her head slightly to meet Serena's eyes, both of them blushing, but Zach pretended not to see it. He didn't want to have to start the whole nonsense from the beginning, wanted it over and done with.

Zach nodded. "Hold out your right arms, palms up." When the women complied, he cupped Serena's hand and made a quick, shallow slice across the tender skin of her wrist. He did the same to Thalia and said to them, "Face each other, and see your future."

The women turned as directed, unable to resist exchanging small smiles as they did. Zach put the knife down on the small table to his side. He reached between them to take Thalia's wrist and took

Serena's in the other hand. Turning their wrists, he pressed the wounds together. "Hold tight to each other."

They grasped each other's forearms, and Zach slowly and carefully wound the soft teal cloth around their wrists to bind them. When he finished, he clasped his own hand around their wrists.

"Thou art bound," he intoned the traditional blessing, determined not to roll his eyes. As soon as he let go of their wrists, the girls sobbed almost in unison and then wrapped their free arms around each other in a tight hug. The crowd cheered, some of Thalia's crewmates whistling obnoxiously. Under the din, Zach smiled at the newly bonded. "Congratulations."

"Oh, thank you, Captain!" Thalia beamed at him. "Thank you so much!"

"Yes, sir, thank you! We're so happy." Serena's smile was a little shyer than Thalia's was.

"I can see you are." Zach forced a warm, friendly tone. "I'm honored to have been asked to perform the ceremony for you. Stay tied for a few minutes—there must be sufficient time for your blood to mingle and begin your connection."

Thalia's smile got even brighter. "I can't wait to feel what she feels, Captain! It will be wonderful."

Zach just nodded. "Go greet your guests, girls. And may your lives be prosperous and joyful."

Guests were already queueing up to greet the newly bonded couple, with Anders at the front of the line. Dressed all in black as usual, Anders wore a short, formal jacket that cut off immediately below his ribs. He had every button polished and fastened up to the hollow of his throat, where the part in the high collar allowed the barest hint of black lace to peek through. The only true color aside from his golden buttons were his epaulets, the same teal as the new couple's bonding sash.

"Congratulations, ladies," Anders said as he approached them with a wide smile on his face, bright teeth flashing against his dark complexion. He bowed deeply to Thalia and Serena in turn. "I'm sure you will have many years of happiness ahead of you." He stepped aside once they'd thanked him, making room for Jackson and Bern to offer their own blessings, and walked over to Zach.

"Very nice ceremony," he said quietly. "It was good of you to do this for them, Zach."

Zach gave him a sardonic look, then turned to pick up his ceremonial knife. "It's not like there are an abundance of people who can do it on board," he said as he wiped traces of blood from the blade with a sanitizing cloth.

"You could have put them off, made them wait until we reached Drion," Anders said, touching Zach's wrist briefly. "You didn't. It never even occurred to you not to do your duty for them, no matter your personal feelings. It's admirable."

"Well, thank you, I guess." Zach sheathed the knife and secured it in its velvet box. He was almost as uncomfortable with Anders's praise as he was with having performed the ceremony in the first place. He rolled his shoulders under the stiff, heavy, navy-blue fabric, then tugged the hem of the jacket back down into place. "If you'll excuse me, I need to put the knife in my safe and get out of my dress uniform."

"You're not going to stay for the reception?" Anders asked. "And here I was hoping to get a dance with the captain."

Zach shrugged. "I have to secure the knife. I hadn't planned to come back, no."

Anders frowned briefly. "I know we're not . . ." He waved a hand as though that would explain what they *were*. "But I can't help wondering why you . . ."

"Why I what?" Zach asked, cocking an eyebrow.

For a few seconds, it looked like Anders might actually let it drop, but he put a bit more steel in his spine and pressed on. "Why you hate bonding so much. There are countless studies showing that bonded couples enjoy longer lifespans and stronger immune systems, especially in matched couples. Not to mention the psychological benefits to having a partner as utterly committed as you are."

"And the psychological benefits of having another person in your head?" Zach said. "And then when one of the pair dies, the other's life is essentially over. I don't see a benefit in that."

"My parents were bonded," Anders said, following Zach as he headed for the exit. Jackson and Bern followed at a discreet distance. "My father never truly recovered from my mother's death, it's true.

But he lived on for another fifteen years. A full, meaningful life, if a little lonely."

Zach kept pace with Anders, not striding ahead like he wanted to do. What was it with Anders and bonding, anyway? He sure hadn't seemed to want it when they first met. "Maybe he did," Zach said, "but what kind of life could that be? He never recovered, you said so yourself. It's different than losing a spouse, no matter how much you might love them. It's pretty much losing the other half of your soul, losing someone after you bond. Why set yourself up for that?"

Anders shrugged. "I . . . I suppose to some it's the ultimate expression of love and devotion. And while he may have missed Mother every day until the day he died, Father never let it stop him from what she would have wanted for him and for us. He always did what he needed to, and did everything he could to be the best father he could be and one of the strongest men I've ever known." He looked at the ground, watching their feet. "I could only hope to love someone as much as he loved her."

"I'm sure he was a great father." Zach hadn't meant to say Anders's father wasn't a good man, only that he couldn't have been truly happy once alone again. His own father, on the other hand . . . "But you do have a choice, that's my point. You don't have to bond and kick that biology into gear."

"I suppose not," Anders said carefully.

Zach smiled at Anders as he let them into his quarters, the guards staying in the hall long enough to be sure Anders was safe inside before peeling off like usual. "That's all. I don't hate bonding, exactly, I just don't see the point, not given the potential consequences."

"I guess not everyone is as practical as you," Anders said with a half smile.

"That's certainly not the first time I've been accused of that." Zach laughed as he crossed the room to open his safe and store the knife. Once he had it secure, he closed and locked the safe again. "If you want to go back to the reception, I will for a little while but not long, and definitely not in my dress uniform."

Anders moved in close, running his finger along the high edge of Zach's jacket collar, tracing along the pips Zach had polished that morning. "I think it makes you look rather dashing," he said in a low voice. "Though I could just have a thing for men in uniform."

Zach put his arm around Anders. "Dashing or not, it's really impractical." He smiled at Anders even though he was still vaguely unsettled from the ceremony.

"I think I need to talk to the admiralty about passing a rule that you in particular need to wear this all the time," Anders said, patting Zach's ass for a moment. "You have no idea how lovely the view is."

"Good luck with that." Zach pulled Anders close and bent his head, rubbing the tip of his nose along Anders's. "I can think of a lovelier view."

Anders responded by kissing Zach, slow and deep. He sucked on Zach's lower lip, nipping briefly before easing the sting with a swipe of his tongue. "We don't have to go back right away," he whispered against Zach's mouth.

Zach tilted his head and pressed his lips to Anders's, slipping his tongue into Anders's mouth. They kissed lazily for several seconds before Zach broke away. "Did you have a better idea?"

"I can think of a few," Anders teased, sliding his hand around Zach's hip and down to cup his groin.

"Oh?" Zach smiled. "Like what?" he said as he leaned into Anders's hand.

In answer, Anders dropped to his knees at Zach's feet, rubbing his cheek against the slowly growing bulge in Zach's pants. He looked up at Zach with dark eyes framed by thick, short lashes, and kissed him through the clothing even as he reached up to unfasten Zach's pants. "Have I mentioned how much I like having your cock in my mouth?"

"Not in so many words," Zach managed. He gasped in a breath as Anders opened his pants and pushed them down. Anders mouthed the soft cotton covering Zach's dick. Zach felt the damp heat, groaned as Anders sucked kisses along his shaft.

Anders curled his fingers in Zach's shorts, tugging them down just enough to free Zach's dick, flushed and full and ready. Groaning happily in the back of his throat, Anders licked up the length to the head, sucking gently and pulling off. "I want you to fuck my mouth."

Zach threaded his hands through Anders's hair and held his head still. "If you insist," Zach said, then because they were a bitch to clean, he added, "but you'll swallow and be careful about it, because if you get spunk on my uniform pants, I'll never fuck your face again."

"Now that *would* be a tragedy." Anders kissed the base of Zach's cock and grabbed his ass. "I'll just have to be neat, won't I?"

"Damn straight," Zach said. "Open your mouth." When Anders did, Zach slid his dick inside, pushing the cockhead into the soft warm flesh of Anders's cheek. He began slowly at first, hips rolling in an easy rhythm that gradually got harder and faster, until he was holding Anders's head in place as he fucked his mouth.

Anders knelt there, mouth open as Zach fucked into him again and again. He fumbled with his own pants, opening them and pulling himself out with shaking hands. Then Anders started stroking himself, jerking his cock in time to Zach's thrusts and moaning helplessly as Zach pushed against the back of his throat.

Zach could feel the orgasm gathering, pleasure sparking up his spine as he hit Anders's limit. Gritting his teeth, he slowed down to an easy roll again, pushing the head of his dick into Anders's throat, groaning harshly as Anders swallowed. Oh god, he was so *good* at this.

Anders coughed and choked around him, adjusted his angle, and then took Zach down to the root. He stayed there for a few seconds before pulling back and going down again, pressing his nose against Zach's pelvis with a moan.

It only took the moan around his dick to finally push Zach over the edge. He shot down Anders's throat in pulse after pulse. Zach curled over him, trying desperately not to choke Anders while coming apart.

Anders tapped Zach on the hip after a few seconds, no doubt needing air. Zach reluctantly pulled back, slipping free from Anders's mouth. He dropped to his knees to face him, quickly opening Anders's jacket before shoving it off Anders's shoulders. The sleeveless black shirt was next, until finally Anders was nude from the waist up, pants open, dick hard, red and leaking.

"Don't come," Zach said, struggling out of his own clothes. About to throw them on the floor, he hesitated, then jumped to his feet to finish stripping, laying his dress uniform carefully over a chair. He grabbed Anders and pulled him to his feet. "I want to make you come."

Anders struggled out of his boots, pants, and shorts, and pulled Zach in, kissing him. "It won't take much," he admitted, voice ragged. "I'm so close, Zach."

Zach leaned his forehead against Anders's. "I'll get you there, baby, make you feel so good." He pushed his hand between them to curl his fingers around Anders's dick. He stroked up and down, a quick, hard rhythm, as he pressed kisses to the side of Anders's face and sucked on his earlobe. "Come."

Whimpering, Anders clutched at Zach's side and shoulder. He trembled, but managed to hold on for a little while before crying out, coming all over Zach's hand and stomach. Zach kept working him through the last of his orgasm until Anders twitched, seemingly too sensitive to do much more than cling weakly.

"We need a shower," Zach said finally, holding Anders close. "And a nap. And when we wake up, you can fuck me again."

"Somehow I no longer mind missing the reception," Anders mumbled against Zach's shoulder, smile clear in his voice.

"I thought you might feel that way." Zach grinned and led Anders into the bathroom.

The shower was small for one man, and almost uncomfortably tight for two. But Anders clung to Zach, still so pliable it was easy to maneuver him around under the spray. "I have a huge shower back home," Anders murmured, head resting on Zach's shoulder.

Zach soaped up, rubbing the suds over Anders's back and ass. "You'll have to show me sometime."

Anders laughed. "Jackson and Bern might force you to get security clearance, first." He ran clumsy hands over Zach's back, returning the favor.

Zach snorted. "I have security clearance already. Starship captain, remember?" He stepped back so he could rub his soapy hands over Anders's chest. He thumbed at one nipple, pleased to see the flesh harden despite the fact that Anders didn't seem to have quite recovered yet. "I'm sure I'm cleared for your shower."

"Royal shower." Anders grinned up at him. "Royal protocol. Any individuals who wish to have extended *personal* relations with a member of the royal family have to go through it."

"Through the royal shower? I can get behind that." Zach grinned back at Anders before wrapping both arms around him to pull him close. He brushed a light kiss over Anders's lips.

"Very cute." Anders kissed Zach's chin, amusement obvious on his face. "Asshole."

"You love my asshole." Zach waggled his eyebrows.

That got a laugh out of Anders, happy and bright even in the tight confines of the shower. "Yeah," he admitted. "Maybe I do. I also love your bed. Shall we?"

"Let's get you dried off first." Zach turned Anders around to rinse his body. Shutting the water down, Zach grabbed a towel and began to rub the water from Anders's skin.

Anders leaned into his touch, relaxed and trusting. He pulled away, though, when Zach tried to dry his left arm, the edges of his privacy patch lifting from the shower. Instead, he looped another towel around Zach's neck and reeled him in. "I don't think I've ever met anyone quite like you before, Captain O'Connell."

"I should hope not." Zach let Anders tug him close until their bare flesh pressed together. "I think of myself as one of a kind."

"Of course you do." Anders pulled on the towel one more time. "Let's go to bed."

Zach kissed Anders lightly. "If you insist."

CHAPTER FIVE

Zach stood on the bridge, overseeing a smooth approach to the transit center at Ciebos. He was pleased at the ease with which his beautiful ship and skilled crew locked into the outdated docking bay. It was old enough that many of the necessary adjustments, automated at other stations, required a deft manual touch.

But just as the ship was locked in, the door to the bridge slid open, and Anders stormed onto the deck, Jackson and Bern right on his heels.

"Anders, what are you doing here? You can't be on the bridge, especially during a docking. You have to leave." Zach moved to counter Anders's approach.

Anders's face was thunderous, but his voice was glacial cold. "Captain O'Connell, I need to speak with you in private. *Now.*"

Zach stopped short, eyebrows lifting. "Very well, Lord Hawthorne, but I must finish securing the ship in place. You may wait here or in your quarters, and I will be able to speak with you in approximately fifteen minutes."

Anders moved in close, voice barely above a hiss. "What part of *now* eludes you, Captain? Are you that backward from all your time in deep space that you don't recognize a royal order?"

"What part of *Captain* eludes *you*, Lord Hawthorne?" Zach hissed back. "You may be a royal cousin but you are merely a cousin and have no authority whatsoever on *my* ship. Now get the hell off my bridge!"

"Why you arrogant, impertinent—" Whatever Anders was about to say was cut off as Bern curled a large hand over his charge's shoulder. With a visible effort, Anders drew himself up and away.

His expression shuttered to a practiced blankness, though the fury was still unmistakable in his eyes. Behind him, Bern and Jackson looked similarly furious, though exponentially more dangerous. Zach didn't understand their anger; Anders had blown up at *him*. "Fifteen minutes," Anders said at last. "My quarters. I expect you to be prompt, regardless of your utter lack of manners."

Zach watched as Anders—*Lord Hawthorne*—spun on his heel and stormed out, Jackson and Bern again on his heels. There was an echoing silence for several moments before Zach shrugged it off and forced a smile for his crew. "Are we locked on?"

It took less than ten minutes for his well-oiled crew to lock in and secure their ship. Zach strode angrily down the hallways until he reached Anders's quarters, where he stopped and rapped sharply on the door with three minutes to spare. He didn't know what had Anders so upset, but he was damned well going to find out.

The door opened swiftly to reveal Jackson's bulk blocking the way. He gave Zach a long, hard look, then stepped aside, whispering, "Be careful."

Zach returned Jackson's hard look with interest before he entered. Anders was seated in a chair across the room, glaring at him as he walked closer. Zach's eyebrows rose. They didn't get as much privacy as they wanted, and usually by now, Anders was in his arms. This time, however, Anders didn't move from his chair, sitting up straighter than Zach had thought was possible.

"You demanded my time, my lord," Zach said, voice cutting through the thick silence. "Now you have it."

Anders scowled, gesturing violently to the porthole view of the Ciebos transit center. "What the hell is that?" he barked. "That is not Drion. I would have thought a man of your . . . *talents* would at least know how to read a star map."

"No," Zach said with exaggerated patience, "that isn't Drion. It's Ciebos. And I would have thought a man of your . . . *intelligence* would at least know not to storm another man's bridge the way you did."

"Ciebos! Our destination is Drion," Anders snapped back. "For *the king's funeral*. That's not the sort of mission you delay to run errands. Ciebos puts us another three days out!"

"I'm following orders, my lord. We were ordered to stop at Ciebos in a communique received almost immediately after we left Gloria." Zach clasped both hands behind his back and took a deep breath. "We've been sent here to pick up troops and high-ranking officials who must attend the funeral. Ciebos is an unscheduled stop, as Gloria was; for *your* benefit, I might add. And you underestimate my ship, *my lord*. We won't be here long, and I have top-notch engines."

Anders laughed, a sharp and cruel sound. "I should hope so, you arrogant bastard. Because the sooner I can get off this bucket of bolts, the sooner I can have you stripped of your pips and your commission. I might be merely someone's *cousin*," he paused to sneer, ignoring the way Bern shifted uneasily behind him, "but I can still see that you are made to answer in full."

"Answer for what?" Zach asked. He still didn't understand why Anders was so *angry*, but it was beginning to spark his own temper. Moving forward, he put his hands on either armrest of Anders's chair, pinning him in. "For following orders? For kicking you off my bridge? What have I done that's so awful that you imagine you, a *cousin*, could take *my* ship?"

Before Anders could voice whatever thought had him turning a lurid red beneath his dark skin, Jackson was there, bodily shoving Zach backward.

"That is more than enough, Captain O'Connell," he said, hand planted firmly in the middle of Zach's chest and propelling him back until they were nearly to the door. "No matter what liberties my lord might have allowed you in the past, I will not permit you near his person again until you can learn how to control yourself appropriately."

Zach took one step farther so that Jackson's hand fell away. "I am in complete control of myself." He shot Anders a sideways glance. "Lord Hawthorne is perhaps the only one on board who has seen me otherwise."

Anders snorted. "Trust me, it's nothing special," he said in that infuriatingly cool voice. "Nor something worth seeing again."

"Don't worry," Zach shot back, "you won't. With my authority as captain of this ship, I order you three confined to these quarters until such time as we are space bound. As I said before, it won't be long, but I can't risk having you storm my bridge while I have troops and government officials settling in."

"How *dare* you order me around like some piece of common trash! I'm your—"

"My *lord*!" Bern's voice cut sharply through whatever empty threat Anders had been about to throw down.

"You need to leave," Jackson said, reaching around Zach to open the door. "And find some other way to entertain yourself for the rest of the voyage before we have you brought up on charges."

Zach stepped out as the door opened behind him, then gave Jackson his own words back, in a much more frozen tone. "Be careful, Jackson. I have to have free access to my ship every day—you don't. Press me further and I will keep you in here until we reach Drion itself."

He looked at the three of them again with a smile that went no farther than his lips. When the door closed behind him, he secured the lock and strode back toward the bridge.

His stride was much slower when he approached Anders's quarters two hours later to release the lock. When he finally reached the door, he paused for a moment before entering his override code. As the lights flashed, Zach pressed the intercom button. "I have news," he said shortly, then sighed and reminded himself to be patient. Anders had lost too much lately.

This time it was Bern who answered the door, although he was moved aside by Anders, smooth-faced and distant as though they had never met. "Yes, Captain O'Connell?"

Zach inwardly sighed. He'd hoped he could talk to his Anders, the one who laughed with him before fucking him blind, whom he was content to merely sit and *be* with, but looking at this Anders, he was hard-pressed to believe the other had ever existed.

"Your cousin, my lord. Prince Philip has been reported missing, feared kidnapped. But we're traveling faster than even I had planned and I *will* get you to Drion as soon as is absolutely possible."

Anders's smooth facade crumbled in surprise. "What? That's not . . ." Anders raised a shaking hand to brace himself on the doorway. "I just . . ."

"I'm so sorry, Anders." Zach's voice softened. "They'll find him."

Anders laughed a little hysterically and stumbled, only to be caught by Jackson before he could fall to the floor. Bern stepped in as his match led Anders back into his room.

"Thank you for the news, Captain," Bern said with a slight nod of his head. "I'm sure you'll understand that my lord needs some time to absorb this."

"Of course." Zach nodded back. "Please tell me if there is anything you need or anything I can do for you. You are, naturally, free to leave these quarters again. At our current speed, I expect to arrive at Drion in two days. Please let him know."

Bern cocked his head as Anders babbled at Jackson in the background. Something about Grand Advisor Tanner. "Goodbye, Captain," he said swiftly, talking over Anders. Then he closed the door, leaving Zach alone in the corridor.

CHAPTER SIX

"**Y**ou need to calm down," Jackson said in that infuriatingly even voice of his.

Anders stopped pacing long enough to glare at him, not that Jackson had the good grace to so much as flinch. "How can you say that? You heard what he said!"

"Which time?" Bern asked. "Because it seemed to me that you were more upset about that delightful lover's spat than anything else. Good job with that, by the way. Very discreet."

"Oh, fuck off," Anders said, more tired than he could express. "You have no room to criticize me when your match is a rational human being." He picked at the edges of his privacy patch, loosening the adhesive. It wasn't as though he'd need to worry about Zach seeing it now. Hell, Anders wasn't sure he even wanted to see *Zach* again.

"My lord?" Jackson asked, so terribly careful.

Anders sighed and peeled off the patch entirely. "He's my match," he confessed, the words much heavier aloud. "He's my match, and he's a complete and utter asshole."

Neither of his old friends said a word, but the agony on their faces spoke volumes.

"Not that it matters right now, though." Anders sat at the desk in the corner and pulled up the screen showing the messages he'd sent and received while Zach had had them locked up. Asshole.

Bern grunted. "It's possible the report was filed before you contacted the grand advisor."

"As much of a jackass as the captain is," Jackson said, "I can't see him bringing such worrying news without thoroughly checking it out first. He has a stellar record, and it's been marked in his file several times how meticulous he is about details."

Anders ruthlessly ignored how his chest warmed at that. Zach was an asshole, and it was just the match making Anders all gooey inside about the littlest things they had in common. All the great sex and attention to detail in the universe wouldn't make up for the fact that Zach was a condescending jerk. As far as Anders was concerned, he never wanted to see Zach again; why would he want to *bond* with him?

"Either way, someone is spreading lies," Anders said in a rush, desperate not to think about how he couldn't even lie to himself. "And I'm sure the story's taken on a life of its own, if the kidnapping rumors are any indication."

"Anyone caught with the prince will be implicated in the kidnapping too," Jackson said, and made long, meaningful eye contact with his bonded.

Bern sighed. "You're going to have to tell the captain, Anders."

Zach found Anders and his guards in a viewing area not more than two hours later, looking out at the sea of stars before them. But he got the feeling that Anders wasn't really seeing anything.

"You sent for me, my lord?" Zach said softly, coming up behind him.

Anders jumped ever so slightly. "Captain." He glanced at Zach over his shoulder, eyes dark and sad. "How goes our progress?"

"We're making good time," Zach replied. "I expect to reach the orbiting point of Drion within thirty-six hours, which would mean docking in under forty."

"Good," Anders said, voice strangled. He coughed once, and turned to make eye contact. "I . . . appreciate the effort."

Zach took a step closer. "Anders, I'm sorry. What can I do?"

"I'm sure there isn't anything you can do about a missing prince," Anders said.

"No, I meant— Damn it." Zach ran a hand through his hair. "What do *you* need? You've had so many shocks recently, too many. Tell me how to help you."

Anders screwed his eyes shut as if he were in pain. "Jackson. Bern," he said at last. "Would you give us a bit of privacy?"

Zach heard the guards moving behind him, then the door closed a moment later, cutting out the flow of sound from the rest of the ship. After a long while, Anders shook his head and opened his eyes. Wet and bloodshot, they were the most raw he'd ever seen them.

"I'll be honest with you, Zach," he said. "I don't think there's much you would be willing to do for me right now. Not after this morning. You made your feelings fairly clear."

"What?" Zach still couldn't figure out why Anders was so upset. Hell, he wasn't sure why they'd fought at all. "This morning on the bridge? Anders, that's a safety issue, it was nothing personal."

"No. You—" He ran a hand through his hair, tousling his curls wildly. "Zach. You all but called me a useless nobody, and then *locked me in my room*. Like a child. What in that is supposed to make me feel like you give a shit about me or my happiness?"

Zach raised one eyebrow. "You stormed my bridge, Anders, and demanded an audience as if you were the king, and then essentially threw a tantrum. I couldn't risk either you or my crew, or the oncoming troops, coming to harm while everything was so busy and on such a restricted time schedule. It really was nothing personal. I have never considered you useless or a nobody, and I wouldn't have asked if I were unwilling to do whatever I could to help you." Zach shifted uncomfortably. He cared more than he wanted to admit about Anders's happiness.

Anders was quiet for a long time, then heaved a loud sigh. "Oh, stop it," he said, his head and shoulders sagging dramatically. "Stop being so calm and perfect while I'm trying to stay mad at your arrogant ass. That's not playing remotely fair."

"I've never played fair," Zach said mildly. The knot in his stomach relaxed, and he only realized it had been there once it was gone. "And I thought you liked my ass."

"A lot more than is healthy for my sanity," Anders said on a chuckle.

Zach grinned but watched Anders carefully. The other man's eyes were still sad and aching. "Are you saying I'm driving you crazy?"

"I keep telling you not to fish for compliments." Anders knocked their shoulders together, but didn't draw away. Instead he leaned into Zach. "Asshole."

"I've been called worse." Zach put his arm around Anders and pulled him in, pressing a kiss to his temple. "How are you really?" he asked, lips against warm skin.

Anders wound his arms around Zach's waist, clinging. "I . . ." He swallowed and tried again in a soft whisper. "I feel like my whole world's been destroyed and I've got nothing holding me together."

Zach hugged Anders close. "Shh," he whispered. "You've got Jackson and Bern, I think they could hold your world together. And I'm here too."

"You keep that up, and I'll try to keep *you*," Anders finally said into Zach's shoulder.

"I'm no one's kept man," Zach said lightly, still holding Anders close. "Seriously, though. Your cousin will be found. The last news alert I received before coming to find you said that there has been no ransom demand, so perhaps he hasn't been kidnapped. Maybe he just wants to grieve alone for a while."

Anders seem to shrink for a moment, before he drew in a deep breath and pulled back just enough to make proper eye contact for the first time. "I want to tell you something. A couple of things, really." He paused to bite his lip. "And I'm pretty sure you won't like either of them a single bit."

"Oh?" Zach loosened his arms but didn't let go. "What am I not going to like?"

Anders didn't move away either. "Well." He closed his eyes for a moment. "There's the real reason I need to get to Drion so quickly, for one."

Zach stiffened. Why would Anders have lied to him? Was his ship at risk? "You aren't going for the funeral?"

"Oh, I am," Anders said, voice heavy and sad. "It's what comes after my father's funeral that's so time sensitive. I can't delay my coronation much longer without risking serious instability throughout the system. I've been raised my whole life knowing that my primary concern during the transition will be to ensure my people have the security and continuous leadership necessary to see us all through this time of change."

"No," Zach dropped his arms and stepped back, out of reach. "No, you are *not* telling me that you . . ."

Something that might have been heartbreak washed over Anders's face for a moment before his expression settled into that damn blank mask. "Crown Prince James Philip Michael Anderson III," he said, pulling a deep bow. "At your service."

"How do I know you're really Prince Philip?" Zach asked suspiciously after a beat of shocked silence. "No one knows exactly what he looks like. You have a family resemblance to the king, but that doesn't mean you're the prince."

Anders unfastened his collar and grabbed a chain from around his neck. "Normally, I wouldn't be wearing this," he said, lifting the necklace over his head. "But I had a feeling it would be necessary today." He held out the chain, a pendant easily the size of his palm dangling free. Gold and tipped in dark-blue sapphires, the eight-pointed star of the House of Anderson was unmistakable. "It was my mother's. Not precisely my usual style."

Zach couldn't believe his prince, soon to be his *king*, was standing before him. Slowly, the horror began to dawn as Zach's mind played back every last thing they'd done together. "Your Highness," Zach said, dropping to one knee in formal acknowledgment. "Please, forgive me."

"Zach, please," Anders put both hands on Zach's arms, tugging up. "I think we're rather past ceremony at this point, don't you?"

"You let— I can't, *shit*." Zach let Anders pull him up. "You didn't tell me, and we, we, god. We're so far past formalities I may as well have run them down at light speed. What the hell, Anders?" Zach threaded his hands through his hair and tugged.

Anders spread his hands helplessly. "Every time I've left Drion since I reached adulthood, I've traveled under an assumed name," he said. "It's a standard security measure. No one pays much mind to a random royal cousin, but the crown prince would be a prize for anyone looking to make a fortune or destroy the monarchy."

Zach shook his head. "It's not *that*, or not only that. I mean, I would have thought you could tell the ship's captain who he has on board. I can keep a secret. But, fuck, Anders, you *sucked me off*."

"I did owe you one."

"Oh, for god's sake."

Anders laughed. "Darling, we didn't do anything I didn't want," he said, voice surprisingly gentle. "Or that I haven't done before, come to think of it."

Zach struggled with a surge of jealousy, on top of everything else. "I can't even think about this right now," he said.

"You're going to have to, though," Anders said. "Because unless there was a miscommunication on epic levels, my father's lead advisors know *for a fact* that I'm not missing. I messaged Grand Advisor Tanner myself when we were at Ciebos, instructing him to tell the rest of the cabinet my travel plans."

"And your advisors would have been the ones to report you missing," Zach said slowly.

Anders nodded. "While I'm reluctant to accuse members of the king's cabinet of some evil plot, you have to admit that is rather suspicious." He ran his hand through his hair, messing the carefully styled curls. "You deserve to know, since having me aboard could put you and your crew in the line of fire."

"You are our prince, soon to be our king." Zach shrugged. When it came right down to it, that was the most important thing, the reason the Royal Navy had been created: protecting the royal family and the kingdom. "Being in the line of fire on your behalf is part of what we signed up for."

"Still," Anders said, catching Zach's hand, "I can't say I'm pleased about asking you to do that. Duty or no, your life is no less precious than mine."

Zach squeezed Anders's hand. "You wouldn't be a good leader if you were pleased about it," he said with a wry smile. "But, if not more precious, your life is infinitely more important."

Anders laughed and kissed Zach's knuckles. The move exposed the black edge of a soul mark on the inside of Anders's wrist, normally covered by one of the privacy patches the rich were so fond of. "That's not all," he said after a moment.

"You did say there were a couple of things," Zach said warily. Something in Anders's tone of voice said Zach was not going to like this any better than he had liked learning who Anders really was.

Anders had barely opened his mouth when an alert klaxon blared across the ship-wide intercom, startling them both.

"*Shit!*" Zach looked up as the room lights flashed red. He pressed a quick kiss to Anders's lips. "Anders, go. Go to your quarters, take Jackson and Bern with you and *stay there.*"

Without another word, Zach took off running for the bridge.

CHAPTER SEVEN

Anders paced a circuit around his quarters, going from bedroom to sitting room and back again, fussing with the perfectly made bed and rearranging the few personal items he'd brought aboard. The red lights had stopped flashing, now a constant red glow since shortly after Zach had left him in the observation room. It was probably a part of the ship's safety system, but it cast a sickly, murderous red that made Anders's heart stick in his throat.

"Everything will be fine," he muttered to himself, adjusting the angle of a picture of his mother.

"Captain O'Connell is one of the finest captains in the Navy," Jackson said. "He'll get us safely out of whatever emergency there is."

"Especially now that he knows his king is aboard," Bern added.

"*Future* king," Anders corrected automatically. He froze on the spot. "Oh god. They must be after me. My message to Tanner included all the details of our trip, from our route to what ship we were on. This is all my fault."

Bern snorted. "If someone on the cabinet is behind this, then it's their fault and no one else's. Stop being so melodramatic and sit down, would you?"

Suddenly, an explosion rocked the ship. Anders stumbled, dropping the picture frame with a *crack* of broken glass. By pure force of will, Anders resisted the urge to point out that they were under attack, and sat on the sofa. He would hold himself together if it was the last thing he did.

Jackson sat next to him, solid and warm as he curled a protective arm around Anders's shoulders. "The *Pallas* is a strong ship. She'll be fine."

"I know that," Anders said. "It's only I haven't had much experience with dogfights in all my years at school."

Another explosion, and this time Bern joined them on the sofa. It was a tight fit, but a comforting one. "Please, someone distract me," Anders pleaded.

"Okay," Bern said. "So when are you planning on telling O'Connell he's the future prince consort of the star Collective?"

"Fuck you, it's not that simple," Anders said, but smiled a bit when he felt Bern chuckle. Before he could say anything else, though, there was a third explosion. The room shook, books flying off the shelves and art crashing to the floor. Bright sparks shot from the communications console as the red lights flickered. Another explosion followed quickly, and Anders, Jackson, and Bern were tossed to the floor. Something struck Anders on the head with a brutal flash of pain, and then there was nothing more.

It had been a bitch of a fight, and a hell of time trying to shake a ship that had kept trying to board. The *Pallas* had taken a lot of fire before being able to get free. *But,* Zach thought fiercely, *we took the whole damn squadron of fighters out.* "That'll teach them to go up against a war-class ship," he said under his breath.

"A very enthusiastic fight. A little over the top, even for you," Oliver said dryly. Zach gave him a look. Olive just smiled. "I know. Shut up."

"Let me gloat a little, Oliver. We *won.* We beat those fuckers down to the last ship."

Oliver nodded. "We did, but we took some heavy fire in the process."

Zach sighed. They had, especially on the aft side . . . the guest quarters. "Oh fuck. Oh fuck, oh fuck, Anders!"

"I'll take the bridge," Oliver called as the lift doors to the bridge slid open. There was just enough time for Zach to scowl and flip him off before the doors shut behind him.

Zach ran down the corridor to Anders's quarters. Burn scars from countless electrical shorts and damaged wall plates gave silent testament to the damage in that section. When he reached the door, he quickly typed in his override code rather than wait for someone to answer. What if they couldn't?

The door slid open, and Zach stepped in to see Jackson, Bern, and two medics gathered around Anders, who had blood all over his face. The medics must have already fixed his broken nose, since the bone mender was lying discarded on the floor at their feet.

One of the medics was taking Anders's vitals with a band wrapped around his lower left arm, and the other was shining a bright light into Anders's eyes.

"Stop that. I'm fine," Anders was saying, though his speech was slurred. He pushed at the medic on his left, only to have his arm caught by the woman. The medic turned Anders's arm, muttering about reading the display for the last of his vitals. Suddenly, both medics froze. Anders pitched a little to the side, no one noticing as both of them gaped at something Zach couldn't see.

"Holy shit," she said. "That's Captain O'Connell's mark!"

Zach moved closer. "What? I didn't give him—"

Everyone looked up at Zach, the medics shifting enough for Zach to see a black mark on the inside of Anders's wrist: a black crown, with a single star cut out right in the middle. The exact same as the mark on Zach's left side. The blood drained from his face. "The fuck?"

Anders pulled his sleeve down, covering the mark. "Surprise," he slurred, scrubbing at his face and wincing.

Zach felt as though he'd been punched in the gut. *Matched.* Zach's mouth dropped open. Anders was his match. *Oh my fucking god.* Anders was going to be *king*, and they were matched, and that meant an end to Zach's career.

"I am not giving up my commission," Zach said flatly.

"I never ..." Anders struggled to his feet. "I never *asked* you to," he growled, words clumsy.

"Sir." The medic with the tiny light fussed around him. "My lord, you have a concussion. Please sit back down."

Zach threw his hands up. "That's what you want, though, what *that*"—he gestured at Anders's wrist—"entails, right? I mean, it's not like you can give up *being king*."

The entire room went deadly silent. The medic on the left dropped his kit, while the second one just stood there with her mouth hanging open. "You have *got* to be kidding me," she said at last.

"Shit." Zach rubbed his hand over his face.

"Oh, good job keeping the secret, asshole." Anders glared at him, the effect ruined by the way his eyes kept trying to cross. Jackson swooped in, herding the two medics out and into the hall, no doubt to put the fear of their god of choice into them. As soon as the door shut behind them, Anders stomped over, shoving Zach in the chest. "If you could pull your head out of your own ass for long enough, you might remember that I have had the good taste *not* to bring up bonding, now haven't I?"

"Yeah, you only let me find out about the whole match bullshit with half a dozen people in the room instead of fucking *telling me*." Zach wanted desperately to shove Anders back, but there was still blood all over his face and his eyes weren't quite focusing. "Sit the fuck down—you have a concussion."

"Don't tell me what to do," Anders said with another shove. "You're not my king. Not my bonded. All we do is fuck when it's convenient for you."

Zach grabbed Anders's hands to keep from being shoved again. "I never heard you complain. Quite the opposite."

Anders yanked his hands free, swaying dangerously until Bern caught him by the elbows. "Don't know why you're mad at *me*," he said, head lolling back against Bern's shoulder. "Just because you're a good fuck doesn't mean I'd want to spend the rest of my life with you. You're an insubordinate asshole."

"I'm not mad at you," Zach muttered. "Sit. Down."

With a huff, Anders let Bern guide him to the nearby couch. Bern settled him before heading to the bathroom, probably to fetch a wet cloth. "It's not like I got this mark on *purpose*," Anders said. "I've seen what happens when people lose their bonded. I don't want that." He scrubbed at his face again, groaning in pain. "Not from *you*."

"I don't want it from you, either," Zach growled. He grabbed the wet cloth from Bern as he came back from the bath, and knelt in front of Anders. "Here. Hold still," he said, carefully cleaning the blood from Anders's face.

Anders flinched and pulled away. "You hate bonding."

Zach curled a hand around the back of Anders's neck. "Hold still! You have blood all over your face," he said irritably. "Yes, I hate bonding."

"That's why," Anders struggled against Zach again, though not enough to break his grip. "Stop. I can get it later."

"I can get it now." Zach kept wiping until the blood was almost gone. "You still should have told me," he said softly. His fingers crept up into Anders's hair, feeling for bumps or blood. "Don't you think I had a right to know?"

Anders leaned into his hands, eyes fluttering shut. "Yes," he admitted quietly. "Not that it changes things either way."

Zach found a large lump and winced in sympathy. "I can't give up my commission," he said. "I can't . . . *need* someone else, not like that." Zach sighed. "C'mon, baby, lie down. But don't go to sleep."

"Could abdicate," Anders murmured, pitching forward to rest against Zach's shoulder. "It's a shitty job, anyway. Been at it less than a week and people are already trying to kill me."

"No, you can't. You know that." Zach rubbed Anders's back. "It's who you are, who you were born to be. And we don't know they were trying to kill you. Stop looking for problems."

Anders snorted. "Stop telling me what to do."

"I will when you start doing it," Zach answered with a grin. He cupped Anders's face and lifted it so he could rub his nose against Anders's. "C'mon, you need to rest, and I need to go start checking the damage to the ship. We can talk when your brain isn't scrambled."

"Come back to me later?" Anders asked, finally stretching out on the sofa. He sighed, closing his eyes. "Never been someone's 'baby' before."

Zach stayed on the floor next to the couch for a minute, then sighed and stood. "I'll come back when I can. You stay awake, okay?" He walked to where Bern was standing. "Make sure he doesn't do anything too strenuous, not with that concussion."

Bern gave him a flatly unimpressed look, but nodded. "I know you have a ship to see to," he said, "but could Jackson have a word in the hall before you leave?"

"Of course," Zach said, lifting an eyebrow.

Zach stepped out to the hall alone where Jackson was waiting, arms crossed as he leaned against the wall. "The medics will keep their mouths shut about everything, at least for the time being," he said.

Zach flushed slightly. He hadn't meant to say anything, but there was no taking it back now. "I know they will."

"We'll deal with it later if they don't," Jackson said with a shrug. "That's not what I wanted to talk to you about. Though it's related."

"I'm listening," Zach said, leaning one shoulder against the wall. "But, I wasn't lying to Anders, I really do need to check my ship."

"Then I'll keep this brief." Jackson fixed Zach with a hard look. "We've been by Prince Philip's side since he turned eighteen. That's eleven years of getting to know our prince as a friend and a person, far beyond a simple assignment. That is to say," he crossed his arms, looming just enough to drive home what a great beast of a man he was, "if you break my best friend's heart, they will never find the body."

Zach stood straight and crossed his own arms, not intimidated, although he could appreciate the loyalty and concern Jackson showed Anders; appreciated it more than he was willing to admit. "I can't promise that," he said. "I can only say that I have no intention of hurting him."

Jackson nodded once, still looking like he was sizing Zach up for a shallow grave. "Good. I know he can be . . . difficult. But he's worth it."

"I'll remember," Zach said after a minute. He didn't know what else to say. Anders *was* difficult, and he *was* worth it. He shrugged his stiff shoulders slightly. "Now, please excuse me. My ship needs my attention."

CHAPTER EIGHT

Zach strode into the bridge, forcing himself to focus on his ship and not the visceral terror he'd felt when he'd seen blood all over Anders's face. Of course, that had been buried under the shock and anger when he'd seen the mark Anders had been hiding from him. Anders had known, *had* to have known almost from the beginning, and the little shit hadn't said a *word*.

"Hadlock," he barked, "report."

Oliver gave him a sideways look, but began to detail the extent of the damage Zach's ship had taken. Fortunately, it wasn't as bad as he'd feared, other than their communications center. Unfortunately, it was going to delay them at least a day, and he vividly remembered Anders's reaction to being delayed before. Then again, it was, probably, ultimately Anders's fault.

"That's it for the damages," Oliver finished.

"Oh," Zach said dryly. "Is that all?"

Oliver merely smiled. "Now for the repairs. Shields should be at full strength again before third shift, the electrical system on gamma deck is still giving engineering fits, and our communications are completely down. Some incoming data might be possible by first shift, but outgoing will take longer."

They'd done well with repairs so far, but it would still be at least a day. He'd make sure it wasn't any longer than that. Anders absolutely had to be at his father's funeral and at the coronation that would swiftly follow. And they needed to announce his non-missing-ness and get to the bottom of the reported kidnapping when the interim government knew damn well Anders was on his way, which they couldn't do anymore from the ship.

"Widen the scope of our alarms, and put some more ensigns on the repairs," Zach said, and held up a hand to stop the protest Oliver would make. "I know it means overtime, but I can't explain here. Get Polito up here to keep an eye on our status; we need to get moving again as soon as humanly possible." Polito was a solid, steady third mate who would follow orders to the letter. "Then meet me in my quarters. We need to discuss something privately."

Oliver nodded, and Zach headed for his quarters. He was exhausted, but there was too much to do for any real rest. He'd have to take a very short nap before going back to see Anders. He both did and didn't want to talk to him—he had no idea what to say.

Oliver entered Zach's quarters after a quick rap on the door fifteen minutes later. Zach gestured for him to take a seat across from him, and steepled his fingers, elbows on his knees. How to begin?

"Oliver," he said, then sat in silence.

"Zach?" Oliver said after a minute.

"Yes." Zach shook his head to clear it. "What I'm about to tell you must stay in this room, in the strictest confidence." Oliver nodded, obviously curious. "We are now, secretly, the Drion One."

Oliver's shock was written all over his face. That was one of the things Zach appreciated about him; he was an open book.

"Remember the three we picked up on Gloria? The royal cousin?"

"Yes, of course," Oliver said, with dawning realization. "He's not a cousin."

"He's not a cousin. He's the crown prince."

"But Prince Philip was reported missing, possibly kidnapped!"

"I know, and that's another problem. There are a very, very few who know where he is, and that same very few would have been the ones to make that report. I suspect that's why we were attacked, and we may have been set up to look like the kidnappers, although I can't imagine how they'd sell that when we're Royal Navy."

"You think the boarding party was a kidnapping attempt."

"Yes. Either that or they were trying to make sure he was dead. Which is part of why I'm telling you. You need to know that we may be attacked again, and you need to know who we have on board."

"How long have you known?" Oliver asked. Zach shot him a look, and Oliver shrugged. "I'm curious. If you're telling me now because I need to know who's on board, why wouldn't you have told me as soon as you found out?"

"I *am* telling you as soon as I found out. I was speaking with An— His Highness—when the attack occurred. He had just told me, when the attack began."

"So you're freaking out because you're fucking the prince."

"*Oliver!*" Zach's face flushed hot.

"What? You thought I didn't know?"

Zach sighed. Of course he knew—Oliver knew him too well. "No," Zach muttered. "But thank you for not saying anything. Also, he's the *prince*. Don't say it's fucking."

Oliver laughed. "What do you want me to call it? Making love?"

The words hit Zach like a brick wall. "That's the other thing that you absolutely cannot discuss. He's my fucking *match*."

"You're joking," Oliver said, eyes widening. "You're not joking."

"I'm not joking." Zach rubbed his hands over his face. "You know how I feel about that shit; I would never joke about it."

"What are you going to do about it? As you so eloquently said, he's the fucking prince. You have to bond. He has to have a consort, and now that he's found his match, he can't marry anyone else."

"I'm not going to fucking *bond* with him, for god's sake. It would be the end of my career! And I'm not going to tie myself to one person who's going to be able to know what I feel and eventually know what I'm thinking."

"You're going to have to, Zach," Oliver said gently. "Maybe you can work out some sort of compromise over your captaincy, but you really have no choice here."

Zach stood and leaned forward, bracing his hands on his desk. "I have a choice," he said angrily. "You're the only one who knows about the match. Well, you and Anders's men and two of our medics who will keep their damn mouths shut. As long as no one else finds out about the match, he can marry someone else. A woman," Zach said, suddenly inspired. "He needs an heir."

"He may not be bi," Oliver said mildly, his cool demeanor stoking both Zach's anger and the fear he couldn't suppress. "There have been royal surrogates in the past; that's not a valid excuse."

"I am not bonding with him," Zach said flatly. "I will not." He shoved a hand through his hair. "I absolutely have a choice."

Oliver sighed. Zach glared at him and waved a hand in his direction. "Go to the bridge. Oversee the repairs, because I have to go back and make sure His Highness doesn't need repairs too."

"Grow up, Zach," Oliver said as he left Zach's quarters.

Zach snarled. There was no way he was going to be calm enough for that nap now. Fucking Oliver.

The first hour or so after Zach left, Anders was happy to sit on the sofa, drifting aimlessly between sleep and wakefulness. He was vaguely aware of Bern doing his own survey of the room and assuring Jackson that it was structurally sound, but Anders didn't much care. As his wits slowly returned, however, along with a brutal headache that Jackson said would only get worse, the dawning realization of just how utterly *fucked* everything was only served to sour his mood further.

"Give the captain time," Jackson said. "He'll come around."

"He'd better," Bern grumbled. Bless him.

No matter what the medics had promised, Anders knew it was only a matter of time before they told *someone*. And then everyone would know that not only had Anders matched, but that he'd been rejected. He'd never be able to marry someone else, not without alienating nearly all of his people. An average man might be able to get away with it, though not without being mocked for it; finding your match was what everyone was raised to hope for, but the fact that the one person who had the exact perfect hormonal complement to his didn't want him would only serve to undermine Anders's authority. As king, he'd be expected to lead by example, to honor their traditions, and to give the people hope with every aspect of his life. It was a complete and total mess, and there was nothing to be done about it.

"We'll have to worry about that later, I'm afraid," he said, despite the knot of something rather like terror deep in his gut. "I don't want to entertain your suspicions, but you're both right. It *would* take someone of a councilor's rank or higher to access the ship's plans in order to locate my quarters. That means we're going to need a solid plan for stopping whoever is behind this when we arrive."

There was a rap on the door of their quarters, and Bern crossed the room to answer. He pressed the intercom button. "Yes?"

"It's Zach. Let me in?"

Bern hesitated, looking at Anders for orders.

"Pissing him off now will only complicate things," Jackson said, and Anders nodded reluctantly.

"Let him in."

Zach entered slowly, as if he'd rather be elsewhere. He walked to the middle of the room and then stood at parade rest. "Your Highness. How are you feeling?"

Anders sighed. "Zach. Have a seat."

"Thank you." Zach crossed to a sofa near Anders and sat, elbows on his thighs, hands working nervously between his knees.

Anders wanted to go to him, to curl around him and smooth the tension out of his shoulders. Instead, he sat as straight as he could with his head trying to split in two and forged on with the most important issue. "We were just talking about the attack. How is the ship?"

"We were lucky. Well," Zach corrected himself, "we were good. There's a fair amount of damage, but the majority of it is either minor or cosmetic. We do have some serious damage in two areas, one of which is communications. It's going to delay us at least a day, and we can't transmit anything until we've made further repairs, I'm sorry."

"Somehow I don't think they expect us to arrive at all, so us getting there according to our original schedule is hardly a disaster," Anders said, waving his hand. "We were wondering about all the damage to this sector. Do you think the attack was concentrated here?"

"It was," Zach said slowly. "There were missiles fired at other parts of the ship, trying to hit the engine, I suspect, but most of the damage is in this sector. They may have been trying to force the ship to jettison the guest quarters." He hesitated, then added, "There was an attempt to board us, Your Highness."

"But taking a ship this size would be impossible, unless . . ." Anders's eyes went wide.

"Unless they were only going to board long enough to take something," Jackson said. "Or someone."

"Fuck," Anders whispered. His ears were ringing, and it took several long seconds of careful breathing to make it stop.

"Yes," Zach agreed shortly. "But we killed the raiding party, destroyed every last ship. You're safe on my ship, Your Highness. I swear."

"I know I am." Anders sighed. What he wouldn't give for Zach to go back to calling him *baby*. "And your crew? Are they well?"

"For the most part," Zach said. "There are a few serious injuries, but we didn't lose anyone."

"Good." Anders relaxed marginally. "Good. When we arrive at Drion, I'd like to do so as unobtrusively as possible. I don't want to lose the element of surprise before I confront my cabinet and begin a proper investigation. We still need more evidence than a few wildly terrifying coincidences, after all."

"It will be difficult; a ship this size is fairly noticeable on radar. Once we dock at Drion Station, we can try to land a shuttle quietly and quickly, if there's a private landing pad. I think we should bring some officers with us and send the higher-ups with the rest of the troops to the central landing pad."

"'We'?" Anders asked, genuinely surprised. "Zach, you're not obligated to go with me. You've more than done your duty protecting me already, and I'm grateful. But anyone who goes with me will have a target on them until we resolve this. I don't want you to think you have to risk your life any further."

Zach stood, back straight. "I am a captain in the Royal Navy. It is my honor to serve and protect the monarchy of Drion. It's part of what I signed up for, and I am proud to do so."

Anders stood as well, legs shaking. "Zach, please. No matter our personal issues, I know you're a loyal man. I didn't mean to imply your honor was anything less than above question." He cupped Zach's shoulder. "I'm sorry," he added softly, swaying on his feet.

"Sit down before you fall down," Zach said. "I never thought you meant that. That's not what *I* meant. Anders." He shifted, breaking eye contact awkwardly. "Of course I'm going to help you."

"Oh." Anders scowled in confusion and shook his head, and immediately regretted it when the room spun around him. "I thought . . . Never mind."

Zach grabbed Anders's arms and forcibly sat him down. "C'mon, baby, you aren't all there yet. Stay in your damn chair."

Anders frowned but obeyed. Just like every other time, that damned endearment had completely disarmed him.

"If you two are done flirting," Bern said, "do you suppose we could get back to planning how to avert an all-out civil war?"

"We aren't flirting, I'm trying to keep him from falling on his ass and possibly hitting his head again." Zach glared at Bern. "I'd think you would be more concerned with his health, given your position." Then Bern's words seemed to actually register with Zach; his eyes widened and he paled slightly. "What do you mean, 'civil war'?"

"It's complicated," Anders said. "You know how the eleven positions in the king's cabinet rotate every five cycles?"

Zach nodded. "Yes? I mean, yes, I knew that. The chief advisor rotates between the ruling families so everyone gets a turn, right?"

"Essentially, yes." Anders rubbed his forehead in a vain attempt to ease the headache. "It's part of the Great Compromise my many-times great-grandfather struck to end the last system war, which solidified Drion as our sovereignty. What everyone doesn't know is that the grand advisor is to act as regent in the event that the king dies without an heir of age."

"Okay," Zach said. "So that explains why Tanner in particular might want you either missing or dead. But if he's regent and in charge, how does that equal civil war?"

"Because if there is no crown prince or princess, then the regent is only supposed to hold power until the nearest royal relative can be crowned." Anders leaned forward, elbows on his knees. "That's why my family is so keen on keeping track of all the random cousins. However, there's a delightful little clause that states that if the first in line cannot be found—not dead, just missing—the grand advisor has the authority to hold the ruling power. Indefinitely."

"But the grand advisor is about to change families, isn't it?" Zach frowned. "Does that mean it wouldn't switch, or that the regency moves with the job?"

"No one really knows. On top of that, the Tanner family has been brewing dissent behind closed doors for well over a decade. My father was forced by a tangled combination of law and tradition to offer the post to one of that family this particular rotation, but he certainly tried to find a way out of it. It only added insult to injury that this particular Tanner won the honor. The Tanners have been running raids on some of the smaller, non-Collective planets on the Outer Edge, trying to expand their holdings in the unclaimed areas. Last year they were forced to disavow an entire squadron when a settlement under the Lee family's protection was leveled in an attack. My father barely averted war then, mostly through some truly amazing diplomacy. But you'll never guess which family is next in line for the grand advisor position when the elections for all eleven cabinet positions run in six months."

Zach's lips quirked in a smile that didn't reach his eyes. "The Lee family?"

"Beauty and brains." Anders sagged back in his chair. "There are factions within factions, alliances and trade treaties, all hinging on the distribution of power among the cabinet. This story that I've been kidnapped, the attack on the *Pallas* . . . it's throwing the power balance off, and I'd be surprised if the other families weren't already gearing up to fight each other for my throne."

"All the more reason to get you quickly and quietly to the palace. You'll need to appear publicly as soon as possible."

Anders nodded. "We still need to investigate the situation. As much as it hurts to even consider, I worry that Father . . . that King James's death was too well-timed," he said, voice cracking slightly.

Zach curled a hand around his and squeezed. "I'm so sorry, Anders."

He kissed Zach's fingers. "Thank you."

"You could always tell them you and your match were taking time to get acquainted," Bern said abruptly.

"Have you lost your mind?" Anders all but shouted.

"What? Everybody loves a good romance; it'll help distract people from fighting."

Zach's fingers tightened on Anders's again. "We aren't matching."

"Bern, let it go," Anders said, shamelessly clinging to Zach's hand. It was like that one part, right where they touched, was the only place Anders could be still. Only a few hours ago, he'd told Zach he felt like his world was flying apart, and Zach had suggested Bern and Jackson could help hold him together. But, really, it was Zach who was grounding him now, better than even his two best friends in the world. And Anders was going to lose him, sooner rather than later if people didn't stop bringing up their match.

Jackson stepped in front of Bern, looking deeply into his eyes as they communicated over their bond. Then he turned around, smiling slightly. "We're going to go see if the repair crews could use some extra hands. Zach, would you take over watching my lord's concussion?"

Zach studied Jackson for a long moment, then nodded. "He just needs to rest. I'd go out and help the crews myself, but I'm not up to much more than resting now, either. Thank you for offering your help, I'm sure we could use it. Find Hadlock, he's my first mate. He'll know who can use you best."

"We will." Jackson nodded, already herding Bern to the door. "And you're right: you need rest too. You look like hell, man."

"Thanks," Zach said wryly. "I look much better than I feel, I'm sure." He watched as the two men left Anders's quarters, then turned to Anders in the sudden silence. "Bed. Now."

"Like that, is it?" Anders said, unable to resist tweaking Zach's nose. "Where has the romance gone?"

"Ha-ha," Zach said. "Very funny. Tell me honestly that you don't have a screaming headache and I won't bug you about getting more sleep."

"It feels like my head's about to explode," Anders admitted. "But I'll go to bed if you come with me."

Zach tugged Anders to his feet and began to lead him back into the bedroom. "You are not up to sex at the moment," he said sternly, almost but not quite hiding the smile in his voice.

"Speak for yourself." Anders wrapped an arm around Zach's waist, shamelessly clinging to him.

"Me either," Zach admitted. He was half leaning on Anders and half holding him up by now. "I'm about ready to collapse." They made it to the side of the bed, where Zach finally let go of Anders so he could take off his uniform jacket, sit down, and take off his boots. "I can't remember the last time I slept."

Anders undressed down to his shorts, feeling terribly awkward the whole time, his limbs clumsy with exhaustion. "I don't know what's worse," he said, falling back onto the bed and staring up at the ceiling. "This headache or the fact you're going to wake me up in two hours."

Zach swung his legs up onto the bed and stretched out fully dressed with a long sigh. "God, it feels good to lay down." He slid over so there was room for Anders to lie next to him. "That's not the best treatment for concussions anyway; I think it's better to just let you sleep."

"Oh, I like the sound of that." Anders crawled up next to Zach, dragging a blanket with him as he curled close. "Why are you still dressed?"

"Because we aren't having sex and I might get called back to the bridge soon. The ship will start moving again as soon as possible, even if some of the repairs aren't finished." Zach yawned hugely and put an arm around Anders. "Sleep."

"You too," Anders shot back. But he was warm and comfortable, so he pressed a kiss to Zach's shoulder. *I love you.* The words almost slipped past his lips, and Anders stopped dead.

"I will, if you'll be quiet," Zach slurred. He was asleep within seconds. It took Anders a few minutes longer, but he truly was exhausted. And he was safe with Zach, as safe as if he had a whole room of guards with him. So Anders let go, falling to sleep as he resolved to look at his inconvenient feelings in the morning.

CHAPTER NINE

Zach woke with a start, instantly awake as fingers opened the fastening of his shirt. He reflexively grabbed the wrist and sat up, ready to defend against an enemy. As soon as he realized what was happening, he rubbed Anders's skin in apology. "Hey," he said, voice rough with sleep. "Sorry."

Anders chuckled. "That will teach me to think I can sneak up on a Navy man," he said, kissing Zach's jaw.

Zach turned his head to capture Anders's mouth, kissing him slowly and thoroughly. He slid his hand up Anders's arm to cup his shoulder and squeezed, then rolled toward him, pressing their bodies close. Zach finally broke the kiss and began to mouth along Anders's jaw, scraping his teeth against skin and stubble.

Humming happily, Anders tilted his head, giving Zach all the access he could want. "I take it you slept well?" he asked, smile ringing through his voice.

"I certainly feel rejuvenated," Zach murmured, lips dragging over the soft spots right behind Anders's ear. He rolled further, laying Anders flat and pressing him into the mattress.

"Glad to hear it." Anders tugged at Zach's shirt, sliding it up until Zach had to shift enough to take it off. He followed it up with freeing Zach of the rest of his uniform before tugging Zach back in and nibbling on his lower lip.

Zach pulled away, licking over his lip, then tipped Anders's head so he could kiss down his throat. He used his teeth between sucking kisses, until he reached Anders's nipple, and used his teeth again. Anders gasped softly, arching up and pressing closer to Zach. His hands ran restlessly over Zach's back and shoulders, urging Zach on.

"Zach," Anders sighed. "Don't you dare stop."

With a final scrape of teeth, Zach raised his head to look up at Anders. "I can stay here, or I can move to . . . somewhere else. Your choice."

Anders laughed, a throaty sound. "Gentleman's choice," he said, still smiling. "So long as it involves you fucking me."

"Well, that was a given." Zach laughed. After nosing at Anders's nipple, he moved down to make a place for himself between Anders's legs. He sucked kisses up Anders's shaft through the silk shorts, sliding his tongue in the opening to taste skin briefly. As he reached the top of Anders's dick, he slid the shorts down so he could suck at the head, tongue pushing into the slit leaking salty liquid.

"Fuck," Anders breathed, lifting his hips. "I didn't realize you were such a tease. And to think I've been missing out for *days*." He cupped the side of Zach's face in his left hand, thumb brushing over his cheekbone.

Zach put his hands on either hip to hold Anders down before he began sucking in earnest, alternating hard pressure with bobs of his head, taking Anders so far in that he almost hit Zach's throat. Zach tilted his head just a bit, and the head of Anders's dick rubbed against the side of Zach's cheek on each slow movement up and down.

Anders groaned again and again, each sound punched out of him as Zach bobbed down. His hips lifted again, and Anders shuddered, whimpering Zach's name. "Zach. *Zach*, I've been dreaming about you fucking me. Marking me up. God, Zach, *your mouth*. Make me feel so fucking good, Zach. So good."

Slowly pulling back until Anders's dick popped free, Zach smiled. "You want me to mark you? Suck hard on your skin until the blood comes to the surface, an obvious claim?" Without waiting for an answer, Zach began to worry at Anders's uppermost thigh, sucking and scraping his teeth over the soft, thin skin. *Mine.*

"Yes." Anders spread his free leg wide, giving Zach room, putting his foot flat for leverage so he could rock up, closer to Zach's mouth. "Yes, just like that," he panted.

Zach kept at it until the mark was dark with blood, then he licked the hot skin. "Roll over, baby, I want to get you all wet and open so I can fuck you."

"Fuck yes." Anders scrambled to obey, lifting up onto his elbows and knees invitingly, his hips canted like he was presenting himself, Anders dropped his forehead to the bed. "I should probably warn you I can be rather noisy when I'm being fucked. I can try to stop it, if you want."

"No, I want to hear you. Wanna make you scream." Zach tugged Anders's legs out from under him and then grabbed his ass, squeezing the firm cheeks and spreading them apart to get to his hole. Zach bent to lick the rim, slide his tongue inside. He alternated thrusts of his tongue with presses of his thumb into Anders's body.

Stretched out on the bed, Anders writhed against the sheets and gasped. "Zach," he managed. "Fuck, Zach. You're going to ruin me for anyone else at this rate."

Zach tugged at the rim of Anders's hole with his thumb. "Isn't that the point?"

"Be careful what you wish for, darling." Anders groaned, forcing his ass back. "You just might get it."

"That's what I'm afraid of," Zach muttered into Anders's skin. He replaced his thumb with two fingers, pushing in and out. "Where's your lube?" he asked more clearly.

Anders lifted his head, dark face flushed and hair a mess. He looked around, confused for a few seconds before he waved at the nightstand. "There. Haven't needed it much this week."

Zach pulled away long enough to get the lube and slick up his fingers, then he slid them back in, stretching and stroking to get Anders wet and ready for his cock. He got three fingers inside and thrust in and out a few times before he couldn't wait any longer. He tugged his fingers free and grabbed his cock, then pressed the head into Anders's hole and worked it inside with short, firm thrusts.

"Oh, oh, *god*," Anders moaned in time, fingers scrabbling, clutching white-knuckled at the pillows. "Fuck! Zach!"

"Yes," Zach growled as he bottomed out. He pressed his hips hard into Anders's ass, holding them both still as Anders adjusted, holding on to control by a thin thread.

Anders was flat on the bed, seemingly unable to do much more than lie there for the long seconds it took his body to relax. Finally, he squeezed around Zach and shifted, moaning.

"I won't break, darling," he said, glancing over his shoulder at Zach. His eyes were barely slits, his mouth swollen from kisses. He looked like a man being fucked hard, and it looked good on him.

Zach started rolling his hips, driving into Anders again and again in a slow, steady rhythm. He licked a stripe up Anders's back and nosed at the damp skin. "Feel so good, baby, god, you're tight."

"I need—" Anders shifted, getting up on his knees. The move changed Zach's angle, and Anders groaned loudly, shoulders shaking as he pushed back to meet Zach's thrusts. "*Yes.*"

"Anything you need, Anders." Zach adjusted, grabbed Anders's hips and began to thrust faster until he was pounding into him. Anders was moaning and crying out almost constantly, writhing under Zach's punishing rhythm. Zach squeezed Anders's hips and then let go of one to reach under him. He wrapped his hand around Anders's dick and stroked in counter-rhythm. "C'mon, Anders, let go. Come on my cock."

Anders gasped, voice cut off and obviously struggling against giving in. For a few thrusts, Anders shoved back, fucking himself just as much as Zach was fucking him, but he couldn't hold out for long. Finally, he buried his face in a pillow and shouted, hand slapping the bed as he came, hot and wet and all over Zach's hand, his ass squeezing brutally around Zach.

Zach growled as he felt Anders come and kept pistoning through Anders's orgasm, chasing his own pleasure until he began to shake and fell over the edge. His body jerked through the aftershocks, even as he curled tightly around Anders and rolled them onto their sides.

"*Fuck,*" Anders rasped, voice shot. He chuckled and covered Zach's arm with his own, holding him in place. "Yep. Definitely ruined me for anyone else." He snuggled back, as close as he could get. "That's not a complaint."

They stayed like that for a minute, until they heard the main door out in the sitting room open and close, followed by the low murmur of Jackson's and Bern's voices. Then someone tapped on the bedroom door.

"My lord," Jackson said. "Captain O'Connell. If you're awake, we have food and updates on the repairs. Perhaps we could discuss the plan for when we reach Drion?"

"Give us a few minutes, Jackson," Zach called out. "I'm not quite coherent yet." He slowly pulled back and out, then nuzzled behind Anders's ear. "I need a shower."

"You *need*," Anders said, squeezing Zach's hand, "to stay right here in my bed for at least a few more days. But since that's not an option, I suppose a shower would be a good idea. I have clothes you could borrow. They'll be a bit short on you, but they're sleep clothes anyway."

Zach kissed the nape of Anders's neck. "Thanks, I'll take you up on that. I'll only be a few minutes."

Anders turned and tugged Zach back in for a lingering kiss. "I'll be waiting for you."

Before heading out into the sitting room, Anders grabbed Zach's hand and kissed his knuckles. He knew Zach had probably only waited for him to finish showering in order to avoid facing Bern and Jackson by himself, but it still felt more significant. Like something he'd do for a lover. Someone he cared for.

"Smells like they brought breakfast," is what Anders said, though.

As if on cue, Zach's stomach growled. "Good thing too," he said with a laugh.

Anders laughed and laced their fingers together before leading the way out of the bedroom. They were both barefoot, each wearing a silk sleep set that was only a loose pair of pants and a flowing shirt. On Zach, the pants and shirt both ended a few inches too soon, but Anders couldn't help the thrill that sight gave him.

Jackson smiled when he saw them, though Bern looked like he'd bitten into something sour. Anders treated him in return with his best Royal Glare; he understood why Bern was so upset with Zach, but Anders was trying to be happy with what he could have. There would come a point where it wouldn't be enough, but he was Not Thinking About It at the moment.

Finally settled next to Zach on the couch with their simple breakfast and tea, Anders leaned forward, elbows on his knees and teacup in his hands. "What news is there?"

Jackson and Bern exchanged a long glance. "The ship's outgoing communications are still down," Jackson said at last, "and probably will be until after we reach Drion. Inbound is working, however."

"And?" Anders prodded.

"And there have been developments in the story of the missing prince," Jackson said.

Bern rolled his eyes. "They're saying that you're so late for your father's funeral because you've been taken hostage by the crew ordered to transport you, Anders."

"That's ludicrous," Zach said hotly. "No military crew worth their commission would harm the prince, and certainly not one with our length of service and experience, our loyalty. I'll kill whoever dares say otherwise."

Anders put a hand on Zach's knee. "I won't let it stand, Zach," he said gently. "But we'll have to be careful how we handle it. Gossip is the weapon of choice in politics, after all." He paused, thinking it over, then nodded decisively. "We'll need to get me on the media streams as soon as we get a solid presence on Drion. Put an immediate end to the story of the kidnapped prince. I don't want to leave even the slightest chance that whoever is behind this will try to make the crew of the *Pallas* into villains a second time."

"And if you're in the public eye, backed by the troops we have on board," Bern added, "as well as those already there for the funeral, our culprit will be forced to rework their plan."

"Giving us time to find it, and them, out," Jackson finished for him.

Nodding, Zach took a sip of his tea. "It's getting that presence without incident that will be the issue. I'm worried that they'll know once we're in orbit and we won't have enough time to get you safely on the ground and hidden away until we can set up that announcement. I think we'll need to come in dark and during the capital city's night to give us the best chance."

"That's a good idea," Anders said, nodding. "I'll be honest, my instinct tells me that Grand Advisor Tanner is involved in this. He's the one I've been in contact with, not to mention he's a complete waste of breathable air."

Bern snorted. "You're only saying that because you're still angry about him trying to kiss you the last time you were home."

Zach raised an eyebrow, teacup halfway to his mouth. "He tried to kiss you?"

"Among other things," Anders grumbled and snatched up a roll, just to have something to do with his hands. "He kept attempting to put me in compromising positions, I assume to manipulate his way into being seen as a suitor. Father wouldn't let me shoot him, though. Something about it being against our laws to shoot someone for being slimy."

Zach's body tensed along Anders's side, then slowly relaxed. "Be that as it may, being an asshole doesn't automatically make him guilty."

"I suppose not." Anders frowned and picked at the roll. "We'll need to flush out whoever is behind this, regardless. I'm thinking I should play just dumb enough that they'll assume they've gotten away with it."

"You've spent your entire adult life in school," Bern pointed out. "Somehow I don't think anyone who knows you will accept you're a clueless idiot."

"They will if everyone believes I'm distracted," Anders said, and faltered on the next bit.

"What can we use as this supposed distraction?" Zach asked absently, reaching for a piece of bread.

Anders breathed in, slow and cautious. This had every chance of blowing up in his face, but it had to be done. "My newly identified match."

Zach froze, then slowly picked up the bread. He took a bite and chewed carefully, clearly struggling with whatever he was thinking. "There has to be a better option," he said finally.

Anders shrugged despite the tension in the air. "We need to have a plausible reason for me to be distracted *and* a reason for me to have suddenly acquired a Navy captain as a part of my entourage. Introducing you to court as my current lover might fool some, but I've never really made a habit of getting attached to bedmates."

"You're the crown prince, soon to be king," Zach said. "Your father just died. I would think those would be sufficient to explain the Navy captain and the distraction, respectively. I don't see how our private sex life is anyone else's business."

"Zach." Anders chanced touching his knee, gratified when he didn't pull away, even if he did tense up some. "I'm in mourning for my father, yes, and I never wanted to take the crown so early, but everyone at court knows I've been preparing for this nearly all of my life. Plus, you know those medics will eventually tell someone. Best to get ahead of it while we can." He paused. "We can use my mourning to put off talk of bonding. And if you want to leave once the situation is taken care of, we can make up some story about it all being a ruse. I won't force you to bond with me. I swear it on my family name."

Across from them, Bern grumbled wordlessly, but subsided with a glance from Jackson.

Zach had visibly twitched when Anders said, "bonding," but said nothing for a long moment. Not looking at Anders, Zach turned to Jackson and Bern. "The three of you know the grounds around the palace well, I expect. Where we can land shuttles?"

There was another pause, Jackson and Bern watching Anders carefully for their cue. Finally, Anders nodded. "Yes."

"We're familiar with the guard rotations," Bern said. "Or at least what they used to be."

"And what we don't know we can find out from friends who are stationed at the palace, once we have transmission capabilities again," Jackson said. "There are more than a few who I know can be trusted to help us once we're on the ground."

Zach nodded. "I don't know how many shuttles we can risk landing without being discovered, so I don't know how many troops we can safely bring with us. I do know who's most loyal and who is marking time until their enlistment is over, so I know who I can count on to have Anders's back for this."

"We should limit ourselves to just the one shuttle for the first trip," Anders said. "Minimize our chances of discovery. All the more reason to make my safe return announcement as soon as possible."

"Yes," Zach agreed. "Another issue I can see is getting the media together for an announcement without alerting our traitor. Unless you have a broadcast room in the palace where we can do it ourselves.

It might be best to do it in front of the palace, though. It would be a visible symbol of your authority."

Anders nodded. "Lord Hawthorne can call the media," he said. "For security reasons, only my immediate family and guard detail have ever known what name I used while traveling. Hawthorne was my mother's maiden name."

"Good idea," Jackson said. "It won't take long for the culprit to figure out what's going on, but by then the palace will be swarming with cameras broadcasting live streams."

"Lord Hawthorne is your uncle, then?" Zach gave Anders a sideways glance. "He can organize a press conference before it's too late?"

"Technically, *I* am Lord Hawthorne," Anders said. "My late uncle never had any children, never spent much time at court. He was glad to pass on the title to me, knowing it will go on to any heirs I have. He died a couple of years ago, not that the media streams really paid much attention." Uncle Philip had been a good man, quiet and calm no matter what came his way, and Anders was grateful for his example now. "We can use his name—our name, really—to call the conference once we land, spreading word through a few back channels that it has to do with the right of succession."

Zach nodded. "Okay. And there's a place to land privately?"

"Yes," Bern said. "There used to be a garden to the south of the palace, but no one's been there in years."

"Mother's garden," Anders said, the familiar ache in his chest when he thought about his mother lingering. "Father walked there at nights even after she died. It should still be clear for landing a shuttle and sneaking onto the grounds."

"Good," Zach said. "I'll pick my twelve best to go with us."

Jackson and Bern nodded in unison. "We trust your judgment completely with that," Jackson said.

"There's one more thing," Anders said slowly. "And, Zach, you're going to hate this, but it's necessary." He fixed Jackson and Bern with a straight look. "As my publically acknowledged match, Zach is to be protected as though he were me. Once we're on Drion, I want you both to assign a security detail to him." Reluctantly, Anders faced

Zach. "I know you can take care of yourself, but you are . . . you're simply too important."

Zach actually growled. "If I need a detail—and that's a *big* if—I can choose my own people."

"Outside of this room, no one on board has the necessary qualifications to make me comfortable trusting them with your back," Anders pointed out. "You might as well let Jackson and Bern pick someone with the appropriate training and clearance, someone who's already been vetted for security work for your temporary guard when we reach the ground. And you will need a guard, I'm sorry. The unbonded match of the not-quite King of Drion would make too tempting a target, and I *refuse* to leave you unprotected. I won't have you hurt because of me."

"I can choose my own people," Zach insisted a little heatedly. "I have more than a thousand men on board, I can spare a couple."

"And I'm sure they will be loyal to a fault," Anders said, doing his best to keep his voice even. The last thing they needed was to start shouting at each other again. "But Jackson and Bern will choose trained and experienced guards for you. Once the situation has settled, we can see about having you vet your own detail, but for now this is the best way I can think of to ensure your safety."

Zach was silent for several long, tense moments, then he nodded shortly. "Fine. Now if you'll excuse me, I need to dress and get back to my cabin to change. I still have ongoing repairs to oversee." He stood and went back into the bedroom, the door sliding shut softly behind him.

Anders stared after Zach, his heart aching. He had asked far too much of his match in too brief a time, and so much of it was more than Zach was willing to give. But give it he had, and now he *owed* Zach the space to breathe.

"Would you let him go?" Jackson asked. "If he wants to leave after all this, would you really let him go?"

Swallowing around the iron ball of emotions in his throat, Anders nodded. "I would. I can't . . ." He tried again. "Just because we're matched by chance doesn't mean he's mine to keep."

"You won't ever be able to marry someone else," Bern added. "You can't risk someone seeing your mark. Too many people have likely seen his. Not to mention you're banking an awful lot on the slim chance people will even believe it's a ruse."

"I know." Anders lifted his hands helplessly. "The least I can offer him after this is his freedom and happiness."

"What about your happiness?" Jackson asked.

Anders just smiled sadly.

At that moment, Zach opened the bedroom door and entered the main room, uniform hopelessly wrinkled. "I'll let you know as soon as we're ready to travel," he said tightly. "It shouldn't be long; I've had people working all night on repairs." He nodded to them, and left Anders's quarters without another word.

Anders held up a hand, stopping whatever well-meaning words Jackson or Bern might have. "I'll be fine," he lied unconvincingly. "Though I rather think I could use some more sleep. Would you wake me if we fall under attack again?"

Without waiting for their nods, Anders stood and went back to his bedroom. The room still smelled of their lovemaking and the bed of Zach in particular. Anders drew a shuddering breath and curled up in his bed, clutching a pillow as he finally drifted off.

CHAPTER TEN

Anders looked up from his media screen when the intercom chimed. It had been eight hours since Zach had walked out, stone cold and anger firmly leashed, and Anders would have been lying if he'd said he wasn't worried. Zach was a strong, proud man, and if he could, Anders would have backed off enough to let Zach breathe, but it simply wasn't an option. Not if they hoped to make it through the next few days.

Surreptitiously wiping his damp palms on his trousers, Anders nodded for Jackson to open the door. Hopefully Zach had cooled down enough that they could finish their plans. But instead of Zach on the other side of the door, it was the first mate.

"Mr. Hadlock," Anders said, standing and bowing despite the disappointment that filled him to overflowing. "How may I help you?"

"Lord Hawthorne," he said as he entered with a deferential bow and a sideways glance that made it clear he knew exactly to whom he was speaking. "The captain asked me to let you know that repairs have progressed sufficiently for us to resume our journey, and I personally wanted to thank you for allowing your men to assist with our repairs."

For a moment, Anders felt as though he'd been struck in the chest. He could barely breathe for how much it hurt that Zach couldn't even look at him for this much. But he still nodded. "You're welcome, Mr. Hadlock. Jackson and Bern were Navy men long before I knew them; I'm glad they could be of assistance," he said after what was probably too long a pause. "And thank you, sir, for updating me. Please let me know if there is anything else we can do to help."

Hadlock smiled. "Thank you, my lord, I'll tell the captain. He's double-checking a few repairs and then will get us on our way, but I believe we have things well in hand." He paused, and then said softly, "He really is just terribly busy right now."

"Of course he is, especially with everything that's been going on." Anders managed to summon up a smile from somewhere. It wasn't Hadlock's fault that his captain was an asshole who couldn't be bothered to face his own match.

"Exactly. Between the repairs and getting to Drion, he's dealing with a lot." Hadlock nodded. "I'm sure he'll come see you as soon as he can. He's quite concerned with your well-being." He paused. "My lord."

"That's kind of you to say so," Anders said, voice dry. His smile twisted a bit, and he laughed. "I take it the captain has filled you in on certain . . . details?"

Hadlock's teeth flashed in a grin. "As few as he could get away with, Your—my lord."

"I'm shocked that Captain O'Connell would play things close to his chest," Anders said. He liked Mr. Hadlock already.

"He's normally so forthcoming, isn't he?" Hadlock was visibly trying not to laugh but quickly sobered. "Speaking of the captain, I should get back to the bridge to assist him. Please let me know if you need anything at all. I am happy to help in any capacity, and please feel free to ask me directly. It's my honor to serve, sir."

Sir. Anders nearly laughed at the way Mr. Hadlock tripped over himself to please. He was so used to being seen as the royal equivalent of a nobody, just another privileged jerk to be pampered. And the fact that Hadlock was also fighting himself from calling Anders *Your Highness* . . . well. Out of all the changes of the past week, this small one was what Anders was the least prepared for, it seemed.

"Thank you, Mr. Hadlock," Anders said, nodding. "I won't forget that."

Hadlock bowed. "Excuse me, my lord."

Anders sat heavily as the door closed behind Oliver, eyes closed for long seconds. After a few beats, he opened them back up, reluctantly facing Jackson and Bern, both of whom looked utterly indignant on his behalf.

"I'll kill him," Bern said, hands balled into fists. "He doesn't deserve you."

"I'm with Bern on this one," Jackson said. "You're not children, there's no excuse for him avoiding you because his precious feelings are hurt."

That startled a full laugh out of Anders, breaking through the hurt wadded up in his chest. Jackson and Bern were the finest friends he could ever have asked for. "Thank you, both of you," he said. "But I think this one is up to me to fix."

The door to the bridge swished open, and Oliver walked through. Zach saw him glance at the ensign, nav officer, and comm officer before approaching Zach.

"Pardon me for saying so," he murmured, "but you're really a dumbass. Lord Hawthorne was clearly expecting you and seemed quite upset that it was me."

"Shut up, *Hadlock*," Zach said between gritted teeth. It was one thing for Oliver to be casual when they were alone; Zach preferred it that way. But on the bridge in front of crew was another story. Besides, what Anders did and didn't expect was both none of Oliver's business and not Zach's current priority. His heart caught at the thought, but he shoved the feeling away. He didn't have time for it right now.

"You're avoiding him, aren't you? What did you do?"

Zach stood so he loomed over Oliver, ignoring the choked gasp from his youngest ensign. "That's enough, Hadlock. I want a status report on the remaining repairs." He turned away and approached the nav officer. "You have our original coordinates, Ronan, but prepare for potential alternatives in the event of another attack."

Ronan's eyes widened. "Are we expecting another attack, sir?"

"No, but I hadn't expected the first. We need to be prepared." Ronan nodded at that, and Zach turned to the ensign. "Coordinates are in and Ronan's monitoring, so get us moving, Ensign, we're behind schedule."

Oliver approached and relayed the repair status with no expression in his face or voice, and Zach inwardly winced. Oliver's insubordination wasn't common but wasn't unheard of, either—Zach counted on him for exactly that kind of reality check. But Oliver was usually smarter about who was around when he mouthed off.

"My office in fifteen minutes, please, Hadlock." He could apologize and explain things to Oliver, and it would appear that Oliver was being disciplined, which would maintain his reputation and standing on board. Two birds, one stone.

After Oliver nodded, Zach contacted his third mate. Polito was overseeing a repair crew that was, fortuitously, just finishing, so the man was on the bridge within minutes. Zach left the bridge in his competent hands and headed for his office, Oliver on his heels.

"What the fuck, Oliver?" Zach said as soon as the door closed behind them.

Oliver sat in the chair facing Zach's desk and steepled his fingers. "I could ask you the same thing."

Zach dropped into his seat behind the desk and scrubbed a hand over his face. "Look, I give you a lot of leeway. You're my friend and keep me grounded when I'm way out of line, but you have to treat me with respect in front of the rest of the crew. It's not an us thing at all; it's part of order on the ship."

"You're right." Oliver sighed. "I'm sorry. Now will you go apologize to Prince Philip?"

"I don't owe him an apology," Zach grumbled. "If anything, he owes *me* one."

Oliver raised an eyebrow. "I know you too well to believe that, Zach."

"It's *true*," Zach insisted. "You have no idea what the fuck he's asked me to do—no, *told* me to do, because I sure as hell have no choice on this one."

"On what one?"

Zach took a breath. Where to start? "We have to get him on Drion, no fanfare, no one aware, so we can get him on the news to prove he's not missing before anything else happens."

Oliver nodded. "Makes sense. So what's the problem?"

"We have to make Anders look distracted and stupid so we can get the attacker out into the open, so we can deal with the kidnapping attempt and whatever plotting is going on behind the scenes before they attack him again."

"And how exactly are you supposed to distract him? More than you already have, I mean."

Zach glared at him. "As his *acknowledged match*," he growled. "He's going to tell the fucking Collective that we have matching birthmarks, and everyone will expect us to bond for the same damn reason that you did when I told you about it."

Oliver watched him. "You may have to get over this thing you have about bonding," he said carefully. "I know your family's experiences with it haven't been good—"

"That's putting it mildly." Zach pushed a hand through his hair. "Dad left us without a backward glance when he found his match, and Kenzie's been like a ghost since Mark died. Mom can barely reach her, and when I video-call, she just looks right through me. She's my baby sister, and I can't do a damn thing to help her."

After a moment, Oliver finally said, "I'm sorry, Zach. I know that's been hard. But Anna and I are really happy. Jackson and Bern seem content at the very least. It isn't all bad experiences."

Zach shook his head. "I'd rather not find out in front of the entire known universe."

Oliver snorted out a laugh. "Or just the Collective?"

"Fine." Zach felt a smile tug at the corner of his mouth against his will. "The Collective. It's still a hell of a lot of people who will feel like they can have opinions on my personal life just because of who I'm fucking."

"You said not to call it that."

"Shut up." Zach grinned at Oliver, tired but grateful he had a friend like him. He had a feeling he was going to need that in the coming days.

When he couldn't reasonably put it off any longer, Zach made his way to Anders's quarters. He took two quick detours to check final repairs that were cosmetic and didn't really need to be checked, but eventually arrived at Anders's door. He pressed the intercom button.

"Yes?" Anders answered, sounding utterly exhausted.

"It's Zach. Let me in?"

The door opened almost immediately. Anders's clothes were wrinkled, his hair a wild mass of curls, and his eyes had that sadness Zach hadn't seen in days. "Come on in," he said, stepping back.

The look Anders gave Zach lodged in his throat, and he couldn't help himself: he moved forward, pulling Anders close and into a kiss. His mouth moved roughly against Anders's, then left Anders's lips to suck at the curve of his jaw. Anders's arms curled around him, and finally he relaxed.

"Hi," he breathed.

Anders gave a small, strangled laugh that sounded more like hysteria than anything else. "Hello," he said back, clinging. He pressed his face against Zach's neck and breathed deeply. "Long day, darling?"

"You could say that. Can we deal with our fight and the plotting after we sleep? I don't think I'm really up for anything else."

"Yes." Anders nodded. "Sleep sounds wonderful. Do I have to move for that?"

Zach laughed softly. "Yeah, 'fraid so." He brushed his lips over Anders's neck. "Unless you want to wake up with bruises when we fall down." He squeezed Anders close, then relaxed his grip.

"I wasn't sure you'd ever talk to me again," Anders said, not letting go of Zach as they made their way to the bedroom. "I wouldn't have blamed you."

"Not your fault," Zach mumbled. "Not happy, but it's not your fault." They entered Anders's bedroom, and Zach pulled free long enough to start stripping.

Anders undressed in an uncoordinated rush, dropping his clothes where he stood. Wearing just his shorts, he crawled into bed after Zach and up against his side.

"I wouldn't make it if I lost you," he breathed, curling closer.

Brain fogged with exhaustion, Zach wrapped his arm around Anders and kissed his temple. "I'm right here, and we're on the way to Drion again. Don't worry, Anders, just sleep."

CHAPTER ELEVEN

Zach stood before a handful of his people: the men and women he most trusted to be loyal to the crown and to him. After studying them for a moment, he smiled. "Sit. We have an extra mission to complete once we pull into orbit."

They all sat, filling the small training room he'd chosen for this discussion. Seven men and five women: they were strong sailors honed by hard work and combat. Zach trusted them with his life, but he was about to trust them with *Anders's* life. Still, he felt sure he could.

"This is, by its very nature, an urgent, secret mission. I have chosen each of you for this mission because of the complete loyalty you have always shown the crown. Because of the delicacy of the situation, nothing you hear today can leave this room." Zach waited for each one to nod their understanding, then he sat in his own seat and leaned forward, elbows on his knees and hands clasped between them.

"First of all, we are actually the Drion One and have been since before the attack." He paused to let that sink in. He was pleased to see each one sit up a little, spines straight and proud. "You will have heard that Prince Philip is missing and possibly kidnapped. He was never missing. We believe that this misinformation and the attack on us are part of a plot that may include not just kidnapping but murder."

Emotion was faint, but visible on their faces, anger warring with protectiveness. He completely understood.

"We have our own plot to put into play. Before the *Pallas* docks at the Drion Transit Center, we will take Prince Philip and his guards in one of the small shuttles and land quietly on the palace grounds. As this is a soft insertion, with no advance notice, we may encounter resistance from guards who either do not know it's Prince Philip arriving or else do not support him. We certainly hope it would merely be the former. In either case, if we do encounter resistance, disable and disarm but do *not* harm them in any way unless absolutely unavoidable. We will not have time to explain or identify ourselves, as he is making arrangements for a media broadcast to take place immediately upon our arrival. We will stand behind him in solidarity during that broadcast. This will serve two purposes: it will prove the prince is not missing and will show him safe with his troops at the palace, preventing any attempt to pin a kidnapping charge on us. Or me, really." Zach smiled grimly. "We believe there will be another attempt on him once we're at the palace, and we must be there to protect him while we catch the perpetrators in the act. We *will* protect him, with our lives if necessary."

They all nodded somberly, and Zach was so proud and knew in that moment he'd made the right choice in each of them.

"We must be ready to go before we get to Drion. Hadlock will have the bridge, and we'll launch from the ship just as it slides into orbit, before the *Pallas* docks. We'll travel at the fastest possible speed to the surface and should be able to go straight from landing to the front steps of the palace for the broadcast. It's imperative that Prince Philip make his speech before anything else happens. Are there any questions?"

There wasn't a single one, and Zach smiled at them. "Good. We will reach orbit in three hours; be ready in two. Dismissed."

As soon as the last one went out the door, Oliver walked in. "You wanted to see me?"

"Yeah," Zach said. "I need you to look into a few things for me."

Quickly, Zach detailed what he needed, and how Oliver's special skills from his time in military intelligence could help. Oliver nodded and asked a handful of insightful questions that reminded Zach all over again just how good his friend was at his job.

Zach scrubbed his hands over his face after Oliver left. He wasn't ready, had never wanted the match he was going to announce on an interstellar broadcast. Oh god, he was going to *announce his match on an interstellar broadcast*. His mother was going to kill him for that, but he wouldn't send a message even if he could, for fear of being intercepted. There was nothing he could do about how Mom would find out now.

Nothing he could do about any of this. He felt like he was being swept away on a tidal wave named Anders. He sat with his face buried in his hands for several minutes. Out of his depth, out of his league, out of his mind. With a sigh, he stood to go find his tidal wave, to make sure Anders at least was ready.

It hadn't taken long for Anders to pack up his belongings. He wouldn't be taking any of them with him on their furtive trip to the surface, but he'd still welcomed the activity. Anything to keep his mind off the fact that not only were they hours away from Drion, but also from upsetting what was looking like an elaborate coup attempt.

Unfortunately, now that he was done, Anders had nothing to take his mind off all the ways that things could go wrong. Especially terrifying was the thought that Zach was not only going to be deliberately putting himself in the line of fire as part of his duty to the Royal Navy, but also that he'd be in very real danger just because he was so important to Anders.

At that moment, Zach swept into Anders's quarters without waiting for permission, but stopped as soon as the door shut behind him. "I've briefed my people. They'll be ready in two hours; we hit orbit in three."

"Good." Anders stood and wrapped his arms around Zach, pulling him in for a kiss. "Are you needed anywhere in particular until then?"

"No, I thought we could go over the details of the plan again, just to be sure. You need to be safe." Zach rubbed his hands over Anders's back and kissed him again. "We'll have to move quickly once we land; there won't be time for debate then."

Anders nodded. "I know the drill. Do exactly as you say, go where you tell me. I won't give you any trouble." He smiled, though it felt shaky at best. "Enjoy it while it lasts, darling."

Zach raised an eyebrow and smiled. "Why, are you going to start telling me what to do instead?"

"As if you'd listen," Anders said with a laugh, bumping their noses together. "Would you do me a favor while you're ordering me around for my own good?"

"I suppose I could do that. It would depend on what the favor was." Zach kissed Anders again and started to open Anders's shirt.

Anders kissed Zach back, drowning in him. Finally, he pulled away enough to cup his hands on either side of Zach's jaw, holding his blue-eyed gaze. "Watch out for yourself too," he said, serious and calm. "I need you in one piece," he went on. "I need you to be as safe as you can. Will you do that for me?"

Zach smiled and rubbed his nose against Anders's. "I need me in one piece too, and I am always careful."

"That wasn't an answer," Anders said, pushing Zach's uniform jacket off his shoulders and draping it over the back of a nearby chair.

"You are my priority, Anders," Zach said. "But I will watch out for myself too."

"Good." Anders kissed him softly. "All of this won't matter for nearly as much without you with me."

Zach sighed. "You're the priority," he said again. "But it shouldn't be an issue. We'll go straight through to the front steps and make the broadcast, and then you'll be safe."

Anders wanted to shake Zach, to spill words of love all over the room until Zach understood. Maybe even until Zach gave some hint how he felt in return. But now was not the time. He couldn't send Zach out into danger distracted. Instead, he just nodded and kissed him again.

"Let's go to bed," he whispered against Zach's mouth.

With a soft murmur that could have been agreement, Zach pressed a kiss to Anders's forehead. "We can rest for a few minutes, but not long. We have to be ready to go soon. I need to be prepared and in the shuttle bay before my troops get there."

"I know." Anders was finally calm, Zach's presence settling him like always. He knew the peace wouldn't last beyond the next few hours, but he embraced the feeling, grateful for the little bit of sanity in a truly insane time. He brushed his hand over Zach's mark. "It's selfish, but I'm glad you'll be with me."

"Where else would I be?" Zach ran his hand down Anders's back. Anders smiled and kissed Zach's shoulder. "Thank you."

CHAPTER TWELVE

The shuttle ride to the surface was quick and quiet—no one seemed willing to break the silence around them. They were all tense, ready to fight but hoping it would be unnecessary. Bern supplied the palace coordinates and, as they approached, directed the pilot to the garden behind the palace. Zach's people were up and out of the shuttle as soon as it put down, falling into formation around Anders and Zach, with Jackson and Bern right behind the two of them.

As they entered the palace, their little core of four moved forward so Anders and his men could direct the group through the building. Thanks to the communications problems aboard the *Pallas*, Jackson and Bern hadn't been able to contact their friends. They were forced to go in blind, although they nearly made it to the front hall before running into guards, a fact that had Zach both concerned and relieved. They shouldn't have been able to get so far into the palace without being stopped—something to talk to Anders about, but for now, it only helped their mission.

Their run-in with the guards was ugly, but not unexpected. The first hint they had of the impending fight was a soft thud from the back of their formation as a guard disabled one of Zach's men.

Without pause, Jackson pushed Anders into a nearby alcove, clear of the action, and then jumped into the fray. He grabbed the first palace guard in a headlock. "Bern," he grunted, holding the guard in place until Bern could knock him out.

Zach had turned at the sound in time to see Jackson get Anders out of the line of fire. He whirled into the fight, immediately engaging a guard in hand-to-hand, the battle no less intense for being soundless. He finally forced a choked sound out of the other man as he knocked him unconscious. A comm crackled to life, one of the guards trying to raise the alarm, but Zach stopped him with a hard jab to the nose. Someone cursed, and two more guards came around the corner.

Two of Zach's people spun to meet them, dropping into identical fighting stances and attacking the guards before they could access their comms. One swung up in a kick that looked more like a round-off than a battle move. It was just as effective, however; the palace guard went down as if he'd been felled when her foot connected with his temple.

In the end, two of the palace guards and one of Zach's crew were left unconscious, a few others bloody but standing, and all of the palace guards were secured with ties and hidden in a nearby alcove. As Zach straightened from arranging the last man in his unconscious sprawl, one of the guards suddenly shouted, "Intruders! Guards, alert! Intruders!"

Zach didn't see who shut him up, just heard the sound of a fist hitting flesh as he moved to Anders's side.

"Hurry," Zach said quietly. "There'll be guards coming now, and more out front; if the media is there as well, we should be able to start Prince Philip's speech before having any other problems."

They ghosted through the halls hearing the faint echo of footsteps behind them as they finally reached the front entrance. Zach glanced out at the media pavilion to see reporters gathered in front of a podium, the buzz of conversation audible even from inside.

"The podium is there, An—Prince Philip," Zach whispered urgently. "They're ready for you. Jackson and Bern will step out first, followed by you and me with my people right behind us."

"We've been over this a dozen times, Zach," Anders whispered back. He grabbed Zach's hand and squeezed it. "I know you'll be with me."

Zach gave Anders the exasperated look that deserved, then gestured to Jackson and Bern, who opened the grand doors and marched outside. With a hand on Anders's back and a gesture to the troops, Zach guided Anders out after them.

Jackson went up to the podium first, his entire body rigid. "Announcing His Royal Highness, Crown Prince of the Drion

Collective, Lord of the Hawthorne Estate and heir to all in his father's name, Prince James Philip Michael Anderson III."

As soon as he stepped outside, Anders tossed back the hood on the black cloak he'd been wearing since they landed. The media, already agitated, exploded into a frenzy of lights and questions. Anders ignored all of them, though, carefully removing his cloak and stepping up to the podium, spine straight and shoulders back.

"Thank you all for coming," he said evenly. His face was that cool, calm mask of cultured royalty, and the media responded with near-instant silence. Anders waited a beat, the cameras whirring around him, and then he started over. "Thank you for coming. First thing, I want to extend my gratitude to all of you for your understanding in this difficult time. My father's death, as sudden as it was, gave me no chance to say goodbye, and I admit to selfishly taking a couple of days to recover from my grief while I made my way home from my studies on Gloria.

"As you can see, I haven't been kidnapped or harmed, despite some of the more wild reports of the past few days." He paused, allowing the reporters a chance to titter nervously. "I have been safely under the care of the crew of the Royal Drion Craft *Pallas* and her captain, Zachary O'Connell, from the moment I left Gloria, and a finer group of men and women in the Royal Navy I have yet to encounter. I wish to take this moment to publicly thank them for their dedication and loyalty both to me and the Collective at large."

Anders looked at Zach and his people, and smiled gently for a beat before turning back to the podium.

"The royal funeral and coronation will proceed as soon as I have had a chance to meet with my father's cabinet," Anders added. "Drion will not be without her king for long, I give you my solemn word."

He paused again. "The other thing I would like to announce is that in this time of loss and mourning, something wonderful has happened. Against all improbability, I have been fortunate enough to meet my match in a man of impeccable honor and character." He held out his hand to Zach, uncertainty flickering in his eyes for a moment.

A roar of shouted questions rose. Zach quickly took his hand, surprised to feel how clammy Anders's palm felt as he pulled Zach to stand beside him at the podium. They stood there for a moment, blinded by the flashing cameras. Eventually, Anders raised his hand, settling everyone back down once more.

"To say it is a bittersweet gain, knowing I would never have met Captain O'Connell if it weren't for the loss of my father, is an understatement. But I still wanted to share this happy news with the Collective as soon as possible. A reminder that life will always go on, that our ways will always continue."

A few reporters raised their hands, but Anders waved them off. "I have had a very long journey," he said, "and the day is just beginning. Over the coming weeks and months, there will be many questions, I'm sure, and I will do my best to answer them. For now, however, I would ask for you to respect our privacy while my match and I get to know each other. Again, thank you all for coming."

Anders stepped back from the podium even as the media erupted into a roaring wall of noise, but he didn't so much as bat a lash. "We can go back inside now," he murmured in Zach's ear.

Zach took him at his word and, turning, led Anders by the hand through the ranks of his troops, trusting them to fall in line. They entered the great hall, and Zach squeezed Anders's hand. "Well, that's step one over with," he said quietly, then raised his voice to normal volume as he gestured to four of his people. "Release the guards we captured and make sure anyone who needs medical attention has it."

Anders squeezed Zach's hand back. "I have a feeling I'm going to be saying this a lot in the near future, but thank you." He took a deep breath. "Zach, I—"

"Prince Philip?" A man, barely into his forties, ran down the hall toward them, clearly shocked and more than a little bit terrified. Two younger men scurried along behind him, tapping madly on media screens. The man's blond hair was askew and his clothes rumpled as though he was still dressing. "I only just heard the news!"

"That's because I only just arrived, Gregor," Anders said, dropping Zach's hand and stepping forward. Jackson and Bern signaled for Zach's people to let Gregor through, although neither one seemed entirely happy about it. "We had trouble with our communications on the way in. I was lucky to even get the word out to the media streams for my arrival once my shuttle entered atmo."

"I saw the end of your broadcast," Gregor said. "Matched! Congratulations, my prince."

"Thank you, Gregor." Anders nodded his head, and moved to the side. "If I might present my match, Captain Zachary O'Connell, of the RDC *Pallas*. Captain, this is Grand Advisor Gregor Tanner, of Ciebos."

Zach nodded coolly at Tanner. This was the man who might have been the one behind the attack on *his* ship, was possibly behind the king's death, and might very well have attempted to kill Anders. He bared his teeth in what could almost be called a smile. "This is your prince, soon to be your king, Tanner, but I have yet to see the respect due his title. Do you no longer bow to your prince?"

Tanner's eyes widened a fraction, then narrowed at Zach for a beat before he bowed low to Anders, the two men behind him scrambling to follow. "Forgive me, Your Highness. I must have left my manners in bed at such an early hour."

Anders returned the bow with a regal tilt of his head, glancing at Zach with a tiny smirk. "Of course, Gregor. Every now and then we must all give protocol a pass, mustn't we?"

"If Your Highness says so," Tanner said. His square jaw was set, and Zach could see a muscle ticking on the side. "So, have you set a date for the bonding ceremony? There will have to be the confirmation of your match first, naturally, but I'm sure we could put something together quickly."

"I am in mourning, sir," Anders said, all humor away. "Perhaps it would be best for me to bury my father before considering something that can most certainly wait while I get to know Captain O'Connell."

The muscle on the side of Tanner's jaw jumped again as he went back down into his bow. "As Your Highness wishes."

"I do." Anders arched an eyebrow. "I will meet with you and the rest of the cabinet this afternoon, once I've rested and the remainder of Captain O'Connell's crew has been comfortably settled. There is much to discuss."

Without waiting for a response, Anders turned sharply and walked away. Zach followed on his heels after a discreet signal to his people. He wasn't convinced Tanner wouldn't try to shoot Anders in the back. They fell in behind, joined by the men Zach had sent to free the guards they had overcome as they came in.

Anders swept through the halls, leading them deep into the palace as they gathered a sizable trail of palace guards in their wake. Once they reached the residential wing, the palace guards began to fall off, taking up posts at corners and doors until it was just Jackson, Bern, and Zach's people following them to an elaborate set of double doors, gilded and conspicuously sporting not one, but two cameras. Anders paused at the door, turning to Jackson and Bern.

"Please make sure the staff see Zach's crew settled properly. Any who came with us today should have rooms in this wing. And find me a proper assistant so the two of you can actually get a break from me?"

Bern snorted. "As if we'd let you that far out of sight, my lord."

Anders laughed softly and waved at the cameras. "I know you'll be watching. Get some rest."

As the rest of their group peeled off down the hall, Anders looked at Zach with a smile. "This is my suite," he said. "I could probably find you your own rooms, if you want . . ." He laced their fingers together. "But, honestly, I can't think of anything I want less right now."

"As if I'd let you that far out of sight, my lord," Zach echoed Bern's words with a smirk.

"Good." Anders opened the doors and led Zach in. "Because I've wanted to kiss you for ages."

Zach shut the doors behind them and pulled Anders into his arms. "Oh really? I think I can do something about that."

Anders sighed, relaxing against Zach. "That's why I like you so much," he said, kissing Zach's neck, his jaw. "You have a plan for everything."

"I'm trained to be prepared and to think on my feet," Zach said, turning his head enough to press his lips to Anders's.

They kissed for a good long while, Anders humming happily into Zach's mouth. "Would you believe that I don't think I actually have the energy for sex right now?"

Zach laughed. "I don't believe you. But there probably isn't time anyway. We need to discuss the next step here. It's too bad we don't have a plan to take advantage of Tanner's surprise, but he was clearly disconcerted."

"He was, at that. Slimy bastard." Anders dropped his forehead to Zach's shoulder. "He didn't like you calling him out like that."

"No," Zach said with deep satisfaction. "He didn't."

"He'll target you," Anders said. "Even if he *isn't* behind all of this, Tanner's never been very good at keeping his pride out of his own way."

Zach nodded. "I know. I've run into people like him before. Usually in the academy. A lot of them wash out because they can't, how did you put it? Keep their pride out of their own way." He curved his arms a little tighter around Anders, pulling him into a hug. "But he won't get you, that's the important part."

Anders made a soft noise in the back of his throat and hugged Zach back. "Or you."

"Or me," Zach said agreeably, although he hoped Tanner tried. He was looking forward to taking that one down a peg or three. "Now, you said something about rest and being too tired for sex?"

"At least we can enjoy these last few moments we'll have to ourselves," Anders said. He pulled away slowly, grabbed Zach's hand, and led him across the sitting room and through another set of doors to a bedroom with an enormous bed. "I have a Collective to run, and you are about to become the most interesting man in said Collective."

Zach shook his head as he sat on the edge of the bed so he could remove his boots. "I suspect people will be far more interested in getting to know their new king."

"I hope so." Anders removed his boots as well, then stood to undress, carefully draping his clothes over the back of a chair. "This will be difficult enough as it is with my every move being watched by friend and foe. The last thing we'll need is to worry about dealing with your own personal media corps. But since we want everyone to believe I'm thoroughly distracted by you, that might not be an option." He paused, smiled. "How do you feel about semipublic displays of affection, by the way?"

"Well," Zach said uncomfortably, "I haven't ever had to consider that question before. Some things should stay private."

"I agree entirely," Anders said, sitting next to him on the bed and holding his hand. "Nothing inappropriate, I promise. But if we're to play the roles of besotted idiots, we should definitely hold hands more." He kissed Zach's knuckles. "And if I can't kiss you breathless in front of my father's cabinet, that will have to do." He smiled. "What do you say?"

Zach nodded. "I think that would be okay." He squeezed Anders's hand. "But you need to sleep now. It's been a stressful morning, and there's still a lot to come."

Anders smiled and kissed him softly. "Only if you join me. I've been spoiled and don't think I can sleep without you now, you know."

"I'd planned on joining you," Zach said with a smile. "It's been a stressful morning for me too."

With a brush of their noses, Anders pulled away, climbing into the bed and sprawling happily across the white sheets, the rich copper of his skin standing out sharply in contrast.

Zach undressed and stretched out next to him with a happy sigh. It felt so good to just relax with him, especially now that Anders was no longer *missing*. He turned on his side and propped himself up on one arm and put a hand on Anders's stomach, caught as always by the difference between his own pale skin against the darker tones of Anders's. He wished he could keep Anders from all risk until they defeated the coup attempt. But poison was a very real risk, and it wasn't as though he could starve him. "Don't eat anything not prepared by your kitchens. Or not vetted by Jackson or Bern."

"Of course," Anders said. "You as well, I'm afraid."

"Damn it." Zach sighed. Naturally he was a target. He wasn't used to having to consider someone gunning for him specifically. "Fine. Me too. Now, go to sleep."

"Yes, darling." Anders rolled over and backed up against Zach, bumping his perfect ass right into the cradle of Zach's hips. "You too."

CHAPTER THIRTEEN

Anders could remember countless hours spent at his father's side, learning how to be the leader Drion deserved. And before he was old enough to sit in officially, Anders would sit in the king's antechamber just outside of the cabinet room, listening to his father's advisors discuss policy. Treaty renewals, trade negotiations, legal debates and more had all been on Anders's curriculum from an early age.

Yet somehow it was all different now that Anders found himself sitting in the king's chair, alone in the cabinet room with Zach and gazing up at his father's face, forever immortalized in paint and canvas on the wall beside the window. Below his father there was a picture of Anders, a rarity even here in the palace. It had been painted less than a cycle ago, during Anders's last visit home. The last time he'd really seen his father, Anders realized with a start.

He must have made a sound, because Zach curled a hand over his shoulder from behind, squeezing briefly, as if in comfort. Before he could so much as dip his toe into the well of grief he'd been ignoring, however, the main door opened and the members of Anders's father's cabinet filed in. Gregor Tanner was first, of course; blond and tall, with broad shoulders and a strong jaw, Anders might have thought Tanner handsome if he didn't have so much firsthand experience with how loathsome the man could be in private. It also didn't help matters right then that Tanner's face was puckered as though he'd bitten into something foul—an expression that only deepened when his eyes flicked over Anders's shoulder, no doubt making contact with Zach's.

Behind Tanner came Bannerjee Reese of Gloria and Omar Nadjem of Lenius, each jockeying to be through the door first. The military and agriculture counselors, respectively, made no eye contact with one another as they took their seats on either side of Tanner. Sofia Garza of Consileen, Natalie Cortez of Iotania, and Sean Kelly of Lithios entered as a single group, murmuring back and forth as they slipped into their seats, the conversation dying abruptly with a sharp look from Reese.

The rest of the cabinet filed in more or less like adults. Reverence Lukas Schmidt of Amasis smiled politely as he held a chair out for Imari Amjad of Sonhadra, who stood as tall as any man. Her long, straight nose twitched with disgust when Bianca Pretorius of Zarine sat beside her, but she remained silent as her eyes danced back and forth between Anders and Zach again and again. Next to her, Priya Mohan of Gael, Counselor of Shared Culture, sat with her hands folded primly as though it was the first day of school.

John Lee of Arkanna strode in last, his head held high no matter that he was short for a man. He had thick dark hair shot with silver, expensive clothes embroidered with gold, neatly accented by the ceremonial dagger of the Head of the House of Lee, and—judging by the expressions ranging from vague irritation to outright disgust— not a single ally in the room. And that made all eleven of the cabinet, and Anders's suspect list.

Anders stared at them long and hard, letting the moment stretch out. The cabinet members looked, to a woman or man, incredibly uncomfortable. A number of them kept shooting one another unreadable glances, and Anders pressed his lips into a tight line; if someone had been making a play for Anders's birthright, then they'd damn well better be prepared for the weight of the true king's displeasure.

Zach stood just behind Anders's shoulder, no doubt trying to glare holes in the side of Tanner's head. It was a tremendously comforting image, and Anders smiled as he placed his hands on the table.

"I gather I've missed rather a lot over the past few days," he said. "Would anyone care to fill me in?"

Silence greeted him. *Cowards, the whole lot of them.*

"Come now," Anders said. "Surely someone knows about the pirates."

"Pirates, Your Highness?" Counselor Nadjem frowned in obvious confusion.

Anders nodded. "The *Pallas* was attacked in deep space. Captain O'Connell would be best to fill in the details, as I was injured during the attack and lost consciousness briefly."

"Approximately two days out from Drion, the *Pallas* came under heavy fire from a squadron of unmarked fighter ships who did not respond to attempts to hail them." Zach's voice was cool and expressionless, a sailor giving a report to a senior officer. "We defeated them without much difficulty, leading us to believe they were mercenaries without the benefit of military training. What damage we sustained was primarily concentrated in the passenger quarters areas. As Prince Philip mentioned, he sustained injuries during the attack."

Zach paused, and when he spoke again, his voice had hardened. "We believe this may have been a targeted strike against Prince Philip, which would mean the mercenaries were given the schematics of my—of the *Pallas*. It would also mean that they were given Prince Philip's confidential travel itinerary. Without that information, they could not have known which ship to attack or where on the ship to focus their efforts." Anders wasn't sure which made Zach angrier: the kidnapping attempt or the fact that it had damaged his beloved ship in the process.

As the quiet of the room broke with the murmur of uneasy conversation, Anders couldn't help turning and smiling slightly at Zach.

"This is all your fault!" Tanner wagged his finger in Transit Counselor Lee's face. "You're responsible for the safety of our travel routes."

"My fault?" Lee was turning an unhealthy shade of red under his normally golden skin. "Two days out from Drion puts them squarely in Ciebos space. If your people weren't such a lawless group of heathens, this would never have happened!"

"Don't blame Ciebos for your refusal to listen to those reports of raiding parties," Military Counselor Reese broke in. "I told you about them weeks ago. And we all know that those raiders must be involved in our recent trouble with the black market."

"Enough." Anders held up a hand when what he really wanted to do was rub his temples. He had no idea how his father had managed for as long as he had. "Counselor Reese, you say there have been reports of raiding parties?"

Reese nodded, eyes flicking to Tanner and back again. "Yes, Your Highness. There's only been nominal damage so far, but perhaps they thought the *Pallas* would be carrying enough nobility for the funeral so as to make the risk worth the potential reward."

Lee snorted. "Everyone here knows those raiders are more likely than not the same squadron that attacked my cousin's settlement last year. Just because you and Tanner are thick as thieves doesn't make it any less so."

"Let's keep this civil, gentlemen," Anders said, even though he agreed entirely with Lee so far. "Rather than assigning blame for what was ultimately a nonfatal attack for everyone but those foolish enough to think they could take on a ship and captain of the *Pallas*'s caliber, we should be planning a proper investigation into the situation. I would hate for a less-prepared ship to fall victim to a similar attack."

"Yes, of course," Tanner said. Anders did not miss the narrow-eyed glare he shot Zach's way. "But perhaps it can wait until we have settled some of the issues a little closer to home?"

Anders resisted the urge to roll his eyes. Instead, he cocked an eyebrow and gestured for Tanner to continue.

"Now that you're here, we can continue with your father's funeral as planned the day after tomorrow, and your coronation the day after that," Tanner said.

"Why the delay?" Anders asked.

"In short? Politics and tradition, Your Highness," Reverence Schmidt offered. "The guest quarters are holding representatives from dozens of the most influential families in the Collective—"

"Not including the ones at this table," Counselor Lee interjected, face pinched and chin lifting sharply.

"Naturally," Schmidt said. Anders was tremendously impressed that the religion counselor didn't roll his eyes when half of his peers did. "Either way, they have come from across the Collective to offer their condolences on the loss of your father. Some have been here for the better part of a week. And, according to tradition and the Temple of the Many's Scrolls of Usmos, you must gather the grief of those who loved your father before his soul is nestled among the Dozen Stars."

"And all of these visitors claim to be Father's nearest and dearest?"

Schmidt lifted his shoulders in an elegant, if helpless, gesture. "That would be where the politics come in, Your Highness."

Now it was Anders's turn to resist rolling his eyes. The last thing he wanted to do was sit and listen to a parade of sycophantic false sympathy. Not when there was so much to be done. Still, he gave a tight smile and a nod of his head. "Of course," he said. "Well, Father's been in stasis this long, I suppose one more day won't matter in the grand scheme of things, will it?" The majority of the cabinet flinched at that. Anders sighed and pushed on. "The coronation must be the day after Father's funeral, however. There have been far too many delays as it is, and the people of this Collective deserve some stability."

"Yes, Your Highness," Tanner said. "Everything is in place for your big event, three days from now. The media streams have been advertising it all morning."

"At least we can count on people to make sure the parties aren't delayed." Anders rubbed his forehead, trying to stave off a headache. No wonder his father had always been so irritable on cabinet days.

"Speaking of parties, Your Highness." The muscle in Tanner's jaw jumped once, twice. "The palace has been receiving numerous inquiries about your match."

"I've told you that I'm not ready to bond while in mourning, Gregor," Anders said firmly. "Nor would I ask Captain O'Connell to bind himself to me after we've only known each other for a single, highly fraught week."

"I understand, Your Highness." Tanner bowed his head in deference, while still managing to leave a note of condescension in his voice. "However, the rest of the kingdom is wildly curious about the man who will be your prince consort when you *do* bond."

"And I assume you have just the suggestion to allay their curiosity?"

"I do." Tanner's smile was far too insincere for Anders's comfort. "A dinner, tonight, with all the visiting nobles and heads of families.

I would suggest a ball, but I seem to remember Your Highness not being overly fond of dancing."

More accurately Anders wasn't fond of dancing with *Tanner*. The man had no concept of proper dancing distance between partners, and obnoxiously wandering hands. Anders, not wanting to cause an interplanetary incident, had pled distaste with the practice of dancing to get out of Tanner's grasp at the last system function.

"Tonight? So soon?" Anders scowled. "I'm not so sure it's in the best taste to have a party during the royal mourning period."

Tanner's smile spread thin and oily across his face. "On the contrary, Your Highness. It's absolutely appropriate. What better way to remind your people that life will go on? You'll provide hope to people all over the system simply by sharing your happiness with others. Besides," he added when Anders hesitated, "people love a good romance."

Anders barely resisted the urge to shudder at hearing words so similar to Bern's coming from Tanner. Still, they did need to promote the lovesick-fool story, even if there was every possibility Tanner was planning some sort of trap. Anders suppressed a sigh and turned to catch Zach's eye. Zach gave a small one-shouldered shrug, as though to say it was entirely up to Anders. Fair enough.

"A dinner would be fine." Anders nodded. "Obviously, the lead officers of the *Pallas* are to be invited as well. You may consult with either Captain O'Connell, or his first mate, Commander Oliver Hadlock, for those details. Now, as to the issue with the pirates," he said, taking a tremendous amount of joy when Tanner's face puckered up, "I will expect more information on the situation, specifically proposals for a remedy, when next we meet after my coronation. Counselor Lee, Counselor Reese, that includes from both of you as well. Rather than throwing blame around, I want solutions. Our people deserve nothing less."

He nodded once and rapped his knuckles on the table, just as he'd seen his father do dozens of times to signal the end of cabinet meetings. "Dismissed, ladies and gentlemen," he said, and stood, exiting through the door to the king's antechamber with Zach, Bern and Jackson waiting for them just on the other side of the door.

They waited in the antechamber while the cabinet left, listening to the counselors bicker on their way out. Anders waited until the last of the voices faded and the exterior door closed for the last time before speaking to his own companions.

"Thoughts?" he asked all three of them.

Bern shook his head. "I hate to say it, but it seems like Tanner has Reese in his pocket."

"That would explain how he would have been able to get the schematics of the *Pallas* without anyone noticing," Jackson said with a nod.

"I can't quite believe I ever admired your cabinet, Anders." Zach was looking at the closed doors to the cabinet room. He shook his head slightly and turned to Anders. "Tanner sets off all kinds of warning bells for me. He oozes guilt; how does he get away with anything?"

"He's his planet's duly elected representative," Anders said. "Even if he *is* a slimy bastard. I've yet to meet anyone who has had close dealings with him and actually likes him, but he's very good at fooling people from a distance."

"Well, we've got to either catch him in the act, or get him or Reese to confess." Zach shrugged. "There has to be an airtight case against him, or he'll keep trying until he kills you."

Anders hesitated. "I've known Banner Reese a long time. I really dislike the thought of treating him like a suspect."

"Better to be safe than sorry, my lord," Jackson said. "We can't afford to give anyone the benefit of the doubt yet."

"Agreed," Anders said on a sigh. "Have you got your contacts in place?"

"We do," Jackson said. "The coverage isn't as complete as we'd hoped, not with so many nobles in house, spreading security thin to begin with. But we've got enough eyes and ears on Tanner that he's going to have a hard time making a move without us knowing."

"But I'm still curious. Why follow only Tanner?" Bern asked. "We have ten other potential suspects. It's a terrible waste of resources if he's actually innocent."

Anders snorted. "I don't think Tanner's been innocent since long before he came of age. Like calls to like. Even if he's not directly involved, I'm sure he'll be able to lead us to whoever is. We just need to know how he spends his time, first."

"We can probably keep eyes on Tanner for a few days," Jackson said. "If he doesn't do anything suspicious, I'd like to revisit this, my lord."

"Fair enough," Anders said.

"And," Bern added quickly, "we don't want you without at least one of us at all times. Fortunately, as your match, the captain is expected to be by your side almost always."

"Somehow, I don't think that will be a problem," Anders said with a smile. Bern rolled his eyes, but returned the smile nonetheless.

"I am concerned about this party, however," Jackson said. "He seemed terribly eager to get you out in the open."

"I'm sure he has something planned," Anders agreed. "But whether that involves trying to kill me or trying to feel me up during a dance again is still up for debate."

"We can address one of those," Zach said. "You won't be dancing with him."

Anders couldn't help the warm feeling Zach's possessiveness gave him, and judging by the exasperated look Bern gave *him*, he failed at hiding it too.

"Speaking of," Bern said, "you two need to work more on convincing people you're stupid for each other."

"Too true—you're both too sharp," Jackson said. "Go for a romantic walk in the gardens. Get your pictures taken. And at least *try* to act like you're falling in love."

Zach laughed. "I'm not really the romantic-walk type, Jackson."

Jackson fixed Zach with a look. "Today you are, Zach. Go, hold our prince's hand. Gaze at him like he's hung the stars."

"That's enough, Jackson," Anders said softly. It wouldn't be acting for him, but he didn't need the reminder that it might be for Zach. "I think we can figure it out from here."

"No, he's right, Anders." Zach held out his hand. "Show me your palace."

Their walk around the palace eventually led them outside, Zach walking alongside Anders, listening to the prince's quiet running commentary on various features and pieces of history as they went by. They both had their hands clasped behind their backs, elbows brushing occasionally, Anders seemingly just as reluctant to break proper etiquette as Zach was, even if it was in the name of their plan.

"And this is the Compromise Garden. The main feature here is the collection of twelve rose bushes, one from each of the twelve original planets in the Drion Collective." Anders paused and smiled ruefully. "I sound like a tour guide, don't I?"

"Well, I need a tour guide," Zach answered reasonably. "I've never been on Drion before, much less in the 'famed' Compromise Garden."

"To be honest, I never really spent much time in this part of the palace when I lived here before Gloria," Anders admitted. "Most often I spent my time in the library or my mother's garden."

Zach nodded. "We can build up your mother's garden again now that you're home." He nudged Anders with his elbow. "I noticed how much more . . . enthusiastic, shall we say, your tour guiding got in the library," he teased.

Anders blushed and glanced over Zach's shoulder at their collection of security: Bern for Anders, two palace guards, and a young man called Grant, who'd been assigned to Zach's detail. They hadn't been farther than fifteen feet away the whole time, but at least it was enough distance to allow for private conversation. "I would love to kiss you right now," Anders said, brushing a speck of lint from Zach's shoulder. "In case you were wondering."

"I wasn't wondering." Zach leaned in to murmur in Anders's ear. "I just knew you'd rather not give our audience a show."

He started to straighten up again when he heard the unmistakable whine of a laser gun shot. "Down!" he yelled, and shoved at Anders. Cursing the fact that he hadn't worn a weapon, Zach turned, and a second blast exploded through his upper arm. The pain was blinding, weakening his knees so that he stumbled to the ground as he shoved at Anders. "Bern, get him inside!"

Security guards rushed in from all sides. While some surrounded Zach and Anders, others ran to search for the shooter. Anders was refusing to budge, struggling against Bern to get back to Zach.

"You've been shot!" he shouted, twisting his slight frame out of Bern's grasp and grabbing Zach's wounded arm. "We need to get you inside. Guards!"

Already fighting the haze of pain that wanted to take over, Zach nearly passed out when Anders clutched his left arm. He grabbed one of Anders's hands with his. "Go inside, Anders," he said roughly. "I'm fine, Anders. Go. *Now!*"

"Not without you," Anders insisted. Bern was still fighting to get a good grip on his charge, no doubt to bodily drag him away if need be, but Anders spun and dropped to a crouch. "Get Zach and I'll go. But I am *not* leaving him. I love him."

"Anders," Zach said evenly. "Let me up and I'll walk in with you. But there is a sniper out here; *we have to go inside right now*."

"Fine." Anders stood and was almost immediately scooped up by Bern and another guard, the pair of them all but carrying him to cover. Two other guards and Grant helped Zach up as soon as Anders was clear, all of them rushing Zach right behind him.

"Sir, are you hurt anywhere else?" Grant was asking in a tight voice as they ran across the garden and back to the shelter of the palace.

"Just the arm," Zach said through gritted teeth. The laser had cauterized the skin, which had done nothing for the broken bone or the pain, or the smell of burnt flesh. "It's broken, but I'll need skin treatment too." He could hear Anders shouting over the roaring in his ears. Fuck, but he'd forgotten how much getting shot *hurt*. "Keep him safe, Grant, we can't lose him too."

"Sir," Grant said, firmly holding on to Zach's uninjured arm, "with all due respect, you're not the one who I'm afraid of most at the moment. His Highness puts a high priority on your safety." They made it inside, though Grant didn't slow. "Let's get you away from these windows, sir."

Wincing with every jarring step, Zach let himself be led farther into the palace. Jackson's familiar bulk came around the corner, his dark face creased in worry.

"Captain!" Jackson hovered as they reached the infirmary and medics surrounded Zach. "What happened? Bern said something about a sniper. Prince Philip is still fighting him to get back here."

"I don't know much more than that, Jackson. I heard the first shot and then got hit. I only know the vaguest direction it came from." Zach sighed as the medics cut away the sleeve of his uniform; at least it wasn't his dress uniform.

"There are guards in pursuit already, sir," Grant offered. "His Highness wouldn't go to safety without the captain, so I stayed here."

"Good." Jackson paused, eyes going distant for a moment. "Bern assures me the prince is safe, but insisting on seeing the captain immediately. Grant, secure the route back to His Highness's rooms and let the prince know Captain O'Connell will meet him there as soon as he's been cleared."

Grant turned a little green, likely at the prospect of facing Anders, but nodded and took off down the hall, a good number of guards following him.

Zach let the medics work, sighing with relief as they repaired the bone before beginning work on his skin. "Tell Bern not to let Anders hurt Grant—there was literally nothing he could have done against a sniper."

"Do you honestly think Anders is capable of being rational right now, Zach?" Jackson arched an eyebrow. "He just saw you *shot*. Surely you must know how he feels about you and how this would affect him."

"Well, that's where Bern comes in," Zach joked weakly. The medic finally patted his arm and pronounced him good to go. Zach thanked them and began the walk back to Anders's quarters with Jackson. "He said he loves me." Zach's voice was soft. "I didn't know."

"Didn't you?" Jackson asked, surprisingly gentle. "Haven't you noticed the way he looks at you even when there's no one but us around? There's no way it's just the match, and you know it."

"No." Zach's eyes were as sharp as his voice. "A match doesn't guarantee love, and, although our sex life isn't any of your business, suffice it to say we certainly enjoy ourselves. I thought that explained it."

"Sometimes I forget you haven't known him as long as I have," Jackson said as they entered the residential wing. There were three times as many guards as had been here this morning, all of them bristling with weapons and ready to lay their lives down for Anders. "If you had, you'd know that until you, Anders was proud of himself for never being more than vaguely attached to his lovers. Trust me, your relationship hasn't just been about the sex since very early on."

Zach shrugged uncomfortably. Jackson was right in that he'd known Anders a lot longer, but Zach had known him *intimately*. They'd had sex pretty much as soon as they'd met and it had been fun, and that's all it had been. Sure, they'd gotten closer the more they'd had sex, and finding out they were matched had added an extra something to the mix, but love? He didn't want to go there.

"You're going to have to face it eventually, even if you don't love him back," Jackson pushed. "When you do bond, you're going to feel what he feels until you both get a handle on shielding your emotions."

"We aren't bonding." Zach felt a little childish digging in, but after everything his sister had been through, after what his father had done to their family . . . Besides, Anders knew Zach's stand on the whole damn thing. "Anders knows how I feel about it too. We aren't."

Jackson sighed as they reached Anders's suite. "And Anders will never force the issue with you because he loves you," he said, blocking the doors. "No matter how disastrous it would be to his rule."

"I'm not discussing this with you," he said. "It's between me and Anders."

Jackson crossed his arms and stepped to the side. "Fine. Then talk to him. But don't storm off when things stop going your way, because you're both going to have to deal with this sooner rather than later."

"Again, not discussing this with you." Zach had no intention of discussing it with *anyone*, least of all Anders, but that, too, was none of Jackson's business. He pushed the doors open and walked into Anders's rooms.

"Zach!" Anders was on him in an instant, his fingers lightly skimming over the ragged edge where Zach's sleeve had once been. "Are you okay?"

Zach rubbed his hands up and down Anders's arms. "I'm fine now, all fixed up. Don't worry."

Anders snorted. "'Don't worry,' he says. How about I get shot next time and I can tell you not to worry?"

"Let's not do that." Zach smiled and hugged Anders. "I told you before, you're more important."

"Not as far as I'm concerned." Anders's face was drawn and pale. "I never wanted my paranoia justified like this."

"Apparently it wasn't paranoia after all. Not if they really are out to get you."

"That's a comforting thought, thanks." Anders brushed their noses together and breathed deeply. "What I said outside is true, if not at all how I wanted to tell you. There's no one more important to me, Zach."

Zach had no idea how to respond to that, so he pulled Anders closer, resting his chin on Anders's shoulder. "Yeah," he said quietly. "I know."

Anders sighed, but held Zach close for a good long while. "Maybe," he finally said, voice a little rough around the edges, "maybe we should cancel the dinner tonight."

"No," Zach said, "we don't have to do that. Let's get it over with before the funeral so we don't have to deal with it later. You won't be up to it tomorrow, and I suspect you'll be really busy after your coronation. And remember," he said softly, "we're supposed to be being stupid in love with each other to draw out our assassin. We can't do that if we're not in public."

"Obviously I've got the stupid part down." Anders sighed against Zach's neck. "I lost my mind a bit when I saw you were hurt. You have no idea how hard Bern had to work to convince me not to banish Grant to an ice planet."

"There was nothing he could have done." Zach eased back and gave Anders a quick kiss. "Not against a sniper. I'm just glad we got you out of the way. Now, I could use some rest before the dinner tonight. My arm's fixed, but it still aches a bit."

Anders smiled, but it was weak. "Why don't you go lie down, then? I have matters to attend to, but at least you'll be able to rest."

Zach grabbed Anders's hand and squeezed. Staring into his eyes, he said, "Be careful, Anders. Stay inside and keep Jackson and Bern with you at all times. You know they're going to try for you again."

"I will, darling." Anders kissed him softly, then backed away. "I'll be back in a few hours, but there will be guards outside if you need to find me."

"I'll see you before the dinner." Zach had to make sure his dress uniform was ready too. He really wasn't looking forward to some big formal evening, but it was for Anders, so he'd deal with it. He was vaguely aware that he was focusing on petty details rather than think about what Anders and Jackson had said, but he'd worry about that later. "Be careful," he said again.

"I will." Then Anders slipped past Zach and out the door without a backward glance.

CHAPTER FOURTEEN

Anders waited as long as he possibly could before going back to his suite. It was cowardly, but all things considered, he was owed a little bit of hiding from the world. Especially when the world contained one very specific Royal Navy captain who did not return some equally specific feelings.

But, eventually, Anders slipped back into his own bedroom, careful not to wake Zach. A long, hot shower worked out some of the knots in his shoulders, helping him tuck away the jagged mass of hurt in his stomach by the time he finished. He stepped out of the bathroom to find Zach just starting to stir. Murmuring a greeting, he crossed the room to his closet, pulling out one of his more formal outfits with a decisive nod; the pale-gray pants and dark-purple jacket with gold epaulets was just what the occasion called for.

"You're not wearing black?" Zach asked suddenly. Anders jumped slightly, then turned enough to see Zach in the mirror. The covers fell down to pool at Zach's waist when he sat up, and Anders could see that Zach had removed his ruined uniform top. Zach's mark stood out, starkly black against his paler skin.

"It's acceptable to break mourning for certain occasions," Anders said, stepping into his undershorts. His left wrist itched, but he resolutely ignored it. "Naming days, weddings, engagements. This isn't any of those, of course, but people will see it as important."

Zach slipped from the bed and approached Anders from behind wearing only his shorts. When he got close, he rubbed his hands over Anders's arms. "I've said it before, but that was before I knew who you were. I'm so sorry about your father, Anders."

"Thank you," he said quietly, looking down at the floor. "That means a lot to me." He couldn't help leaning back into Zach's touch, no matter how much he reminded himself that it didn't mean anything.

"I know how much it hurt when I lost my dad, and he didn't die. I can't imagine what you're going through." Zach pressed a kiss to the back of his head. "But I'm here for you."

No, you're not. Anders swallowed the words down. Instead, he turned in Zach's arms and dropped his forehead to Zach's shoulder. "You've never mentioned your father before."

Zach shifted uncomfortably. "He left us when he met his match and hasn't bothered with us much since his bonding, although I suspect that's more Mom's doing than his. He has three other kids, last I heard."

"Ah." Anders wound his arms around Zach's waist. "I'd wondered. I'm so sorry, Zach."

"Thanks," Zach said, curling his arms around Anders's shoulders in a hug. He left them there, holding Anders loosely. "At least he's happy, I guess. My sister's been like a ghost ever since her bonded died. She just looks right through us."

"Losing your bonded is probably one of the worst things that can happen to a person," Anders agreed. "It took years for my father to even begin to wake from losing my mother. He kept it out of the public eye except for never breaking his mourning, but he missed her every day." Then again, he and Zach would never bond, and Anders was fairly sure he wasn't going to recover once Zach left, either. So maybe it had less to do with science and more with hearts. Anders swallowed hard and vowed that he'd pull away in just a few more seconds.

Zach squeezed Anders again before bending to kiss his forehead. "I should hit the shower so I can get ready."

Anders nodded. "Of course," he said, but didn't let go.

With a soft laugh, Zach bent farther and pressed his cheek to Anders's. "You gotta let go first, baby," he said into Anders's ear.

"Sorry. Yes. Of course." Another beat, and then Anders managed to unpeel himself from Zach. He stared up into Zach's warm, fond gaze, and couldn't help smiling back. "Go shower, you smell terrible."

"Yes, bad enough that you might need to shower again after hugging me." Zach kissed Anders lightly and then turned away, dropping his shorts on the floor on his way to the bathroom. "They should probably change the sheets too."

As much as he hated the thought of Zach leaving, Anders had to admit he loved watching him walk away. Laughing unkindly at himself, Anders dressed quickly and headed out into the sitting room, where Jackson was waiting. He must have looked terrible if the concern on Jackson's face was anything to go by.

"I'll live," Anders said, collapsing next to Jackson on a sofa. "But I won't want to."

"What's going on?" Jackson curved one big hand over Anders's knee.

"Not only does he not love me," Anders said, not caring how bitter he sounded, "but bonding ruined his family. There is no way this is going to end well, is there?"

"Oh, Anders." Jackson, bless him, knew exactly when to break the rules. He wrapped his arm around Anders's shoulders, pulling him in close. "Bern's right. The bastard doesn't deserve you."

"There are some things that can't be helped," Anders said, leaning into Jackson's comforting bulk. "I don't know if it makes him a bastard just because we're not meant to be. At least not like that."

"He's an emotionally constipated ass," Jackson grumbled. "And I'd be honored to assist in pulling his head out of his backside."

That got a laugh out of Anders. "I don't think that will be necessary." He sat up straight again, feeling a bit better. Yes, his heart was broken. But he had friends like Jackson and Bern to watch out for him. And, besides, soon enough Anders wouldn't have any time to worry about petty things like a personal life. Sublimation had worked for his father, it would work for him too.

Zach sat stiffly in his seat, uncomfortable with all the pomp and circumstance surrounding a state dinner. Everyone had been eager to meet him; they'd formed a long and stuffy receiving line as soon as he and Anders had arrived. Zach couldn't remember anyone's names, except for the members of Anders's cabinet, any one of whom could be ass deep in the plot to kill their prince.

The mere thought of Anders's death sent a spear of rage and something that might have been pain through his gut. He was right there, though, and Jackson and Bern were close by, so Anders was safe for the moment. He ignored the little voice in his head that reminded him he'd been right next to Anders when he himself had been shot this morning.

His thoughts were interrupted by the arrival of yet another course that wasn't dessert. Zach had been trying not to eat everything they brought him, which was directly counter to what he'd been taught. There was no room for waste on a ship or in his mother's home. He leaned over to speak quietly in Anders's ear. "How many courses are there?"

Anders laughed. "Two more," he murmured back. "Be glad they didn't have time to plan; the dinner when I came of age had *twenty* courses."

"Well, fuck." Zach shook his head, amazed. "No one can eat that much food. Or this much food."

There was a high-pitched giggle, and Zach turned slightly to see a group of ladies watching him talk to Anders, whispering to each other behind their hands. He sighed. "They're talking about us, aren't they?"

Anders took Zach's hand and kissed his fingers. "Without a doubt. It's rather the point, though."

Zach leaned in to touch his forehead to Anders's. "You're right. I'll do better. We should talk tonight about our plans, though. We need to catch these bastards."

The tittering of their audience grew as Anders smiled gently, the expression lighting up his face. "The sooner I get to put my boot on the throat of the man who shot you, the better."

After I beat him into the ground, maybe. But Zach just smiled back. Anders was truly beautiful when he smiled, and Zach wanted to pull him out of his chair and lead him back to bed. They really needed to put that big, comfortable bed to good use. "Tell me what to expect tomorrow."

"Tomorrow," Anders said on a sigh, "I get to sit through a parade of meetings with people who barely knew my father, listening to their condolences. Most likely, they'll use their allotted time to curry favor, or put some agenda forward. You don't have to join me for that, if you'd rather not."

"Sounds like it would be far too much fun to miss," Zach said grimly. "Don't forget—I'm your shadow until we get this fucking plot rooted out and killed."

"You might change your mind after tomorrow," Anders said, offering a small smile. "But I can't say the company won't be welcome. I'm not sure how I'm going to make it through people talking about the funeral, much less the funeral itself."

"We'll make it through, Anders. I won't lie to you; it won't be easy, but you can do it." Zach sighed and poked at something green on his plate. He put down his fork. "I want to leave room for dessert," he said, then smiled at Anders. "What about the day after tomorrow? What will happen?"

Anders put his fork down and dabbed his mouth with his napkin, even though he hadn't touched the last two courses. "There will be a funeral procession through Dryax to the Temple of the Many." He leaned in close, probably to look like he was murmuring sweet nothings. "The route will be long in order to cover as much of the capital as we can. If it's anything like Mother's, it will take a couple of hours at least. At the temple, there will be the usual rites and then some. Probably another two hours or so." Anders picked up Zach's hand, staring intently down at their tangled fingers. "Then another procession—" his voice cracked, but he kept going "—this one to the royal tomb."

Zach covered their hands with his other one. He felt helpless, had no idea what to say. Knew there was nothing he *could* say to make it better. "You're strong, Anders. We can do this."

"I do wish you wouldn't—" Anders started, but stopped abruptly when Counselor Reese approached.

"Your Highness," Reese said, bowing to first Anders and then Zach. "Captain. Please forgive the interruption, but if I might have a moment of your time?"

Anders arched an eyebrow. "I assume this can't wait until after dessert?"

Reese nodded. "I'm sorry, Your Highness. It is a matter of importance to you both."

Anders hummed thoughtfully. "Very well." He gestured to the space just behind their chairs. Reese hurried around, crouching down for the three of them to have some measure of privacy. He was a tall man, almost of a height with Zach and nearly half a foot taller than Anders, so the position put him at the perfect level to murmur into Zach's and Anders's ears and close enough to hurt Anders if he was of a mind to. Zach watched him closely; he didn't trust anyone on the cabinet, not yet. Anders extended his hand, as if to wave Reese on. "What is it, Counselor Reese?"

"I'm pleased to report that the sniper from the gardens this afternoon has been detained," Reese said.

Zach sat up straight, instantly alert. "Has he said anything yet? Do we know if he was working alone, or on another's behalf? I need to question him." Zach paused. "Or, sorry, I guess that's the job of your guards. I forgot I'm not the one in charge here."

"Good questions, though," Anders said. "Has the capture given us any more information?"

"Not yet, Your Highness," Reese said, then hesitated. "I believe that when he does talk, it will be to implicate me, however."

Anders turned in his chair to look directly at Reese. "I beg your pardon?"

"The sniper is a former member of my security staff on Gloria," Reese said. "I terminated his employment shortly before my rotation here, due to concerns I had about some missing items. I think he was hired to implicate me in an assassination plot once I became too suspicious of Grand Advisor Tanner."

Zach raised an eyebrow at Anders. Who should they believe?

"Grand Advisor Tanner?" Anders asked. "Do you have any proof?"

"Nothing solid, I'm afraid," Reese said with an elegant shrug. "I do, however, suspect that His Majesty's death was no illness, and have been investigating this for the past several days."

Anders returned Zach's look for a long moment. "That's a very serious suggestion. What makes you think His Majesty died from anything other than a simple illness? My father's physician was the best in the Collective, you know."

"That's true." Reese nodded his head. "But your father had been researching several potential sources of corruption within the cabinet. He brought me into his confidence after his illness made acting on his own too difficult, and it wasn't long after that, that he lost his battle. He never had a chance to fully share his suspicions with me, so I've been forced to fly blind ever since. I've tried to be subtle about my queries, but obviously not subtle enough."

"But why Tanner?" Anders asked, sounding only vaguely interested at best. "As I'm sure my father would have said, there are no laws against being a dislikable human being."

"Sadly, that's true," Reese said with a fleeting smile. "But right until you showed up with your match in tow, Gregor Tanner seemed utterly convinced that he was going to marry you and help you adjust to your new rule."

Zach raised an eyebrow. "Somehow I doubt Anders would need Tanner's *help*, and it's a moot point now," he said, somewhat smugly. "He won't be a problem; *I'm* here."

Anders said nothing, but looked away, refusing to meet Zach's eyes. Reese shifted, obviously sensing Anders's sudden turn in mood.

"Yes, well," Reese said at last, "Gregor Tanner's infatuation with Prince Philip, not to mention Your Highness's obvious distaste, was part of what made me suspicious. The fact that I'm most likely about to be framed for today's assassination attempt tells me I must be on the right track."

"You do understand," Anders said, "that if you were guilty of participating in an assassination plot, it would be a wise move to ingratiate yourself with me now by pretending to be loyal."

Reese nodded. "I am no traitor. But I know that proving a negative is a tricky proposition. I would ask that you at least give me the chance to refute any claims against me."

"And my father's alleged murder?"

"His symptoms, Your Highness. I have seen poisons with similar behavior patterns. Very rare, obscure poisons that would be unlikely to innocently find their way into His Majesty and would be able to mimic natural illness closely enough to fool most."

Zach's fists clenched. Anders did not need this on top of everything else right now, but if their suspicions were correct, if his father *had* been assassinated, it was just further proof that the attack on the ship and the shot at Anders earlier really had been deliberate attempts on Anders's life, that someone was targeting the royal family.

Anders was quiet a long while. "Fine," he said with a decisive nod. "If you are implicated, I am willing to give you the chance to defend yourself. However, be warned that I cannot appear to be lenient on anyone, especially when my match was so publicly wounded while protecting me."

"That's another thing, Your Highness," Reese said. "I suspect the sniper was after Captain O'Connell. It's no secret that he and Tanner haven't gotten along from the start, and I've never met a more prideful man than Grand Advisor Tanner in all my life."

"After me?" Zach raised an eyebrow. "There's no reason for him to target me other than sheer spite because I don't buy his brand of bullshit. Killing me would do nothing to harm the royal family."

"Don't be dense, Zachary," Anders snapped. "You're my match and I'm in love with you. Killing you would destabilize both my political standing and my emotional well-being."

Oh. For all his military training that had taught him to plan, to see all the angles of a situation, Zach had never had to take emotions into consideration. He thought about how angry he'd been when he thought the sniper was after Anders. "I'm sorry, Anders, you're right."

Lips compressed into a tight line, Anders nodded once. "Is there anything else, Counselor Reese?"

"Nothing that can't wait, Your Highness," Reese said, shifting awkwardly.

"Thank you for letting me know. I will keep this conversation in mind as events unfold." Anders waved his hand, dismissing Reese.

Zach waited until Reese left before leaning over to murmur in Anders's ear. "I really am sorry. I wasn't thinking. I'm still not sure I was the target, but killing either one of us would be devastating, and the resulting uproar would be disastrous. I'm not used to having to take emotion into account when planning for and analyzing a dangerous situation," he finished awkwardly.

"I'm sorry my emotions are so inconvenient for you," Anders said, his hands tightly fisted in his lap, arms trembling.

"C'mon, Anders, that is not what I meant." Zach was just making it worse, but he had no idea how to fix it. "I meant that I'm deficient in—in dealing with feelings, okay? It's my fault."

Anders snorted but relaxed marginally. "Jackson called you emotionally constipated."

Zach laughed. "He's not wrong," he said, rueful. He curled his fingers through Anders's again. "Be patient with me. I don't know what I'm doing here."

"I don't either." Anders sighed, but gave Zach's hand a squeeze. "I'm simply hoping you'll figure it out before this all blows up in our faces."

"I certainly hope so too. Jackson and Bern might have to come to my rescue. They seem to have their lives much more together than I do." Zach smiled. "Oh god, another course. I'm not going to have room for dessert."

Anders laughed softly. "It's the last one, I promise," he said. "The worst part is that there will be dancing after this."

"All the better to work some of the food off, I guess." Zach pressed a quick kiss to Anders's lips. "And you'll show Tanner that it's just him you don't like dancing with."

Anders sat there with a stunned look on his face for several seconds before blushing fiercely. "I . . ." He paused, cleared his throat, and licked his lips. "I suppose I will, at that."

Zach grinned at him, then turned back to his food. They managed some small talk through that final course and dessert, and then they moved from the dining hall to the ballroom. Zach didn't waste any time, swinging Anders into his arms as soon as they walked through the doors.

"So you *can* dance," Anders said with a laugh as Zach took the lead, guiding them around the floor with nimble steps. "And here I thought you distracted me with sex during Thalia and Serena's reception so you wouldn't have to show me a flaw."

"Haven't you noticed? I have no flaws." Zach grinned. "Just many talents."

"I love you, but even I know that's up for debate," Anders said, but squeezed Zach's hand in his. He flinched. "Sorry, I'm trying not to bring that up."

Zach pulled Anders in close, breaking out of the dance's pattern. He pressed his forehead to Anders's, unwilling to put a name to what he was feeling. "It's okay, Anders," he said, then tilted his head to kiss him.

Anders curled his hand around the back of Zach's neck, holding him close while they kissed. "You always make me forget myself," he murmured against Zach's mouth. "It's a good thing we're supposed to be stupid for each other."

Supposed to be? Zach wasn't sure they weren't actually stupid for each other. "Sometimes forgetting yourself is a good thing." He rubbed his nose against Anders's. "Forget yourself tonight and just dance with me."

"Gladly." Anders kissed him once more, then pulled them back into formation. People around them whispered and giggled, but Anders kept his head high as he moved in Zach's arms.

CHAPTER
FIFTEEN

They danced for what felt like hours, Anders safe in Zach's embrace. He was sure they scandalized more than a few of the stodgier members of court, but Anders didn't really care much tonight. Not when it looked like Zach might one day actually love him back, if Anders could just be patient.

Pressing Zach against the door outside of his suite and stealing kiss after kiss, Anders figured he'd find some way to be patient if the waiting was all like this.

"I hope you're not too tired, darling," he murmured, brushing their noses together.

"Too full, maybe," Zach said with a smile. "But not too tired." He tipped Anders's face up into another kiss, big hand cupping his jaw.

Anders hummed happily and nibbled on Zach's lower lip. "I told you not to eat all of your dessert." He kissed Zach's jaw, working his way around to whisper in Zach's ear. "We should work off some more of that dinner."

Zach pressed his lips to the juncture of Anders's neck and shoulder. He nipped lightly at the skin with his teeth and then started to suck hard, seemingly determined to bring blood to the surface. Anders groaned softly at the thought of wearing Zach's mark.

"We need to get inside," he said, hand on the back of Zach's neck, holding him in place. "There's a large bed inside."

"Yeah," Zach murmured into Anders's skin. "I had a wonderful nap on it earlier, but I'd like to see if it's just as comfortable when put to . . . other uses."

"God I hope so," Anders said. "Wouldn't know, though. I've never tried out those particular uses in that bed." His bedroom at the palace had always been his space and no one else's. He'd never wanted someone he was sleeping with to be there with him. Zach, however, was an entirely different story.

Zach gave a low, husky laugh. "Well, we'll have to change that right away, then."

"Indeed." Anders kissed Zach once more as he fumbled for the door knob.

They stumbled into the sitting room of Anders's suite, giggling and clinging to each other like a couple of pubescent fools. Anders was about to grab Zach for another round of kissing up against the door, when he spotted movement across the room.

"Please pardon my interruption, Highness," Tanner said as he unfolded himself from the chair he'd been waiting in.

Zach blocked Anders's way, getting between him and the other man. He'd drawn himself up to his full height, imposing and intimidating in his dress uniform. "I believe these are His Highness's rooms, and I don't remember hearing him give you permission to be here tonight."

Tanner looked at Zach like he would a bug in his path. "Captain O'Connell, I'm pleased to see you've recovered from the excitement this afternoon."

"Gregor," Anders said, putting his hand in the small of Zach's back to remind him not to attack the grand advisor just yet. "How did you get in my rooms?"

"Oh, that," Tanner said with a smirk. "There are still some people in the palace who recognize the royal regent's power. Besides, unlike Advisor Reese, I know the importance of holding private conversations in private."

"The crown prince is here and will soon be king. Your extremely limited power is almost nonexistent," Zach said. "And these are not your quarters. You can schedule time with us tomorrow for your *private* conversation, Tanner. Get out."

Tanner turned to Anders, face bland as though Zach had never spoken. "Highness?"

"You heard my match, Gregor," Anders said. "It's extremely inappropriate for you to be here uninvited, and we *will* talk about that. Later."

"As my prince wishes," Tanner said, bowing deeply. He placed a small wooden box on a nearby table. "I simply wished to give you this. I've been ensuring its safekeeping since your father died, and wanted to be sure it made it to the right hands as soon as possible."

Zach reached back to put a hand on Anders's hip and moved him as Tanner approached, shifting to keep himself between Tanner and Anders. Once Anders was away from the door, Zach stepped forward to open it, gesturing for Tanner to leave.

"And Tanner?" Anders said just as Tanner was crossing the threshold. Tanner paused, looking back. "Captain O'Connell and I might not be bonded, but showing my match such disrespect is showing the crown disrespect. He speaks for us both, and I'd *appreciate* it if you would behave accordingly."

Tanner turned a violent shade of red, but only nodded in acknowledgment. "Your Highness. Captain O'Connell. Enjoy the rest of your evening," he said, and left, shutting the door behind him.

"There's something not right about him," Zach mused.

"There's very little that *is* right with him." Anders pressed his mouth shut. "But I think he might have gotten worse since the last time I was home."

"We've got to pin him down. He's definitely up to *something*." Zach shrugged. "He's out of our way for the evening, though, and I think we had some interrupted plans." He turned to Anders and began to open his jacket.

Anders glanced over at the box Tanner had left. Whatever it was could wait. Instead, he pulled Zach in for a hard kiss. "You have no idea how unbearably attractive you are when you're dangerous," he groaned against Zach's mouth.

"I'm always dangerous," Zach said. "It's just not always obvious." He took charge of their kiss, running the tip of his tongue along Anders's bottom lip before sucking it into his mouth. He shifted, scraping his teeth over Anders's lip, soothing the sting with his tongue before sliding it into Anders's mouth to explore and claim.

Opening up willingly, Anders fumbled with the rest of the snaps holding Zach's jacket closed and pushed his hands under it, grabbing fistfuls of Zach's pristine white undershirt. They needed to be in bed. Naked. Now.

"You," he gasped. "You need to take off your uniform before I ruin it."

"I could say the same to you. But you have to let go of me first."

Anders laughed and stepped away, grabbing Zach's hand. "Let's go, then." He led a very willing Zach into the bedroom, only letting go once Zach had shut the door and locked it one-handed.

Zach slid his jacket off and, probably because it was his dress uniform, hung it up carefully. He opened his trousers and did the same with them. Anders copied his movements despite the distraction of Zach slowly revealing miles of pale skin over lean, toned muscle. Zach tugged his undershirt off over his head and dropped it to the floor before sauntering over to Anders wearing only his shorts.

His own undershirt forgotten, Anders ran his fingers down Zach's chest and across his firm stomach. "God," he whispered, kissing Zach's shoulder. "You are so beautiful."

"Have you looked in a mirror lately?" Zach pushed his hands under Anders's undershirt, moving them over Anders's body in a firm caress, then lifted the fabric up until Anders raised his arms so Zach could pull the shirt off and toss it to the floor.

"I've been looking at myself my whole life," Anders said, tracing the slightly raised edges of Zach's soul mark. "You, on the other hand . . ." He stumbled closer, pressing their bare chests together, and tugging Zach in for another kiss. "You I could look at for the rest of it."

Zach didn't answer, diving into the kiss instead. His hands were strong on Anders's back, holding him close. He slid one hand down teasingly, working his fingers under the waistband of Anders's shorts to cup his ass. He squeezed in time with the slow thrust of his tongue into Anders's mouth.

Anders groaned, shoving his shorts down one-handed. Zach's fingers pressed at Anders's crease, and Anders had to bite down on the solid muscle of Zach's shoulder to keep from crying out over something so simple. It was too much, and there was no way he'd be able to handle being fucked by Zach right now. Not with everything that had happened that day. Fortunately, there were options.

"Zach," he whispered. "Zach, I want to fuck you tonight. Please?"

"Yeah," Zach gasped. "Yeah, want you to, want to feel you inside me." He shifted his grip and lifted Anders, who automatically wrapped his legs around Zach's hips. Zach walked them to the bed and dropped Anders onto the mattress, before quickly crawling up next to him.

Anders rolled to meet him, kissing fast and messy up Zach's neck, his jaw. "Touch me first," he begged. "Make me yours first."

Zach turned his head to meet Anders's mouth. "Yeah." He bit Anders's chin, mouthed kisses down his throat, and licked a path down his chest. "You *are* mine."

A split second later, Zach's mouth was on Anders's dick, sucking it deep into his mouth, teasing the sensitive spot on the underside every time he bobbed his head down. He hollowed his cheeks on each slide up, creating suction that was almost too much for Anders to bear.

"*Fuck.*" Zach's hair was too short to grab properly, so Anders held on to the back of his head instead, guiding him. "Zach, you look so good with my cock in your mouth," he crooned, lifting his hips in small thrusts. His whole body was thrumming out of control, and Anders loved every second of it.

Zach put both hands on Anders's hips and held him down, pulling off Anders's dick with an obscene *pop*. "Fuck my face," he rasped. "But don't come—I want you to fuck me, so let me know when to stop." He wrapped one hand around Anders, stroking fast and rough, rubbing over the top of his cock on each pass. When Anders was dripping over his hand, veins standing out, Zach put him into his mouth again.

With a guttural noise Anders barely recognized himself, he surrendered, moving in and out of Zach's mouth slowly, going deeper and deeper each time. Zach's mouth was so wet, so hot, that Anders was barely holding on to his sanity by the time he reached the back of Zach's throat, the head of his cock bumping hard enough to make Zach choke.

"Sorry, sorry," Anders gasped, but didn't stop. Hands on either side of Zach's face, he kept going, fucking in and out and in again until he was shaking, desperate for more, desperate to come. He was close, very close, and he needed to stop soon if he was going to fuck anything else. "Zach," he ground out. "I can't . . . I need . . . *so close.*"

Zach groaned low in his throat before tugging free of Anders's grip. He pulled off completely, strings of saliva and pre-come connecting them still. "Hold on, baby," he said, voice wrecked. He licked up the underside of Anders's cock. "Just need some lube, okay?"

Hands shaking, Anders brought Zach up for a sloppy kiss. "You are so fucking sexy," he managed. "Lube's over the headboard. Panel on the wall."

"Okay," Zach panted. "Okay." He crawled up to the headboard, reaching for the panel Anders had indicated. He shoved his shorts off and grabbed the lube, shifting up onto his knees, slicking up two fingers that he pushed into himself without ceremony. He rolled his hips back into the thrust of his fingers as he worked himself open.

Anders gave a heartfelt curse and kissed the sweat-slicked spot between Zach's shoulders. "You are so hot," he growled. "Fingers in your ass and getting ready just for me." He rubbed his fingers down between Zach's cheeks and felt Zach pumping his fingers in and out with quick, jerky motions. "Going to be even hotter when you're riding my dick, Zach. Going to feel so good."

Zach groaned. "I want your fingers too, Anders, want you to help me get ready to ride you."

"Yes. Whatever you want, darling." Anders grabbed the lube and slicked up several fingers, though he only pushed one in first. He dropped his head to Zach's shoulder. "You're so tight," he praised. "Can't wait to fuck you."

Zach's head fell forward, and he panted. "Give me another one, baby, stretch me wide open."

Anders groaned, adding the second finger. He had to wiggle them in around Zach's, but the *sound* Zach made when he did was what nearly undid Anders. "Make you feel so good," he promised. "So good. Tell me, Zach. Tell me when you're ready."

"Almost," Zach breathed out. "Almost there, Anders, god, I love the way that feels." Zach thrust his fingers in, moved them against Anders's. He widened his stance and pushed his hips back into their hands. Two, three more thrusts and he shuddered convulsively. "Now, Anders, wanna come on your cock, want you to fuck me through it, fuck me hard."

"Yes, *god*." Anders slicked himself quickly, carefully. Then he sat up against the headboard, gently tugging Zach onto his lap. "Come here, Zach. Ride me. Let me see you take me."

Zach put his hand around Anders's cock and guided it to his hole, slowly lowering himself, letting his weight push him down onto

Anders, let it push Anders inside. He let out a long, rough groan as Anders filled him completely.

"Zach," Anders gasped, fingers flexing on Zach's hips. He wanted to move. Wanted to pound into that perfect, tight heat. Wanted this to never end, to stay there, suspended on the edge of bliss forever. "Fuck yourself, love. Take whatever you need."

With another groan, Zach started to move, small circles and figure eights, before setting a steady, rolling rhythm, working himself on Anders's cock. He tried to kiss Anders, but the hard slam of their bodies made it impossible to do more than just share breath.

He wrapped his hand, still slick from opening Zach up, around Zach's cock. He wanted to praise Zach, to whisper dirty things to drive him crazy, but he could barely remember his own name, much less how to form sentences. All he could do was grunt each time Zach slammed down onto his lap. He tightened his fingers, wanting to see Zach's face as he came.

Zach cried out. The smooth, hard roll of his hips became a rough, uncoordinated jerk, and he grit his teeth in a grimace of pleasure. Anders's hand worked him faster, and Zach's body seized up as he finally came, spurting over Anders's chest and hand.

Anders stroked Zach through his orgasm, milking the last out of him until Zach slumped against his chest, still trying to ride him. "Got you," Anders groaned, and flipped them so Zach was on his back and Anders kneeling between his legs. Before he pushed in again, Anders leaned down and kissed Zach's mark once.

Zach's breath hitched. "Inside me, Anders. C'mon, wanna feel you come inside me." He lifted his hand to grab Anders's arm and tug. "Fuck me."

"Gladly." Anders lifted Zach's leg for better access, throwing it over his shoulder as he pushed in deep with one hard thrust. Zach moved with him, thoroughly relaxed from his orgasm. Anders took advantage of Zach's pliable state and pounded into him, quickly losing himself.

"Zach," he gasped. His own orgasm was growing, almost ready to break, and he chased it. When it crashed over him, dragging him under, Anders could only give a wordless shout, shaking as his body pulsed and he came, emptying himself into Zach at last. "So good, love. So good."

Anders collapsed on Zach, and Zach turned his head to share a slow, easy kiss and wrapped his arms around him. "*So* good," he agreed. "Go to sleep, and I'll fuck you when you wake up."

"Always said you were brilliant," Anders murmured, snuggling close. He wanted to sleep, very much so, but the spunk was drying on their skin, and it would be tremendously unsexy when they did finally wake. "We should clean up, though. Much as I adore you, don't want to be glued to you."

"I'd suggest a shared shower, but I think you fucked all the energy out of me." Zach laughed softly. "Maybe we could lean on each other while we wash."

Anders snorted into Zach's shoulder. "I have a better idea. Be right back."

Reluctant to leave both the bed and Zach's embrace, it took some doing before Anders was walking across the room on shaking legs. In the bathroom, he grabbed a couple of cloths and wet them. After a quick but thorough wipe down of his own body, he brought the remaining cloth back out to Zach.

"It's occurred to me," he said as he lovingly cleaned Zach's skin, dipping the cloth into his crease, "that now we're no longer on the ship, we have a shower big enough for the both of us."

"Hell, we have a *bed* big enough for the both of us." Zach was completely sprawled out but still wasn't even taking up half of the huge bed. "We're definitely taking advantage of the shower. Tomorrow."

Anders laughed and dropped the cloth before crawling back into bed, lying half on top of Zach regardless of all the extra room. "Sleep, darling. We can talk about your filthy plans for my body later."

"Later," Zach agreed on a yawn. He wrapped his arms around Anders, grip loosening as he fell asleep.

Anders was a few minutes in following, though. His mind, briefly quiet thanks to his orgasm, turned over a dozen worries about his meetings in the morning, and the last thought he had as sleep took him was of the box in the sitting room. Whatever was inside had to be important for Tanner to show up like he had.

Zach drifted awake, missing the warmth of Anders's body even before he was alert enough to realize he was alone. He looked around the empty room and noticed light under the door leading to the sitting area. Slowly rolling out of the bed, he stretched, yawned, and scratched his stomach, then dug in his bag for a clean pair of shorts.

Once he put them on, he crossed the room and opened the door to find Anders standing in a pair of silk pants and nothing else. The light from the lamp caressed his smooth, dark skin, and Zach wanted to touch. He was on his way to do just that when he saw that Anders was staring at something in his hands: the box Tanner had lain in wait to give him.

Anders glanced up and into Zach's eyes, that sad, haunted look in his. "My father's signet ring," he said, lifting the box. "It goes to each head of our family in turn. It's mine now, I suppose."

Zach put his hands on Anders's shoulders and squeezed before sliding his hands up and down Anders's arms, pressing his chest to Anders's bare back. "Yeah," Zach said, hooking his chin on Anders's shoulder, "it is."

Sighing, Anders opened the box to show Zach its contents. "He never let me touch it when I was a boy. I feel like I should ask permission even now."

The ring was large, not the sort of thing anyone would wear willingly on a daily basis; gold and covered in intricate scrollwork, the familiar eight-pointed star of the House of Anderson covered an oval sapphire more than half as big as Zach's thumb, and twelve diamonds for the twelve original Collective members studded the bezel around the edge of the stone. Though not the official symbol of rule, the king's signet ring was both an instantly recognizable item and strangely mundane for something almost mythical to the average person.

Zach reached around Anders to brush a fingertip over the ring. "It takes a while to realize he's really gone," he said, remembering times when he'd turned to ask his father a question or when he'd needed something and his father hadn't been there.

"Yeah." Anders's voice was thick, and he cleared his throat twice before speaking again. "He was going to pass the rule to me in a few years, you know. Help me through the transition. And now . . ." He pulled the ring out of the box, holding it up to the light. "I kept telling myself I'd deal with it later. Too many people are expecting me to be . . . something I'm not certain I'm ready to be. And I don't know if I can be that person without his help."

"Be yourself," Zach said simply. "That's all you can do. And, Anders, it's enough. *You* are enough."

"I hope so," Anders murmured. He set the box back down, ring on top of the closed lid, and turned in Zach's arms, resting his head on Zach's shoulder. "I don't know what I'd do if I hadn't met you. I can't imagine going through this alone." He sighed and kissed the underside of Zach's jaw. "Thank you."

"You're welcome," Zach said, "but no thanks are necessary." His arms tightened around Anders; it felt right, having Anders close. Zach mentally shrugged the thought off. "You aren't alone."

Anders hummed low in answer, winding his arms around Zach's waist. "I think I can sleep again," he said after a long while. "Take me back to bed?"

Zach kissed Anders's temple. "Of course." He eased out of the hug and took Anders's hand, leading him into the bedroom. When they reached the bed, Zach put his hands on Anders's hips and pushed the silk pants down until they fell at Anders's feet, then took his own shorts off. When they were both nude, Zach guided Anders down onto the bed and wrapped his arms around Anders. "Go to sleep, baby. We've got a long day ahead."

Anders gave a shuddering sigh, face hidden from Zach. "Thank you," he whispered. "Love you."

Zach pulled Anders closer. He didn't know how he felt, but he wasn't as uncomfortable with Anders's feelings as he thought he should be. He wasn't excited about the next day but found himself looking forward to spending more time with Anders. A lot more time. And that didn't bother him as much as it should, either.

CHAPTER SIXTEEN

I f the rest of the day continued the way the first hour or so had gone, Zach was going to die of boredom. He pulled a face at the back of the pompous ass who was finally leaving, and waited for the next pompous ass to come in. "Really?" he said to Anders. "Are they all going to be like that?"

"Most likely." Anders set aside the ornate box holding the second ceremonial dagger of the day. "I will never understand the obsession with gifting weapons to new matches," he murmured. "Seems like a recipe for disaster. What if we hated each other?"

"At least we both have one now," Zach said, teeth flashing in a quick grin. "Fair fight."

Anders huffed a laugh at that. "I could take you, with or without the knife," he said, eyes playful. "I've had years of self-defense training. There wouldn't be anything fair about the fight."

Zach's grin turned a bit fierce. "No, you're right. Nothing fair about a fight with someone who has combat training."

Unfolding himself from the high-backed chair that looked more than a little like a throne, Anders prowled across the short space between them to seat himself firmly in Zach's lap. "I do like you competitive," he said, rubbing their noses together. "We'll have to see which one of us is better some time."

"Not," Zach said, tilting his head enough to brush his mouth against Anders's, "with knives. Hand-to-hand, *maybe*." He wrapped his arms around Anders and squeezed. "I don't want to hurt you, civilian." He grinned. "Well. Not civilian, but not military either."

"Captain O'Connell, are you suggesting wrestling with your future monarch?" Anders teased. "Because if you are—" A sharp rap at the door signaled their next visitor, and Anders sighed, slumping against Zach briefly.

Zach squeezed him again, oddly reluctant to let go despite knowing that whoever was on the other side of the door would be thrilled to see Anders in his lap and would immediately tell everyone who would listen. Of course, that might not be the worst idea. He shook his head and forced a smile. "We've *been* wrestling, Your Highness," he purred into Anders's ear. "And I'm absolutely suggesting we do it again. But not, unfortunately, right at the moment."

"I'll hold you to that." Anders nipped at Zach's neck once before climbing out of his lap. Instead of going back to his own chair, though, he settled next to Zach on the sofa, their knees pressed together. Then he called for the visitor to enter, and the door swept open to admit Sofia Garza, leading in an ancient, petite woman with snow-white hair and swathed in yards of iridescent fabric.

"Your Highness," Counselor Garza said, hesitating when she saw Anders wasn't in his appointed seat. "May I present the head of my family, my great-aunt Valeria Garza?"

Anders rose slightly and gestured to a pair of nearby chairs. "I am honored by your presence, Madam Garza."

The dowager waved off Anders's gallantry. "I'm glad to see you inherited your father's manners as well as his looks," she said as she settled in her seat. "He was a good man, your father."

"The best I've ever known," Anders murmured.

"He always said you'd do his legacy proud. Even when you were a boy."

"I . . ." Anders swallowed audibly. "That means more to me than I could possibly express, Madam Garza. Thank you."

"You'll call me Valeria, just as your father did," she insisted. Her niece sighed and closed her eyes with a soft mutter that might have been a prayer. The old woman rolled her eyes. "If it pleases Your Highness, that is."

Anders snorted quietly. "Valeria, then," he said with a hint of a smile. "I'm pleased to meet you."

"And is this your match?" Valeria said, pinning Zach with a steely gaze.

"I am," Zach affirmed with a small smile. "I'm pleased to meet you as well."

Valeria looked him over. "Huh. Our prince certainly got himself quite the soldier, didn't he?" she cackled.

Zach inclined his head. "I like to think so, madam. And I've caught myself quite the prince."

"It remains to be seen, boy. You haven't bonded him yet, so he's not quite caught, now is he?"

"Close enough," Zach said, shifting uncomfortably. So far, everyone had asked, some more subtly than others, about bonding. He didn't get the fascination people had with the ritual, didn't get their willingness to dive so deeply into a relationship that way. "We have time, and His Highness is in mourning, after all."

Valeria harrumphed, while her niece darted sharp glances between Zach and Anders. "If I'd matched the leader of the entire Collective, I'd have dragged him to the temple myself," the old woman muttered, shaking her head. "Sofia," she said abruptly. "Give the happy couple my gift and then we'll be off. I'm sure Prince Philip has far more important duties to see to than entertain an ancient old thing as me."

"I can't think of anything more enjoyable than spending time with you, Valeria," Anders said, standing and offering her a hand as Sofia handed Zach a box containing a jeweled pair of cufflinks, done in the style of the Anderson crest.

"Aren't you a pretty liar," Valeria said, patting Anders's hand. "Now take my advice and sneak off and bond that captain of yours before a passing ship snaps him up."

"My mother would turn in her grave," Anders said in a serious tone, but smiled as he inclined his head. "But I appreciate the thought."

Zach watched them go in silence, then spoke as soon as the door closed behind them. "There it is again. And again."

"Did you expect something different?" Anders asked, voice cool as he refused to meet Zach's eye.

"I guess not." Zach rose and crossed the room to pour himself a drink. "I have to admit, though, I didn't really expect people to be so brazenly nosy. Do you want anything?" he added, lifting his glass in question.

Anders shook his head. "If you think this is nosy, wait until the media streams start speculating on our sex life. Everyone's raised to think matching is the be all and end all, an instant engagement between two perfectly matched halves. Naturally people want to know when we're making it official." He looked out the window for a few seconds. "This was a terrible idea."

"I just don't understand why they can't understand that you're in mourning and leave us—*you*—alone. And of course it was a terrible idea," Zach said irritably. "But I don't see any way we could have gotten out of it."

"Most people don't see bonding to their match as something to get out of," Anders sniped.

"I didn't mean bonding," Zach sniped back. "Although that's a terrible idea too. I meant this whole—" he waved a hand, gesturing around the room "—day of receiving people."

"It's a good thing you won't be sticking around, then, because *this* is my life now," Anders snarled, spreading his arms wide. "My life stopped being my own the very second my father died. It's expected for the king's heir to obey tradition, so obey tradition I will. And if part of that tradition means smiling and nodding while well-meaning old biddies tell me to elope with someone who wants none of that, then I will smile and nod. Doesn't mean you have to stay if it makes you so damn uncomfortable."

Zach jabbed a finger at himself, pointing at the place his mark rested. "*This* means I kind of do; this and the fact that I promised I would. And stop saying that like I'm going to sneak out the back door in the middle of the night, never to be seen again." He rolled his shoulders, feeling uncomfortable and petty, with a small corner of something that might have been hurt. Something that he didn't want to be his.

"Please, as if you haven't been planning to leave as soon as we're done." Anders laughed, short and sharp. "I'm not that blinded by my emotions, Zach."

"You're blinded by something," Zach muttered. "Stop putting words in my mouth and trying to put ideas in my head. *I* don't know what I'm going to do when we're done. It's not like I can just go back to my ship, not when the entire Collective knows that we're matched."

"You can't even hear the word 'bond' without flinching, and staying here means *we will have to bond*. And you have made your stance on that inescapably clear," Anders said. "Let's not go back to lying to each other now."

"I'm not lying!" Zach nearly shouted. "I told you I would be here and I will. I *am* here, and I'm not going anywhere no matter how much you bitch at me." The hurt had grown, making his stomach clench. "Just because I don't want to run away together doesn't mean I'm running somewhere else."

Anders scoffed and folded his arms across his chest. "I promised you your freedom when this is done," he said, chin tilting up defiantly. "I fully expect you to take it once I'm safe. I can't imagine anything making you more miserable than being dirt-bound and soul-bound for the rest of your life."

"Then you have very little imagination," Zach muttered. "I haven't *tried* to imagine anything else," he continued. "I never thought about it. I didn't have to—there weren't any other options for me. Now everything has changed, and I have to decide things I never considered before, so get off your fucking high horse while I adjust."

Anders huffed wordlessly. "You are such an asshole," he said. "I honestly don't know why I'm in love with you sometimes."

Zach shook his head. "Yeah, *I'm* the asshole."

A sharp knock at the door stopped Anders from saying whatever he might have returned fire with. Instead, Anders drew his shoulders back and backed even farther away from Zach, his face going carefully blank. "We don't have time for our personal bullshit right now."

"By all means," Zach said, resisting the urge to sneer, to strike back at Anders for pushing him so hard when he hadn't even had time to fucking *think*. Anders really loved him, and that was the hardest shove of all. Fuck. "Can the bullshit. Oh, wait. It's just a different kind of bullshit."

"Yes. It is." Anders's face stayed smooth and unreadable, but his eyes went so terribly sad for a few seconds before he turned away and reclaimed his original seat.

Zach sighed. He wasn't sure he could fuck things up any worse, but he *was* sure if he could, he would, intentionally or not. "Well, bring it on, then. No point in us ripping on each other when we can have some nosy old ass do it for us."

Anders snorted, but called for their next guests to enter. A pair of middle-aged men from Arkanna, they each wore full diplomatic dress, from the floor-length robes to the embroidered skullcaps over their shaved heads. Both men bowed deeply to Anders and barely acknowledged Zach except to hand him their gift—another knife.

At first, the conversation went pretty much the same as all the others before. Everyone thought King James had been a wonderful man, taken too soon, although *of course* Anders would do his legacy proud . . . and then:

"Your Highness," one of the men said. He must have a name, but to be honest Zach hadn't been paying attention. "Your Highness, there's a matter of grave concern we wish to discuss with you while we have the chance."

"Oh? And what might that be?"

The man slid a look at Zach, his thin upper lip curling in disgust. "The sanctity of the royal lineage, Your Highness."

Anders's shoulders went stiff. "Is that so?" To someone who didn't know him, Anders might have sounded politely interested, but Zach could hear the anger beneath it all. "I didn't realize it was such an issue."

"Oh yes," the other man said, nodding so hard his skullcap shifted. "We have a list of more . . . suitable, more political options for your bond."

"Gentlemen, I think there's been a misunderstanding," Anders said. "The captain here is my exact match. There won't be any need for me to bond with someone else, nor could a reasonable person expect I do such a thing."

"I'm sure he is," the first man said, though he looked like he'd tasted something nasty. "But surely Your Highness must recognize that it's unheard of for the head of the House of Anderson to bond so far beneath his station. My nephew is a distant cousin of yours, raised from birth to know the proper behavior for a man of the prince consort's station—"

"Sir, I'll thank you to stop there," Anders said. "Captain O'Connell is a decorated naval officer who has proven himself dedicated to not only his calling but to my own personal safety time and again. He is well aware of what it means to be by my side, especially in these confusing days of transition, and has repeatedly expressed his commitment to the grave responsibilities he's inherited through the accident of birth. And, I might add, *he is standing right here* while you propose I throw him over like some casual acquaintance. I would have thought your dedication to tradition would have extended to common courtesy, but it would seem not."

Zach raised an eyebrow at Anders's impassioned defense after the near-shouting match they'd had just minutes ago. *Politics*, he thought sardonically. "Thank you, Your Highness," he said aloud. "But, by all means, let them keep digging the hole they find themselves in."

The one with the single nephew turned purple and sputtered incoherently even as his companion jumped up, jabbing a vicious finger in Zach's general direction. "Is *this* what you imagine the right sort of bonded to be, Your Highness? He was probably raised wild on some backwater planet, with no notion of how proper manners work, and you're willing to risk the good name of your house and the support of one of the oldest houses in the Collective for a foolish notion of romance? Our allies and enemies alike will laugh us out of the stars, Prince Philip."

"That is more than enough, sir," Anders said, standing and drawing himself up to his full height, arms clasped behind his back in a white-knuckled grip. "Believe it or not, I have a very comprehensive understanding of our traditions and our history, and I am completely aware of the irregularity in the king's spouse being from a common station. However, I am *also* aware that it is a tradition among the House of Anderson to bond as our marks direct us. King Drion Ands the First bonded with Queen Gloria, the daughter of his sworn enemy, in the midst of all-out war—a fact that is often ignored by so many self-described historians these days. If my ancestor can be so successful with his own bond, then I sincerely doubt I will bring about the society's downfall by bonding with a brilliant man who is overflowing with loyalty, honor, and morals. Now, if you will excuse us, Captain O'Connell and I have plans for our midday meal that do not include either of you."

"You flatter me," Zach murmured as he watched the men make their way across the room and out the door.

"Asshole you might be when we're fighting," Anders growled, "but I'll not let them treat you like some subhuman piece of trash just because you're nothing like how a bunch of hidebound traditionalists expect my spouse to be."

Zach laughed in spite of himself. "Oh, I'm an asshole all the time," he said. "It's part of my charm." He stood and moved to stand behind Anders, absently rubbing a hand over the tense muscles of Anders's upper arm. "I would tell you not to let them bother you, but I can tell they don't."

Anders nodded once. "They're not the only ones who feel I'm unworthy because I'm walking my own path, and it's hardly unexpected. It only bothers me that they could honestly think I'd be able to cast you off. No matter what else happens between us, you deserve far better."

"Don't let that bother you, either. I know you aren't like that—the idea speaks to their moral failings, but it would never occur to you." Zach shrugged. "Forget about them, all of them. Now, I believe you mentioned lunch."

Relaxing by increments, Anders nodded and turned to face Zach, tangling their fingers together. "I thought we could eat in my suite," he said. "Just the two of us."

Zach squeezed Anders's fingers between his own. "Perfect."

CHAPTER SEVENTEEN

Afterward, Anders had only the vaguest memory of dressing on the morning of his father's funeral in his finest all-black clothes, slipping on his father's ring and walking out to the waiting ground shuttle, Zach's hand a solid and steadying brace at his back. The shuttle was a newer model than the one he'd ridden in for his mother's funeral so many years before; that one had been dark and enclosed, hiding him from view as they'd made the long way through the capital city's streets. This one was open, with a clear, laser-proof cover the only thing between Anders and all the people of Drion.

As the procession pulled away from the palace and out the gates, they were immediately surrounded by a sea of people pushing up against the barriers along the shuttle's path. Anders gripped Zach's hand in his own, glad for the warm touch to ground him. Tradition be damned, Anders was certain he'd lose his mind without Zach's touch, and he didn't much care what anyone might say about it. He looked over at Zach, unable to muster much more than a poor copy of his best blank face.

"We'll have to do this tomorrow too," he said. "I can see about shortening it, however."

Zach squeezed Anders's hand. "However long it needs to be, Anders. It's important."

Anders smiled as best as he could, then faced forward. The crowd stretched on and on ahead of them, countless people pressing in, a smothering weight of eyes and expectations. His vision swam briefly, and he had to close his eyes to catch his breath and calm his heart. "I can do this," he whispered to himself. "*We* can do this."

"Just breathe, baby," Zach said quietly. "And you're right. We can do this."

For a moment, Anders felt filled with love for Zach, but he said nothing. Just nodded and breathed carefully until he was calm again. He didn't speak for the rest of the ride, but somehow he knew Zach understood.

Finally, the enormous white bulk of the Temple of the Many loomed above them, its countless spires gleaming in the sunlight. Some people said there was one spire for each god, a unique path for each worshiper to reach their own special heaven. Others said that the spires channeled Divine messages to the priests below for delivery to the masses.

To Anders, they had always looked like a wild mess of architecture. He'd never been a particularly devout man, not when logic and reason had served him so well, and the idea that he was in a galaxy where a man as good and true as his own father might have been murdered over something as petty as power didn't much help him to believe in a higher power.

Resolutely ignoring the twist of nausea in his gut, Anders released Zach's hand and straightened the signet ring before climbing out of the shuttle. Wordless, he waited for Zach to join him, pathetically grateful when Zach put his hand on Anders's back again without a word. Then they climbed the temple stairs, Anders's father's casket leading the way.

A follower of Usmos, the God of a Dozen Stars, the king's funeral went the same as the queen's had. The priest moved around the Altar of the Great Circle, the casket his axis, stopping at each of the holy points. The prayers washed over and around Anders, a jumble of platitudes and meaningless words that in some corner of his mind Anders was sure were beautiful and inspiring.

Once the rites were complete, Anders stood and walked across the temple to the altar. His father had been well-preserved, so well in fact that Anders had a brief, hysterical moment where he wondered if this all hadn't been a colossal mistake and his father would wake any moment, ready to set things right. But his father's hand was as cold as the marble floor Anders had been kneeling on, his pulse just as still.

He had no words, not for his father and certainly not for the people watching. So he nodded once, swallowing thickly around the stone in his throat, and moved to the side to make room for the bearers who would take the casket away.

Zach might have murmured a soft question to check on him; Anders wasn't sure. All he knew as they left the temple to make their way to the royal mausoleum was that he absolutely was not okay. Just as he knew that he could never let anyone see.

By the end of the day, it was all Anders could do to keep his spine straight and his eyes up. He'd thought, in the rare moments he'd let himself imagine it, that the act of sealing his father behind all of that marble would be the moment that broke him. In reality, by the time it came, he was utterly numb from everything else that had happened.

Zach hadn't left his side for more than a moment all day, and he didn't leave then either, gently nudging Anders where he needed to be, just as he had all day, breathing reminders in his ear that he was strong enough to do this. In a distant part of his mind, Anders wondered if this was what grief was supposed to feel like. A numb, empty sensation that never seemed to do anything.

But then they got back to the suite, and Anders slowly became aware of his hands trembling more and more. Fortunately, Zach was there to catch him when his knees gave out, and Anders clung to him, gasping as the last of his strength evaporated.

Zach crooned soft encouragements to stand up, to just make it a few feet to the bedroom. It still took Anders longer than he cared to admit to get his feet under him without falling, to make it across the room. He sat on the bed, slumping and unresisting as Zach carefully undressed the both of them, setting the signet ring back in its box before walking Anders into the bathroom and under a warm shower.

"Come on, baby," Zach said, his hands gentle as he pulled Anders close. "It's okay. I've got you." He held Anders, rubbing his hands up and down Anders's back as Anders finally broke, tears rolling silently down his cheeks to mix with the water flowing over them. He felt so weak and shaky, nauseous. After a while Anders stood straight, easing away from Zach.

"I think I need to lie down," he said.

Zach nodded. "Sure, baby, let's get you dried off first." He turned the water off and used his hands to sluice some of the moisture away before opening the shower door and reaching for a towel.

Anders stood still and silent as Zach rubbed the towel over his body and then his hair before drying his own body. Docile with his hand in Zach's, Anders let himself be led back to the bedroom and eased down onto the bed. Zach rolled onto the mattress next to him and wrapped him up in strong, muscled arms. Anders felt Zach's chin come to rest on the top of his head, and he closed his eyes, exhausted yet safe in Zach's arms.

CHAPTER
EIGHTEEN

Zach watched Anders kneel at the altar before the Priest of the Many as he placed the formal crown on Anders's head. Anders had been right; the coronation was much the same as the funeral had been. The same people, the same procession route, the same priest and altar. The atmosphere was different, however. Many of the people there were joyous, excited to have a new king and an excuse for celebration. Some were still somber, yet carried an air of pleased anticipation. There was a marked difference in Tanner's countenance, however. His smile was almost predatory, definitely unfriendly, and it made Zach even more determined to protect Anders from the man and to catch and punish everyone behind the attacks.

Finally Anders stood and turned to face the audience, pausing briefly before taking measured steps forward. He walked down the aisle in the temple with more of the same careful steps, the mantle of royalty fanning out behind him much like a bride's train. It was a fitting comparison, Zach thought, because in a way Anders was now married to his kingdom, bound to act in his people's best interests and lead them as they lived their daily lives, protect them from threats they frequently knew nothing about. Zach's eyes drifted to Tanner again and found him staring back, malevolence in his eyes. It sent a shiver of warning down Zach's spine.

Attention caught by a cheer from the crowd, Zach turned to see Anders wave solemnly from the door of the temple. The ceremony was over. As his match, Zach was the first to rise and start down the aisle toward Anders, followed by the nobility in order of importance. It meant Tanner was directly behind him, and he could feel Tanner glaring daggers at his back. Zach reached Anders and took his hand, bringing more cheers from the crowd even as he gave a short bow with his head. They stood there on display for a minute or two, horribly exposed, before Zach was able to lead Anders away toward the open-top shuttle they'd arrived in. The same cheers and waves as the ride to the temple followed them on their way back to the palace, but Anders remained solemn. Threading their fingers together, Zach felt the hard press of the signet ring. Anders's skin was chilled. Zach put his other hand over their clasped hands, rubbing briefly.

They arrived at the palace to more fanfare. Anders stumbled slightly as they left the shuttle, but Zach caught him and pulled him close in a hug that disguised the misstep and brought another cheer from those in the palace courtyard. "We're almost inside, and then you can sleep for a bit before the party tonight." Zach pulled a face. "I wish we could skip it."

Anders laughed weakly. "That makes two of us. I feel as though I haven't slept in days. There's no way I'm eating two dozen courses tonight."

"Two dozen? Good grief, where do you come up with all this food?" Zach guided Anders inside the palace. The counselors followed them in, fanning out around them. Zach raised an eyebrow at them. "Excuse us, please. King Philip needs rest after all his recent stress. I'm sure you understand."

Pressing a hand to Zach's chest, Anders stepped forward, his head held high and the crown shining in the light. "Thank you," he said to the small crowd around him. "Thank you, all of you, for your support and understanding over the past few days and in the days to come. I can only hope to do justice to the legacy of the great man who came before me. His legacy, of course, would be incomplete without you. Something I will strive never to forget, for I am blessed to have you at my side."

The counselors smiled and nodded, some more genuinely than others. Their murmurs of approval turned to gossip, however, when Anders swayed on his feet, like he might collapse then and there.

Zach put his arm around Anders again; he was pale and shaking slightly. Zach wouldn't have known about the shaking if he hadn't been pressed against Anders's side, which Anders would consider a small mercy. Zach kissed Anders's temple. "As I said." He looked around at each of them individually. "Excuse us."

Without waiting for a response or objection, Zach turned and led the two of them to their private quarters. When the doors were finally shut behind them, Zach hugged Anders close. "Are you okay, baby?"

Anders shook his head. "I don't know what's wrong with me," he said quietly. "This is worse than yesterday."

"You probably just need to rest. You've been through a lot in the last few weeks." Zach helped Anders remove the mantle and hang it carefully in the closet, then locked the crown up in the safe in the bedroom once Anders put in the combination to open it for him.

"Of course," Anders mumbled, collapsing on the bed in an inelegant sprawl. "Seems the king is human after all, hmm?"

All too human, and that was part of the problem. He could so easily be taken out. Zach shook his head slightly. *Not on my watch.*

"C'mon, let me help you get undressed before you fall asleep, okay?" Zach propped Anders up into a sitting position. He smiled. "You're getting your clothes wrinkled."

"Always trying to get me naked," Anders joked weakly. "All you had to do was ask."

There was a knock at the main door, followed by the sound of it opening soon after. "Your High . . . Your Majesty?" Jackson called. "Captain O'Connell?"

Zach helped Anders stand before calling out, "In here, Jackson, we're coming." Lowering his voice, Zach leaned over to murmur, "Good thing he didn't come in a few minutes later, right?"

Anders laughed quietly. "Sadly, it would not be the first, or worst, compromising position he and Bern have caught me in."

"Oh? You'll have to tell me about it sometime," Zach said. They walked out into the sitting area to find Bern and Counselor Lee with Jackson. Zach raised an eyebrow. This looked a little more serious than Jackson checking up on Anders.

By the sudden stiffness to Anders's posture, he thought the same. "Gentlemen. What has happened?"

Jackson and Bern looked somber, more so than usual, and Zach noticed anger banked in Bern's eyes. "Counselor Lee has something to report, Your Majesty."

"Your Majesty," Lee intoned. "I have news."

"So Bern said." Zach turned to Lee impatiently. "What is your news?"

Lee's face flushed. "Your Majesty," he repeated. "I have news."

"Very soon," Anders said, voice like ice, "I am going to have to talk to each member of my cabinet about the proper way one treats the match of their king. In the meantime, Counselor Lee, I do believe Captain O'Connell, my *match*, asked you a question. And please be prompt with your answer, as I have more important matters to attend to than your complete lack of manners."

Lips pressed so close they were nearly white, Lee nodded shortly, and it still took several moments before he spoke. "The sniper has confessed, sire. He did not act alone; he was hired by another to kill your match."

Zach absorbed the shock of the news quickly. It was good that the target hadn't been Anders, but that meant he really did have to watch his own back now too.

"And? Who hired him?" Anders demanded.

Lee drew himself up to his full height. "Counselor Reese. Apparently, the sniper was on his personal staff back on Gloria, and Reese brought him here a week before your father died. He says the counselor was offended in your choice of match and wished to overthrow a weak rule that had no respect for our ways."

Anders scoffed. "Nonsense. Captain O'Connell is an excellent match."

"The captain is as common as they come. He'd only pollute the royal bloodline by being there." Lee nodded his head in Zach's direction. "Or so the gossips say."

"It's a good thing I don't listen to gossip, then," Anders said, voice chilled. "And it's highly unlikely I'll be getting him pregnant."

Zach snorted out a laugh, turning it into a cough. "We do always use protection," he said as solemnly as he could.

Though Anders laughed, Lee didn't seem to find it funny in the slightest. "Not to mention your refusal to bond does have our more traditional citizens up in arms."

"I wasn't aware the court had latched on to that bit of information already. And whether I bond or not is neither your nor anyone else's business," Anders said, all traces of humor gone. "Especially not when my father is barely in the ground. I have hundreds of royal duties to see to, more than a dozen planets and colonies to oversee, and years' worth of political machinations to catch up on in a matter of days. I assure you, Counselor Lee, my love life is the very least anyone should be worrying about."

Zach briefly put his hand at the small of Anders's back in silent support.

"Be that as it may," Lee said, a hint of a smile lifting his mouth, "Counselor Reese is far from the only person who sees this," he gestured vaguely between Zach and Anders, "as an unforgivable sign of weakness. Though it does seem he is the first to take it as a call to violence."

"You seem rather happy for a man discussing an assassination plot." Anders's voice went straight from chilly to utterly frozen.

"My apologies, Your Majesty." Lee bowed. "I'll be the first to admit that there is no love lost between me and Counselor Reese."

"That seems to be the case with you and several people," Anders mused.

Lee went deathly still but for the throbbing vein on his right temple, but only bowed again. "Perhaps so, Majesty. But the fact remains that Counselor Reese has been accused of an attempt on the life of your match. And as Your Majesty has mentioned, Captain O'Connell is to be treated as your equal, though you have not yet bonded."

Zach twitched at the repeated mention of bonding. "What proof have you that the sniper is not lying?"

Lee waited a long beat before answering, and even then he addressed Anders directly. "I'm not certain Your Majesty can afford to entertain the thought. The longer you delay, the greater chances are that the counselor will run. Or worse, you leave yourself and the captain open to further attack."

"I am more than capable of determining what I can and cannot afford," Anders said with an arched brow. A knock sounded at the door. "Now what?"

"Your forgiveness, Majesty," Lee said, a small smile tickling at the corners of his mouth. "Once I heard the accusations, I sent palace guards to collect Counselor Reese from his home in Dryax, so you might pass your judgment in person."

"How very . . . proactive of you," Zach said dryly. "It seems to me you should be asking Reese's forgiveness instead."

Anders turned his head to murmur in Zach's ear, hand over his mouth for privacy. "I still must entertain the idea that Reese is guilty. There have been too many witnesses to the accusations—the guards, most likely Lee's staff, anyone they might like to drink with, they all probably know by now. This could be seen as a direct challenge from Gloria to my new rule."

To the rest of the room, Anders nodded. "Bring in Counselor Reese."

Zach stood straight next to Anders, once again offering silent support as Reese was brought into the room between two guards. He looked more resigned than upset or afraid.

"Counselor Reese." Anders's voice was firm, though Zach could feel a slight tremble running through him where they touched. "You have been accused of attempting to assassinate Captain O'Connell. In addition, there has been an implication that you are involved in a coup plot. Have you any evidence of your innocence?"

Reese frowned and spread his hands as far as he could with his elbows gripped by the guards. "I'm sure Your Majesty is aware," he said, "of how difficult it is to prove a negative."

"We have the sworn testimony of one of your conspirators," Lee put in.

"*Thank* you, Counselor Lee." Anders's mouth was a thin, straight line. "Now, Counselor Reese, loathe as I am to give any weight to the words of a hired killer, you have to admit that this is suspicious, especially given the still-unresolved attack against the *Pallas* targeting the very section of the ship I was in, a location the raiders could never have known without help from someone with clearance just like yours."

"I would never—" Reese spluttered. "I never even knew what ship Your Majesty was traveling on!"

"Your life is full of unprovable negatives, isn't it, Counselor Reese?" Anders's mouth twisted irritably. "Guards, please escort Counselor Reese to the holding cells in the security wing, and see that he is comfortable."

"Your Majesty!" Reese eyes were wide and panicked now. "Surely there isn't enough evidence to prove my guilt! Especially being as I'm innocent!"

"I will have these claims investigated," Anders said, still trembling. Zach pressed his hand to the small of Anders's back to steady him. "But, in the meantime, I must insist that you stay under the custody of the Royal Guard."

"You have to let me defend myself!" Reese struggled free of the guards, only to be grabbed once more. Jackson and Bern formed a solid wall of muscle between Reese and Anders.

Zach wanted this over now; he wasn't sure how much longer Anders could stand. Leaning in, he murmured in Anders's ear. "You did promise, Anders."

"And defend yourself you will," Anders allowed. "But this is clearly nothing that can be resolved here and now. And on the chance you don't actually have innocence to prove, I can't put my life, or Captain O'Connell's life, in any unnecessary danger. I'm sure you understand."

At Anders's nod, the guards took Reese's elbows again. Reese tugged free, already babbling. "You're making a mistake," he insisted. "I'm a loyal ally. By locking me up, you're only putting yourself in *more* danger. Your Majesty, your life is on the line!"

"Watch your words," Bern growled. "They sound like threats."

Anders waved a hand. "Take him away. This will still be an issue in the morning."

The guards pulled Reese away, his desperate attempts to prove his innocence not slowing even as Anders turned to Zach, rubbing his temples. No sooner had the door closed behind Reese and his escort, when Anders swayed dangerously, falling into Zach's side without warning. "I think," Anders said, his words slurring, "we should send for the physician."

"Bern!" Zach caught Anders close. "Jackson! He's right. He can barely stand." Zach wrapped his arm around Anders's waist and nearly carried him back to the bedroom. Helping him sit on the edge of the bed, Zach began to undress him. He opened Anders's jacket and tried to remove it, but the sleeve caught on the large stone in Anders's signet ring. Irritably, Zach tugged the ring off and put it on his own finger until he could get it safely back into its box.

"How long has this been going on?" Jackson demanded. They could hear Lee running out of the sitting room and into the hall, shouting for help and no doubt raising panic through the entire palace.

"Since yesterday," Anders said, pushing at Zach's hands. "Stop trying to get me naked, darling. We have guests."

"Why is this the first we're hearing of any problems?" Bern hovered close as though he wanted to snatch Anders out of Zach's arms.

Zach grabbed Anders's hands and leaned forward to touch Anders's forehead with his. "Stop, baby. I'm trying to save your fancy uniform. You'll be more comfortable without it." He winked. Without turning to Bern, Zach added, "We thought it was just stress. It hasn't been an easy few weeks for him."

"Not a delicate flower," Anders mumbled. "Only tired... need..." Between one breath and the next, Anders went limp and unconscious.

Moving quickly, Zach let Anders's body sag into his as he pulled off the jacket. Bern helped him lift Anders up onto the bed. Once he was lying down, Zach let Bern and Jackson check Anders for fever (he was a little warm, but not inordinately so) while he hung the jacket safely in the closet.

The palace physician ran in then, and convinced Jackson and Bern to step back so he could check Anders. Zach watched all of them carefully. He still wasn't sure if it was just stress, or if it was one of those fancy poisons Reese had mentioned. But if it were...

"Test his blood for toxins," Zach said, voice loud in the relative quiet of the room.

"I beg your pardon," the physician said, turning his head to pin Zach with a look.

"I said, test his blood. He may have been poisoned."

"What?" Jackson and Bern bellowed in unison as they straightened, fixing Zach with matching glares.

Zach's eyes flicked to Jackson and then Bern before focusing on the physician again. "It was suggested to Anders that his father may have been poisoned. With the attempt on the ship and then the one on my life, I don't think we can take the risk. Test his blood."

The physician continued checking Anders over. "Well, some of the symptoms King Philip is exhibiting are similar to his father's last days. It could be the same genetic disease."

"That wouldn't explain why Anders's symptoms came on so suddenly after we arrived here." Zach folded his arms. "It won't hurt to test him for poison. Do it. And test for the more exotic ones too."

"Can we speak to you outside?" Jackson said abruptly, his face a study in fury.

Zach raised an eyebrow at Jackson. "You can speak to me here, or you can wait until the physician is gone. I'm not leaving Anders alone."

Bern snorted. "If you actually gave a *shit* about the king's safety, you would have told us there was a threat to his life."

"What, you didn't notice the attack on my ship?" Zach asked.

"Poison, you ass," Jackson said as the physician drew a sample of Anders's blood. "You are not in charge of the king's security, *we are*. And we can't do our jobs with some commitment-phobic asshole standing in our way at every turn."

Zach merely stared at them both. "There was no threat of poison against Anders," he said coolly. "There was only discussion of the possibility that his father had been poisoned. All things being equal, I don't think it's unreasonable to test for poison despite there being no specific threat of poison among the other threats against Anders."

"That was not for you to decide," Jackson said, his hands balling into fists. "No matter what the king has said, without a bond between you two, you have no authority here. He gives you too much leeway, and it will destroy him." He turned to the physician. "Run your tests. Submit your report to me and no one else. And tell *no one* what you've seen tonight. Is that understood?"

The physician nodded. "I can only recommend rest for now. I may have more answers after I run those tests."

Zach smiled at the physician. "I'll make sure he rests," he said easily. "Let Jackson know what you find out, as soon as possible, yeah?"

Jackson held off until the physician left, breathing deeply while Bern kept shooting him worried looks. Once it was the three of them and Anders, he rounded on Zach again.

"Just stop it," he growled. "Stop overreaching, and stop acting like he's yours to care for. You've turned that—and him—down rather firmly, and you're just going to hurt Anders all the more when you tire of him and go back to your ship."

"Jax—" Bern said, but Jackson shrugged off his hand.

Zach moved next to the bed and reached for Anders's arm. He lifted it so the mark there was starkly visible. "This makes him mine to care for, for however long I'm here, which is something between me and Anders, not you."

"Don't pretend you care about that," Jackson growled. "If you did, you wouldn't be making him look a fool in front of the entire galaxy by refusing to bond with him."

"They're laughing at him," Bern added. "For being unable to win over his match, for ignoring a cornerstone of our way of life. They say he's weak and unworthy of the rule. And it's your fault."

"He's our charge," Jackson went on, taking half a menacing step forward. "Our friend. And since we clearly care more about his happiness and heart than you do, you need to *learn your place*."

"My *place*," Zach said, fighting for calm, "is by his side. And, from what I understand, the only people who know I won't bond with him are in this room. I certainly haven't told anyone, and all Anders has said is that we're waiting because there are a few other important things going on. So if anyone is laughing, whose fault is that really?"

"Oh, fuck you," Jackson snarled, but this time subsided when Bern touched his arm. "We're not the one who flat out refused him in front of two witnesses, who looks physically ill every time someone mentions the word 'bonding.'" He pointed angrily to Anders, who was shifting on the bed, frowning in his sleep. "Royalty doesn't wait to bond if and when they match. They can't, not when their power and social standing with the noble families rely on how strong they appear, how dedicated to our ways.

"But he's let you put him off, even set up plans to tell everyone this was a lie to lure his enemies out in the open. He's doggedly loved you, despite being rejected time and again, so if you want to assign blame, *Captain O'Connell*, I would suggest you take a long, hard look in the mirror first."

"He needs rest right now," Zach said, intense but quiet. "Get out."

This time it was Bern who stepped forward. "If you make one more call involving my king's safety and security without consulting us first, I will have you removed from his side and placed next door to

Counselor Reese. You seem to think you're untouchable, but we have the palace guard on our side. You'd do well to remember that."

As one, they turned away and stormed out of the bedroom, leaving the door ajar as they crossed the sitting room and left.

"I'll talk to them later," Anders said, his voice weak.

"Hey," Zach rushed to sit on the side of the bed next to Anders and carefully pushed the hair out of his face with one hand. "Don't worry about them. How do you feel?"

"Embarrassed." Anders gave a rueful smile. "I hope not too many people saw me lose my feet like that."

"Just the three of us." Zach smiled, but it quickly faded. "The physician came. He said rest. But I told him to test you for poison, which was when your boys completely lost their shit."

Anders flinched. "They would," he admitted. "Part of our bargain for the freedom I have is that I'm to tell them if there's even a hint of danger. They trust me to be alone with a devastatingly handsome ship's captain," he gave a half smile, "and I trust them to make the right calls on what is or isn't a credible threat."

"There wasn't a credible threat," Zach argued. He couldn't help feeling a bit smug at being called devastatingly handsome. He gave Anders his best smile. "It was just me being cautious after what Reese said about your father. Not you. Your *father*. Which I explained, but it didn't seem to get through to them."

"Unless it *is* poison, and my security detail has just been caught wrong-footed because we didn't take five minutes to tell them." Anders grabbed Zach's hand and kissed his fingers. "They're right to be frightened and angry."

"Well, it didn't occur to me that there might be a problem until you passed out, at which point I told the doctor to test you." Zach pressed a quick kiss to Anders's lips. "They're absolutely livid, and they blame me, and it's really not my fault. At least not entirely, and that's assuming there's even fault to be had in the first place."

"Don't be childish, darling," Anders said, eyes drooping. "I seem to remember you threatening to throw me in the brig for getting in the way of you doing your job on Ciebos."

Zach raised an eyebrow and sat up straight. "That was a completely different situation," he said. "If there had been an accident hooking up to the transit station, there potentially would have been thousands dead and millions in damages. Plus, I had no idea who you were, and whose fault was that?"

"If I've been poisoned," Anders said, pushing up onto his elbows, then struggling to sit up. Zach helped him, but Anders still had to pause for a moment to get his breath back, leaning against the headboard. "If I've been poisoned," he said again, "and we took away Jackson and Bern's chance to stop it, I could die, Zach. And while my life has never truly been my own, now it belongs to billions of people. People who will be living in an utterly destabilized kingdom when they lose their second king in a month. There will be war, Zach. People will die."

"Then you should have told them," Zach said flatly. "But it's moot at this point. The physician will test your blood, and I told him to test for the more exotic poisons after what Reese said, and we'll have an answer one way or the other. You might just be exhausted and stressed."

Anders sighed, but shifted closer so he could rest his head on Zach's shoulder. "Either way," he said, "I'm still going to tear into them for the rest of what they said. I love them like brothers, but that was not their place. What you and I have is . . . ours. I'll deal with the fallout later if there is any."

Zach couldn't stop himself from rubbing Anders's back. "I told them it was between us," he murmured. He tightened his arms around Anders briefly, then pulled back enough to look him in the face. "But that's not important right now. What *is* important is that you rest like the physician directed."

"Yes, darling." Anders didn't move, though. "Do you suppose we can get away with postponing the party? I'm sure the entire palace knows what a frail, ill creature I am now; the last thing I want is to be stared at like some bug under glass."

"It's your party," Zach said. "You can cancel it if you want to." He kissed Anders's forehead. "Rest, please. I'll take a nap with you." He started to open the jacket of his dress uniform. He hated to hear Anders sound so unhappy. "Lie down, okay?"

Anders hummed softly and stretched back out on the bed. "If I do have whatever killed Father," he said, dark and sleepy eyes watching

Zach hang up his jacket, "I'm glad I got to find you first. Never thought I'd match, much less fall in love."

Zach took off his uniform pants and hung them up as well. "Stop talking like that," he said irritably. "You aren't going to die." In his shorts, he climbed into the bed and took Anders into his arms. "I won't let you."

"My hero," Anders said on a laugh, curling close.

"Oh, shut up," Zach muttered. He pressed another kiss to Anders's forehead. "Go to sleep."

"Yes, darling," Anders sighed, already drooping in Zach's arms. "Love you, even if you leave."

Zach waited until he was sure Anders was out cold, then he brushed the hair off his *match's* forehead and sighed. Anders had turned his world around in every possible way, and he was struggling to accept it, to adjust to what it meant.

After several long moments, Zach shook his head and sighed again. "I'm not going anywhere," he said quietly. "I love you too."

CHAPTER NINETEEN

Anders woke slowly to the rustling of someone moving around his bedroom. He blinked his eyes open to see a servant switching out an untouched dinner tray for a second tray loaded with a hot breakfast for two. The girl jumped when she saw he was awake, nearly dropping the old tray in the process.

"Your Majesty!" She fumbled some cross between a curtsy and a bow, blushing furiously. "Good morning, Your Majesty!"

"Good morning," Anders croaked. "Did I sleep the whole night through?"

She nodded so violently, it was surprising she didn't lose the little cap perched on her head. "You both did, Your Majesty. I know everyone will be so glad to hear you're awake. Shall I get the guard, Majesty? Mr. Grant hasn't budged from your sitting room all night."

Zach stirred next to Anders with a quiet groan. "Too much noise," he mumbled.

Anders rubbed Zach's arm before turning back to the girl. "You may let the necessary people know we're awake," he said, head pounding, "but we're not to be disturbed before the noon hour. Is that clear?"

"Yes, Your Majesty," she said, trembling so hard the dishes on her tray rattled. "As you wish, Your Majesty."

Anders waved her off, waiting until the door was closed until he turned back to Zach. "Are you all right, darling?" He cupped the side of Zach's face. "You're normally up at the first noise."

"Jus' tired," Zach said, voice a little more clear. "And dizzy, god. I don't remember drinking that much last night." He put his hand on his forehead.

Whatever Anders was about to say vanished when he saw the signet ring on Zach's finger. He laughed, burying his face against Zach's chest. "If you want the family crest that badly, darling," he said through the giggles, "we could just get married and you can have your own."

Zach lifted his head and stared at Anders blankly. "What?"

Anders laughed again, lifting Zach's hand so he could see the Anderson signet ring plain as day. "It's a good thing the guys didn't see this," he said, pulling the ring free and kissing the back of Zach's hand. "Jackson might have actually hit you then."

"Oh shit." Zach let his head fall to the pillow. "I was going to put it away after I got you settled."

"It's fine. I know you only meant well," Anders said, placing the ring back on his own hand. "Just don't let anyone else see. Remember what Counselor Lee said last night? A noble family's line is some pretty serious business. You don't want to be accused of trying to usurp the crown from your sickly, deluded lover."

Zach laughed. "That sounds like the kind of plot Jackson or Bern would accuse me of."

"They've both had diplomatic training," Anders said. "That way they know what people are saying about me." He wound his arm around Zach, squeezing until his muscles protested the use. "God, I feel like I've been run over by a shuttle."

"Yeah, me too," Zach agreed. "Can we go back to sleep? Or maybe I should go to another room, I think you're contagious," he said with a wink.

Something cold formed in Anders's stomach. "You feel sick too?"

Zach shrugged one shoulder. "More dizzy than sick, really. What about you—how are you feeling?"

"Sore all over. Dizzy. Like I should *definitely* avoid that breakfast." Anders swallowed around the queasy knot just talking about food gave him. "Headache." It was also painfully bright in the room, and Anders wasn't sure he'd be able to stand at any point in the near future, but there was no point in causing panic.

"Let's stay in bed, then," Zach said, wrapping himself around Anders. "I could eat, but I'm not feeling hungry enough to make the effort to go get the food."

Something wasn't right, Anders was certain of it. But he was so warm, so comfortable in Zach's arms. Surely it wouldn't hurt to take a few more hours to themselves. But, just then, the outside door banged open, bringing with it a storm of angry voices.

"Where is he?" Bern's voice boomed in the next room. "O'Connell, you get your skinny ass out here and answer to me this *second*."

"Oh, fuck off," Zach said quietly. He cleared his throat and called out, "My ass isn't skinny."

"Don't antagonize him," Anders whispered. He could hear the servant girl and Grant both arguing with Bern to keep him out in the sitting room, but it would be a futile fight. "Come in, Bern."

Bern came in, his face red with fury. "*You*," he pointed at Zach. "Get out of bed."

"No." Anders pushed himself up by holding Zach down. "That is more than enough, Bern. You and Jackson think you're being helpful, but my relationship with Zach is *not your business*. Nor is it your place to order him around, regardless of our lack of a bond. *Is that clear*?"

"My king," Bern said through gritted teeth. "The physician says you've been poisoned, and he can't identify the cause. You're *dying*, and this bastard could have helped us stop it."

"And would you have had any idea if I hadn't told the physician to run blood tests?" Zach asked coolly.

"I might have known to be watching for it specifically if you'd bothered to let me do my job, you arrogant bastard." Bern flexed his fingers, balling them into a tight fist.

"Stop it, both of you." Anders stood, keeping his balance only by holding on to the bedpost. Bern hurried to bring him a robe without asking, at least preserving *some* of his dignity. "It's already happened, and the only innocent person here is probably Grant. So how about we stop arguing over who's to blame and move on to the facts?"

He took the sullen silence as assent. "Good. Now, what do you mean you don't know what it is? How do we know it's poison in the first place?"

With one last dark look at Zach, Bern gave Anders his full attention. "All of the tests came back negative, but there were irregularities. Levels of radiation in your blood that shouldn't be possible. In addition, your blood is entirely off from your normal healthy baseline. What tests they *did* for your father had the same readings, leading us to believe that you've been exposed to the same toxin."

Anders breathed deeply, trying to stave off the panic. This was different than what happened to his father. They had some warning, they could fix this. "You said I was dying."

Bern's face crumpled. "Your body is shutting down, Anders. If we can't stop this, you'll be dead within the week."

"I see." Anders took a stumbling step forward. "I—I need to sit."

"Come back and lie down, Anders," Zach said. "You need rest. Have Bern get Reese out of his cell. He's the one who first mentioned poison, maybe he knows more."

Anders shook his head as he made his way across the room. He needed to be alone, needed to think. "I think," he said, voice shaking, "I'm going to take a shower."

Bern caught him by the elbow and steered him back around. "Not when I can't trust that you won't fall and crack your royal head open," he said, walking Anders back to the bed. "You're going to want it when you're better, my lord."

Zach held out his hand. "Come on, Anders. Lie down with me. I need Bern to go away so I can go back to sleep."

"Fuck off," Bern said. "You don't deserve to stay here. First you think you're in charge of his security, now you're the prince consort? Why don't you just get on your ship and—"

"Bern. Please." Hysteria rose inside Anders, choking him, the constant bickering only making it worse.

Bern subsided. "I'm sorry," he murmured, helping Anders sit back on the edge of the bed.

"I need some time," Anders managed, hands knotting in the covers. "Have Counselor Reese brought to me in an hour, along with all of that testing data." Something occurred to him then, and Anders started trembling. "Have someone come test Zach too. He's been sick this morning."

"I'm not sick," Zach said, "just a little dizzy. Maybe hungover."

"You didn't drink last night, Zach," Anders said, struggling to keep his breathing under control, to hold the panic at bay. "Thank you, Bern. If you could close the door on your way out?"

Mouth a tight line and eyes full of worry, Bern nodded and left without another word. Anders, for his part, stayed on the edge of the bed, white-knuckled and barely able to breathe. He wasn't sure what the wrong move would be, but he *was* sure it would send him to pieces when he made it.

Zach's hand was suddenly on Anders's back, slowly rubbing over his spine. "Breathe, Anders, nice and easy. In. Out. Why are you panicking?"

"You, Zach." Anders could barely get the words out. "What if they got you while trying to get me? You could be dying and it would be my fault. Oh god," he gasped, bending over. "You could be *dying*, Zach."

"Then we'll go out together. Anders, come on. According to Bern, you *are* dying. I should be the one panicking here." There was a tug at Anders's robe. "You told him to come back in an hour. We should rest while we can."

Anders crawled across the bed. "Why are you so calm?" he asked, shaking. "I don't understand."

Zach wrapped Anders tightly in his arms. "I'm not calm," he whispered. "You're dying."

Anders laughed, not caring that it sounded at least half as hysterical as he felt. "Yeah," he said, unabashedly clinging to Zach. "I know how that feels."

By the time their hour was up, Anders had calmed considerably, though Zach could still see the anxiety around his eyes. He hugged Anders and kissed his cheek. "We're okay," he said, crossing to the closet where his uniforms were hanging. He pulled one out and started to dress.

"Yeah," Anders said as he tugged off the signet ring and put it away in his safe. "Everything's fine."

"Well, I wouldn't go *that* far." Zach waited while Anders dressed and then went to him, rubbing his back again. "But, as of now, we're okay. Reese will have an answer, right? He said he'd been investigating, surely he knows of an antidote."

Anders breathed deeply and nodded. "He was a chemist, back on Gloria. We met when I was working on my first graduate degree. I was a new fellow, and he was a first-year professor. We bonded over the special torture that is staff parties."

"*First* degree?" Zach asked, happy to have the diversion. "How many do you have?"

"Two. Law and History." Anders smiled. "I'll have my third in Literature once I've finished my book: A History of the Drion Collective."

"Wait, you're writing a book too? Damn." Zach couldn't help the small surge of irrational pride he felt, learning about Anders's accomplishments and goals. He forced it down and grinned. "We should really get to know each other sometime."

"That sounds like a plan to me," Anders said, kissing Zach once, twice, the third one lingering until Bern knocked on the door. Then he pulled away slowly, his smile sad. "Here's hoping we get that chance."

Zach grabbed his hand as they walked out of the bedroom. The first thing he noticed was the physician, reminding him that he would have to get stuck with a needle soon. He grimaced. Grant was attempting to melt into the wall as though trying to stay out of the way as Bern paced the sitting room. Reese watched the whole scene warily as Jackson stood next to him, one hand just above his elbow.

"Let him go," Anders said as he and Zach sat side by side on the sofa. He gestured to a chair. "Counselor Reese, would you have a seat?"

Reese sat, still looking suspicious. "Your Majesty, I'm sorry to hear you're not feeling well."

Anders waved over the physician, who immediately set to drawing Zach's blood. "And neither is Captain O'Connell," he said. "There is suspicion of poisoning, so you can imagine that I wanted to talk to you."

"Poison?" Reese's eyes went wide. "Surely you don't think I would—"

"No, of course not," Anders said. "To be honest, I don't think you are a dissident, either. However, I've been encouraging my enemies to underestimate me, and couldn't afford to slip up at such a crucial point. I hope you understand?"

Reese frowned. "I do, not that I like it much."

"Fair enough," Anders said with a regal nod. "I wanted to talk to you because you were the one to mention poison in the first place, and I was hoping that you might be able to shed some light on our symptoms. Jackson, the file please?"

Jackson handed Reese a media screen. "This contains all of King Philip's tests as well as what data we have from King James's bloodwork before he died."

Reese flipped through the screens quickly. He paused on the last page. "His radiation levels are that high? Are you sure that's not an error?"

The physician harrumphed as he ran Zach's blood through a small machine. "I did the test three times. It's a miracle His Majesty doesn't glow in the dark." The machine beeped, and the physician frowned at the screen. "The captain's aren't much better."

"Well, hell," Zach said. "So how do we fix it?"

Reese sighed and looked back down at his screen, flipping back and forth between the pages. "I wish I'd had King James's tests before this," he said. "Perhaps we could have stopped this from happening."

"Pointless wishing," Anders said. "Do you know the poison?"

"I do," Reese said. "It's called sarna. A very rare, very expensive poison that was accidentally discovered during the nuclear refinement processes." He sighed again. "I read a study a few years ago about a group of power plant workers who had been accidentally exposed. They nearly all died. Considering our recent problems with smugglers, I'm not as surprised as I'd like to be that sarna has found its way to Drion."

"And the antidote?" Anders sat perfectly still, his knuckles white as he gripped his knees. Zach put his hand over Anders's and squeezed.

Reese shook his head. "There is none, Your Majesty."

Across the room, Jackson cursed once. Anders froze for a moment, just staring at Zach with wide eyes. Zach threaded his fingers through Anders's. "We'll just ride it out, okay? We're stronger than some refinement byproduct."

"I'm afraid not, Captain," Reese said. "You might have a chance, depending on your level of exposure, but according to these readings,

King Philip is beyond any window of opportunity to 'ride it out.'" He hesitated. "There is one chance, however."

"What is that?" Anders asked, his voice rough.

"You two bond as soon as possible," Reese said with an elegant shrug. "The only cases with high exposure where the affected survived was when they had a solid, healthy bond with their match. There's every chance that's it's too late for even that to work, and that it might kill the both of you to try, but it truly is your only chance, Your Majesty."

Zach had never been this terrified before in his life. His hand tightened on Anders's until it had to be painful, then he forced himself to let go. He'd sworn he'd never bond, but that was before Anders. In that moment, he realized that summed up his whole life, and what was before Anders didn't matter nearly as much as what had come after. "Yes, okay," he said. "Someone send for Hadlock to be my witness. And we need a priest; I can't do the ceremony myself, not for the king."

"Wait, what?" Anders turned to meet Zach's eyes. "You don't have to do this. I know how you feel about bonding. Don't think I expect you to."

"*I* damn well expect it," Bern growled. "It's the least he could do."

"I know you don't expect me to," Zach said, ignoring Bern. "I am doing this of my own free will and choice. *Choice*, Anders." He shifted sideways and took Anders's hands in his. "Bond with me," he said softly.

A single tear escaped Anders's eye before he buried his face against Zach's neck. "You won't be able to leave," he cautioned.

Zach pulled back so he could cup Anders's face. He met Anders's gaze steadily. "I wasn't planning on it."

Anders smiled and brushed their noses together. "Stop being so perfect. You know I can't resist you like this." He took a deep, shaking breath and nodded. "Yes. Okay. Let's do it. I don't suppose anyone knows a Priest of the Many we can trust? I can't have word of this getting out before we're ready."

"Your Majesty?" Grant stepped forward timidly. "I have an uncle in the temple. He's just visiting for your coronation, so no one will know he's a priest."

"Excellent." Anders nodded. "Send for him at once, as well as Captain O'Connell's first mate, Oliver Hadlock. Reese, would you be my witness and verify our marks before the bonding?"

"It would be my honor," Reese said, looking both pleased with himself and flustered.

"Good." Anders squeezed Zach's fingers and leaned in, stealing a single lingering kiss before returning to the matter at hand. "In the meantime, let's see if we can't figure out how Zach and I were poisoned."

"Tell Hadlock to bring my bonding knife with him," Zach called after Grant. "He knows where I keep it. Now," he said, turning back to face Reese, "how is the poison administered? And how is it possible for Anders's symptoms and levels to be so strong so quickly when his father lingered for weeks?"

"Sarna is absorbed through touch," Reese said. "And I'd assume that the person who killed King James wants King Philip to go much faster. An increased dosage, a heavier coating on something the king touches daily would do it." He paused. "Are we all on the same screen about who might be behind this?"

Anders shook his head. "Only that it's most likely someone on the cabinet. No one else outside of the Navy would have had access to the blueprints of the *Pallas*."

"I vote for Tanner," Zach growled.

"Whether it is Tanner or not," Anders said, "we'll have to be very careful. Even without his position in the cabinet, he'd be too powerful and influential for us to accuse him of assassination without evidence."

"Oh, he'll confess," Zach said darkly. It might take his hands firmly around Tanner's neck, but he'd confess.

"Not if we don't have proof," Anders insisted. "Reese, you said it could be something I touch daily? I'd say it could be something in my rooms, but there's not much I have that isn't handled by at least three or four other people, and none of the staff appear to be ill."

"It could be something Tanner gave you, Anders." Zach was pretty sure he knew exactly what it was—the only thing he and Anders had *worn*. "Something we," he paused, saw Bern and Jackson watching him, and realized he really shouldn't finish that sentence the way he'd meant to, "... touched. Something you wore."

Understanding dawned on Anders's face. "Of course," he whispered. "The signet ring." No sooner were the words out of his mouth than Jackson and Bern were both rushing into the bedroom. "Tanner gave it to me the night before Father's funeral," Anders explained to Reese over the *click-thunk* of his safe being opened.

"You wore it for the funeral and your coronation," Reese said, nodding. "And it's reasonable to assume that there's been sufficient—" he coughed delicately "—contact between the two of you. Easily enough to inadvertently poison the captain."

Neither one of them had been up to the kind of contact Reese was referring to, not that it mattered. "We can test the ring, I assume, but would it be possible to clean it?" Zach asked. "Anders will need to wear it for state functions."

"It will take time," Reese said, accepting the ring box from Jackson when he and Bern returned, "but yes. In the meantime, I believe there are other options?"

"Yes," Anders said. "My family has always kept costume versions of essential items from the royal collection. In the event something breaks, the public will never notice it missing. They're little more than fancy glass pieces, but will do the trick."

"Then we'll get it cleaned." Zach turned to Reese. "If sarna is that rare and that dangerous, there's no way it made it here, to the center of the Collective, without certain precautions. Not legally."

Reese nodded. "Correct. On his first day back, His Highness mentioned the threat of pirates along our shipping lines, but I'm afraid it's much more serious than that. There have been increased reports of raids on our outlying settlements, violent deaths, people being conscripted, impossible ransom demands. I wouldn't be surprised if one of those pirates had taken to smuggling rare and deadly poisons."

"How has this gone unchecked for so long?" Anders demanded.

"They've managed to keep their activities spread out enough to avoid detection," Reese said. "I only saw the pattern when you mentioned the raiders who attacked you on the way here. That's not something a rookie would attempt."

"A rookie mercenary would try it for the right price," Zach said dryly.

"Would they?" Reese cocked an eyebrow at Zach. "As the military counselor, I'm privy to a number of reports, and I can tell you it's vanishingly rare for a private ship, or even a small squad of private ships, to pick fights with our Navy. Especially with a ship as impressive as the *Pallas*."

"Rare, but not impossible. Not unlike sarna poisoning." Zach's smile was faint and unamused. "As it happens, I agree that it was probably a party of raiders. The real question is motive. Were they paid to attack us, or paid to try to kill Anders? Or were they not paid at all, but attempting to protect their organization? And if so, who has enough authority and insecurity to order such an attack? Because they wouldn't order it if they didn't feel threatened."

"They did seem to target the very section of the ship I was on," Anders pointed out. "Not to mention at least one of the ships attempted a boarding. That seems disturbingly specific, if you ask me. Not to mention the level of clearance that would have been needed for that much information."

"Gods above," Reese whispered. "The break-in."

Zach immediately straightened. "What break-in?"

"There was a break-in at my home here in Dryax." Reese ran a shaking hand through his hair. "I filed a report with security, but it seemed like a run-of-the-mill crime. A few trinkets stolen, nothing disastrous. But now that I think about it, my computer was destroyed. If someone had hacked my system and then destroyed the drive to hide their tracks . . ."

"They could have easily found the information necessary to target me," Anders finished for him.

"And that would enable someone who has access legally to hide the fact that they'd pulled the plans." Zach nodded. "It's certainly a possibility."

"Are you saying the raiders have a sponsor in the cabinet?" Reese pulled back. "Because I was going to suggest they were connected to the piracy plaguing our more isolated citizens, not to mention the recent surge in smuggling and its related violence. That level of corruption goes far beyond even what King James suspected."

"That is ... terrifying to contemplate," Anders agreed. "We already suspected there was at least one person behind the attempts on my and Zach's lives, but if there's this much money on the line, we might be looking at a fully-fledged conspiracy."

"They overplayed their hand," Zach said. "If they'd left it at the attack on the *Pallas*, I might have believed it was just related to piracy. But since they've tried to kill us—and may succeed—it ruins the illusion that it isn't about the monarchy."

"We'll have to proceed carefully," Reese said. "If your bonding is successful, you both are going to be in even greater danger."

Zach looked up as Grant returned with a priest, presumably his uncle, with Oliver close on his heels. "Gentlemen," he said, "my first mate, Oliver Hadlock."

The other men murmured greetings, which Oliver answered with a bow of his head. "Zach, can I talk to you for a minute?"

Zach turned to Anders. "Can we borrow the bedroom?"

Anders nodded. "Of course."

"Thank you." Zach jerked his head toward the bedroom door and Oliver followed him in.

"The kid insisted I bring your bonding knife. Whose bonding are you officiating?" Oliver waited for Zach to drop onto the bed before taking a seat on a chair close by.

"I'm not officiating. And don't you dare say I told you so."

"*You*?" Oliver gaped at him. "*You're* bonding? You were adamant that you would never bond, not ever."

"Anders and I could die if we don't bond. We might die anyway." Zach gazed steadily at Oliver. "We've been poisoned."

Oliver's face went from shock to rage. "Who? I'll kill the fucker myself."

Zach stood and put a hand out. "No. We don't know for sure but we have a good idea, and killing him could cause a war."

"I don't care." Oliver started pacing. "We've never fought anyone except smugglers and the assholes who attacked us on the way here. I could use the adrenaline rush."

"Oliver," Zach said softly.

Oliver slumped and then walked over to drop onto the bed next to Zach. "What do we do?" he asked. "There's got to be an antidote, right?"

Zach shook his head. "Not for this poison. It's radioactive, and from what they said, the only people who have ever survived exposure were strongly bonded with their match. Even then, there's no guarantee."

The light dawned on Oliver's face. "So that's why—"

"Not entirely." Zach put his face in his hands. "I've fallen in love with him, Oliver. He's become more important than my career, more than everything."

"Wow." Oliver patted Zach on the back. "You really have fallen—hard."

Zach nodded miserably. He loved Anders, but that didn't mean he was happy about losing his ship, his ability to *fly*.

"When's the bonding?"

"Now. We can't let the traitor know that we might survive his assassination attempt until after we've taken the steps to try to do so. That's why we needed my knife. I wanted it to be mine. And I want you to be my witness."

"Of course," Oliver said immediately. He patted Zach on the back again and stood. "Well, come on, buddy, let's go do this."

"Yeah." Zach sat for another minute, and then took Oliver's extended hand and let him pull him up. Zach led the way into the sitting room, and smiled at Anders. "You ready for this?"

Anders stood, reaching for Zach even as he wobbled. His skin had gone a bit gray under his usual sepia complexion, and his eyes looked almost feverish. "Trembling with anticipation, darling," he said with a wry smile.

"I'll need to confirm your match before continuing," Reese said. "Shall we do it here, or do you need privacy?"

Zach shrugged. "Here is fine," he said, and took off his uniform jacket, lifting the shirt underneath to show Reese the mark over his ribs. "My middle name is Benjamin."

Anders pulled up his cuff and held his left arm out so Reese could compare the two marks side by side. Reese smiled and turned to the priest. "Let the record state that I have confirmed the match between King James Philip Michael Anderson III and Captain Zachary Benjamin O'Connell."

"More people have seen this mark in the past week than in all the rest of my life combined," Anders murmured as he rolled his cuff back. "It's an odd sensation."

Zach pressed a kiss to Anders's temple. "You don't have to cover it anymore, not if you don't want to." He put his jacket back on. "Let the record show that my witness is Oliver Roarke Hadlock, first mate of the Royal Drion Craft *Pallas*."

"And your witness, Your Majesty?" the priest asked.

"Counselor Bannerjee Reese of Gloria," Anders said as he smoothed his sleeve down. He brushed their hands together and kissed the corner of Zach's jaw. "My parents' sash is in my safe, if you don't object?"

"He'd better not object," Jackson muttered. Anders shot him a look that was more amusement than anything else, and Jackson subsided.

"That's perfect," Zach said, ignoring Jackson. He murmured in Anders's ear. "Do you want me to go get it? You'd have to give me the combination. Or would you rather I help you go in?"

Anders smiled. "Always trying to get your hands on the family jewels, aren't you?" he whispered with a laugh. "Some help getting there without embarrassing myself would be greatly appreciated, though."

Zach laughed too. "*Those* jewels are about to be mine," he whispered back. "We'll go get it," he said loudly enough for everyone to hear. He helped Anders across the room and into the bedroom so Anders could open the safe again. Zach grabbed the sash and locked the safe. They returned to the sitting room to stand before the priest, Reese and Hadlock moving to either side.

The priest was pale, taking the knife Oliver handed him with shaking hands. Zach held out the sash, which the priest nearly dropped as he took it too. His wide eyes flew to Anders, who smiled gently and nodded. The priest blew out a breath and began.

"Thou art matched?"

"Yes, Reverence," they said in unison.

"Thy wish is to bond, to join thy lives, to be ever faithful and true to one another? Thy wish to join thy minds, hearts, and souls ever more tightly together as thou dost age, to care for one another and to live for one another for the rest of thy lives?"

"Yes, Reverence," they said again.

"Hold out thine arms, that I might bind thee." Anders's arm trembled slightly as he held it out; Zach didn't know if it was from fear, excitement, or the poison. Zach held out his arm next to Anders's. The priest made quick slices across each wrist before handing the knife back to Oliver. "Face one another and see thy future."

When they turned, the priest took their arms and pressed the wounds together. "Hold tight to each other."

It stung a little, but Zach didn't move as the priest took the dark-purple sash and carefully wound it around their wrists, binding them together with the wounds bleeding into each other. When the sash was secure, the priest clasped their wrists with his right hand.

"Thou art bound," he said solemnly.

Anders smiled brilliantly, his hand gripping tight to Zach's forearm as he pulled him in for a kiss. "I love you," he breathed.

Zach kissed the words off Anders's lips, then pressed his face against Anders's neck. With a kiss behind his ear, Zach muttered, "I love you too."

Anders laughed, clutching Zach close. "Asshole," he murmured. "Of course you'd wait until I can barely hold my own dick to say that. I owe you one hell of a wedding night."

"Let's get through the next few days before we worry about your dick," he whispered back. He kissed behind Anders's ear again, then swayed with a sudden head rush. "And let's sit down before we fall down," he added.

"It will take some time for the bond to heal you both, if it can," the physician said as they made their careful way to the sofa. "And you, Prince Consort, will almost certainly feel much worse before you feel better."

Reese was nodding along. "Yes, the bond will mean you share in King Philip's illness before the hormonal reaction has a chance to gather enough strength to purge the radiation from both of your bodies. A process that is likely to be tremendously uncomfortable in and of itself. I'm afraid neither of you will feel like celebrating your new union for at least a few days."

Anders managed a smile despite his drooping eyes. "That's fine. We'll have to do this again for the ceremony of things once our problems are dealt with, anyway. My mother would roll over in her grave if we didn't."

"Oh god. My mother is going to kill me," Zach groaned. He slumped against the back of the sofa. He really was going to have to do it all over again, because she wasn't here and oh god, he was fucking *Prince Consort*. "I can't think about that right now, Anders."

"It's okay, darling," Anders said, curling against his side as best as they could with their arms still bound. He yawned, jaw popping audibly. "I'll protect you."

"Oh thanks," Zach said dryly. He squeezed Anders's forearm. "Tell everyone to go away so we can sleep in peace."

"You'll want to stay tied together as long as possible," the physician said, already packing up his equipment. "Studies have shown that bonds deepen faster the longer matched pairs stay tied." He checked the sash, tugging on the knot with a sound of approval. "You might as well sleep in the meantime, Majesties. I'll come back to check on you in a couple of hours."

Anders hummed in agreement. The faintest traces of something alien filtered in through the back of Zach's mind, dragging him down. It wasn't until Anders yawned again that Zach understood what it was.

"Reese, I'm sorry," Anders said at last, "but I'm going to have to ask you to return to the cell for the time being. You're not under arrest, nor are you under suspicion, but . . ."

"We want to keep Tanner—or whomever—underestimating you." Reese sighed. "I understand, Your Majesty. If we could send someone to my home in Dryax to collect my research into Tanner's activities, I would appreciate it."

"Would Oliver be willing?" Anders asked Zach softly.

"Of course," Oliver said instantly. "Anything I can do."

Zach smiled. "There you go."

"Excellent." Anders waved his unbound hand. "Everyone else can go, as well. I'm too tired to be as gracious as you all deserve, but thank you for everything. All of you have gone above and beyond today."

"Yes, thank you." Zach yawned. He patted Anders's leg with his free hand. "Stop talking and go to sleep," he said. "I can feel how tired you are, and it's making me exhausted."

"Lost the romance already," Anders whispered, resting his head heavily on Zach's shoulder even as their guests all filed out.

Zach snorted. "Don't worry, we have plenty of time to find it again."

CHAPTER TWENTY

"**Y**our Majesty, you need to wake up."

No.

"Majesty, at least drink this. You need to keep your strength up."

Too tired. Go away.

"You've been asleep for days, Majesty. Please wake up and eat something."

Leave me alone.

"Anders, wake *up*. Zach is sick."

"Zach," Anders slurred, his throat so dry it felt like he'd been through a wildfire. He stretched, blindly seeking Zach, but was restrained.

"Hold still, Majesty," someone said. "You're connected to a lot of machines."

"Zach." Anders tried to look around, but it was too bright to keep his eyes open. "Where's Zach?"

"Your bonded is here, Sire," the physician said. "He's unconscious, and we can't wake him. You've both been unconscious for more than three days, and we've had to feed you through tubes."

The spot behind Anders's right ear burned, exactly where a bond mark would be. "The bond," he asked, reaching out slowly until he encountered a hand, slack on the bed beside him. *Zach.* "Did the bond work?"

There was a long pause, and Anders was sure he heard people moving around.

"Who's there?" he demanded, lacing his fingers with Zach's even as he tried to sit up.

"It's me, Anders." Jackson pushed Anders back to the bed. "I'm here, Bern's here, we're not going anywhere."

"The bond," Anders repeated.

Jackson sighed. "We're not sure yet."

The exhaustion was already dragging Anders back under. "Zach?"

"It doesn't look good, Anders," Jackson said, squeezing his shoulder. "He keeps getting sicker. I'm sorry."

"No." Anders shifted over toward Zach, trying not to dislodge any of the machines, but not caring if he did anyway if it got him closer to his bonded. "He's too strong for that. You'll see."

Gentle fingers brushed hair off Anders's forehead. "I hope you're right," Jackson whispered.

For the first time in what must have been at least a year, Anders didn't hurt. He was well rested, mildly hungry, and was actually looking forward to getting up and getting dressed. *We did it. It worked.* He rolled over, blinking his eyes open, eager to share the victory with Zach.

There was no one there. The bed was neatly made, with only the barest hint of an indent on the pillow. Anders couldn't help the surge of panic. Who had taken Zach? Where had they taken him? Oh god, had Zach not pulled through? If Zach hadn't made it, how would Anders get through the next sixty years with only half a bond to sustain him?

"Anders? What's wrong?" Zach came hurrying out of the bathroom wearing only a towel, face half shaved. "What's happened?"

"Zach? You're okay?" Anders jumped out of bed, wobbling on his feet for a few seconds before he remembered how to stand properly.

Zach reached Anders and pulled him close. "Yeah. Well, 'okay' might be a stretch. I feel like I've been hit by a shuttle, but I'm here. We got through it."

Anders turned Zach's face to the side, wiped a bit of shaving cream out of the way, and laughed joyously at the sight of the crown-shaped bond mark behind Zach's ear. "It worked," he breathed.

"It worked," Zach agreed. He cupped Anders's face, rubbing his bond mark, and brought their foreheads together. "I wasn't sure you were going to pull through," he added quietly. "You were out a lot longer than I was—god, eight days."

"I woke up, and they told me you might not make it," Anders whispered. "Just now, waking up alone, I . . ." He shook his head, refusing to even voice it. Instead, he copied Zach and rubbed Zach's bond mark. "When did you wake up?"

"A couple of days ago. I must not have had as big a dose; I was only out for six days."

Anders kissed Zach's shoulder. "Did you feel it? When I woke up?"

Zach nodded. "I felt it when you panicked. Which is, I guess, when you realized I wasn't next to you." He lowered his voice to a whisper. "I can feel how much you love me."

"Yeah?" Anders closed his eyes and concentrated. After a moment, he found a mass of emotions that weren't quite *his*. There was happiness, concern, a touch of sadness . . . and so much love Anders was overflowing with it. *Zach.* He smiled, kissing Zach full on the mouth, completely uncaring that he was getting shaving cream all over both of them. "Yeah," he laughed. "I see what you mean."

"Now," Zach said, rubbing his nose against Anders's, "if you'll excuse me, I need to finish shaving this mess off my face. And since you've got shaving cream on yours, you might as well do the same."

"Only if there's a shower in my near future too," Anders said, stealing one last kiss.

Zach made a face. "Yeah, you need a shower."

Anders snorted. "Asshole," he said, hooking his fingers in Zach's towel and yanking it free before heading to the bathroom.

In no particular hurry, Zach sauntered into the bathroom after him and picked up his razor as Anders dropped Zach's towel and detoured to the sink, quickly cleaning his teeth. Every last inch of him felt scummy from his sickbed, and he just wanted it all off his body. Teeth finished, he pushed his sleep pants off his hips and headed for the shower. He did want a shave, but more than anything else, he *needed* to bathe. He slid open the glass door to the large shower, not remembering to close it in his haste to get clean.

At last, the hot water pounded down on Anders's head and shoulders, and he couldn't help the guttural moan that escaped his mouth. For a long while, he just stood there, face tilted up into the spray as he rinsed away several days' worth of illness and stress. "God, that feels so fucking good," he groaned.

Zach laughed. "You sound like you're having sex without me in there," he called out.

"I'd much rather be having sex *with* you in here," Anders called back as he shampooed his hair. "But I know how you are about your uniform standards, Captain."

Anders turned to watch Zach in the mirror as he scraped another stripe of cream and hair off his face. "Are you implying you want beard burn, Your Majesty?"

"Only if it's on my ass." Anders grinned; he could feel a growing curl of arousal separate from his own. "Take your time, darling. I can always start without you."

"Go ahead, if you're in such a hurry. You must really be better," Zach said with another careful swipe of the razor.

"I did promise you a proper wedding night," Anders said, leaning back against the wall. He ran a hand down his slick chest, fingers teasing his cock as he gradually hardened. He imagined it was Zach's hand touching him, Zach's fingers ghosting over his nipples. "I figured we might as well get a jump on that."

Zach scraped the last of the shaving cream off, and grabbed a towel to wipe at the remnants of white on his jaw. He dropped the towel to the floor. "Well, let me know when you're ready for that wedding night. I'll go catch a nap while I wait."

Anders wrapped a lazy hand around his dick, stroking gently. "What, not interested in shower sex, darling?" He spread his feet and arched his hips, thinking about how good it would feel to wrap his legs around Zach's narrow hips while Zach fucked him up against the shower wall.

"I already had a shower," Zach said reasonably, shoulder propped on the doorframe. "And you didn't invite me into yours." Zach's hand curled loosely around his own dick, stroking the slowly hardening flesh.

"What's mine is yours." Anders chuckled breathlessly. "Get over here and kiss me, would you?"

Zach sauntered over to the shower. "If you insist," he said, stepping under the spray. As soon as he closed the door behind him, he lost the nonchalance and grabbed Anders, pushing him against the wall as he pressed their mouths together.

With one hand pulling Zach in closer at the small of his back and the other on the back of his neck, keeping him close for more kissing, Anders grinned against Zach's mouth. "God, I love the way you kiss," he breathed.

"Oh yeah?" Zach panted. "Well, I love the way you ride my dick."

"Another thing we have in common." The sex between them had been electric before, but now that Anders could feel how turned on Zach was, it just moved everything higher. Anders straddled one of Zach's legs, rubbing his cock against the slick skin of Zach's hip. "Fuck me, Zach," he whispered between kisses. "Please."

"When I'm ready," Zach said. He began to slowly kiss down Anders's throat, nipping at the skin, soothing each scrape with his tongue. He sucked at Anders's nipples, teased them with his fingers, then traced the lines of Anders's abs with his fingertips as he kept moving down Anders's body.

Anders gasped. "Whatever you want, love," he said, biting his lip. "Always make me feel so good. No one else could ever light me up like you."

Zach scraped his teeth a little harder just below Anders's navel. "I would hope not," he said, and took Anders into his mouth.

Anders cried out, hands latching on to Zach's shoulders. A dark emotion leaked through the lust, and Anders realized with a groan that it was *possession*. It shouldn't be so hot, shouldn't make Anders squirm, but at the same time it thrilled Anders to know Zach felt just as jealous as Anders did. He nodded, forgetting Zach couldn't see him. "Yes," he whimpered, hips twitching under Zach's hands. "I *am* yours. Forever."

Humming around Anders, Zach grabbed Anders's hips to hold him still and started bobbing up and down, sucking hard when he reached the tip, digging his tongue into the slit before taking Anders all the way to the root again.

"*Fuck.*" Anders couldn't move under Zach's strong hands, could only stand there, rapidly losing his mind under the onslaught. He gazed down at Zach, watched those perfect lips sliding up and down his length, saw how Zach's cheeks hollowed from the amazing sucking. It was too much; Anders closed his eyes and knocked the back of his head against the shower wall. "Look so beautiful with my cock in your mouth, Zach."

Zach pulled free and started kissing up Anders's chest. "Yeah?" he panted. "You look even better riding my dick."

"Yes, *yes*." Anders tugged Zach up, desperate to taste Zach's mouth. "Let's do that. Right now."

"We don't have anything in here." Zach took Anders's mouth in a hard, fierce kiss.

Anders growled in frustration. "We're going to have to fix that," he said between kisses. "Let's go back to bed."

Zach turned off the water and tugged Anders out of the shower. After grabbing a towel, he haphazardly wiped himself down and then dried Anders off much more thoroughly, rubbing the fabric over Anders's sensitive skin. Anders hadn't even known it was possible to feel this way, wrapped up in soft fabric and Zach's warm, possessive love. There was a rush of need and love before Zach dropped the towel, grabbed Anders's hand, and pulled him from the bathroom into the bedroom. He kissed Anders, quick and urgent, and hurried to the bed, pulling the lube out of the wall panel before lying down. "C'mon, baby, let me fuck you."

"*Finally*." Following Zach to the bed, Anders crawled over him, straddling his hips. He snatched the lube from Zach's hand and opened it, holding it out. "Would you like to do the honors?"

"I'd planned on it," Zach said, letting Anders squeeze some onto his fingers. "Lay down and tilt your hips up so I can open you up for me."

Anders stretched out on top of Zach, nosing at his neck, his ear, his bond mark. "I love you," he murmured. "So very much."

There was a burst of love over the bond as Zach pressed a kiss to the curve of Anders's jaw. "Yeah," Zach whispered. His hand pulled at Anders's ass, spreading him for the two fingers that unceremoniously shoved inside, fingertips curling in. Zach started a slow, steady rhythm, fingers sliding in and out, working Anders open.

Whimpering, Anders pushed his hips back, trying to get Zach deeper. He needed more, needed to be fucked, needed Zach. He focused on all his desire, all the ways he wanted Zach, and then shoved it into the bond as he mouthed down Zach's neck, latching on to the strong cord of muscle where neck met shoulder, sucking and biting to leave a bruise.

Zach cried out, arching his neck under Anders's mouth as his hips jerked up, dick rubbing hard against Anders's stomach. He dug his fingers deeper into Anders's ass, finding his prostate, and stroked it relentlessly.

"Zach!" Anders let go of his mouthful to pant against Zach's shoulder. "I could come like this," he warned. "Want to come on your cock, want to feel you. Split me open, Zach. Fuck me. It's enough, just let me ride you. Please."

"No one's stopping you," Zach said with a low laugh. His fingers slipped free, and he helped Anders kneel up, then, taking his cock in one hand, started to guide Anders down. "Put me in you, baby."

Anders pushed down, mouth working open and closed in tiny gasps. Zach was a big guy, thick and long, and Anders hadn't really been stretched enough. The intrusion burned, singing through his veins, and all Anders could do was throw his head back and ride the perfect feeling out. "God, I hope you can feel this," he managed as he slid completely down, to rest flat against Zach's pelvis.

Zach grunted, hips rising in a quick jerk that lifted Anders up. "Yeah," he growled. "God, I can feel how good that feels to you."

"Yeah." Anders circled his hips, adjusting to the stretch before he pushed up on his knees and slid back down Zach's length. Up and down, Anders slowly fucked himself on Zach. He rolled his hips, shifting to press Zach's cock against his prostate, and moaned. "*Zach.*"

"C'mon, baby, just like that," Zach said. He lifted up as Anders pressed down, working them both in rhythm. His hands covered Anders's on his chest and pressed down. "Kiss me, I want your mouth."

"Kiss. Yes," Anders said, groaning as he leaned forward, mouth to mouth. "Taste so good." He licked at Zach's lower lip, sucking on it even as he kept rocking his hips, kept riding Zach.

Zach suddenly rolled, pulling Anders underneath him, fucking into him hard and fast. "Sorry," he muttered into Anders's mouth. "I can't wait."

"Thank fuck," Anders breathed, hooking his arms under his own knees to open himself up to Zach. "You feel so good," he gasped. "I'm close, love. So close."

"Let go." Zach bent and pressed his mouth to Anders's in a rough kiss that became little more than panting against his lips. "Let me feel you come, show me how it feels."

Anders knew how close Zach was; he was hanging on by a thread, lost in how good it felt to pound into Anders again and again. But there was determination there too. He wouldn't come without Anders.

"You are so hot," Anders said, grabbing his own cock and stroking himself hard and fast. "So perfect. God, Zach, I can't . . . I have to . . ." And then he came, arching up under Zach and pulling him deep, coming hard on the both of them.

"*Fuck!*" Zach yelled as Anders squeezed around him, hips jerking as he fucked Anders through his orgasm, finally shoving in one last time as he spilled inside Anders's body.

Zach collapsed on top of him, and Anders wrapped him up in his arms, running gentle fingers up the sweaty length of Zach's spine. Anders pressed a kiss to Zach's temple, still panting and quivering from the aftermath.

"Best belated wedding night *ever*." Anders laughed softly. "I can't imagine how making love's going to be when the bond gets deeper."

"I'm not sure we'll survive it." Zach braced himself up on his elbows to smile down at Anders. "But what a way to go."

Anders kissed Zach's smile, warm all over and not caring which one of them the feeling came from. "We need another shower, darling. You've gotten us dirty again."

Zach looked at the mess between them and snorted out a laugh. "Yeah," he said dryly, "*I'm* the one who got us dirty."

"Shush," Anders said. "Don't you know it's bad manners to contradict the king?" He rubbed their noses together and hummed happily.

"Get used to it," Zach said, leaning in for a quick kiss. "I'm a contrary man." Another kiss, and then Zach shifted, pulling out of Anders's body. Anders pouted, but let him go. Zach rolled them, Anders sprawling over his body, and his hands reached down to squeeze Anders's ass. Two fingers teased at Anders's puffy hole, pushing the leaking come back into his body.

"Just give me five more minutes." Anders yawned and settled more fully against Zach's chest. His eyes drooped, a nap beckoning, no matter that he'd already slept for so many days. "We can fuck again then."

Zach laughed. He pushed his fingers in and left them there. "I'll take longer than five," he said, pressing a kiss to the top of Anders's head. "I'm a fair bit older than you are."

"Oh, this will never work." Anders grinned as he kissed the hollow at the base of Zach's neck. "Do you suppose I could trade you in for a newer model? There must be one who can keep up with me."

"Good luck finding one who'll put up with your baggage." Zach wrapped his free arm around Anders. "I hear you've recently acquired extra baggage in the form of a rather possessive Navy captain who's more than capable of defeating a pretender."

"True," Anders said. "I wouldn't put anyone against him. He's a tough bastard, stubborn as hell. But I love him, so I suppose I'll keep him. Even if he is terrible about keeping me from my postcoital naps."

Zach laughed. "I thought you were gearing up for another round."

Anders made a negative sound in the back of his throat. "Seems my ass is currently occupied. I might as well enjoy my afterglow with a nap. Then a shower, and possibly a shave."

"Start with the nap, and we'll go from there." Zach slowly pulled his fingers free of Anders's body. "Sleep."

"Yes, darling." Anders concentrated on how happy he was, how much he loved Zach, and pushed it on down the bond as he nuzzled Zach's jaw. Zach sent an answering pulse of love back, and Anders smiled as he drifted off to sleep.

CHAPTER TWENTY-ONE

Zach checked the time and sighed. Intellectually he knew that his nap had been more than long enough, but physically he wasn't quite as sure. Anders was awake, Zach could feel it, but he didn't seem willing to move yet. "Why are we awake?"

Anders groaned into the pillow. "Because we slept for a week and our bodies hate us, is my best guess." He sat up, rubbing his face. "At least it's not the middle of the night."

"If it were, we could go back to sleep. Since it's not, we'll have to get up and actually do things." Zach yawned. "I can't believe how tired I still am."

"Hopefully there will be enough time to rest before flushing out our would-be assassin," Anders said. "But I doubt it. I've most likely missed a dozen small disasters already."

"I should get up too." Zach sat up and wrapped his arms around Anders, for support as much as anything else. His weight tugged Anders back down next to him. "Oops."

Anders laughed and kissed Zach's shoulder. "I need another shower, not to mention a shave," he said, pulling away slowly. "Then we should probably talk to Jackson and Bern and check the lay of the land. We've got a lot of work to do, Prince Consort."

Zach ignored the twinge of annoyance at Anders's words. He'd never wanted to be a prince, only a pilot. He summoned up a mock scowl. "Jackson and Bern, really?"

"They are my friends," Anders said, each word measured. "And until we have this all sorted out, they're at the top of a very short list of people we can trust." He took a deep breath and relaxed marginally. "Once we're safe again, I'll get a proper assistant and the guys will settle in to choreographing palace-wide security while we're in residence. I can even see about getting you an assistant of your own, though your schedule won't be as packed as mine."

It was more than a twinge this time. "I don't need an assistant. I have a first officer." Zach threw off the covers and climbed out of bed nude. "I should go check on my crew."

"Zach." Anders's voice was careful. "They're not your crew anymore. A man who can't fly can't captain a ship."

"Of course I can fly," Zach said sharply. "And captain or not, they are still *my* crew. *My* people. *My* friends. Or am I not allowed to have my own friends anymore either?"

"I never said you couldn't have friends." There was rustling as Anders got out of bed and came around to face Zach, already shrugging on his robe. "But your responsibilities have got a whole lot larger than just one ship in my—*our* Navy. The prince consort doesn't run training maneuvers or ferry dignitaries from planet to planet. He stays where he belongs. Here."

The twinge had grown to full-blown anger. "You've effectively imprisoned me, is that what you're saying? I can't go or do anything I want to do, it's all about *you* and what *you* want. I never asked for this."

Anders drew back. "You knew exactly what you were signing up for, *Captain*," he said. More anger, and not Zach's, started leaking across the bond, tinted with something akin to panic. "I told you that you wouldn't be able to leave, I *warned* you that staying with me would keep you dirt-bound. Don't you dare blame me because you've got buyer's remorse."

"I signed up for *you*." Zach poked a finger in Anders's chest. "Not the rest of this shit, just you." He poked Anders again, annoyed and overwhelmed by the emotions swirling in his head. He could no longer separate his from Anders's. He stepped closer to Anders, close enough for the robe to brush against his bare skin. "Don't you dare blame me for not wanting your baggage."

"My 'baggage' is who I am." Anders looked up at Zach, and a sudden burst of sadness and anxiety washed over the bond. "I'm not the uncomplicated Lord Hawthorne you first fucked. I'm King Philip, responsible for the well-being of the Drion Collective and anyone in my life has to share in that burden." He turned away. "If you hate it so much, you should have left when you had the chance."

Zach grabbed Anders's shoulder and pulled him back. "The baggage is what you do," he said irritably, "not who you are." He let go of Anders and shoved his hands through his hair. "It's a lot to get used to. You've known your whole life. Give me a break, here." After a pause, he quietly said, "I'm not going anywhere."

"I know. I'm sorry." Anders smiled, nearly convincingly. But Zach could still feel that sadness, like Anders was swimming in it. "I wish I could give you your freedom to fly, Zach. But it's not something people like us can have, I'm afraid."

"Just . . . stop reminding me for a while." Zach wrapped himself around Anders. "Let me deal with this my own way."

"I'll see what I can do," Anders joked weakly. He leaned into Zach, though, so it was as close to a win to be enough. "I don't want to fight with you. Can't we have today to be newlyweds?"

Zach hugged Anders tightly. "Not if you bring Jackson and Bern in here," he returned. "But fighting isn't so bad, is it? Not when making up is so much fun."

"I suppose I could wait to bring them in," Anders said, voice muffled by Zach's chest. "It's not as though they mustn't already know we've been up all this time. It'll keep until morning."

"Then yes, we can have today to be newlyweds." Zach didn't mention the fact that Anders was the one who'd initially brought up work. His flash of annoyance was met with more anxiety from Anders. At least he could tell whose emotions were whose now. He waggled his eyebrows suggestively. "Let's have a nap, then we can be newlyweds again."

"We did just wake up. Might as well skip the nap." Anders's arms wound around Zach's waist. He nuzzled the underside of Zach's chin, the bristles on his unshaven jaw scratching Zach teasingly.

Zach brushed a quick kiss over Anders's lips and walked them the few steps to the bed until the backs of Anders's knees hit the mattress. "Good point. You're a smart guy."

"I didn't do all that school for nothing." Anders finally started to relax, his bitter emotions fading.

"I would hope not." Zach eased Anders down to sit, then sat beside him. He pulled Anders into a deeper kiss, sliding his tongue past lips and teeth to tangle with Anders's tongue. Keeping it slow and easy, Zach leaned over him, guiding him to lie down as they kissed.

Anders hummed softly into Zach's mouth, the faintest tendrils of love replacing any remaining sourness. Then he pulled Zach in closer and nothing else mattered for a long while.

"You're feeling at me again," Zach complained mildly the next morning, shifting restlessly under the sheets as he stretched and looked over at Anders. "You're all—" he made a sweeping motion with one hand "—frustrated. And bored, and worried. And you're tired. Come back to bed so I can sleep."

A burst of Anders's irritation washed over Zach at that. In contrast, though, Anders barely ticked up a single eyebrow as he glanced up from the media screen in his lap. "I missed over a week to not-dying, darling," he said with a patience Zach knew for a fact he didn't feel. "I don't have the luxury of napping now. But I can try to be less . . . emotional."

Zach snorted. "Emotional is part of who you are, so good luck with that. Just don't, I don't know. Broadcast everywhere." He patted the mattress next to himself. "I can help you stop thinking for a while."

"I'll still be broadcasting," Anders said with a smirk. "Even if it *is* about how much I like the way you fuck me."

"But then I'd be right there with you, and it wouldn't matter who was broadcasting what," Zach said reasonably.

"Speaking of," Anders said, cocking his head to the side, "why can I hardly feel you except for when you're randy or angry? Doesn't seem fair if you're stuck getting my emotions all over you." Another burst of Anders's feelings, which were bitter and frustrated this time.

Zach rolled onto his back and tucked his hands behind his head. "I don't know. It's not that I don't feel things, it's just—I don't know. Maybe I'm more self-contained than you are." He smiled faintly. "Someone in academia has more luxury for emotion than someone who has thousands of lives in his hands on a daily basis."

"But then I've never really been just an academic, have I?" Anders asked, a twisted feeling thrumming under both their skins. He huffed, forcibly relaxing. "It must be strange, then, experiencing things as much as I do. I didn't realize it would be like this."

"Maybe we can teach each other," Zach said. "After all, I no longer have thousands of lives in my hands and now you do."

"Try billions, darling," Anders drawled, the knot of his emotions yanking Zach almost painfully. "Aside from the populations of the twelve core worlds, there are four settled moons and six Outer Edge planets officially within the Collective, along with one or two border worlds that no one's entirely sure are ours that I am, on any given day, responsible for leading."

"Good for you," Zach said flatly. "And I am very well aware of the boundaries of the Collective. I used to fly between them daily." He curled around a pillow, turning his back to Anders. "Be responsible for them more quietly."

"Don't be an idiot," Anders huffed. "Just because I can sense you're in a pissy mood doesn't mean I know why."

Zach yawned, deliberately ostentatious. "Didn't say you did. Interesting, though, isn't it, that now that you can, you're bitching about it? What I *did* say, however, is that I want to sleep. Nap with me or don't, just stop feeling so loud."

"For fuck's sake, what did I do wrong?" Anders's frustration boiled between them. "You knew exactly what I was like when we got into this; you do *not* get to be angry with me for not changing. Just because emotions are such a foreign concept for you . . ."

"So you're the only one who gets to be angry?" Zach rolled over and raised an eyebrow at Anders, keeping his face calm and cool with an effort. "Remind me to add that to the marriage rules I'm trying to learn."

"I'm only angry because you're angry and *you won't tell me why*." Anders stood and tossed the media screen into the opposite chair. The anger was there, confusion too. And underneath it all was something hard and tight that sat in the back of Zach's throat. "What did I do to piss you off this time, or do I not get to know?"

"It's rather arrogant of you to assume that you're what pissed me off." Zach sat up and rolled his shoulders. "This is part of why

I didn't want to bond before. No privacy but plenty of room for misunderstanding, especially before you can control the bond or speak through it."

"What the fuck am I supposed to think?" Anders demanded. "It's not like there's anyone else here to blame your bad mood on, and I am well aware of how much you despise the idea of bonding, thank you."

"That maybe it's internal and there's no one to blame? That maybe it's none of your business?" Zach got out of bed and stalked toward Anders. "Yes, I despised it—emphasis on the past tense, there, thank you, although it still seems creepy—and yet I did it, for you, because I love you." Zach voice rose as he spoke until he professed his love at the top of his lungs. "That doesn't mean I have to explain myself, or that everything is your fault. Back the fuck off."

All of the rage melted out of Anders in an instant as he blinked up at Zach. Something fragile came across the bond, almost tentative. "Do you still?" he asked softly. "Even after I took your wings?"

Zach let all the confusion and frustrated love he felt flow through him. "You didn't take my wings," he said, voice quiet. "I gave them to you."

"Can you forgive me for that?" Anders asked, guilt and love all tangled up as he reached up to cup Zach's cheek.

"There's nothing to forgive, baby." Zach pulled Anders's hand away from his face and curled it into his own, giving it a light squeeze. "I made a choice, because I love you more than I love flying." Heat crawled up his face, and he forced a smile. "And that's something I can't say about anything or anyone else. But we have got to figure this thing out before we drive each other crazy. There has to be some way other than time to get control."

"Under normal circumstances, we'd have spoken to another bonded pair before the ceremony," Anders said. "Not that there's a lot of people we can talk to now, not without giving the whole game away. In fact, I'm pretty sure there's only . . . Oh dear. You are going to *hate* this."

Zach had come to the same conclusion as soon as Anders said *bonded pair*. Anders's guard dogs were the only pair who knew they were bonded, and Anders was right. He was going to hate it. "Not as much as Jackson will."

Anders sighed. "I know it's counter to your nature," he said, moving more into Zach's space. "But please play nice."

"That wasn't a threat, just a statement," Zach said.

"I know, darling," Anders said, kissing Zach's jaw, his amusement clear across the bond. "But I also know you two haven't spoken since we were poisoned. Bern either. *And* I know how much you like to torment people who call your abilities into question."

"I can behave myself if he can." Zach kissed Anders on the lips, soft and chaste at first but quickly deepening until it slid into hard and dirty. He eased back again, enjoying the soft sound of protest Anders made as he did. "He hates me for risking you, but I would have told him if I'd known there was risk. It really wasn't my fault."

"We'll never really know if the extra notice could have made a difference," Anders said. "Once everyone accepts that, we'll be able to move on. I, for one, think a case of near-death might have been worth it just to hear you say you love me."

Zach rolled his eyes. "Nothing is worth being near-death that way. Besides, I said it before then, and I would have said it again. Eventually."

"You screaming it at me a few minutes ago is only the second time those particular words have crossed your lips," Anders said, wrapping his arms around Zach's waist. "Trust me, I'm keeping count." Warmth and love flooded the bond, completely open and unrestrained.

"You may or may not have been asleep at the time," Zach said, hugging Anders close. Then he sighed. "Let's get the guys and get this mentoring thing over with."

Anders laughed softly and rested his head on Zach's shoulder. "Yes, darling," he murmured. "I love you too."

Anders and Zach sat across from Jackson and Bern, but no one spoke. *This is never going to work*, Anders thought as Jackson glared at Zach for the tenth time since walking into the room. Some of Anders's frustration must have shown on his face, because Bern relented at last, touching Jackson's knee.

Jackson huffed but nodded. "You're both going to need shields, or you'll drive each other insane inside of a month," he said. "All the telepathy in the world won't make up for being powerless against every last stray emotion being shared indiscriminately."

"Yeah, we've experienced some insanity already," Zach drawled. "Will you help us create shields so we don't kill each other?"

"We can talk you through it, but in the end it's up to you," Bern said. "And there's a lot of literature on shielding techniques, in case what we do today doesn't work for you. No one expects bonded pairs to share everything. I mean, can you imagine having the one you love getting a front-row seat for the worst, most unworthy thoughts you have?"

"Yeah, that could be fairly horrible," Anders said, shifting. He could feel all the fear and anxiety brought on simply by talking about this building. He couldn't help but wonder if Zach would be the first bonded to leave his match in however many years. Not that Anders would really be able to blame him, if he kept *feeling* at Zach so much.

Zach put his hand on Anders's knee under the table and squeezed. "We have enough incentive already without thinking about unworthy thoughts, thank you."

Jackson shot Zach another narrow-eyed look, but Bern held up his hands peacefully. "I'm only saying that those kinds of thoughts are natural and don't dictate who we are, not if we don't act on them. Which is why there's no good to be had from sharing them."

"Thank you for the reassurance." Anders covered Zach's hand with his own. "So how do your shields work?"

"For most people," Jackson said, "it's a matter of visualization. I see mine as a tall, impenetrable wall."

"I think of it in terms of windows and doors," Bern added. "The trick is to find something that allows you to maintain control over the ebb and flow of the bond."

"Doors would probably work," Zach said thoughtfully. "I'll have to think about that a little."

"Initially, you're going to have to work at keeping the shields up, but after a day or two, it'll be mostly automatic," Bern said. "It will take a few tries to get them to stick too, so we might as well get started."

He was right about it taking a few tries. The first few times, Anders felt ridiculous. He didn't see how picturing a wall or a gate in his mind could help at all, and for the better part of an hour, nothing worked. It didn't help, either, that he could both see and feel the frustration the whole process was causing in Zach. Of course, matters also weren't helped by the way Jackson talked to Zach, either.

"You're not *concentrating*," Jackson told Zach as Bern walked Anders through yet another breathing exercise.

"Oh, *fuck* you, I'm not concentrating! How goddamn easy was this for *you* when you first tried to learn it?" Zach's fists clenched then slowly relaxed as he took deep breaths.

Bern snorted. "It took us both a while," he admitted. "But we wanted to bond in the first place, and learned how to do this *before* we had the chance to start driving each other insane. So how about you ease up on my bonded and listen to the advice he's giving you?"

"Bern." Anders kept his voice quiet, but firm. "That's not helping. Please stop."

"Yeah, Bern," Zach sneered. "Please stop."

Anders couldn't help his annoyance at that, and spitefully hoped Zach felt every bit of it. "We all need to work together on this. And no matter what anyone's personal feelings are about underlying matters, I think we all can agree that these shields need to be our top priority."

Zach took a slow breath in, held it for a moment, then blew it out. "Fine. You're right, we have to get the shields down."

"Let's try again," Jackson said, voice frosty. Always the more placid of Anders's friends, it was surprising, but especially gratifying that someone cared about how Zach's behavior was affecting Anders.

But thoughts like that weren't going to help, and eventually there would be a telepathic link between Anders and Zach, which meant Anders needed to get his shields working. Needed to block off those unworthy thoughts Bern had mentioned, before they caused even more problems.

Anders closed his eyes and pictured a collection of windows and doors, mentally moving them to block thoughts and feelings before they could bleed through. Suddenly, the background hum of grief-anger-bitterness-love cut off, and Anders gasped at the abrupt change. "Oh. So *that's* how it works."

Zach's eyes widened. "You're gone," he said. "I mean, you're there, but I can't *feel* you anymore."

"Nicely done, Your Majesty," Bern said. "It's going to take practice keeping them up, and strong emotions are going to tear through them like paper, but it should give you some privacy."

"And the protection will only improve once you've both got the skill under your belts," Jackson said, sparing a smile for Anders.

And then Anders lost control, and his shields fell. Zach's annoyance nearly knocked him over, and Anders pulled away slightly. "Sorry. I'll work on keeping them up longer."

"Yeah, you do that," Zach muttered. He closed his eyes and blew out a breath again. "I'm done for now. I know the basics and I can practice by myself."

"Yes. Of course." Anders scrambled off the couch and away from Zach, his guards following.

Jackson was the first to break the uneasy silence as they reached the door, his voice pitched low for privacy. "Anders—"

"We're all stressed," Anders said, trying to convince himself as much as his friends. "And you've seen Zach's file: top of his class, early promotions, overachiever his whole life. He's probably in a mood because I learned faster than him."

"He shouldn't take it out on you." Bern frowned tightly. "Deliberately projecting negative emotions can cause actual pain in bonded pairs."

Anders shook his head, sure about this much. "Zach would never hurt me deliberately. Ever." He touched both Bern's and Jackson's forearms. "He'd leave before it ever came to that. He's a good man. Stubborn, angry at being forced into this, and easily as slow to forgive as you two. But he'd sooner cut off his own hand than harm someone who loves him."

Jackson frowned, but Bern nodded reluctantly. "You would know him better, I suppose."

"I would. Now, why don't you two send Grant over to watch us, and get some rest? The physician was here earlier and told me how you two never left us alone. Spend time together not worrying about me, sleep in the same bed. Tomorrow we have the cabinet meeting, and we'll all need to be at our best."

After seeing Bern and Jackson out, and confirming there was the now-usual complement of four guards in the outside hall, Anders went back to Zach, who was still frowning on the sofa. "How's it going?"

"I'm working through my mood just fine, thank you." Zach kept his eyes closed.

"Trust me, *I know*," Anders shot back. He could feel Zach's turmoil and wished desperately to be anywhere but there. "They were worried about you abusing me, you great sulking asshole."

Zach opened one eye enough to send Anders a searing glare. "I heard. And *I'm* the asshole." He huffed out a laugh and closed his eye. "If you don't want to feel me, throw up those shields again and go."

Anders's own rage took his breath away. *How dare he?* He'd never felt this furious in his entire life. But Bern's warning about projecting negative emotions stopped him, and instead, Anders yanked up his shields. They were haphazard at best, but at least they provided some relief from Zach's mood.

"I was going to offer to help you," he snarled, walking away. "But maybe a visual aid is what you need." And he slammed the bedroom door behind him, shutting himself away from Zach and Zach's anger as much as he could.

Anders spent the rest of the day working on his shields. Once he had them solid enough, he moved on to keeping them up while distracted, flipping through screen after screen of reports on the supposedly isolated piracy incidents over the past few years. Reese was right: there was a pattern. People were losing everything they had, even dying at the hands of these pirates. And at least one of the border worlds had been making noises about independence, citing the rampant lawlessness of criminals who called the Collective home. Something had to be done, and fast.

Zach didn't come to bed until very late. When he did, he came in quietly and sat on the edge of the bed to take off his boots. "I got it," he said. "And I'm sorry."

Keeping a tight rein on his shields, Anders set aside his media screen and settled back in his chair. "Oh?"

"Yes." Zach stood to finish stripping off his uniform. He hung it up carefully and climbed into bed nude.

Anders bit off the first three *unworthy* responses that came to mind. Instead he settled for, "What for?"

Zach finally turned at Anders, raising an eyebrow. "For losing my temper, despite overt provocation from your guards. For taking it out on you when I did. They may have deserved it, but you didn't."

"Oh." This time the word was quiet, and Anders looked down at his hands.

"Oh?" Zach said, voice clearly trying for teasing as he echoed Anders's earlier response.

Anders sighed around the residual anger lodged in his chest. "Thank you. I . . . needed to hear that."

"Come to bed, baby. Tomorrow will be a long day."

"Yeah, okay." Anders stood and undressed, climbing into bed next to Zach, but still maintaining a small distance between them.

Zach tugged him close and wrapped him up in strong arms, not allowing the distance. "Sleep."

CHAPTER
TWENTY-TWO

Zach watched with interest as the cabinet filed into the room. Most seemed concerned about Anders, relieved to see him whole and healthy at the head of the table, but Tanner looked a little off. Zach smiled slowly. It was good they'd taken the extra day to learn how to shield themselves, because the last thing either of them needed was Anders feeling exactly how furious it made him to see Tanner there.

Once everyone was in and seated, Zach pushed himself off the wall he'd been leaning on and sauntered over to the table to stand behind Anders's right shoulder.

Anders looked around the room, his pleasure singing across the bond despite the calm air he projected. "Now that everyone is here," he said, "I would like to formally introduce you to Captain Zachary O'Connell, Prince Consort of the Drion Collective and heir to all that is in my name."

The bond opened a little, letting in Anders's amusement at Zach's own smug pleasure as the room absolutely erupted into pandemonium. He watched Tanner carefully—the other man was glaring at Zach as if Zach had stolen his favorite toy. Zach just smirked at him. He could feel Anders's glee in the situation, and it was all he could do to stand there with a straight face.

"Your Highness," Lee sputtered. "This is highly irregular!"

"Your *Majesty*," Zach firmly corrected. "He is your king."

Anders smiled at Zach over his shoulder, his delight clear even through their brand-new shields as Lee turned purple with absolute fury. "I suppose we can forgive the counselor for a single slipup, especially given the circumstances," he said before turning back to the room at large. "We recognize that this is a complete breach of protocol and tradition. However, it was necessary in order to save my life and preserve stability within the kingdom."

The cabinet members shifted uneasily and began muttering among themselves. Anders silenced them by raising his hand. "Long story made unforgivably short: soon after my arrival, I began to suffer from the same ailment that took my father. The royal physician determined it to be a rare form of genetic illness, as yet unidentified. The captain and I chose to bond quickly and quietly once Counselor Reese advised us that very few illnesses could stand up to a strong and healthy bond."

"Reese?" Tanner spat. "Your Majesty had that bastard locked up on suspicion of treason!"

"I did," Anders said. "But after careful investigation, we determined that there was no evidence beyond the word of an assassin that the counselor was involved in anything sinister."

"Not," Zach interjected, "that it's really your place to question His Majesty's decisions. Counselor." He smiled again and knew it looked as predatory as he felt. Tanner shrank back into his seat.

Anders nodded to Jackson. "Please show the counselor in to his rightful place at the table." When Jackson opened the door to the king's antechamber to admit Reese, more than one person gasped, scandalized. A few of the others shot Tanner anxious looks, but it was Lee who spoke up first.

"Counselor Reese," he said as Reese sat across from him. "How fortunate for you the king was willing to clear you of all charges."

Reese shot Tanner a smirk before answering Lee. "Indeed," he said, folding his hands on the table. "King Philip is already proving to be a wise and thoughtful ruler."

"Thank you, Counselor Reese," Anders said. "Now. We will announce the happy news of our bonding to the rest of the kingdom soon, but I think it best that we take a few days to plan a proper bonding ceremony for tradition's sake. In addition, it will allow me to regain the rest of my strength before appearing in public again."

Zach rested his hand on Anders's right shoulder and squeezed. It would be good to regain *his* strength before Anders appeared in public too. He gaze flickered back to Tanner. The other man kept shooting him angry glares. Zach just lifted an eyebrow at Tanner, who subsided once more, looking slightly sick.

Anders covered Zach's hand with his own, leaving it there. "And for those of you who might be concerned, I would like to assure you that our bond was properly blessed by a Priest of the Many and witnessed by multiple parties." Anders turned his head to show his bond mark. "We are fully and legally bonded, and any additional ceremony will be to satisfy tradition and pay the respect due to our ways. Since it's highly unlikely this is a secret even now, the prince consort and I will make the announcement to our people tomorrow over the media streams to take care of any budding rumors."

There was a round of congratulations, some more genuine than others, Anders broadcasting how wildly amused he was at how it seemed to physically pain Tanner to do so. With a last squeeze to Zach's hand, Anders sat forward, bracing his elbows on the table.

"Now, on to other business," he said.

"I agree, Your Majesty," Reese said. "If I may?" He waited for Anders's nod before continuing. "As noble a man as the prince consort is, I'm afraid we can't have a mere captain as the next in line to the throne. That's just too common for a man of your position."

Zach stiffened. He was proud of being a "mere captain," had worked hard to get there, and he hoped Reese had a point beyond insulting him, otherwise Anders might throw Reese back in prison. He could feel Anders's fury and indignation through their bond, felt Anders's control begin to slip before he ruthlessly pulled himself back from the edge.

"Go on," Anders said in a low voice. "But choose your next words carefully."

"It had been widely rumored that the prince consort had no desire to bond," Reese said. "Yet when it became clear that a bond was your best chance at recovery, Majesty, he did not hesitate. He saved your life, and not for the first time. Such selfless—" he paused when Tanner snorted "—such selfless heroism deserves the proper recognition. I have spoken to the necessary parties, and the prince consort's military record is presently being updated to reflect his new rank as admiral."

Zach gaped at Reese. He was shocked to the core, and all he could think was *I really won't ever fly again.* He could feel Anders's shock amplifying his own. The bond was getting stronger. Zach shook his head, not in denial but to pull himself together. "What did you say?"

Reese smiled. "I admit it's a tremendous promotion, especially during peacetime," he said, "but the man at my king's side deserves it. Consider it a bonding gift."

"I . . ." Anders paused, then started again. "That is a most generous gift, Counselor. And I happen to agree wholeheartedly that my bonded deserves such recognition and reward." He looked back over his shoulder, sending love and soothing feelings. "Although I am admittedly rather biased."

"Thank you," Zach said numbly. He had, in the farthest corner of his mind, thought that admiral might be in his future, but in the far, far future, not now. Despite Anders's earlier denial, he'd still thought someday he'd fly again. Being a captain meant flying a ship. But admiral—admiral meant riding a desk. He wasn't ready to give up the expanse of space and stars for a desk. "Thank you very much, I—I don't know what to say."

"It's the least the Navy could do for you, Majesty," Reese said.

Anders made a low noise of agreement. "Indeed. Now, as I was about to say, we have other business to discuss today. Have there been any developments on the situation with the pirates?"

Silence greeted him.

Anders's anger surged, bitter and sharp in the back of Zach's mind. Judging by the way two of the counselors flinched, the expression on Anders's face wasn't much better.

"Nothing?" Anders asked, looking around the table. The silence held, and Anders's temper finally snapped.

"Unacceptable!" He banged the table with the flat of his hand. "Piracy is a very real threat to all of us and all of my people. They prey on the unwary, they flood our market with substandard and illegal goods, and they promote crime everywhere they go. As the king's cabinet and as the elected representatives of your planets, it is your sworn duty to address this danger when directed by your king. By me. And I distinctly recall issuing that instruction over a week ago. So what, pray tell, could possibly have been more important?"

"Your Majesty," Reese ventured, "in all fairness, the whole cabinet has likely been focused on your health for the past several days."

"And it took all eleven of you to sit at my bedside and hold my hand?" Anders scoffed. Zach squeezed Anders's shoulder again, determined not to let Anders's temper spiral completely out of control. He sent calming, loving feelings through the bond. Even though he actually agreed with Anders, yelling wouldn't accomplish anything, especially not with his power so recently gained.

Anders took a deep breath, forcibly relaxing. "I am strong and healthy now," he said after several excruciating moments of silence. "And I expect each one of you to do your jobs as instructed and to the best of your ability. That includes each one of you investigating this issue as it pertains to your counsel, ready to report back and discuss at our next meeting. Now," he added, voice going arctic as he leaned forward, "barring an act of the god of your choice, I expect to hear *something* besides my own voice next time. Is that clear?"

There were a few murmured assents, and more than a few flushed faces. Tanner looked like he was about to detonate, and Lee wasn't much better. Reese was the only one able to sit comfortably, probably by virtue of his having been in jail for nearly the entire time.

"Good." Anders nodded once, then glanced down at the notes on the table in front of him. "The next order of business is the prolonged rainy season on Amasis. Counselor Nadjem, what projections do you have from the Agriculture Office? How severely will this impact the stores of our citizens there?"

It was two long hours before they'd covered enough and Anders was willing to let his cabinet go. "A reminder," he said, "that I am utterly serious about those reports on our piracy situation. I will not be nearly so pleasant about it next time." He glared down each counselor, then rapped his knuckles once on the smooth table. "You are all dismissed."

Zach waited until everyone had filed out the door before murmuring in Anders's ear. "You were a bit hard on them, baby." He pressed a kiss to the skin there, behind Anders's earlobe.

"They deserve it," Anders grumbled as Jackson left the room as well, pointedly closing the door behind him. "I sincerely doubt half of them cared I was ill at all. They presume to think they can test me. They *will* fail."

"Yes, but pushing them like that will only backfire, I'm afraid." He smiled against Anders's ear. "I thought Tanner was going to be sick."

Anders relaxed slightly, tilting his head to give Zach more access. "I noticed you enjoyed that."

"I did, a little." And wasn't *that* an understatement. Zach laughed and kissed the crook of Anders's neck. "I'm not," he said quietly, lips moving on warm skin, "going to make out with you in your cabinet room."

Cupping the back of Zach's head, Anders chuckled. "I never thought you would." He turned, catching Zach's mouth in a kiss.

Zach kissed him back slowly, savoring the feel of Anders's teeth nipping at his lower lip, then the slide of Anders's tongue into his mouth. He let it keep going longer than he probably should have, enjoying himself, but eventually he eased back far enough to speak. "I said no," he teased, "and no means no."

Anders laughed against Zach's lips. "Somehow, darling, I don't think even a royal decree could make you do something you don't want to."

"Well, I don't know; you *do* outrank me."

Another lingering kiss, and then Anders pulled away. "Well, if you're not going to make out with me here, then I'm going to have to take you back to bed. I'm on my honeymoon, you know."

Zach took Anders's hand and pulled him up, leading him out of the room. "Oh you are, are you? What a coincidence, I'm on my honeymoon too."

The whole way back to their suite, Anders kept sending lust at Zach along with long, hooded glances. Right outside of the residential wing, they ran into a group of counselors, all eager to make their congratulations to Zach on the bond and his promotion. Anders, for his part, stood off to the side, projecting so intently that the two of them were in serious danger of causing a scandal with their tight trousers.

Trying to ignore Anders, Zach accepted the congratulations graciously and tried to extricate himself as quickly as possible. After several too-long minutes, they were finally able to get away, Zach pulling Anders through the halls until they reached their rooms.

Anders's grin stretched from ear to ear by the time he locked the door behind them with a chuckle. "In a hurry to get somewhere?" he asked, winding his arms around Zach's waist.

"Not really." Zach rubbed his nose against Anders's. "But you sure were."

"Only because I have a fondness for your beautiful, naked body," Anders said, nipping at Zach's chin. "Along with all the rest of you."

Zach laughed. "I'm so glad you realize I'm more than my dick." He pressed a light kiss to Anders's lips and grabbed his ass in both hands. He was just about to deepen the kiss, when there was a discreet knock at the door. "Your Majesty?"

Anders sighed. "Of course," he whispered before calling out an answer. "Yes? What is it?"

"I'm so sorry, Your Majesty. Commander Hadlock and Counselor Reese are here to see you and Admiral O'Connell." Zach could hear regret in Jackson's voice.

"I used to really like Oliver too." Zach sighed, kissing Anders's jaw and stepping back. "Come in," he said, not sounding at all as disappointed as he felt.

Oliver stepped into the room. "Sorry for the interruption," he said repentantly. "But we have news of Tanner and his 'business' practices."

Anders straightened. "Please come in, gentlemen," he said, waving Oliver and Reese farther into the room. Jackson and Bern followed behind them. Once they were all seated, Anders leaned back against the sofa and Zach's arm. "I wasn't aware you were conducting an investigation, Mr. Hadlock."

Zach nodded. "Oliver was in military intelligence before I convinced him to join me on the *Pallas*. He still has contacts who were willing to help."

"Excellent." Anders waved to Oliver. "Please do continue, sir."

"I found someone who says he knows a guy who's getting really rich off a partnership with Ciebosian smugglers who, according to him, never get caught because they always know the safe routes to take." Oliver raised an eyebrow. "I also found out that Tanner goes to a lot of parties in a lot of places and throws money around like there's an endless supply, but his stipend and his allowance from his trust fund don't add up to the amount he's spending, even when combined."

Zach nodded. "Can we access his bank records, see where the money's coming from? Maybe he's just drowning in debt. We can't discount the possibility."

"I considered that, and I'm working on it," Oliver said. "He has standard accounts showing his stipend and allowance, of course, but there are traces of other financial dealings too. He's not hiding them very well; I'll find more soon. Then we'll know if it's debt or something else."

"We won't be able to use that information publicly, though," Reese said. "Not without risking serious repercussions from the Tanner family. They would have a field day about illegal investigations and improper documentation."

"I can take care of that. At least going forward." Anders stood, walking across the room to a desk and pulling out a media screen. He tapped away even as he returned and sat next to Zach, pressing close almost absently. "There. I've just authorized you to *legitimately* investigate the financial records of anyone suspected of being involved in the piracy issue plaguing the kingdom. Do you have anything more concrete on Tanner to justify him being a suspect?"

"I've got nothing else concrete, Your Majesty, only rumors," Oliver said. "The only other one of note is the rumor that he's involved with the raiders attacking non-Collective planets. It's kind of an open secret among traders, actually."

"It doesn't seem like much by itself," Reese said. "But Tanner's been making frequent trips home, supposedly for family-related issues according to the flight logs he's filed. However, the corresponding logs at the Ciebos Transit Center don't always match up. Arrival dates, departures, travel times. They're just slightly off in a few places, and further investigation has yielded proof they've been altered. It could simply be his involvement with raiders, or it could have something to do with the financial discrepancies Commander Hadlock is investigating. I have a feeling that we'll find out soon. Also," he added, "it will come as no surprise that Your Majesty's ring tested positive for sarna. Considering the direct chain of custody involved, I'd say it's safe to say Gregor Tanner tried to assassinate you."

Zach frowned. "Everything about this, and everything I've seen of the man, screams incompetence, immaturity, and impulsivity. He doesn't have the temperament for plotting. His kind of assassination attempt is hiring a disgruntled sniper with a rifle, not dealing with massively dangerous poisons."

Bern nodded. "I agree," he said, only sounding a little grudging. "Tanner's never been a particularly crafty person. I seem to remember that being part of the problem when he was trying to court you, Anders."

Anders shuddered. "Thanks for the reminder, Bern."

"Don't think about it," Zach said. "You're taken now."

A brief pulse of satisfaction and love washed over Zach as Anders smiled for a couple of seconds. "So if Tanner isn't alone in this, that means we're missing another suspect. But who?"

"Imari Amjad in Finance is too good with money to align with someone stupid enough to leave fingerprints in his accounts," Reese said. "Sofia Garza in Interplanetary Affairs, though, has been siding with Tanner in his feuding with Lee. Omar Nadjem in Agriculture, too," he added.

"Does it have to be one of the counselors, though?" asked Oliver.

"I think we can fairly safely rule others out. There's nothing to be gained by assassinating Anders for anyone else. In fact, there's really nothing for anyone other than Tanner. Why is someone else even working with him?" Zach asked.

"Unless he's been deliberately acting like an idiot to make us underestimate him," Anders pointed out with a wry twist of his lips.

"Well, you know him better than I do," Zach said with a small smile. "Is he smart enough for that?"

Anders snorted. "Highly unlikely."

Even Reese laughed at that one. "Then we'll need to broaden our investigation."

"Start with his enemies," Jackson said. "They're the ones who will be happiest to air any dirty laundry."

Bern was already nodding. "Counselor Lee. Lee doesn't like anyone, but especially not Tanner."

"I don't know Lee," Oliver said, "but can we trust anyone? Should we investigate him before taking him into our confidence?"

"Tanner and Lee have been feuding publicly for over a year," Reese explained. "Lee blames the Tanner family for a raider attack on a Lee settlement outside of the Collective, and Tanner takes offense at his kin being called lawless monsters."

"That doesn't necessarily mean he's trustworthy," Oliver said.

"But it does mean it's unlikely he's in this with Tanner," Anders said. "Still, you have a point. We won't mention that we suspect Tanner has an accomplice to anyone, not even Lee."

"Good," Zach said. "It's best we keep all our suspicions within this group until we know what's actually going on."

"It's worked so far." Anders took Zach's hand in his. "I'm thinking I shouldn't be there when you start questioning people. It'll just be a casual conversation without the king sitting there, after all."

"I agree that it shouldn't be Anders," Zach said, "but who will do the questioning? It might be casual without the king there, but it won't really be idle conversation."

"I'll do it," Reese said. "With Commander Hadlock. Admiral, you should be there too. If only to irritate our subjects into talking as much as possible, since you seem to have that talent."

Zach's smile was all teeth. "I don't put up with any bullshit, if that's what you mean." He could feel Anders's amusement through their bond, so he elbowed Anders not quite gently.

Anders completely failed to hide his grin. Still, he nosed at Zach's ear, kissing his neck once. "You've only gotten under people's skin when they've been disrespectful to me," he murmured. "Of course you'd protect your king and bonded."

"It's actually quite entertaining to watch from the outside," Reese said. "I didn't know Lee and Tanner could turn so many shades of red."

"Let's see if I can help them find more shades. I can probably even get them to go purple." Zach nudged Anders again. "Stop laughing, it's really not that funny."

"Darling, I love you," Anders said, "but you have to admit it is a *little* bit funny. You once pissed me off so much I nearly revealed my identity in front of your entire bridge crew." Still, he subsided, sending a warm pulse of love over to Zach. "Mostly because I knew I wasn't completely in the right and it frustrated me to see you knew it too."

Zach sighed and turned to Reese. "When is the best time to talk to the cabinet members?"

Reese pulled out a small media screen. "Lee's in meetings out of the palace all day. But maybe we should check his finances first. Mr. Hadlock has a point about making sure we can trust him."

"Maybe I should check all of them for financial discrepancies before any meetings occur," Oliver said. "We still don't know which, if any of them, could be helping Tanner, and I may as well investigate them all while I'm poking around."

"All right," Zach agreed. He could see Oliver fighting back a smile and shook his head. "Be here at oh eight hundred the day after tomorrow. Hadlock, you can present your findings then."

Once Oliver had nodded in understanding, Anders stood. "I think we should break for now, in that case," he said, looking back at Zach for a moment.

"Yes," Zach agreed. Oliver was staring at him. Zach glanced back to see him raise an eyebrow and subtly jerk his head to the right. He stood. "Hadlock, don't leave."

Oliver stayed where he was as Reese stood and left, followed by Jackson. Bern took up position at the door as he did whenever there was anyone but Zach there with Anders. When the door was shut again, Zach walked over to Oliver as Anders headed to the other side of the room, grabbing a pair of glasses and pouring them drinks. "What's with the staring and the eyebrow?"

"*Admiral*?" Oliver asked. "Is there something you aren't telling me?"

"I haven't had a chance, they literally sprang it on me this morning," Zach said. "Because captain isn't a good enough rank to be prince consort."

Oliver snorted. "I could have told you that." He sobered then. "It doesn't mean you wouldn't have earned it on your own."

Zach waved a hand. "Oh, I know. It's just a lot to take in. I fully intended to be an admiral, but not for about thirty years."

"You're a little old to wait thirty years," Oliver pointed out.

"It's not an issue anymore," Zach said.

"That so?"

"Yes." Zach kept his voice firm. "I'll miss flying, though. It's all I've ever wanted, all I've known for most of my life."

Oliver nodded. "I think Anders is a fair trade, though."

Zach looked over at Anders. "Yeah, most of the time."

Anders snorted and tossed Zach a rude hand gesture before casually leaning against the wall, drink in hand.

Zach winked at Oliver, who laughed. "We don't know these people," Zach said, serious again, "so we have a different perspective, hopefully an unbiased one. I want you to people-watch when we're meeting with the counselors. You might see something the others will miss. Trust no one."

"Even Anders?" Oliver's lips twitched.

"Okay. Anders." Zach rolled his eyes as Anders called out thanks for the endorsement. "Reese is probably okay, but keep an eye on him too."

"Aye, sir," Oliver said with a little bow.

"Get out of here," Zach said. "Go see what you can dig up."

"Aye, aye, Admiral." Oliver patted his arm and walked out of the sitting room, Bern following and leaving Zach and Anders alone.

Anders set his empty glass down on a nearby shelf and offered Zach a small smile. "Forgiven me yet?"

"I don't know." Zach sauntered across the room to where Anders stood. "Should I?"

Anders looked up at Zach through his thick lashes with a hint of a smile. "I think you should," he said, reaching out to lace their fingers together.

Zach squeezed Anders's hand. "I don't know," he said again, lips quirking up at the corners. "You shouldn't laugh at me, at least not in front of Jackson and Bern. They already think I'm an idiot."

"They think you're an asshole," Anders said, moving closer until they were barely a breath apart. "But you'll prove them wrong just by being you. You're a strong, intelligent man. Frustrating as hell, true, but I love all of you. Jackson and Bern will be won over once they accept how happy you make me."

"Except I *am* an asshole," Zach said. "I'll keep being an asshole, can't help it. That doesn't speak well for my ability to win them over." He rubbed his nose against Anders's, sending love through their bond. "And I was *really* an asshole on my ship. Justifiably," Zach said with a raised eyebrow. "But that doesn't matter to your boys. I saved your life, nearly gave mine in the process, and they still don't trust me."

Anders sighed. "I know," he said, wrapping his arms around Zach. "I'm sorry. But *I* trust you. Give them time to come around?"

Zach smiled. "Somehow I don't think I have much choice in the matter," he said. "I can't see them going away anytime soon."

"Or you." Anders kissed the corner of Zach's mouth. "By the way, congratulations, *Admiral.*"

Zach couldn't help himself. He laughed. "That one's going to take some time to sink in," he admitted. "But thank you."

"Will you get a new uniform that's as unreasonably attractive as the one you have now?" Anders asked, kissing down Zach's neck.

"Well, it'll be a new uniform that's as unreasonably uncomfortable," Zach said, tilting his head to give Anders room. "And I expect an admiral who is prince consort will have to wear his dress uniform far more often than a mere captain who spends most of his time in space did." Zach couldn't help the twinge of loss that hit him at the thought of never flying again.

Anders leaned back, a frown puckering his forehead. "What's wrong?"

Zach shook his head. "Nothing's wrong."

"That's not true at all." Anders scowled and backed away. "You'll need to work on your shields if you're going to start lying to me."

"I'm not lying to you, Anders. Calm down. I'm fine." Zach slowly rubbed his hands up and down Anders's back, trying to soothe. "Being an admiral is a big deal, and it's going to be a big change for me. It's a little overwhelming, that's all."

"But I feel . . ." Anders hesitated, then wrapped his hand around the base of his throat. "Loss. Right here. I am very familiar with the various aspects of grief, Zach, and I just . . ." He sighed. "I hate the idea of you hurting, and I can't make it better if you avoid the question every time I ask you."

Zach kissed Anders's forehead. "You can't make it better," he said into Anders's skin. "Leave it alone."

"When has telling me what to do *ever* worked out for you, love?"

"Hope springs eternal." Zach smiled ruefully. He eased back so he could see Anders's face. "I'm fine, I really am."

"I'm sure you will be." Anders smiled, just for a second, then sobered. "We're going to be together a long time, so let's do this right.

Please tell me why you're upset, and I promise not to be angry if it's nothing I can fix."

Zach clenched his teeth and pulled away to pace. "So this bond means I have no privacy whatsoever? Sometimes I just don't want to talk about things, and you need to respect that."

"No, I didn't mean . . ." Anders reached for him. "You keep feeling sad at odd moments, and it makes me feel so helpless. I should be there for you." Zach got a sloppy mess of love and anxiety and worry from Anders.

"I know you're here for me." Zach tried to send calming thoughts to Anders and wasn't sure how successful he was. He didn't want Anders's sorrow or guilt at the loss of his wings and didn't want to hash it out. "But, seriously, *leave it alone.*"

Anders nodded and offered a weak smile. "You're testy when you're grounded, aren't you?"

Zach actually *felt* his burst of anger hit Anders and saw the comprehension light up Anders's eyes. "I said I didn't want to talk about this. Why do you have to keep pushing?"

"It was a *joke*," Anders said. Zach could feel him withdrawing, pulling everything away from the bond. "How was I to know to avoid it if you don't tell me?"

"You could have backed off." Zach shoved his hands through his hair. "It wouldn't have mattered what the problem was, not really. I told you I wanted privacy and told you to stop pushing. But apparently that's not allowed." Choking on his own emotions, he deliberately opened himself to the bond in a way he hadn't since Jackson had taught him how to shield, how to start to control the bond. He let go of all the grief and loss and fear, left everything out in the open for Anders to see. "Happy now?" he snarled.

"Stop, Zach," Anders begged. The tears in Anders's eyes didn't fall; instead he scrambled to the other side of the room, hands fisted in his hair. "It's too much. Please."

Zach shut the inner door he'd learned to build with a slam. "You wanted to know," he said sardonically.

He watched as Anders curled further into himself, still shaking.

"Yes, I'm sad sometimes." Zach sighed, aching at the sight. "Look, I'm losing the life I always wanted. In exchange I'm getting a life I never dreamed I could have, with someone who is becoming absolutely necessary, but it's still difficult. Such an abrupt change would frighten anyone."

Anders wrapped his arms tight around himself, all of his doors shut tight, a disconcerting blank wall in the back of Zach's mind. "If you say so," he said, voice low and weak.

Zach walked carefully toward Anders. "I say so. I don't know what you want to hear. I can't change how I feel, it's not like flipping a switch."

"I know it's not." Anders sighed, still looking anywhere but at Zach's face, still a blank wall of nothing in Zach's mind. "Just like I can't stop worrying you're going to decide to hate me for this whole mess, either. And who could blame you if you did? All I do is push buttons you've told me to leave alone."

"I can't hate you for something that isn't your fault." Zach took a few more steps forward. "And this is not your fault. But sometimes you've got to just let things go. Let me come to this in my own way."

"I'll try, but I've never done anything like this before, so I'm going to fuck up. A lot, most likely." Anders lowered his arms so he was less hugging himself and more holding his own elbows. "But you can't ever project like that again. Bern wasn't exaggerating when he said it could hurt."

"I'm sorry." Remorse stabbed through Zach, hitting sharply in his gut. "I'll never hurt you on purpose, Anders. Never."

"I know." Anders sounded tired. "I did ask for it, to be honest. What with all the demanding you share what you were feeling and all." He sighed again, and this time finally met Zach's eyes. "I was out of line too. I'll try to listen better when you tell me to give you space."

Zach finished crossing the room, stopping in front of Anders. "Fair enough. Keep in mind that I will fuck up a lot more than you will. I already have." He put a tentative hand on Anders's arm, freezing as Anders tensed. Then Anders suddenly relaxed, and Zach pulled him close. "Be patient with me, baby. I'm sorry."

"I was completely out of line. You should be furious with me," Anders muttered against Zach's shoulder. But he looped his arms around Zach's waist, holding lightly.

"Who says I'm not?" Zach hugged Anders.

"But you're—" Anders stopped himself. "Backing off. Got it."

"Teasing, Anders." He sighed. "We both have some work to do to get comfortable with each other again, don't we?"

Anders laughed, a dry sound. "Well, we have been fighting for days. On the upside, the makeup sex should be pretty spectacular."

Zach huffed out a chuckle. "Regular sex is pretty spectacular." He squeezed Anders again and then eased his grip. "We okay? For now?"

"At least until the next time you're an asshole."

"Won't be very long, then." Zach kissed Anders's temple. "Let's go back to bed, baby. I'm suddenly exhausted."

"Yeah. Let's go. We are still recovering, after all." Anders's shields loosened, letting through a trickle of love.

Zach relaxed with Anders's shields. It wasn't perfect, or even all better, but it wasn't completely fucked up, and that was good enough for now.

CHAPTER
TWENTY-THREE

Z ach settled in behind the video screen. He was surprised his mom hadn't contacted him already—even she would have heard about the king's match by now, despite the fact that she didn't pay much attention to the news. This was, unfortunately, more than news. It was something that could potentially impact everyone in the Collective.

And wasn't that just mind-blowing.

Scrubbing a hand over his face, he sat forward and input the coordinates that would ring in his mother's home on Zarine.

She answered almost immediately. "Zachary Benjamin, what have you done?"

"Hello to you too, Mom. I'm great, thanks for asking."

"Hi, sweetheart, you look well." Alexandra O'Connell laughed at him. "Now tell me what the hell you've done. Matched? The *king*?"

"Yeah." Zach sighed, then laughed helplessly. "I don't even know what happened. I didn't know who he was for a long time. He was pretending to be a cousin."

She nodded. "I can understand that. It'd be hard for him to travel freely." She gave him a sly look. "Is he good in bed?"

"*Mom*!" Zach blushed. "I'm not going to tell you about my sex life. Besides, he's the *king*. I'm not telling you about the king's sex life."

"I suppose that would be a little awkward when I meet him, knowing what he likes." She laughed at the flush Zach could feel rising in his face. "When am I going to meet him, by the way?"

Zach shook his head. "Soon, I promise. There's something else. We've bonded."

She gaped at him, then smacked the screen like he knew she wanted to smack him. "You *bonded*? You said you would never bond, not with anyone, and then you went and did it without me?"

"There were extenuating circumstances, Mom," Zach said seriously. He wasn't looking forward to sharing the whole story. "I'll tell you everything when I can."

"Damn straight, you will," she said firmly. "Wait. I know I don't always watch the news, but I would have heard if the king had bonded, just like I heard about the match. Why haven't I heard about the bond?"

"We haven't announced it publicly yet. I wanted to call you first."

Alex snorted. "Well, I suppose that's something. So what you're telling me is that you met your match without knowing it was the king and then you bonded him secretly without the entire universe finding out?"

Zach laughed. "When you put it that way . . ."

"What other way is there, Zachary?" She made a face at him. "You're going to have to have the ceremony again. He's the king. Oh my god, my son-in-law is the king of the Collective."

"Think how I feel! I just wanted to fly, and now I'm married to the king. The prince consort, for crying out loud. Oh, and that's another thing."

"There's more?" she asked warily.

"I got a promotion. Captain isn't good enough to be prince consort; I've got to be an admiral too."

She brightened. "That's wonderful!"

"So you're excited about that but not being the king's mother-in-law?" Zach grinned at her.

"A promotion is *earned*, a reflection of your service and capabilities. The king is the king; that's really weird."

Zach shook his head. "I didn't earn it, Mom. They gave it to me because of Anders."

She made a face at him again. "Oh, I doubt that. They don't just throw those ranks at people for nothing, honey. You did something to earn it, even if you can't tell me. So that's the king's name? Anders?"

"Yeah," he said, "it's short for Anderson. He has a ridiculous number of names. Philip is his official name. King Philip."

"Well, when do I get to meet my son-in-law King Philip?"

"Soon, Mom, I promise." . . . *even if you can't tell me* . . . His mom was sharp, much more than she let on. Still, although she suspected something, she wasn't going to be happy about the mess he was in. "You'll meet him and I'll tell you everything."

She nodded. "Are you happy, baby?"

Zach thought of Anders and smiled. "I really am."

"Then it will all work itself out." Alex raised an eyebrow. "I suppose you can't send Oliver to pick us up."

"He's a little busy, but I'll make other arrangements to make sure you get here. It'll be faster to have you come directly rather than send him out to Zarine, anyway. You'll bring Kenzie?"

Alex sighed. "I'll try. She's doing better than she was the last time you saw her—she really is."

Zach nodded. "Good, that's good. I can't wait to see her. I've missed you both."

"We miss you too, honey." Alex put her hand on the screen, and Zach put his up too, palm to palm from millions of miles away. "Let me know when we're leaving. I can have us packed and ready to go within a couple of hours at most."

"I'll arrange it," he promised, "and send you a message to let you know."

She gave him a stern look. "You had better not have the bonding without me again, Zachary."

Zach laughed. "I'll do what I can. I think we can put it off a few days under the guise of planning a big, obnoxious ceremony. Be ready to leave shortly, I'm going to try to get you on a ship tonight if I can. I want you to be here."

"Then make it happen, baby."

"I will. I love you, Mom."

"I love you too, Zachary. I'll see you soon." The screen winked out, and Zach sighed.

Anders peered around the doorframe, finally emerging from his hiding place in their bedroom. "Will you live to see our first anniversary?"

Zach turned laughed. "Oh, I will. You might not." He winked and stood, stretching before crossing the room to pull Anders into his arms.

"Is that so?" Anders asked.

"I'm teasing," Zach said. "She's going to love you."

Anders relaxed slightly, some of his anxiety easing off their bond. "I hope so." He kissed Zach's neck, the corner of his mouth. "Otherwise it might be terribly awkward for me to ask if you wanted to move her to the palace."

Zach tilted his head to kiss Anders, keeping it slow and chaste. "I would love to have her here, but it would be up to her. Kenzie would have to come too."

"I wouldn't have it any other way." Anders laughed, a stilted sound. "Unless they hate me on sight. That might be a problem."

"Stop it, Anders." Zach kissed him again. "They aren't going to hate you, on sight or otherwise."

"Sorry." Anders shook his head. "I only . . . I'm sure they want the best for you. I just want them to see me as that, king or no."

Zach nodded. "You're my bonded, Anders, my one true match. How could you be anything but the best for me?"

A wave of love came across the bond, and Anders rubbed their noses together, smiling. "Thank you."

"Anytime. Now. I need to arrange transport for Mom and Kenzie to get them here ASAP, and there's a rather important announcement to make." Zach squeezed his hand. "We need to get busy."

Anders chuckled. "If I'd known going into the family business would mean making so many speeches, I think I'd have joined the Navy instead."

Zach cocked an eyebrow. "Apparently the Navy entails speeches as well, or at least an admiralty does." He squeezed Anders's hand again and then let go. "You'll do fine. And I'll stand behind you the whole time." He winked.

"Of course you will," Anders said. He straightened his gray coat and tugged on his cuffs, the dark purple of his shirt shining royally. "I know how much you like the view."

"I'll have to be good, though. People would notice if I spent the entire time staring at your ass." Zach wandered back over to the computer and sat down, starting the search for transpo that could bring two to Drion.

There was a perfunctory knock at the door, and then Jackson and Bern entered. "The media room will be ready soon, Majesties," Jackson said. "We've limited the number of staff for security reasons, so the broadcasts will be mostly automated."

"Thank you." Anders paused, then huffed a laugh. "I should probably wear my ring and crown. Do try not to kill each other while I'm gone."

There was an awkward moment of silence as Anders left the room, broken when Jackson sighed irritably.

"Thank you, Zach," Bern said at last. "My bonded is a stubborn jerk, but we both wanted to thank you."

"For what?" Zach asked absently. Aha! He found a ship leaving that afternoon. He quickly booked passage.

"For saving Anders's life," Jackson said slowly, as though he were forcing the words out between his teeth. "Anders told us . . . We know you didn't want to bond with him, and you did anyway."

Zach turned his chair around and raised an eyebrow. "He saved mine as well. And if I hadn't wanted to bond with him, I wouldn't have done so."

Jackson rolled his eyes and turned at Bern as though to say *See?* Bern shook his head and tried again. "Fine. Look, you're not going anywhere and neither are we. If we agree to stop bringing up the fact you broke our friend's heart over and over before getting your shit together, can you agree to dial back the asshole attitude to a five or so?"

"Wow, what a charming and diplomatic offer of truce." Zach bared his teeth in what might, loosely, be called a grin. "This is who I am. Deal with it or stay out of my way."

"Enough, all of you." Anders strode into the room, glowering. With the thin gold crown resting on his dark curls and the costume version of his signet ring glittering on his hand, he looked every inch the irritated monarch. "I don't expect you guys to hug this out, but I do expect you to stop actively sniping at each other. I will *not* choose between my only friends and my bonded, and you will not put me in the middle again. Is that clear?"

Zach stood, folding his arms across his body as he leaned back against the computer console. "I would never ask you to choose, nor put you in the middle. That wasn't my intent. But that goes both ways, Anders."

"Every time you three antagonize each other, I'm in the middle," Anders said, gentle for a moment. He turned to Jackson and Bern. "I appreciate you two trying to apologize, but perhaps you might want to save it until you actually mean it. You'll only succeed in pissing yourselves off and making the whole situation worse, and all this when we've got a much more serious situation on our hands than an assortment of bruised egos and overgrown mother hens."

Bern flushed. "But Anders—"

"I swear to the Great God Usmos," Anders said, "if *anyone* says anything remotely resembling 'He started it,' I will lose all semblance of noble behavior. Is that clear?"

Bern and Jackson both nodded, mute, and left the suite, waiting just outside the open door.

"Yes, dear," Zach said dryly. "I just need to let Mom know when she and Kenzie are leaving, then I'm ready to go." He turned back to the computer and typed quickly.

"Asshole," Anders muttered, but sent a warm pulse of affection tinted with amusement across the bond.

Zach sent the message and then crossed the room to Anders. "You love my asshole," he whispered in Anders's ear, then he patted Anders's ass. "Let's go get this over with."

Anders snorted. "One more thing," he said, pulling a cloth pouch out of his pocket and offered it to Zach. "I can't give you a crown yet, not until everything is official in the eyes of our people. So, until then, this will have to do."

Zach opened the pouch and slid the contents out into his palm. It was Anders's pendant, the one Anders had shown him on the flight to Drion. The one that was his mother's. He handed the pouch back to Anders and lifted the pendant over his neck. "I'll take care with it," he said seriously, "until I can return it after the broadcast."

"You keep it," Anders said. He placed his hand over the pendant, pressing the metal and stone against Zach's chest. "You're part of the House of Anderson now."

"But it was your mother's, Anders." Zach covered Anders's hand with his.

"And now it's yours." Anders kissed the back of Zach's hand, a lingering caress of lips. "I know you'll take good care of it."

"I will." Zach leaned in to kiss Anders lightly. "Let's go tell everyone."

The media room was set up to look like what most people expected the king's study to look like. Large media screens that mostly only displayed the royal crest were on one side of the room, and on the other an entire wall of shelves made up as though it held dozens of paper books. A large, ornate desk sat in the middle of the room, a ridiculously wasteful use of wood that was the only thing between Anders and dozens of automated cameras sending his image to streams all across the Collective.

Still, it was easier than the press conference he'd held his first day back on Drion. Maybe it was because he didn't have the weight of so many strange eyes, expecting the world *from* him. Maybe it was because his power was solidifying, weakening whatever plots had been in place before his coronation. Or maybe it was just that now he had Zach willingly at his side, hand on his shoulder as Anders took his seat behind the desk.

Either way, Anders was exponentially more relaxed as the small red light on the far wall flipped to green, letting him know the broadcasts were live.

"People of the Drion Collective," Anders said, using the same address his father always had. "The past few weeks have been a trying time for us all, and I want to begin by telling you how blessed I am to have each and every one of you as a citizen of the Collective. Despite tragedy and great change, you have all worked tirelessly to keep Drion strong. Without you, I would be nothing. Thank you.

"I come to you today with happy news. Two weeks ago, on the day after I was privileged to be made your leader, I bonded with my one true match. It was a small, private ceremony, witnessed by those closest to us and blessed by a Priest of the Many. I had fallen ill with the same sickness that took my father, and was advised that bonding was the best way to save my health and preserve stability for the kingdom."

He glanced over his shoulder at Zach, smiling softly for a moment. "Fortunately, my match is a strong one, one of love, and Admiral O'Connell and I are pleased to tell you all of my clean bill of health. We also would like to announce that there will be a traditional ceremony broadcasted publicly in the near future, so that you might share in our joy. Again, I want to assure you that I am in perfect health now, and that I look forward to leading all of you for many years to come. Thank you all for watching, and may the blessings of the Many fill your lives and days."

Anders smiled and nodded his head once to signal the end of the broadcast. As soon as the light went back to red, he slumped back in his chair. "That went well, but I've decided that I really hate giving speeches," he muttered. "Always left wondering if I sounded as much like an asshole as I felt."

Zach laughed. "I'm afraid you'll probably have to get used to it."

"No need to be so smug about it. I could pass a law," Anders said. "Make the prince consort the Royal Voice or something."

"Nope." Zach shook his head. "I'm the Royal Support System." He put his hands on Anders's shoulders and squeezed. "If it's any consolation, you appeared very confident and in control."

"Thank you, darling." Anders heaved a sigh and stood, pulling Zach into a brief hug. They might have been alone, with Jackson, Bern, and Grant standing guard just outside the door, but it was them and a wall of recording devices; better to be safe than a public spectacle. "Let's go."

Once they were out in the hall, Anders pulled Zach down for a lingering kiss. "I love you," he breathed against Zach's lips.

Zach kissed him again, love flowing across their bond. "I know," he said, rubbing his nose against Anders's.

Anders hummed happily, leaning into Zach for a moment. He was remarkably relaxed for a man who had just told the entire Collective, complete with a number of rabid traditionalists, that he'd eloped with a sailor. He laughed softly, forehead pressed against Zach's shoulder. "At least now Daniel knows why I missed his bonding."

"Oh? Who's Daniel?"

"We saw each other for a while," Anders said. The memory stung much less now, and he didn't fool himself as to why. "He broke things off with me the day Father died and asked me to come to his bonding."

Zach stiffened slightly, but after a moment he relaxed and hugged Anders. "Well. It's a bit much that he'd ask you to go to his bonding after that."

"My thought exactly." Anders kissed Zach's neck once and sighed. "It was just as well. Daniel was possibly the most uninspired fuck in the Collective. Not to mention tremendously dense when it came to people."

"Clearly," Zach said. "I do have a question, though. Why fuck him if he was so uninspired?"

"Boredom, I suppose," Anders said with a shrug. "Besides, it's not as though I wanted to be attached to anyone when I wasn't even allowed to tell them my name." He sent a wave of love with a hint of the lust he'd felt the first time he'd touched Zach. "As always, you were the one to break the rules."

"That's me," Zach said. "The rebel." He took Anders's hand and tugged lightly, leading him down the hall, their guards trailing at a respectable distance. After they'd ambled along for a minute, Zach asked, "How'd you meet him?"

"Over a pile of reference materials in the campus library rare books section," Anders said. "I was working on my thesis paper, and he was trying to find new ways to fail his first-year students. In retrospect, we should have stayed friends rather than adding sex to the mix, but sometimes a convenient arrangement is simply too tempting."

Zach shook his head. "He sounds like a jackass. One thing you'll never have to worry about with me: I'm rarely convenient." He nudged Anders with his hip.

"True." Anders squeezed Zach's hand. "And certainly never boring." He pulled them to a stop. "You do know you were never like him in my mind, right? Maybe it was the match, maybe it was that you're so much *more* than he could ever hope to be, but from the first time we kissed, I knew there was something special about you."

"Oh, I know I wasn't—for one, you'll never find me in a rare books section of a library." Zach looped his arm around Anders's shoulders, pulling Anders's arm across his own body in the process. He pressed a kiss to Anders's temple. "You were special too," he murmured into Anders's skin. "I don't usually fuck passengers, and definitely not the first time I meet them."

"I should hope not." Anders glanced up the hall to be sure they were alone except for their guards, then wrapped his arms around Zach, holding him close. "For a while there," he whispered, "I thought I was just another fuck for you and that you'd leave me when this was all over. I like being special to you instead."

Zach hugged him. "I wanted you to be just another fuck," he said honestly. "It would have been easier if you had been, for both of us. I know I'm not the best choice for consort, and your bodyguards hate me."

"Maybe," Anders allowed. "But I love you. I think I'd love you even without the match. Everything else will sort itself out."

"It'll have to, won't it?" Zach rubbed a hand down Anders's back. "You're kind of stuck with me now." He stepped back enough to smile at Anders. "So what's on the schedule next?"

Anders sighed. "We have to go to the Temple of the Many and talk to a priest about how we're going to do our second bonding ceremony. Not to mention we have to see about getting you properly crowned as prince consort. Until we choose a surrogate, you're going to be my heir, after all."

Zach made a face. "That all sounds fun."

Laughing, Anders pulled away and grabbed Zach's hand, kissing his knuckles. "Tomorrow you can go back to being a menacing naval officer, I promise."

"Hey," Zach protested mildly, "I was never menacing to anyone who didn't deserve it."

"I'm not criticizing, darling," Anders said, guiding them to the underground shuttle bays where their ride waited. "I actually find you even hotter than usual when you're being menacing. It's a struggle to keep my hands to myself, you know."

Zach followed Anders to their shuttle, waiting for him to enter before following. "I notice it's a struggle you don't win very often," he teased.

Anders activated the privacy screen on the shuttle windows, blocking them away from the whole world, driver and all three of their guards included. Then he climbed into Zach's lap, straddling his thighs. "Is that a complaint?" he whispered against Zach's lips.

"Never," Zach promised. He cupped Anders's ass with both hands and squeezed. "You know we can't do this here, right? I mean, there isn't enough time to do anything before we get to the temple."

"I know," Anders said. He kissed Zach lightly. "Still, we can always take the long way back to the palace."

Zach kissed him back. "Why fuck in the shuttle when we've got a huge bed at the palace?"

"True." Anders nibbled on Zach's lower lip. "But then I've never fucked in a shuttle before. I'd imagine it's a lot of fun."

"It's not as fun as it sounds," Zach admitted, "but it's not without its charms."

Anders frowned, jealous and pouting more than a little. "I suppose I'll have to take your experienced word for it, then."

"Not if you don't want to." Zach shrugged, then leered. "I'm happy to initiate you on the way back."

"So generous." Anders laughed and got out of Zach's lap before he could wrinkle their clothes too badly. "We're almost there already."

Almost as soon as Anders settled back in his seat, the shuttle began to slow. "It's still kind of weird to not be at the helm myself," Zach mused. "I guess it's something I'll have to get used to now."

An awkward silence fell, lasting until they pulled up in front of the temple. Anders straightened his clothes and smoothed his hair with quick, practiced movements. Then he reached out and fixed Zach's collar, even though it was perfect, smoothing his fingers over the new golden pip telling Zach's new rank. "Ready, darling?"

"As I'll ever be." Zach stood and stretched, swaying slightly as the shuttle came to a stop. He took Anders's hand and tugged him up out of his seat. "Let's go see what the priest says. Do you think he'll be upset that we didn't call him in to do our bonding?"

"I'm certain of it," Anders said as they stepped out of the shuttle. "But being the one to do it again in front of the Collective should ease most of his ruffled feathers. Just don't apologize. If he thinks we feel guilty, we're sure to hear all about how we're damned and doomed if we don't come to services for the rest of time. You should have heard the lecture I got when I was ten and tried to beg off acolyte duty."

"I missed that particular pleasure myself," Zach said with a grin as they walked away from the shuttle toward the temple, their guards in close formation around them. "And don't worry. I don't feel guilty and I don't apologize unless it's truly warranted."

Anders laughed as they headed up the steps. "True," he said. "I don't think I've ever heard you apologize to anyone other than me, and even then—"

Something blasted behind them, throwing all of them forward like rag dolls. Anders barely managed to catch himself in time to save himself another concussion, as Zach covered him with his own body. Something was on fire, close enough Anders was sure they'd cook themselves. He tried to move, to look around, but Zach held him firm.

"Don't move," Zach shouted, voice muffled by the ringing in Anders's ears. "Goddamn it, the fucking shuttle just blew." He curled more tightly around Anders as a piece of the shuttle landed on the steps behind them. The crash of metal abruptly stopped, and Zach slowly released Anders, hands skimming over his body and up to cup his head, fingers testing his scalp for lumps. "Are you okay? How's your head, did you hit it again?"

"I'm fine. A few bumps is all, I swear." Anders twisted, taking his turn to check Zach out. "What about you? Are you all right?"

"I'm pissed as all fuck," Zach said, anger clear in his voice. "We were almost incinerated. We've got to do something about Tanner soon, regardless of what Oliver is able to find."

Security guards came running from around and in the temple, their captain shouting orders. Jackson, Bern, and Grant moved in to help Zach and Anders to their feet, barking questions as they checked both of them over.

"We're *fine*," Anders shouted over them. "Zach protected me from the blast."

That set Grant off, looking his charge over again, but Bern relaxed marginally, and nodded to Zach. "Good. Is everyone accounted for?"

Zach shook his head. "The pilot was still inside."

Anders closed his eyes at Zach's words. "I am done with innocent people paying the cost of this," he said, jaw clenched and hands balled tight.

Bern frowned. "This makes no sense. It's too public, too obvious."

"And now word will spread," Grant said. "No one will believe this was an accident."

"No," Zach agreed. "Even if we wanted to present it as some kind of malfunction, there are too many here as witness to keep it quiet. Tanner is getting desperate."

Anders couldn't tear his eyes away from the blaze. He imagined he could see the charred remains of the pilot, although the man had likely been blown to pieces in the explosion.

"There hasn't been an execution for treason since my grandfather's time," he said, deathly calm, "but this cannot go unpunished. It will not."

CHAPTER
TWENTY-FOUR

When they got back to the palace, Anders and Zach were immediately bundled off to the security wing. "We have to clear the building for explosives," Jackson had said in a no-nonsense voice. Not that Anders would have dared to argue. Not when Anders's guards and Zach were finally in agreement.

"This is going to take hours," Anders said, if only to say something. Jackson wouldn't even let them out of the hall until every room in the sector had been cleared. He took Zach's hand. "I'm glad you're safe."

Zach tightened his grip on Anders's hand. "You could have been killed," he said hoarsely. "You could have *died.*"

Just then, Jackson came out of the office at the far end of the hall, nodding to Bern and Grant as they flanked Anders and Zach. "Your Majesties can wait in here," Grant said, gesturing to a nearby surveillance office. "We'll be out here while Jackson oversees the rest of the sweep of the palace."

Zach pulled Anders into the office, shut the door behind them, and slammed Anders against it. He tangled his fingers through Anders's hair and cupped his head, tugging him into a brutal kiss.

"Yes," Anders panted. The adrenaline roared through his body, fingers and toes tingling, and he hauled Zach closer, sliding his hands under Zach's jacket. "I *need* you so fucking much."

"I need to fuck you," Zach growled. "I need to be inside you, feel you hot and tight around me, *now.*"

Beyond actual words, Anders groaned, opening up eagerly for Zach, sucking on Zach's tongue like he wanted his cock. Grabbing fistfuls of Zach's shirt, Anders pulled it up until he could touch skin, his fingers digging into the sinewy muscles of Zach's back even as he straddled one of Zach's thighs and rocked against him.

Zach grabbed Anders's hips and hauled him roughly into the solid strength of his thigh. "You gonna come for me, baby? How hard are you?" He used his free hand to cup Anders's crotch. "Can feel you getting hard for me."

"Yes," Anders panted, thrusting desperately into the heat of Zach's hand. "*Fuck.* I always want you, Zach. Please, make me come. Make me come and I'll suck your dick until you see gods, I swear."

"Oh, I will," Zach growled. He began to rhythmically squeeze Anders's cock through his clothes, sucking at the juncture of neck and shoulder with the same steady pull.

"Can't believe I almost lost you, *fuck*," Anders grunted. Their combined desperation only shoved him higher, mind buzzing with the need for more. "Not . . . not in my pants, love. Please."

"Why not?" Zach nosed up the cord of Anders's throat, bit his earlobe.

Why not, indeed. Anders pressed his head back against the door, considered just giving in and coming like Zach wanted. "Because," he gasped. "Because then everyone we see will know you made me come in my pants. *Oh god*, Zach!"

Apparently, Zach liked that idea, because a possessive wave of desire washed over the both of them, nearly breaking Anders's resolve. Instead, Anders fumbled with his pants, jerking them open and pushing them to the side. "Like this." He urged Zach's hand under his silk shorts.

Zach curled his fingers around Anders's cock and started to tug and stroke the hard flesh. "So where do you plan on coming, baby? Since you don't want to come in your pants."

Anders shuddered, forehead dropping to Zach's shoulder. "I *want*," he ground out, "to come on your cock, screaming your name."

"Then we shouldn't be doing this in here," Zach said, biting Anders's earlobe again. Suddenly he pulled away and spun Anders around to face the door. "You can't scream now, or our guards will come running. You don't want them to see us, do you?"

"You promised to fuck me." Anders barely recognized his own voice. "*Do it.*"

"Then suck my fingers, get 'em nice and sloppy wet. I don't have any lube."

"*Fuck yes,*" Anders groaned, and opened his mouth wide to suck Zach's fingers. He shoved his pants and shorts down, tangling them over his boots. He was hobbled, trapped between the cold door and Zach's hot, strong body.

Zach made him suck on his fingers for several long moments before freeing them from Anders's mouth. He trailed them over the very base of Anders's spine, then using his free hand, Zach spread Anders's cheeks and slid one finger steadily inside him.

"Zach—" Anders barely managed to keep from shouting. He bit his knuckles and pushed back, wanting more, wanting everything Zach could give him. "You're going to have to gag me when you fuck me," he warned. "You feel so fucking good."

"You'll have to be quiet." Zach pushed a second finger inside, slowly fucking them in and out of Anders's body. "I don't have anything to gag you with. Someday I'll gag you," he promised. "Tie you up too, if you want."

"Yeah," Anders said, already completely Zach's. "I want. I want it all." He shrugged out of his jacket and tossed it over a nearby chair. "Give me another, Zach. You know I'm gonna need it. Fill me up so good."

Zach immediately worked a third finger into Anders, spreading him open and loose, fingers moving faster. "You ready for me, baby?"

"Yes," Anders groaned, rocking back into Zach's hand. "Let me suck you, get you wet for me. Then you can fuck me like I need."

"You think you can finally be quiet if my dick is halfway down your throat?" Zach's fingers pressed hard and sudden against Anders's prostate.

Anders cried out, barely muffling the sound with his forearm. There was no way Grant and Bern hadn't heard that, but Anders didn't care at all. Instead, his cock jumped, already eager and leaking—he wasn't going to last much longer. "I make no promises," he rasped, pushing all the love, lust, and even some of his lingering fear across their bond.

Zach roughly pulled his fingers free and grabbed Anders's arm, spinning him around and forcing him to his knees in one smooth motion. He cupped Anders's cheek, tilting his face up, giving him a dark, hungry look. "Suck me."

"Anytime," Anders said, yanking Zach's pants open and down just enough to expose his cock and balls. "Anyplace." He nuzzled Zach for a few seconds, kissing his balls a couple of times, and then opened wide, sucking Zach all the way down to the root without pause.

With a low growl in the back of his throat, Zach tangled his fingers in Anders's hair, tightening his grip to guide Anders's movements. He kept the motion slow and steady, thrusting into Anders's mouth. Anders gazed up at him through his lashes, slurping wetly every time he slid up, and sucking hard every time Zach pushed him back down.

Zach fucked Anders's face for several long minutes, letting Anders get him wet, dripping with pre-come and saliva. He sucked in a breath before abruptly pulling Anders off. Then, grabbing Anders's arm, Zach tugged him up and around, shoving him against the door again. "Gonna fuck you," he muttered into Anders's ear. "Split you wide open on my cock."

"Do it," Anders rasped back, his voice wrecked. His pants kept him from spreading his legs, though, and Anders growled in frustration. "The desk," he said. "Over the desk."

"Move and strip." Zach helped Anders lose the boots and pants as they maneuvered across the short distance to the nearest desk. When they got to it, Zach shoved Anders down across the surface and kicked his feet apart. The head of his cock teased at Anders's hole, pushing slightly in, easing back. "Love to watch you take me."

"Yeah?" Anders gasped, pushed up onto his toes, trying to take more of Zach. "Tell me."

Zach's hands fell heavy on Anders's hips, pinning him down. "You stretch so wide to let me in. Your rim thins to almost nothing, it stretches so far." His thumbs dug into Anders's crack, tugging his cheeks apart, as Zach worked himself in a little farther.

Anders whined, a high and needy sound that might have embarrassed him if he hadn't been able to feel how absolutely crazy this was making Zach. Instead, he jammed his fist into his mouth and bit down on his knuckles. Zach felt bigger than usual, the pull and drag of not enough lubrication so fucking perfect Anders didn't know if he'd be able to last.

"Shhh," Zach murmured absently. He started thrusting deeper, a long slow push in, and even slower tug back out. He used his grip on Anders's hips to tilt them up and back, then began to shove into Anders's ass in short, hard thrusts, finally working himself all the way in before stopping again. "So fucking tight," he growled.

"Oh *fuck*," Anders moaned, far louder than he should have. He scrambled with his hands, trying to find some leverage, but the desk was too wide, too slippery. He could only lie there, pinned by Zach's hands, his hips, his *cock*. "It's like you're, fuck, like you're splitting me in half. So fucking good, Zach. Give me more."

Zach wrapped an arm around Anders's waist and pulled him back, curling his other hand around Anders's dick and starting to stroke. "I don't think so," Zach said, "I think I want you to come like this, wanna feel you come apart just having me inside you."

"Oh god," Anders moaned, clenching down fiercely on the hard length inside him. It wasn't going to take much. "You're going to fucking kill me, and I'll only beg you for more."

"Don't say that too loudly," Zach said with a low laugh. "I'm sure Grant and Bern can hear you." He jacked Anders steadily, swiping his thumb over the crown and digging into the weeping slit. "Come on, baby. Bear down on me, use me."

The thought of people listening to him getting fucked, of them hearing how good Zach was giving it to him, sent lightning through Anders's body, and he could only groan through it as he held on a little longer. He stood up from the table and leaned back into Zach, the new angle forcing Zach that much deeper into his ass. "So close."

When Anders stood, Zach shifted his grip, arm coming up across Anders's chest, hand curling over Anders's shoulder. His mouth brushed the juncture of Anders's neck and shoulder again, and his hand started jacking Anders faster, squeezing on each upstroke. "Let go, Anders," Zach ordered against Anders's warm skin. "Come."

"Yeah," Anders managed, his whole body lighting up as soon as Zach latched on to his neck. "Oh, fuck, Zach!" And then he was coming so hard he could see stars. Zach's hand was brutally perfect, wringing every last drop out of him while Anders squeezed down on the hard length splitting him in two. Through sheer force of will, he managed to only leak a little of his orgasm across the bond. "Fuck me, Zach. *Please*."

"Turn around and lay down on the desk." Zach pulled out, wiping his handful of Anders's spunk over his own dick as Anders scrambled up on the desk. He hauled Anders to the edge of the desk and guided himself back into Anders's open body. "Think I can last until you come again?"

"I'm going to need more than a few minutes for that," Anders said, not caring how stupid his grin was. He groaned as Zach bottomed out. "But either way, I'm going to enjoy the hell out of it."

Zach grinned fiercely. "You have such little faith in my stamina," he said, but he set a hard, fast pace, one that almost certainly meant Zach wouldn't last much longer. He hooked Anders's legs over his arms and bent forward, forcing Anders almost in half.

Anders ran his hands over Zach's face, his shoulders, his chest. "Feels so good," he moaned, and stretched out as much as he could, pressing his hands against a media screen, shoving it at the wall before using the leverage to push back, to bear down on Zach once more. "Come for me, love. Want to feel you coming in me, leaking out of me."

"God, you're so tight," Zach groaned, hips pumping harder and harder, almost brutally fast, then pausing to circle and grind before thrusting again. He began losing rhythm quickly, hips stuttering as he lost control. "All mine," he growled, sending a tangled wave of love and lust and possession through their bond as he came, hips jerking helplessly as he filled Anders up.

Anders sighed, relaxed for the first time all day, blissfully grateful for how pleasantly empty his mind was. "I love you too," he whispered, sitting up to pull Zach in for a kiss.

Zach kissed him back slowly, easing his weight off Anders. "So," he finally said, nose rubbing along Anders's, "we have a problem."

"Hmm?" Anders draped his arms over Zach's shoulders. "Do we?"

"We do," Zach said solemnly. Bone-melting relief followed by a spark of amusement danced across their bond. "You wouldn't let me make you come in your pants because you didn't want people to see the mess. Now we have a different sort of mess, literally on my hands. And leaking out your ass."

Anders kissed Zach lazily. "That *is* a problem." He grabbed one of Zach's hands, salty-smelling from Anders's come. "I suppose we'll have to get creative, won't we?"

Zach grinned. "Do you think Bern would bring us a wet cloth if we asked nicely?"

"Oh, absolutely," Anders said, dissolving into uncontrollable giggles. Bern was the bigger prude of his two guards, and had never had any patience for Anders's sex life even *before* it got so damn good.

"Or I might have a better idea," Zach said. "Well. Maybe not *better*, necessarily, but less inconvenient for Bern." He began to kiss a path down Anders's neck.

Anders hummed happily. "Any idea that starts with your mouth on my body is a good one."

Zach kept slowly kissing down Anders's body, pulling out of Anders as he bent, and mouthing up Anders's soft cock. He mouthed at the head a little, and sucked small kisses back down the shaft. Kneeling, hands pressing Anders's legs up and out, Zach tongued at the spunk leaking out of Anders's hole.

"Fuck," Anders said, voice weak. "That is the best idea I've heard all day." He leaned back on his elbows, watching Zach through heavy eyes. "Feels good."

"You're a little puffy," Zach said, running a fingertip around the swollen rim before tracing the same circle with his tongue. He lapped at Anders's rim a few times, rubbing the flat of his tongue over the hot skin, and then finally eased his tongue fully inside.

Anders's cock gave a valiant effort, twitching as Zach ate him out, but he was too spent. All he could manage was to lie there as his nerves sent wave after wave of pleasure up his spine. "What a way to go," he moaned.

"Don't ever die on me," he murmured. He started to alternate thrusts inside with sucking kisses along the rim. Sliding one hand down, Zach pressed a thumb into Anders alongside his tongue.

"I won't if you won't," Anders breathed. He hissed when Zach tugged at his rim. "Easy. I'm still all lit up."

"You love it," Zach said, but he slid his thumb free and cupped Anders's hips, lifting him up into the thrust of his tongue. He kept working at Anders's hole, licking and sucking and thrusting, until Anders was writhing against him, riding his face.

"Zach," Anders moaned softly. Against all odds, Anders's cock firmed slowly, more of a question than a need. "God, darling, if you're going to fuck me again, I insist on lube. And a bed. And a chance to take my time."

Zach huffed a soft laugh and pulled away, licking a final stripe up the length of Anders's cock. "I can live with that."

"So long as you stay living for a good long while," Anders said quietly, then shook himself. "Now help me get dressed so I can go out there and be respectable."

"How embarrassed do you think Grant and Bern are?" Zach asked, grasping Anders's hand and pulling him to his feet.

"On a scale of one to mortally so and never forgiving me?" Anders took a moment to get his balance. God, but he loved it when Zach got rough. "Probably about a seven. Bern's always hated being so much as in the same building whenever I have sex, and that was *before* I met you and your uncanny ability to make me lose my mind."

Zach helped Anders into his pants, rubbing a hand down the back of one calf before standing and taking Anders into his arms. He brushed a light kiss over Anders's lips. "You ready?"

"I am not," Anders said firmly, "going out there in just my socks to deal with treasonous pirates and mad bombers."

He pulled out of Zach's arms and reached for his jacket. Then he bent and tugged on his boots swiftly, straightening his clothes as best as possible as he stood. A quick finger-combing tamed the absolute worst of his hair, but judging from the fucked-out expression on Zach's face, there was no way everyone wouldn't know precisely what they'd been up to.

"We're going to need a shower before anything else," he said ruefully. Still, he refused to regret what they'd done.

Someone knocked on the door, two sharp raps. "If Your Majesties are ready," Grant's voice crackled over the intercom. "Jackson has cleared the residential wing and we're ready to take you back to your suite."

"Never done a walk of shame quite like this before." Zach raised an eyebrow. "Shall we?"

Anders adjusted Zach's shirt. "Me neither," he confessed, and slipped his hand into Zach's as they headed for the door.

CHAPTER
TWENTY-FIVE

All things considered, Anders decided to join Zach's meeting with Oliver and Reese in the morning. It wasn't as though no one knew he was under threat at this point. Still, he insisted they gather in a small meeting room that no king had likely entered in fifty years or more. It was a simple room with a single round table big enough for half a dozen at most, all the chairs the same size with the same displays on their in-table media screens.

It was all terribly symbolic.

"Well," said Oliver, "I found a few things. Your agriculture counselor is making some random deposits into his accounts that don't match up with any of his officially reported income. He's dumb enough to use his regular accounts instead of using off-planet accounts the way Pretorius is. She's taking in regular payments, in much larger amounts than Nadjem's random ones."

Anders frowned. "Unscheduled and unrelated deposits sound like bribery, though what for I don't know." He drummed his fingers on the tabletop. "Reese?"

"Nadjem receives crop reports, Majesty," Reese offered. "Early access to that could be worth a lot to the right people, but it's not the sort of thing worth regicide." He turned to Oliver. "Pretorius has off-planet accounts?"

"Healthy ones too," Oliver said. "At least from what I was able to find quickly. I found three; there may be more. And then there's Tanner, of course. He has his regular accounts, which also don't mesh with reported income, and at least one off-planet account."

"So they're dirty," Reese said, clearly pleased.

"But we don't know how," Anders cautioned. "The only concrete evidence we have against Tanner so far is that he gave me my father's ring that *someone* poisoned. And how is Pretorius connected to all of this?"

Oliver shrugged. "She may not be. I'm working on following her deposits back to their origin to see if I can find out where they're coming from. We might be looking at extortion, rather than bribes, or I suppose it's possible it's family money she doesn't want taxed. Still working on it."

"I want to be frustrated by the slow pace, but you've actually uncovered a lot in only a day, Oliver. Thank you." Anders nodded once. "What about the rest of the cabinet? Anything interesting there?"

Before Oliver could answer, the door burst open and Imari Amjad stormed in. "What in the three hells do you think you're doing, investigating me?" she demanded, looming over Oliver.

He leaned back in his chair and eyed the finance counselor coolly. "There is a royal directive on record to investigate anyone who might be involved in our piracy problem." He smiled faintly. "Nothing personal."

"Just because your former captain is bonded to my king does not mean that his antisocial attitude gives you free rein to—"

Anders stood abruptly. "Counselor Amjad," he snapped. "Please close the door and join us."

She shut her mouth with an abrupt *click*. "Your Majesty," she said, bowing her head. She did as Anders ordered, but sat as far away from Oliver as she could manage. Unfortunately, that put her next to Zach, a fact that gave Anders no small amount of spiteful joy. "My apologies, Your Majesties," she said. "But I still feel I am owed an explanation as to why a naval commander has been trampling through my financial records with all the grace of a water mammal on land."

"Commander Hadlock already explained, Counselor," Zach said neutrally. "And I personally know that he has a light touch with a computer, which you must as well, as you're the only one who picked up on it."

Amjad sniffed. "Not so light I couldn't trace him back to this room the moment he logged on."

"Yes, I've heard how good you are with computers," Anders said, manfully resisting the urge to roll his eyes.

"I'm also smart enough not to risk my freedom, my family's fortune, or my social standing for something as petty as money, Majesty," Amjad said, spine ramrod straight. "So investigating me was a waste of time."

Anders turned to Oliver. "Commander Hadlock, would you agree?"

"I suppose," Oliver said, "except for two points. One, we needed to eliminate her as a potential threat, and two, if she's clean, an investigation shouldn't be an issue."

Reese nodded in silent agreement.

"That you would even consider me suspect is offensive," Amjad insisted. "Do you honestly mean to tell me you suspect a conspiracy because of one explosion that only *might* have been a bomb?"

Zach and Oliver looked at each other and then at Anders. "It's not just the explosion, although that adds weight to the theory," Zach said, facing her. "And it definitely was a bomb, although we aren't sure if it was meant as a scare or if, as is more likely, all things considered, the bomb simply didn't explode at the right time."

"If you'll recall," Anders said, "the *Pallas* was attacked en route shortly after the cabinet was notified I was aboard. Not to mention the assassination attempt against the prince consort the same day we arrived on Drion." He pushed down the wave of rage. "There is a definite pattern of murderous behavior here."

"Not to mention the poison," Reese added.

Amjad blinked. "Poison?"

"Come now," Anders said. "You didn't honestly believe that story about a rare genetic illness, did you?"

The counselor was quiet for a long minute, then nodded decisively. "My apologies, Majesties. Commander Hadlock. You were obviously doing what needed to be done. I assume my name has been cleared from your list of potential suspects?"

Oliver nodded. "Yes, Counselor. Your finances are," he smiled faintly, "as meticulous as one would expect from the finance counselor. I found no indications of anything that wasn't above board."

That seemed to mollify her somewhat. "In that case," she said, pulling her chair closer, "I offer my assistance. Your father was a good man, Your Majesty, and his legacy deserves better than this nest of vipers. I expect my proven innocence is enough for you to trust me?"

Looking at Anders and then Zach, Oliver shrugged. "Bianca Pretorius has suspicious deposits into off-planet accounts. We need to follow that money and discover where it's coming from. Tanner also has at least one off-planet account, and deposits into his regular accounts that don't match up with his reported income."

"Gregor Tanner has all the foresight of a piece of below-average garden statuary," Amjad said with a wave of her hand. "There won't be much challenge there. Bianca has been terribly smug lately, however. Give me her records, I'll find out what she is up to."

"We didn't think Tanner was doing this on his own," Zach said. "We need to know if she's the one pulling his strings or if there's another person behind him."

Amjad sighed. "In that case, you'd better give me both of them. And order us a lunch."

Zach had thought Oliver was good with computers, but watching Amjad work was like watching an academy grad after spending the day with a kid fresh out of school. He still wasn't entirely sure they could trust her, but Oliver hadn't found any reason not to, and Anders seemed okay with it. She'd been right about one thing—he couldn't imagine her jeopardizing her life over something as simple and petty as money. From what Oliver had found, she didn't need to worry about money in the slightest, but for some people, there would never be enough. Money or power, actually, which brought him right back to Tanner. Obviously Tanner thought he could take over the monarchy if Anders was dead, otherwise he wouldn't bother trying to kill him. But whoever was pulling Tanner's strings had to have other motives, be looking for power in other ways. Then again, who had more power than the man—or woman—behind the throne?

"This is fucking ridiculous." Amjad pushed back from the table, scowling.

Reese glanced up from his screen curiously. Anders hadn't so much as twitched, he was so thoroughly engrossed in whatever he was reading.

"I'm sorry?" Zach said. He and Oliver looked at each other and then back at her. "What's the problem?"

"Money is clearly moving between Bianca and Gregor here, here, and here," she said. "But it's these transactions that I can't track." With a wave of her hand, she copied her view onto everyone else's screens. "There's no way either of these two are smart enough to block me, so whoever is running their mysterious enterprise is the sneakiest bastard I've ever met."

Zach had to smother a smile at the owl-eyed look Anders gave them as his reading was interrupted. He reached under the table and put a hand on Anders's knee. "That's kind of what I was afraid of," he admitted. "We'll have to flush them out to track them down, and we have no idea who it could be or what they're capable of. Although the fact that they're going after the king means they're probably willing to do just about anything."

"I think I know how Counselor Pretorius is involved," Anders said, finally getting his bearings. "I've been going through the records of the known instances of smuggling and black market goods. A number of the items confiscated are copies of products so new they've barely touched the market. Someone is getting our pirates copies of schematics belonging to some of the most secure companies in the Collective. The most vulnerable point for them would be here, with Industry Counselor Pretorius. She has virtually unfettered access to the complete details of even the most closely guarded plans . . ." He paused, then nearly jumped out of his seat. "The recalls!"

"Pardon?" Reese asked when Anders didn't elaborate.

"The recalls they were talking about on the media streams a couple of weeks ago," Anders said, punching up information on his screen and copying it onto everyone else's. "There has been a series of recalls from multiple companies, citing manufacturing defects. I wouldn't be surprised if further investigation showed the defective products were more counterfeit goods, made with substandard materials and cut corners."

Amjad nodded. "Bianca could make sure the counterfeits received tariff marks, and Gregor could use his connections to smuggle them onto freighter ships at Ciebosian transit centers."

"Shit." Reese slumped back in his chair. "The sheer size of the criminal enterprise this must be funding is terrifying. No wonder they were so quick to kill King James."

Zach felt Anders's grief and anger spike at the mention of his father's assassination, and he reached for Anders's hand, tangling their fingers together. "But who's running it? We're still missing a huge part of this picture. We've got to pin it down somehow."

"Gregor is the key," Amjad said, her grin as sharp as a knife. "He knows who's in charge, and he's not nearly good enough to be able to withstand questioning. Once we have a name, Commander Hadlock and I will be able to trace the money. Just having the name won't do much without evidence."

"We should pick up Counselor Pretorius too," Anders said, squeezing Zach's hand. "While I doubt that our mastermind will run—they've covered their tracks too well—it certainly won't hurt to put as much pressure on them as possible."

"Plus it will keep her from contacting whoever it is and warning them. We don't want to give them any time to bury themselves deeper to avoid detection." Oliver was leaning back in his chair now, hands folded over his stomach, sharp, observant eyes belying his relaxed pose.

"Of course." Anders glanced at Zach's wrist unit for the time. "It's not too late; Tanner and Pretorius should both still be on the palace grounds. Zach, I'd rather use your people for this, since we know they're clean."

"They're yours," Zach said simply. "Anything you need them to do."

Anders nodded, sending warmth over the bond. "Counselor Amjad, I want to thank you for your assistance. There's no way we could have made so much progress so quickly without you."

"Of course not," Amjad said. "Though I have no doubt the commander would have gotten there in the end."

"Thank you," Oliver said, voice just dry enough that only one who knew him well would hear it. Zach smothered a grin. Oliver winked at him.

"Oliver, gather up our people and put them at the king's disposal," Zach said.

"Right away." Oliver sat up straight, ready to leave. "And, naturally, I am also—anything you need, Majesty."

"Thank you, Oliver," Anders said with warmth. "You're dismissed."

Oliver stood, bowed, and strode from the room with purpose. Zach leaned in to whisper to Anders. "He'll make an excellent captain for the *Pallas*."

"I was thinking the same thing," Anders murmured back. "Besides, I can't imagine you'd trust her to anyone else." He took a deep breath, pulled back his shoulders, and rapped his knuckles against the table. "Let's put an end to this."

CHAPTER TWENTY-SIX

They met up less than an hour later with Oliver and a dozen of the *Pallas*'s finest officers, all bristling with weapons and sporting the same grim, determined looks. Anders had already confirmed with palace security that Counselor Pretorius was on the grounds. Tanner, who was still under surveillance, had been confirmed as *entertaining* a guest at his private residence in Dryax.

Anders did *not* want to think about what that would entail. Instead, he focused on other things.

"I'm going with you to arrest Pretorius," he murmured to Zach in quiet tones.

Zach gazed at Anders steadily, then finally nodded. "You have a weapon?"

Anders smiled and turned, lifting his short jacket enough to show Zach the pistol secured at the small of his back. "It's been a few months since I've fired it, but I'm fully trained."

"I trust you are." Zach rubbed a hand down Anders's back. "Still, I wonder if we should stay back and let Oliver take her into custody."

"You're right; we should," Anders said, kissing Zach's jaw. "Besides, it will help when you make your recommendation to assign him as the *Pallas*'s new captain."

Zach met Oliver's eyes and gave him the signal to move out, and as soon as Oliver moved, their men fell into line behind him. He and Anders took up the rear, with only Jackson and Bern behind them. The guard who had kept tabs on Pretorius walked next to Oliver, directing him to the wing where she had been seen talking to Counselor Lee.

They quickly found her just as reported. She was speaking with Lee, whose head was bent toward hers. She was gesturing urgently with her hands but stopped abruptly when she saw the contingent of men heading her way.

"What's going on?" she demanded, using her unusual height to look down her nose at Oliver.

"Counselor," Oliver said neutrally, "you're under arrest. Please come with us now."

"What? How dare you!" Lee shouted. "Counselor Pretorius is a respected member of King Philip's cabinet!"

Oliver pitched his voice to carry above Lee's bluster but otherwise ignored him. "You are under suspicion of treason, piracy, and tax evasion. You may come with us quietly or forcibly, Counselor. Your choice."

"It's not much of a choice, now is it?" Pretorius said, stepping forward calmly.

"Thank you, Bianca," Anders said as Oliver bound her wrists. He waited until Oliver finished securing her, then stepped forward. "I hope you're as reasonable in questioning."

Lee's face had gone sickly pale at the mention of treason. "Your Majesty," he said, scraping the floor with a bow. "Of course I'm happy to cooperate with any investigation."

Pretorius shot him a dark glare, but said nothing. Anders resisted the urge to roll his eyes at Lee's desperate attempt to curry favor. "I'm sure you will, Counselor Lee," he said instead. "If you would, please bring any records you have of your interactions to me at the guard station."

Oliver took hold of the woman's elbow and began to lead her away, the men once again falling into step behind him.

"Lee," Zach said with a short nod. He turned to follow Oliver, taking Anders's hand with a light tug.

Anders followed, holding his silence until Pretorius was led into the interrogation room, leaving Zach and Anders alone with only Jackson and Bern.

"Is it wrong that I took an incredible amount of satisfaction from that?" he asked Zach, grinning wildly.

Zach pulled his fingers free so he could hook an arm around Anders's neck instead. "Not at all," he said, grinning in return before reeling Anders in to kiss his temple. "Do you want to go with them to lock her up until she can be questioned?"

"Oliver can handle it," he said, tangling their fingers together as Jackson approached.

"Majesties, while Commander Hadlock secures the suspect, I request leave to search Counselor Pretorius's office here at the palace."

Zach nodded. "Of course, Jackson. Excellent plan. You could search Tanner's office after you finish with hers."

Jackson hesitated until Anders nodded in agreement, and then headed down the hall, collecting two security officers to follow. Anders sighed. "It's an improvement, I suppose."

"What's that?" Zach asked absently, watching them go.

Anders shook his head. "Just people adjusting to your new rank. I suppose it's natural there'd be a period of adjustment."

"Makes sense," Zach said. "I'm the new guy in town and no one really knows who I am."

"Something like that." Anders smiled and kissed Zach's knuckles. Zach would eventually figure out he was the second most powerful man in the Collective, god help them all. "Now what?"

"As soon as Oliver's got Pretorius settled, I'll go with him to pick up Tanner." Zach squeezed Anders's hand. "We'll have this wrapped up soon."

Anders stilled, Zach's words hitting him unexpectedly. "I beg your pardon?"

"This part of things will be over soon, and Tanner will crack once we've picked him up." Zach smiled. "We'll get whoever is behind this and get it all wrapped up."

"Once Oliver's picked him up, you mean," Anders said carefully.

"Well, he'll lead our team, so yeah, I guess." Zach shrugged.

The mere thought of Zach going after a man who had tried to kill both of them and had killed Anders's father made Anders queasy. "No."

Zach raised an eyebrow. "No? No, what?"

"You—you can't go with them," Anders said. "I won't allow it."

Straightening, Zach pulled his hand free of Anders's and folded his arms over his chest. "You won't *allow* it? You don't control me, Anders. I'm going."

Painfully aware they were still standing in the middle of the hall and far from being alone, Anders pulled his hands behind his back. "Fine. Then I'm going with you."

"Ah, no." Zach shook his head as if to emphasize the words. "That wouldn't be a good idea. Oliver and I can take care of it; we'll have a good team, and I doubt Tanner will resist."

"If it's safe enough for you, it's safe enough for me." Anders fought to keep his voice even.

"Anders, I'm a naval captain, trained to handle situations like this. It's not automatically safe for you just because I'm going." He held up a hand as if to halt whatever Anders was going to say next. "I know you can take care of yourself under normal circumstances, but we're going to take down a criminal who was dumb enough to try to take a shot at me. If he'd go after me, he'd kill you without a second thought, and I can't do my job if I'm worried about you."

"You're not just an *admiral*," Anders snarled. "You're the fucking *prince consort*. You're my bonded match. And the fact that Tanner has tried to kill both of us is precisely why you have to stay here. I won't have you giving him another chance at you."

Zach shook his head and pulled Anders into an office, closing the door behind them. "Fine. *Admiral*. And prince consort. But trained for battle, Anders. With a team of my best men behind me and Oliver next to me. I'll be fine, and so will you. Because you are *staying here*."

Anders tried to hold his temper back, and for the most part failed. "I think you'll find I'm king of the Collective. As such, I *do* control quite a lot. You can't go into battle anymore, because you can't take those kinds of risks anymore. Not with billions of people relying on the both of us. If it's not safe enough for me, it's not safe enough for *you*. You're staying here. With me."

"No," Zach ground out, "I'm not. You may control a lot, but you do not control me." He shoved a hand through his hair. "Sorry, Anders. It won't take long. I'll be back soon, and I'll send Bern to stand with you. He'll keep you safe and secure."

"After the disaster with my father's ring, I'd expect you to understand how important it is we follow basic safety protocols. Or are you that dense that you still think you're invincible after everything we've been through?"

"I know I'm not invincible," Zach said with hints of temper. "That's why I'm not going alone. Oliver and I have had each other's back for years. We've got this, Anders, and nothing is going to happen to me—"

"You have no way to guarantee that, and you know it!" Anders was definitely shouting now, and he couldn't stop himself.

"Okay, no," Zach snapped. "No guarantees. Just training and experience and an abundance of caution. I have to leave soon, Anders. I don't have time for this."

Anders shook his head once. "You have all the time in the world. Because I won't allow you to go. I know you think you're better than having to listen to your spouse, so you'll have to listen to your king and stay here, you stubborn asshole."

Zach took a step back. "You can't stop me, Anders. You'd better get used to not having everything your way. I'm not a child you can order around." Zach's voice started to rise even as his tone went tight and hard. "Listen carefully. I am going with my team to arrest someone suspected of attempted murder and piracy, at the very least. You are staying here where I know you're safe so you don't distract me."

"Do you even understand how important you are to me?" He jabbed Zach in the chest once. "To the Collective?"

"Do you understand how much more important you are to the Collective? To say nothing of how important you are to me. That's why you're *staying here*." Zach's hands flexed at his sides.

"You're next in line for the throne, asshole," Anders snarled. His shields were cracking, and he knew he was leaking emotions all over the place. He didn't care. "But unlike you, I actually take personal safety seriously, and if the situation is that dangerous, I know better than to go sailing on in. That's my point. I'll fucking stay put if you do."

"Sailing on in has been my responsibility for two decades," Zach said. "I take personal safety very seriously, yours more than anyone else's. I have to go secure someone dangerous to help keep you safe. I will be back, *safely*, soon."

"That's not your job anymore!" Anders bellowed. "You're not a captain, you're not just another Navy man. You don't get to fly off whenever you want anymore, and you need to grow the hell up and accept that!"

"No, I don't get to fly off anymore, do I? You've seen to that. I have tried to accept that I will never fly again, but I will be damned if I will be treated like some tame pet to be ordered around and caged."

"For fuck's sake—" Anders paced away, hands in his hair. "If something happened to you, I would *lose my mind*. Stop being such a selfish bastard."

"Oh, *I'm* selfish?" All remnants of Zach's calm fled, anger lashing out with his words. "I'm selfish. You're the one insisting I stay here just because you want me to, because you're king. I'm trying to fulfill my duties as a naval officer, possibly the last opportunity I'll ever have to do so now that I'm going to be stuck riding a fucking *desk*, by pursuing and arresting a suspected smuggler. Stop arguing with me so I can go do my fucking job."

"Your *job*?" Anders scoffed, not caring he was shouting. "If you could listen to me over the sound of your ego, you'd know that your fucking job is to support me, you arrogant, *ignorant* . . ."

"No," Zach snarled, "my job is to protect the king and the Collective. To protect trade routes and boundaries, and the people of the Collective. None of which entails supporting you." He spun on his heel and started for the door. "Now, if you'll excuse me, Your *Majesty*, I have work to do."

"If you go, if you choose your stupid pride over *us*, over your real responsibilities—" Anders sucked in a breath. "As prince consort, you're not really in the Navy anymore, and you know it. You don't get both, Zachary. If you insist on being in the Navy, then you don't need to come back to me."

Zach's step hitched, but he didn't stop until he reached the door. He turned back to face Anders, his own expression cold and unreadable. "I am a naval admiral, precisely *because* I am prince consort. If I can't be trusted to fulfill those responsibilities, then I am not the right man to be consort. Good day, Your Majesty."

Without another word, Zach left, door closing quietly behind him.

"Oh, no, you don't," Anders growled, chasing after him and opening the door. Two of Zach's officers blocked his path, looking painfully determined to hold Anders back. *Oh that just fucking does it.* "I'm dead serious, O'Connell!" he shouted. "Do this and we're done. I don't care what happens!"

Zach kept walking, collecting Oliver as he passed the other man standing in the hall. Oliver gave Anders a quick look before turning to walk with Zach until they disappeared around a corner.

CHAPTER
TWENTY-SEVEN

They walked in silence for several long moments, Oliver having fallen naturally into step with Zach like they'd done so many times before. Zach sensed as much as saw Oliver open his mouth to speak and raised a hand to stop him.

"Don't," he said, still fighting for calm. "Don't say a word about it, or about Anders. We had a disagreement, and I'll have to deal with the fallout when we get back with Tanner in restraints."

Oliver nodded. "I'll only say this—I'm here to talk if you need me."

Zach shook his head. "Not now. I have to focus on our mission, not my personal issues."

"Fair enough. At last report, Tanner was entertaining at home. I have a shuttle ready to take us."

"Good," Zach said. "Hopefully he's still there. It will make things a lot easier if we don't have to chase him down."

There were several of Zach's crew waiting, and they all made the quick trip to Tanner's residence. With a single gesture, Zach sent his men to surround the house. He and Oliver took the front door, bursting in quickly. "Gregor Tanner," Zach called loudly, "you are under arrest on suspicion of piracy, treason, and tax evasion."

There was a crash upstairs, followed by the thud of running footsteps. Another crash, the buzz of a laser shot, and then one of the crew out back shouted in alarm. "Polito's down! I need back up!"

"Goddamn it," Zach roared. He and Oliver raced through the house to the back. "Take him down! Get a medic for Polito!"

Oliver paused when they reached Polito. "I'll stay with him, Zach. Go get Tanner."

Zach nodded and ran. When he reached the rear of Tanner's property, he saw Tanner facing away from him, shooting wildly at Zach's men, not hitting anyone but not letting anyone close enough to catch him, either. He was nude. Zach made a face at the sight of Tanner's pale ass and tried to grab his arms to cuff him. As soon as he touched an arm, Tanner whirled, sending another wild shot that sheared off a limb from one of the giant trees just inside the perimeter wall. Zach reached forward and snagged Tanner's wrist, tightening his grip until Tanner dropped the weapon with a yelp. He swung around and caught Zach's chin with a fist, distracting him enough to get loose.

Shotwell, a tall, strong woman who was Zach's best at hand-to-hand, stepped up with a kick that caught Tanner directly in the gut. He doubled over, and she gave him a quick jab that broke his nose. He spun and ran, apparently forgetting that there was no escape from the back, and ended up in the far corner. Zach embraced the fierce satisfaction of cornering a suspect. Face and chest bloody from his broken nose, Tanner alternated between covering himself and raising his hands in response to all the guns pointed at him. He swiped at the blood with the back of a hand, then raised that hand and used the other to cover his groin.

"I am filing charges against every last one of you!" he sputtered, face and skinny chest a blotchy red.

"You go right ahead," Zach said. "I'm sure the king will address those charges as soon as he's dealt with the charges against *you*, which now include attacking an officer of the Royal Navy and resisting arrest." Zach grabbed Tanner's wrists and bound them behind his back.

Tanner stumbled, but jerked to a stop, looking at Zach over his shoulder. "If you kill me, you might as well kill Anders too." He smirked. "I've been hearing rumors of trouble in paradise; are you sure you want to 'fix' things that way?"

"The rumors of trouble are greatly exaggerated," Zach said. He refused to think about their most recent fight, but anger and *fear* curled through him at Tanner's words. "We're fine, not that it's really your concern. Keep moving." He jerked Tanner's arms, forcing him forward again.

"That's what I love about Navy men. Blessedly lacking in anything resembling imagination and conveniently shortsighted." Tanner pulled his shoulders back and picked up a strut. "Men like you will always make it possible for men like me to get ahead. And get rich."

"Yet you're the one in restraints with his dick hanging out. Besides, you aren't getting ahead, you're getting used by whoever is tugging your strings." At the thought of that someone, Zach's fear grew, tangling with the anger building at the idea of a plot against Anders. He kept his expression insolent and careless with an effort, refusing to let Tanner see what he felt. He shook himself. "It will be better for you if you're the one who spills the details before they roll on you." Zach kneed the back of Tanner's leg, making him stumble and lose his strut.

"I might be in chains now, but by the time we get to the palace, I'll be regent again and you'll be single. We can talk about my dick more then, if you want to stay prince consort."

Zach snorted. "Your dick is too small to be interesting. And you seem to be forgetting something, Tanner. As prince consort *I'm* the next in line. Killing Anders will not make you regent." Even saying the words sent a cold freeze through his blood. Anders was fine. Bern would never let anyone near him. "I'll say it again. Whoever is behind this plot is using you and won't—*can't*—give you the power they say they can. Tell me who it is, Tanner. They'll give you up in a heartbeat. Do you want to take the fall?"

Tanner stopped and turned to face Zach fully. "You're uncrowned, and in a matter of minutes will be the only surviving witness to the bonding that I have at least three witnesses ready to swear never happened because—" he smirked, a slow and oily expression "—King Philip was in my bed that night. How was I to know he'd succumb to the stress of the past few weeks and hallucinate an entire bonding with you? Besides, half the court knows you'd rather chew off your own arm than accept your new life. Let me go now and start cooperating, and I'll get my friends to let you live after we solve your marital problems."

"You forget our bond marks, something that cannot be faked. You forget the required witnesses to our bond, whose names you do not know. You forget that it had to be officiated by a Priest of the Many, who again, you do not know. You can't erase everything, Tanner." Zach glared at Tanner, a hint of pity winding through the anger. "You're a patsy, Tanner, and too stupid to see it. I can't help you if you won't help yourself."

"Your bodyguard's uncle," Tanner said, suddenly serious. "Bannerjee Reese. Oliver Hadlock. Your assorted meathead shadows. The king's clueless physician." He glanced over to where Oliver watched over the injured Polito. "Well, we might not get him. But maybe you two boys will be able to share a cell. For shame, conspiring to take advantage of poor Anders. Or that'll be the story when the media get hold of pictures of the king's mangled body and the story of how you destroyed him. Speaking of, have you heard from your bonded lately?"

Zach jerked Tanner up by his wrists and plowed another fist into Tanner's face, crunching his already broken nose as his anger boiled over. He followed that up by a quick sweep that caught Tanner's legs and took him to the ground. "You're pathetic, Tanner," he growled. "Do I have to beat the answers out of you?" Zach punched him in the gut, forcing an explosion of air from Tanner's lungs. "Because I would be happy to break every bone in your body. Talk. *Now*."

Tanner coughed, spraying blood on the ground. "Fuck you," he gasped in between dry heaves. "*He'll* kill me."

"Him or me," Zach said harshly. "The difference is, I can protect you if you talk. Anders may go easy on you if you talk. We'll put him away permanently—if you talk." He gut punched Tanner again, then, settling between Tanner's legs, pressed his knee lightly against Tanner's balls. "Decision time, Tanner."

Air whistled wetly through Tanner's bloody nose. "Lee," he said in a strangled voice. "John Lee. Not that it matters, because you're here and he's across Dryax with better explosives than last time. And Anders trusts him."

It was a punch to the gut. *Lee*? Still reeling, Zach hauled Tanner up and forced him into a trot. Lee and Tanner *hated* each other. And Anders might not like Lee, but Tanner wasn't wrong about Anders trusting him. Fear rushed through Zach, replacing the anger. He had to get to Anders. *Now.*

"That arrogant, selfish, emotionally stunted bastard." Anders paced the narrow width of the windowless office, grumbling to himself. "Running off after a murderer as if nothing matters but what he wants. And why shouldn't it? If you ask that damn asshole, he'll tell you he knows better than anyone else because he's in the Navy and obviously has a far better grasp of politics and law than, say, a king who has spent his entire adult life studying it!"

"I can't believe I'm about to say this," Bern said, "but being a naval officer isn't something a person can simply turn off. Not any more than you can stop being you."

"Don't you think I know that? I've always admired his sense of honor. But he's just so narrow-minded. He thinks he's the only one who can save us all, *and* he thinks he can do that by making a single arrest, which is ridiculous. And so very Zach." Anders tugged at his hair. "He refuses to acknowledge how irresponsible he's being. The kind of disaster his death could bring."

"He still doesn't understand why Jackson and I were so upset about the poison."

Anders waved his arms wide. "See? Stubborn!"

Bern sighed. "But you love him, Anders. Even without the bond, I don't think you could live without him."

"I may have to." Anders choked on a small sob. "If he can't be responsible, if he can't accept how many people rely on us both, I can't . . ."

"Easy there." Bern pulled Anders into a stiff, awkward hug. "He's an asshole, yes. And I would love to see the last of him, yes. But he's your bonded, and he's not an idiot. He might very well come around."

Anders sighed. "I know. And there's going to be a period of adjustment. But if he can't accept that he's out of his element and needs to actually listen to other people . . ."

Someone knocked on the door. "Your Majesty," Lee called through the wood. "I have those records I promised you."

Reluctantly, Anders stepped free of Bern, smoothing his hair and clothes. He took a deep breath, sat in the nearest chair, and nodded for Bern to admit Lee into the office. Entering, Lee hesitated as he glanced first at Anders, then Bern. He lifted a media screen in one hand. "I haven't had much business with the counselor, but I brought what I have, Majesty."

Anders nodded. "Excellent. Please come in, Counselor. Bern, please have Counselor Amjad join us so she can begin reviewing them." Bern nodded and sat at the nearest communication console.

"Counselor Amjad, Majesty?" Lee asked as he took a seat, looking as though he'd bit into something sour.

"Yes." In the back of his mind, Anders felt a tentative brush from Zach. Scowling, Anders braced his shields even further. "Imari has been assisting with the investigation into some very serious issues. If it weren't for her, we would never have been able to tie Bianca to Gregor's particular illegal activities."

"Gregor Tanner?" Lee's voice was oddly strained; Anders would have thought that with their ongoing feud, Lee would have been pleased.

"Hmm? Oh, yes," Anders said distractedly. What could Zach have possibly wanted? Did he really think Anders would welcome him back into his mind after what had happened? "We have substantial evidence to implicate Gregor in my father's murder and in an almost successful attempt on me, as well."

"I wouldn't have thought Gregor capable of such machinations," Lee said, shifting in his seat.

"You'd be right," Anders said, still focusing on his screen. "We're working on uncovering whoever is pulling the strings—"

A great boom rocked the floor, the lights flickering, then going black. Anders jumped, then jumped again at Lee's incoherent shout, and gripped the arms of his chair, heart racing. *Not again.*

"Anders!" Bern shouted across the sudden silence. "Your Majesty, are you all right?"

"I'm fine," Anders said over the pounding of his heart. "John?"

"I am well, Majesty." Lee's voice was clipped.

"The emergency lights should come on soon," Bern said, his voice moving closer. Moments later, the room filled with amber light. Bern's face was pale and grim. "Jackson says the explosion was in the cabinet offices. There are dead and wounded and . . . *Jax*. Anders, Jackson is hurt."

"Go." Anders pointed to the door. "I'll stay here." When Bern hesitated, Anders stood. "Jackson needs you. Go!"

Bern tossed Anders a tight, grateful look, and ran out of the room. Anders watched him go with a knot in his own throat, part sympathetic, part his own lingering fear for Zach. He could do nothing but push it down, acutely aware of how keenly Lee was watching him sit back down.

"That was kind of you," Lee said.

"They're bonded," Anders replied by way of explanation, still focused on the door. *Perhaps I should check on Zach.*

"Like I said, kind of you." Lee shifted, his clothing rustling. "But tremendously stupid."

A sudden move and a flash of light finally drew Anders's attention. Lee was standing, his family dagger in hand. He rushed Anders, pressing the surprisingly sharp tip against his neck.

"You," Anders snarled. "You *traitor.*"

Lee pressed harder with the knife, cutting off anything else Anders might have said. "You should have stayed hidden away, Philip," he said. "You should have just run away with your precious *common* match and left the governing to those of us who actually know how to do it."

Anders ignored the panic threatening to take control. Instead, he just glared up at the man who'd had his father killed and cracked open a narrow line to Zach, hoping his bonded wasn't still so angry he'd be blocking.

"Fuck you," he ground out.

"So eloquent," Lee sneered. "I see that upstart bonded of yours has been a true positive influence." He angled the blade until Anders didn't dare breathe. "Stand."

Slow and careful, Anders stood. "You and Tanner both have hated Zach from the beginning," he said, mindful not to make any sudden moves. "It really bothers you that he isn't from a noble family, doesn't it? It's not as though we had much of a choice."

Lee grabbed Anders's arm, tugging him out from behind the desk. "I detest your pet pilot," he said, "because he never minds his place and he's been a wrench in the works from the beginning. You were supposed to marry that idiot Tanner and go back to your school and let us take care of things."

Anders couldn't help a derisive snort. "Have you *met* Gregor Tanner? There isn't enough ice wine in the entire Collective to make marrying him sound like a good idea."

"Which was why I sent those raiders to kill you on the *Pallas*," Lee said, shifting the knife to Anders's side. "Now shut up and move, Your Majesty. I want to be out of here before your hulking guard comes back, and you're going to walk me right out the door."

"Really? You're taking *me* hostage?"

"I don't have to let you live after, you know." The knife cut right through Anders's shirt, far enough back that the blood from the long, deep slice across Anders's ribs was hidden under his jacket. Bleeding, Anders held up his hands in surrender and let Lee force him through the door and into the hall.

"Hands down," Lee hissed. "We're just going for a walk to look at some documents on my private server."

"Your Majesty?" One of Zach's people, no doubt ordered to babysit Anders, trotted up. He was young and fresh-faced, and the earnest concern on his face was almost as painful as the wound in Anders's side. "Did you need anything?"

Anders shook his head. "I'm fine. The counselor and I just need to go look at something."

The officer shook his head and advanced. "I'm sorry, Majesty, but it's not safe. This wing is secure, but the rest of the palace needs to be cleared both structurally and for further explosives before you can go out there. I need to ask you to stay here, sir. Sire. Majesty."

Then he made the mistake of moving within reach, and Lee struck. Free hand darting out, Lee grabbed the young man, yanking him off-balance. The blade flashed again, and the boy fell, clutching at his throat and gurgling through the blood rapidly staining his uniform.

Anders stared in horror, unable to look away as the boy died. "You didn't have to do that! I could have made him leave."

"Says you, Majesty, but my way is much faster." Lee sneered, kicking the body out of his path like so much garbage.

Anders stared down at the poor kid, mind still refusing to accept the casual violence. Then Lee yanked him through the door, disabling the lock with his own cabinet clearance code. "Come along," he snarled. "We have a shuttle to catch."

CHAPTER
TWENTY-EIGHT

Zach had barely gotten Tanner secured in the shuttle when he felt a burst of terror followed by a stabbing pain in his head. While the pain had been his, the terror wasn't. "Go, go, go!" he yelled at the pilot. "Get to the palace as fast as you can."

Tanner, still naked and bloody, sat back with his bound hands draped casually between his legs. "Something the matter, *Admiral*?"

"I'm just in a hurry to get you in a cell, Tanner," Zach said. His own fear was growing quickly enough that it would soon match the terror he'd felt from Anders. He kept himself calm with an effort and sent Tanner an easy smile. "You're going to spend the rest of your life in one. We'll put you right next to Lee, would you like that?"

Before Tanner could come back with whatever idiocy he had planned, the shuttle's communication system lit up. "Admiral, are you there?" Grant's voice was strained. "Your Majesty, come in."

Zach leaned forward. "I'm here, Grant. I'm almost at the palace. I have Tanner. Listen to me, Grant, you need to take Counselor Lee into custody immediately. Do you copy?"

"That's going to have to fucking wait, sir," Grant said. The background noise surged, static resolving into a *crackle-pop* sound, punctuated by distant shouting. "The palace has been bombed, and the fucking place is on fire."

"Find Lee," Zach snapped. "There are others who can deal with the fire and the damage." Zach kicked Tanner's ankle hard when the other man started chuckling. "The bombing was a distraction. King Philip is in danger. He is your first priority."

"*Shit.*" Grant paused. "Sir, Jackson's hurt and Bern's here with him. Stand by, I'll check with the other guard." There was an agonizingly long silence, only broken by Tanner's soft chuckle. Then Grant's voice returned, shaking. "Admiral, the other guard's body was found outside the office. His Majesty is somewhere else, alone with Lee. You need to warn him yourself."

Zach growled. "I can't warn him," he said with exaggerated patience. "Let Bern take care of Jackson. You grab some of my crew and protect your king."

"But I thought you were *bonded*," Tanner singsonged.

Grant's breathing picked up. "I'm on my way, sir. But there's a lot of damage between here and security. It's going to take time."

"*Fuck*," Zach said harshly. "Run, Grant." Zach turned to Tanner. "We are *bonded*, not *telepathic*." Just then pain swam through his head and then centered over his ribs. He gasped. "What the hell?"

"I've heard bonded couples can share pain. Especially when one is near death." Tanner smirked. "But that wouldn't apply to you, would it? You're too weakly bonded to even reach your precious Anders."

Zach hadn't considered trying to use the bond—it was too new for telepathy, wasn't it? And that kind of contact would mean letting Anders in all the way, never going back from that, never truly being alone again. He shuddered, torn between love and the fear of such a complete bond. But this was *Anders*. A quick wash of images flooded his mind: Anders laughing; Anders's quick smile and his shy one; Anders angry; Anders as he came, pleasure riding his face. He *loved* Anders. Taking a deep breath, Zach let it go. He didn't have time for his own issues. He had to get to Anders. He closed his eyes against the fatigue and fear that washed over him and concentrated fiercely on the corner of his mind that was the source of the pain. *Anders!* he screamed silently. *Can you hear me?*

There was the usual jumble of emotions he was used to from Anders, and then a sharp burst of unmitigated panic. Anders was alive, but terrified, and it was several long seconds before the terror faded enough for a vague sense of recognition to filter through the mess. *Zach?* he heard, faint and echoing. *How?*

Because you're mine, Zach sent fiercely. *I've got Tanner. Lee is behind it. Stay away from him.*

After an agonizing delay, Anders responded. *Too late.* His voice was still distant, like with a crappy comm connection. *Sorry, love. That kid . . . He's dead.*

Zach felt a burst of sorrow at the thought of the lost guard, but he couldn't let it worry him now. Anders was the priority. *Where are you? Where's Lee?*

Shuttle. Mother's garden. There was another burst of phantom pain across Zach's ribs. *Hurry, Zach. Bring a medic. Too much blood.*

This time Zach couldn't tell whose panic, whose *terror* he felt. It nearly pulled him under. With an effort, he hit the comm again. "Grant, take a medic and guards and get to the queen's garden. Be prepared to be attacked. Counselor Lee has taken the king hostage. You must be careful."

Grant let loose a string of swear words. "Copy, sir. Now get your ass here."

"We're almost there." Zach shut off the comm and swore. "New destination," he barked at the pilot. "Queen's garden behind the palace. Push this thing as fast as it will go."

Zach barely heard the pilot's acknowledgment of the change in orders and ignored Tanner completely as he struggled to contain both his rage and Anders's fading fear.

Beyond Anders's closed eyes, he was dimly aware of Lee moving around the shuttle, securing containers and running through preflight checks. Anders groaned, his head screaming from the sudden telepathy. There was no way it should have worked this early, but of course Zach was a stubborn bastard who only obeyed rules when it was convenient for him.

"I'm still fucking bleeding," he griped, chancing a look around. Preflight was almost done and the engines were nearly primed. He needed to stall Lee, keep them on the ground until Zach could get there. "I need a skin treatment if you don't want to be stuck using my dead body as leverage."

Lee snorted. "It's not that bad, princess."

"I'm pretty sure I know excessive blood loss when I experience it." The hard line of Anders's pistol dug into his back. But Lee was still too close, had too good of a chance to overpower him if Anders were to go for the weapon now. "At least give me a fucking bandage, then. I'm bleeding all over your seat, you know."

Lee spat out a curse, then got out of his seat. Anders waited until Lee was across the narrow confines before he twisted, reaching behind his back. The move pulled at his wound, and Anders hissed as his vision swam with black spots. He could feel Zach's anxiety rising through the bond and tried to reassure him. *Fine. Getting stabbed sucks, though.* The answering burst of fear and rage told him that had been a *very* bad idea.

Anders twisted again, his blood-slick fingers slipping along the smooth grip of the pistol handle. He must have made another noise, because Lee came back in a rush.

"What are you doing?" he demanded, shoving at Anders's shoulder, then reaching behind Anders. "What do you have?"

In the same moment, Anders got his hand around the pistol. He kicked out at Lee's shins, earning a satisfying *pop* of a dislocated kneecap for his efforts. Lee howled in pain but didn't let go as they grappled for the gun. "Should have killed you when I killed your father!" he roared in Anders's face.

Pure fury rose up in him, and Anders surged out of the seat. He threw himself at Lee, forgetting he was armed until the pistol went off with a wild shot that hit the control panel in a shower of sparks. Lee pushed forward, slamming the crown of his head into Anders's face. The sudden burst of pain disoriented him, and Anders lost his grip on the gun for a few precious seconds. Lee snatched the pistol away, cracking Anders's nose with his free hand.

"Hold still, you little shit," Lee panted. Just then, the engines cut off abruptly, and Anders laughed, manic. He stumbled backward, vision swimming from the head butt, and fell against the exterior hatch, sliding to the floor in a heap.

"Should have left me behind, you stupid bastard," he snarled, spitting blood. "Now you're stuck, and my bonded is on the way. I hope he kills you slowly."

Lee growled. "Gods, you are such a pain in the ass. It's a miracle you made it through puberty. How has no one killed you already?"

Before Anders could respond, though, Lee brought the butt of the pistol crashing against the side of his head. There was a sharp burst of pain, and then Anders slipped into darkness.

Zach *felt* Anders abruptly vanish. He shouted wordlessly, then growled at the pilot. "Faster! Fast as you can to save your king." He knew the burst of speed wouldn't be enough. Anders wasn't dead, not yet; Zach would feel *that*. But Zach was afraid it was going to be a close thing, because something had happened to make that improbable connection disappear.

They winged around the palace to the garden, setting down next to the shuttle already there. "Keep Tanner here," he said to the pilot. "Don't let him loose for any reason." Then Zach ran for the other shuttle, mentally screaming Anders's name.

The connection clicked back into place, but it was too many long seconds before Anders's voice returned. *Head fucking hurts. Where are you?*

Feeling Anders once more made Zach weak at the knees with sheer relief. Fortunately, he'd reached the shuttle and could lean against it for just a moment. When his legs could hold him again, he slapped at the controls that should have opened the door. It stayed sealed shut. Zach pounded helplessly on the shiny metal. *At your shuttle. Can't get in. Can you open the hatch?*

I shot the control panel. He felt Anders's pain and fear, almost eclipsing the sheer relief Anders was broadcasting at Zach. And still Zach's ribs hurt, though the phantom wound was slowly going numb. *Glad you're here. I'm sorry. Love you.*

Zach roared with pending grief. *No! Do* not *give up, Anders. Can you get to the hatch? There's a manual latch under the panel by the hatch. Get to the hatch and let me in!*

Already there. Lee's here too. I can't . . . He's got my pistol, Zach. He thinks I'm out, but if I move, he might use it.

I have guards everywhere. I can try to distract him. Be ready. You can do this, Anders. You have to do this. I love you. Zach pushed away from the shuttle and screamed at the guards and his crew. "Attack the nose of the shuttle! Use whatever weapons you have to destroy it."

Most of them jumped into action, following orders immediately. Even the ones who side-eyed Zach first began to attack. The laser guns didn't do much damage to the shuttle, which was designed to withstand the heat of atmospheric entry, but their attacks screeched against the hull until the air was bitter with ozone. Shotwell had focused on one spot on the window, and it was slowly giving way.

It was enough. It had to be; Zach had no other options. *Go, Anders! Go, go, go!*

Anders held as still as he could when the sound of laser fire started at the front of the shuttle. He could feel Zach's roiling emotions—all the rage and grief and fear being forced into such fierce determination that even Anders couldn't help but believe they could do this.

"What the hell are they doing?" Lee growled, turning away and looking out the front view. Anders didn't need Zach's urging to know this was their only chance.

He tried to stand, but slipped, hands and knees dragging smears of blood across the floor and down the bulkhead. *Shit!* Fortunately, the racket outside of the shuttle masked the noises of Anders's own struggle. The cut on his ribs screamed in agony, and Anders bit his lip to hold back anything louder than a whimper. He couldn't fail. Zach needed him to do this.

It took long seconds of fruitless searching along the smooth metal wall, but Anders's fingers found the panel at last. He pried it open and had his hand around the latch when Lee saw him.

"Get away from there!" Lee grabbed Anders by the shoulder, shoving him away even as Anders yanked on the emergency release lever.

Anders laughed as the hatch stuttered open. "Too late, asshole."

Zach charged through the hatch in full rage and fury, flying at Lee, hitting his midsection and taking him down hard. Lee's head hit the floor with a loud *thud*, and Zach followed it up with a sharp jab to the jaw. Lee's eyes rolled back, and his head lolled to the side. Zach punched him again. His fist rose for another but he stopped, curled hand in midair. He shook his head as if to clear it and then turned to Anders, leaving Lee unconscious on the floor. "Anders." Zach rushed to his side. "Anders!"

"Hey, baby," Anders slurred, tasting the metallic tang of his own blood. "Missed you."

"Medic!" Zach screamed. "Get a medic in here!" He gingerly put his hand over the slice in Anders's side, and it came away covered in blood. Putting it back, he pressed hard. "Stay with me, baby. Medics are coming to take care of you; you've got to stay with me."

Anders gazed up at Zach. "Always. I thought you knew that." The room pitched dangerously, and Anders had to close his eyes. "Hurt my head again, Zach. Have I mentioned how much I fucking hate concussions?"

Zach brushed the hair off Anders's forehead with his free hand. "I vaguely remember hearing something of the sort." He kissed Anders's temple, lips staying there for a moment before he pulled away and screamed for a medic again.

Someone dropped to their knees next to them, and Anders opened his eyes to see a grim-faced young woman in a medic's uniform. Without a word, she shoved Zach's hand and the remnant of Anders's jacket away from the wound, nimble fingers already tearing Anders's shirt apart. "This is going to sting like a bitch, Your Majesty," she said at last, grabbing a spray from her bag.

"Oh?" Anders asked. When the spray hit his side, stars exploded in his vision, and he hissed, grabbing for Zach's hand, fingers clenching. "*Fuck*, you weren't kidding."

"Antibacterial spray. This wound's been out in the open too long to risk it." The medic pressed a thick white bandage to Anders's side. "I'm afraid I can't close the skin for at least another day. Not until you're in the clear."

"We need to get you to bed, Anders." Zach squeezed Anders's hand then leaned down and kissed his forehead again. "You're going to be fine, you hear me?"

"Anders!" Bern's shout from outside was agonized even from a distance. He ran into the shuttle, stopping dead when he saw the scene. Utter horror stood out on his face as he stumbled closer. "Oh god. No. Majesty, I'm—"

Anders tried to sit up straighter, but gave up when he got twin glares from both Zach and the medic. "Hold it right there. Jackson needed you, and I told you to go. And I'm *fine*."

"I wouldn't go that far, Your Majesty." The medic had finished affixing the bandage to his side, and was brandishing a small light in one hand. "You've lost a lot of blood and are at risk for serious infection. Not to mention your second broken-nose-and-concussion combination inside of a month. With proper medical care, you *will* be fine, but you're certainly not walking out of here."

Bern went pale at that. He knelt on the floor on Anders's one free side, eyes darting to where Anders was clutching Zach's hand like a lifeline. "Grant says Lee was behind everything?"

"Yes." Wincing, Anders held still as the medic closed the small cut on his temple with a skin treatment. "It's a long story, and my brain's a bit scrambled right now. But Zach figured it out. He saved me."

"Yeah?" Bern managed a small smile and clasped Zach's shoulder. "Of course he did."

"And I got to beat the shit out of Tanner and Lee in the process." Zach gave Bern a grim smile. "Speaking of which, someone needs to get Lee in restraints before he comes to again. Lock him away with Tanner, after we get Tanner something to wear."

Bern stood. "With pleasure."

"Do I want to know why Tanner's naked?" Anders asked as Bern walked away, hauling the still-unconscious Lee up and over his shoulder like a sack of laundry.

Zach made a face. "He was . . . *entertaining* when we arrested him." Zach looked up as another medic brought a gurney in. "Time for bed, baby."

Anders scowled at his ride. "You'd better be coming with me."

"Not like that, he isn't," the medic put in, closing up her bag. "I'm putting you on strict bed rest for the next twelve hours until you're cleared for a skin treatment. Microbes don't care that you're the king of over a dozen worlds."

"I'll go take a shower while they settle you in, then I'll sit by your bedside like a doting husband, I promise." Zach smiled shakily at Anders. "You've got to heal. You have to get better, baby. I need you here."

Anders wanted to fuss, but he could feel everything Zach could right then, and it was too much like Anders's own frantic worry for Zach's safety. Instead, he let the pair of medics help him up and onto the gurney, and said nothing until they were buckling him securely in place. He reached out for Zach again, needing him close more than he needed just about anything else right then. "At least we'll get twelve hours of sleep out of the deal."

Zach laughed. "If you can keep it uninterrupted. Good luck with that."

"I have two words for you," Anders said as they picked their way out of the shuttle, heading back to the palace. "Royal. Decree."

EPILOGUE

Anders wasn't surprised that, in the end, Bianca Pretorius was the one to hold her silence the longest.

Tanner had scrambled to implicate every criminal he'd ever known, of which there were a disturbing number. He not only turned on Lee and Pretorius, but also confirmed that Omar Nadjem most definitely was selling advance crop reports to businesses, though he was completely uninvolved in the assassination attempts and the piracy.

Lee, after recovering from his wound, had mostly spat venom at Zach during interrogation. He'd said he had no interest in the throne, so much as he wanted the power, but he was downright offended that Anders hadn't dropped his common-born match at the nearest space port and married someone with a "decent" bloodline.

Zach thought that was hilarious.

He'd convinced Anders to wait to officially promote Oliver until after Alex arrived. She considered Oliver as another son, and it was bad enough that he and Anders had bonded without her—they couldn't let her miss Oliver's big day too. Since she was already on the way, it was safer for all involved to hold off on the ceremonial advancement.

Which was why the three of them were waiting in the shuttle bay, Anders still holding himself gingerly despite having his skin treatment over a day earlier. The ship carrying Zach's family had arrived and settled in orbit, and the men were just awaiting the shuttle bringing the two women to the surface. It slid into the bay smoothly, Zach barely giving it enough time to stop before he was striding toward the door.

"Mom!" Zach swept a small woman into his arms and spun her in a circle before giving her a smacking kiss on the cheek. He curled his arms more tightly around her when she slapped his back, finally letting her go so he could carefully take a fragile-looking version of his mother into a solid hug. He kissed her cheek too, murmuring something into her ear as he released her. She smiled up at him, which earned her another hug, and then he was leading the two of them toward Anders and Oliver.

"This is Anders. King Philip. Anders, this is my mom, Alex, and my sister, Kenzie." Zach hugged Kenzie close again and pressed a kiss to the top of her head, watching as Alex gave Anders a thorough look.

"You'll do," she said after a long moment, then laughed. "You'll do very well, especially if you can keep Zach in line. I never could." She gave him a quick hug before pulling a laughing Oliver into a longer one.

Anders blinked for a couple of seconds, thrown. He'd spent the past few hours working himself up, absolutely sure that after everything that had happened, Zach's mother would decide her new son-in-law wasn't worth the danger he brought into her son's life. Finally, he shook it off enough to offer his sister-in-law a bow. "I'm happy to meet you at last," he said, smiling at Kenzie.

She smiled up at him, still leaning against Zach. "I'm happier to finally meet *you*," she said softly. "We didn't think anyone would ever catch Zach."

"I don't know if 'catch' is the right word," Anders said, fighting back a chuckle. "More like waited patiently for him to decide to come to me on his own." He leaned in enough to faux whisper. "I'm told it's rather like fishing, but we won't talk about the bait I used."

Alex choked on a laugh as Kenzie smiled at Anders. There were hints of Zach's mischievousness in Kenzie's expression.

"I'm sure," Alex said. "Zach always did do exactly what he wanted to do on his own timetable, regardless of what I said."

Oliver held a hand out to Kenzie, and she left Zach's side to give Oliver a hug. "Congratulations to you too," she said. "I can't imagine Zach letting anyone else have his *Pallas*."

"He deserves it," Anders agreed.

Oliver laughed. "I've earned it, putting up with Zach all these years."

"Hey!" Zach protested with a grin. Alex smacked his arm.

"If that's what it takes, maybe I should be the one getting the captainship," Alex said, to which Oliver nodded somberly. Zach pinched her side, and she yelped.

Anders laughed. "I don't think there are enough awards for you . . ." He hesitated. "What should I call you, by the way?"

"Whatever you'd like, honey," Alex said. "Alex works."

"Alex, then. And please, you both should call me Anders." He smiled at Zach, definitely a little longer than he should have. "Since we're family now."

"Anders," Kenzie repeated, and smiled again. "I always wanted another brother, especially given the one I have."

Zach tickled her. She yelped just like their mother had and squirmed away, hiding behind Oliver.

"Let's get your luggage and get you to your rooms before this devolves any further," Oliver said. "Once the tickling starts, all bets are off."

Anders offered Kenzie a conspiratorial wink. "You have to tell me embarrassing stories from Zach's childhood," he said. "I was an only child and always wanted an older sibling to torment, you know."

"I'd offer you mine, but you've already taken him," Kenzie answered. This time her smile was sly, and Zach choked and turned red.

"Kenzie!" Zach's voice was scandalized, and both Alex and Kenzie laughed. Oliver grinned widely.

"Well, hasn't he?" Kenzie asked.

"I'm not discussing my sex life with you," Zach said gruffly, "and neither is Anders. Stop embarrassing me."

Kenzie took Anders's arm and smiled up at him sweetly. "I have a lot of stories."

"Fantastic." Anders smirked at Zach over Kenzie's head before spinning them out of his bonded's reach. "Please allow me to escort you, then."

Zach shook his head. "This can't possibly end well," he said, but he was beaming at Anders, love and pride and relief coming across the bond.

Anders paused long enough to use his free hand to pull Zach in for a brief kiss. "I do so love it when you're wrong."

"Enjoy it while you can," Zach said. "It hardly ever happens."

"I heard that," Alex said. Oliver laughed.

"Yes, darling." Anders glanced over at Alex, grin still wide on his face as he winked at her. She winked back.

"I don't think it's safe for you to talk to my family," Zach said. "Maybe you should go walk with Oliver, Kenzie. He already knows all your stories."

"Come on, Kenzie," Oliver said, holding out a hand. "Let's not terrorize Anders until after the bonding."

She patted Anders's arm. "He's right," she said, "I don't want to scare you off." Turning away, she took Oliver's hand.

"It's a little beyond that already," Zach said, but Kenzie just waved a hand at him as the three of them started to walk, leaving the women's luggage behind with Zach and Anders.

"She looks so good, Anders," Zach said quietly, watching as Kenzie smiled up at Oliver. "So much better than the last time I saw her. Still not the same as before Mark died, but better."

"I don't think anyone's ever the same after losing someone they love, bonded or not," Anders said, taking Zach's hand as servants gathered up the luggage. "That's why your mother is probably going to be furious when she finds out what's been going on."

Zach looked guilty. "What she doesn't know won't hurt us."

"I'm pretty sure she's smart enough to get a good idea on her own once the streams break the story on three of my cabinet going to prison for treason and attempting to kill both of us." Anders sighed. "Sometimes I wish I was a little less reasonable so I could justify bringing back executions for high crimes."

"It's better for them to sit in prison for years. Death is too quick a punishment," Zach said. "Unless I get to kill them personally."

Anders huffed through his nose and squeezed Zach's hand. "Still, it's all far from over. If half of what Gregor and Bianca told us is true, there's a criminal empire out there without Lee to keep it all in check."

Zach squeezed back. "If half of what they've said is true, we know where to start taking it apart."

"I can't say I'll be happy," Anders said, pulling his arm free and looping it around Zach's narrow waist, "with you flying to the far reaches of the Collective to do that dismantling."

Zach stopped, eyes widening at Anders's words. "I thought you'd be sending Oliver," he said slowly.

"For much of our efforts, Oliver will certainly be leading the charge, as it were," Anders said, fighting off the smile. "But you have to admit that there are some things that just need a wiser, more experienced commanding officer. Someone who will know my mind in even the most complicated situations."

Zach's smile was bright and eager and surprised all at once. His eyes gleamed with excitement. "I'd need a new ship. Something smaller and faster. To keep tabs on as many operations as possible, of course."

"And to bring you home as often as possible." Anders's stomach knotted at the thought of not having Zach there with him, safe and sound. At the thought of Zach flying off into danger completely beyond Anders's control. But Anders would survive. "Fortunately, I have an entire Navy for you to pick from."

"I know just the model I want. But only," Zach said, "if there's something unassigned, or one with a retiring captain. I won't take another man's ship." He kissed Anders's temple. "Until then, Oliver can handle almost anything himself."

"We'll figure something out." Anders pulled Zach in for a kiss. He kept it brief, considering they were surrounded by people, but brushed his nose to Zach's as they parted. He could feel Zach's joy across their bond, and that was worth more than a few lonely nights. "I can always commission a new one for you. Still, you must promise me one thing before you go flying away."

"Anything," Zach said immediately.

Anders hugged Zach close and rested his head on Zach's shoulder. "That you will always do everything you can to come back to me," he whispered.

"Always, Anders." Zach stopped them and turned Anders toward him, cupping his face. "Always."

"Good." Anders relaxed into Zach's touch, sending all of his love across the bond even as Zach did the same. "Otherwise I might have to make it an order, and we both know how well it works when I try to order you around."

Zach brushed their noses together, then hooked an arm around Anders's neck and got them walking again. "Oh, I don't know. Depends entirely on the order," he said with a leer.

Anders snorted. "Insubordinate asshole," he said fondly.

"You love my asshole," Zach murmured in Anders's ear.

"True," Anders laughed. "That doesn't make you any less insubordinate. Now, come on; I bet your mother is just full of ideas for our bonding. And wait until she finds out about your coronation after!"

Zach smirked. "Mom isn't much of a party planner. Kenzie's bonding was about as much as she ever wanted to deal with. Besides, I think she'd faint if she had to plan a royal bonding ceremony."

"Never underestimate the motivation of revenge, darling," Anders said. "Even I know she was *not* happy to find out we'd bonded in secret. And she's had days to think of ways to make us pay."

"Oh, you don't know Mom. She'll give me crap about it, but trust me; she's laughing at me behind my back for having to have a big ceremony at all." Zach looked forward as his mom glanced back at them with a huge grin and a wink.

Anders hummed happily. "You'd know better than me. It's your family, after all."

"Your family now too," Zach said. "You're stuck with her."

"Good." Anders let his happiness wash over the both of them.

They watched Alex squeeze Oliver's arm before stopping. Oliver and Kenzie continued on without her as she waited for Zach and Anders to catch up. When they finally did, she looped her arm through Anders's free arm and walked with them. "We know you're still in the honeymoon phase," she said with another grin for Anders. "You don't have to show us all the time."

Anders laughed. "This is us being restrained, I'm afraid."

She leaned forward to stare at Zach around Anders, eyebrow raised. Zach raised an eyebrow back at her but flushed. "This is Zach restrained?" she asked.

"Now it is," Anders said, grinning broadly. The time when Zach avoided touching him at all in public was so far gone it might as well be a distant memory. "I'm very fortunate to have earned such a loving heart."

Alex laughed as Zach choked. "Okay! That's enough of that from both of you," Zach said. "I can still make you help plan the bonding and rank advancement ceremonies, Mom."

"Ooh," she wrinkled her nose at Zach. "Threats, now? What did I do to deserve such an ungrateful son?"

"Woe is you," Zach agreed amiably.

"Don't be such a jerk while I'm trying to get your mother to like me, darling." Anders pinched Zach's side.

Zach raised an eyebrow again. "She already likes you. Although that might change if you keep pinching me."

"Nope," Alex said cheerfully. "I've spanked you enough times to not be terribly worried about a pinch or two when you deserve it."

Anders threw back his head and laughed. "Alex, I can't tell you how wonderful it is to meet you at last."

"Just wait until she starts bugging you about grandchildren," Zach muttered.

"I have never bugged you about grandchildren," Alex protested.

"I've never been bonded before," Zach said reasonably.

"True," Alex agreed. "So, have you thought about having children, Anders?"

"Of course he has," Zach said, "he has to have heirs."

"I wasn't talking to you, Zachary," Alex said primly. "Anders?"

"I have, yes," Anders said, fighting back a grin. "As soon as I told my parents I was gay, I was thoroughly briefed on the time-honored tradition of royal surrogates. I imagine Zach and I have perhaps another week or two before people start making recommendations."

Zach and Alex were both silent for a few moments. "Well," Alex said, "that's actually sooner than I was expecting."

"You and me both," Zach said, eyeing Anders.

"There's no rush," Alex said suddenly. "I can wait to be a grandma until the two of you are ready."

"Ha!" Zach said. "Caught by your own cleverness, Mom. I'm not the only one whose tongue gets ahead of their brain."

"I'm teasing you both," Anders said, giving in to the smile. "I've already talked to Reese in his role as temporary grand advisor, and he agrees with me that there's nothing wrong with waiting a few months before we begin considering heirs."

This time it was Zach who pinched Anders. "Maybe we should wait until after things have settled down some," he said. "I'd like to be here for our kids."

"You'd better be," Anders said mildly as they entered the residential wing. "Surely by now you know I have no idea what to do with a child."

"And you think I do?" Zach asked.

Anders rolled his eyes. "Darling. I was raised by nannies. I never even *saw* a child my own age outside of official court functions until I was at least ten."

"Trust me. Having a little sister in no way prepares you to raise a child."

"Boys," Alex interrupted. "You're never prepared. You just make sure they know you love them and do the best you can."

"I'd be an idiot not to listen to you," Anders said, and kissed Alex's cheek. "You did raise my favorite person, after all."

She patted his arm. "He's one of my favorite people too."

Zach rolled his eyes at them, but his lips held the faintest curve. "I *am* awesome," he said seriously.

"Yes, darling, of course you are." Anders pulled them to a stop outside of Alex's suite. "Kenzie is in the adjoining room," he told Alex. "Zach and I are down the hall."

"Thank you, Anders." Alex patted Anders's arm and then turned to hug Zach. Zach held her close for several moments, letting her go when she patted his back.

"Thanks for coming, Mom," he said, serious in truth this time.

"Where else would I be?" she asked with a smile. She studied them both for a moment, then nodded and went into the suite of rooms, closing the door quietly behind herself.

"She's wonderful," Anders said, taking Zach's arm as they headed to their own suite. "They both are."

Zach nodded. "They really are. I'm lucky to have them."

Anders hummed softly, leaning slightly into Zach's comforting warmth. They walked in companionable silence back to their rooms, and as soon as they were safely behind closed doors, Anders pulled Zach in for a kiss.

"Thank you," he whispered against Zach's mouth, "for sharing your family with me."

Zach smiled into their kiss. "You're welcome," he said. The smile widened into a grin. "I hope Mom doesn't make you regret it."

"Not possible." Anders laughed. "Not even if they think I'm a complete idiot because I can't stop looking at you."

"Mom's much more likely to think I'm the idiot, regardless of the situation," Zach said with a laugh.

"I love her already." Anders grinned, and let his hands drop to the top swell of Zach's ass. "We have over an hour before dinner, you know."

Zach kissed Anders slowly, thoroughly exploring his mouth before easing back. "Oh?" he said, voice husky. "Whatever can we do to pass the time?"

"I'm sure we'll think of something," Anders said, tugging Zach toward the bedroom. He laughed, overflowing with happiness. They had a lot of work ahead of themselves to set things to rights in the Collective, to set their own boundaries with each other. But this, Anders knew, this would always be right between them.

Anders fell back on the bed, Zach landing on top of him with a laugh. "My one true match," Anders murmured, cupping Zach's face between kisses. "Mine alone."

Zach pulled back just enough to rub his nose against Anders's. "All yours. And you're all mine."

"Forever," Anders agreed. "Now get undressed. We have a schedule to keep."

Dear Reader,

Thank you for reading Elizabeth Silver and Jenny Urban's *In His Majesty's Service*!

We know your time is precious and you have many, many entertainment options, so it means a lot that you've chosen to spend your time reading. We really hope you enjoyed it.

We'd be honored if you'd consider posting a review—good or bad—on sites like **Amazon, Barnes & Noble, Kobo, Goodreads, Twitter, Facebook, Tumblr,** and your blog or website. We'd also be honored if you told your friends and family about this book. Word of mouth is a book's lifeblood!

For more information on upcoming releases, author interviews, blog tours, contests, giveaways, and more, please sign up for our weekly, spam-free newsletter and visit us around the web:

Newsletter: tinyurl.com/RiptideSignup
Twitter: twitter.com/RiptideBooks
Facebook: facebook.com/RiptidePublishing
Goodreads: tinyurl.com/RiptideOnGoodreads
Tumblr: riptidepublishing.tumblr.com

Thank you so much for Reading the Rainbow!

RiptidePublishing.com

RIPTIDE
PUBLISHING

ACKNOWLEDGMENTS

Thank you to Elin Gregory for the beta, the honesty, and the encouragement; to Mia for the cheerleading and capslocky feedback; to Mr. Silver for not complaining about the hundreds of hours of lost quality time; to our assorted cats for supervision; and to the makers of a wide assortment of caffeinated beverages. Every last one of you made it possible for us to get here.

ALSO BY
ELIZABETH SILVER
& JENNY URBAN

The Fae Haven Series
A Year and a Day
Truth of the Heart
Promises Kept

ABOUT THE AUTHORS

ELIZABETH SILVER is a writer, a tarot reader, a Level Two Cat Lady, and an internet junkie. Her day job is terribly dull, her hobbies oddly specific and quirky, and her husband the most patient person a writer could ask for.

A New Jersey native, Liz is a proud nerd and an awkward human being. She likes to think it makes her endearing. When not writing, Liz can be found collecting tarot cards, chasing Pokémon, fighting her way out of YouTube spirals, and/or performing online searches that will probably land her on a government list somewhere someday.

Join Liz online!

Web: idkmybff.com

Facebook: facebook.com/lizsilverauthor

Twitter: twitter.com/lizsilverwrites

JENNY URBAN is a card-carrying crazy cat lady who lives not too far from Las Vegas. She likes a show about dysfunctional monster-hunting brothers, tall men, and driving her family up the wall. When she's not writing, she's singing or playing the piano, reading other people's books, or providing chatroom commentary on awards shows.

Join Jenny online!

Web: www.idkmybff.com

Facebook: facebook.com/JenUrbanWrites

Twitter: twitter.com/JenUrbanWrites

Enjoy more stories like
In His Majesty's Service
at RiptidePublishing.com!

The Tide of War
ISBN: 978-1-62649-265-3

No Quarter
ISBN: 978-1-62649-400-8

Earn Bonus Bucks!

Earn 1 Bonus Buck for each dollar you spend. Find out how at
RiptidePublishing.com/news/bonus-bucks.

Win Free Ebooks for a Year!

Pre-order coming soon titles directly through our site and you'll
receive one entry into a drawing for a chance to win free books for
a year! Get the details at RiptidePublishing.com/contests.